"Who are you?"

"My name is Annika."

In the flickering torchlight, long, thick, honey-colored hair fell to her waist, a veil over her face and shoulders, shielding her from his gaze as she knelt to one side of him. A pale, flowing dress clothed her slender form, but she was all woman: rounded breasts, a narrow waist, and curved hips. She was everything he'd imagined a Handmaiden of the *Lady* to be.

Delicate, graceful hands untied a pouch and removed several jars and pots. They gave no clue as to the identity of the woman, but the clean, fresh scent of herbs and oils told him she was a healer.

"You waste your time." The Light Blade warrior's voice was hoarse. He tried to swallow, but his mouth was dry. "I thank you for your concern but there's little you can do for me that won't be undone by 'morrow-eve. Save your salves and potions for another who would benefit from them more."

The woman raised her head, a gentle smile curving her lips. All pleasure fled as his gaze met hers.

Lady's Breath, she had demon eyes . . .

VENGEANCE BORN

KYLIE GRIFFIN

BERKLEY SENSATION, NEW YORK

THE BERKLEY PUBLISHING GROUP
Published by the Penguin Group
Penguin Group (USA) Inc.
375 Hudson Street, New York, New York 10014, USA
Penguin Group (Canada), 90 Eglinton Avenue East, Suite 700, Toronto, Ontario M4P 2Y3, Canada
(a division of Pearson Penguin Canada Inc.)
Penguin Books Ltd., 80 Strand, London WC2R 0RL, England
Penguin Group Ireland, 25 St. Stephen's Green, Dublin 2, Ireland (a division of Penguin Books Ltd.)
Penguin Group (Australia), 250 Camberwell Road, Camberwell, Victoria 3124, Australia
(a division of Pearson Australia Group Pty. Ltd.)
Penguin Books India Pvt. Ltd., 11 Community Centre, Panchsheel Park, New Delhi—110 017, India
Penguin Group (NZ), 67 Apollo Drive, Rosedale, Auckland 0632, New Zealand
(a division of Pearson New Zealand Ltd.)
Penguin Books (South Africa) (Pty.) Ltd., 24 Sturdee Avenue, Rosebank, Johannesburg 2196,
South Africa

Penguin Books Ltd., Registered Offices: 80 Strand, London WC2R 0RL, England

This book is an original publication of The Berkley Publishing Group.

This is a work of fiction. Names, characters, places, and incidents either are the product of the author's imagination or are used fictitiously, and any resemblance to actual persons, living or dead, business establishments, events, or locales is entirely coincidental. The publisher does not have any control over and does not assume any responsibility for author or third-party websites or their content.

Copyright © 2012 by Kylie Griffin.
Cover illustration by Gene Mollica.
Cover design by Lesley Worrell.
Interior text design by Kristin del Rosario.

PUBLISHING HISTORY
Berkley Sensation trade paperback edition / February 2012

Library of Congress Cataloging-in-Publication Data

Griffin, Kylie.
    Vengeance born / Kylie Griffin.—Berkley Sensation trade paperback ed.
        p. cm.
    ISBN 978-0-425-24536-1
    I. Title.
    PS3607.R54836V46 2012
    813'.6—dc22

                                                            2011040958

PRINTED IN THE UNITED STATES OF AMERICA

10 9 8 7 6 5 4 3 2 1

To Mum, Dad, and Michelle,
you put up with my obsession for all things paranormal
and supported me as I pursued my passion and dreams.

I love you.

ACKNOWLEDGMENTS

To my editor, Leis Pederson, whose belief in this story changed my life. To my agent, Elaine Spencer, for your enthusiasm for my work, patience, and sharing of knowledge.

To Mrs. Wendy Jackson and Miss Julie Simmington, two wonderful high school English teachers, who encouraged a novice writer to pursue her passion.

To Robyn and Darryl, Michelle, Dee, Gracie, and Jem, and the local post office staff—for making sure I remembered to eat, for all the visits/emails and long phone calls, and for not hiding behind the shop counter when you saw me coming with yet another load of manuscripts.

To the BILDers—my support group, shoulder to cry on, cheerleaders, wielders of ugly-sticks, and sisters-in-madcap mayhem. What an amazing group of writers!

To Valerie Parv, incredible mentor, wonderfully generous lady, and fountain of knowledge—your prediction came true!

To three amazing writing organizations—Romance Writers of Australia, Romance Writers of New Zealand, Romance Writers of America: You've given me knowledge, professional support, and lifelong friendships.

And last, but not least, to all contest judges and readers, thank you for your feedback and encouragement. I listened, I learned, and you helped me achieve my dream.

You have all encouraged, guided, and pushed me to reach this milestone. I couldn't have done it without you. Thank you, from the bottom of my heart.

Chapter 1

ANNIKA hated visiting the dungeons. The dank cells reeked of pain and fear as well as blood. Anyone unfortunate enough to be imprisoned here risked dying of exposure if the torture inflicted by the *Na'Reish* guards didn't claim them first.

"This had better be worth it, Hesia," she muttered and tugged the skirts of her dress away from slime-covered walls.

The furious squeaking she heard coming from a shadowed corner made her glad she was wearing her knee-high boots. Bare feet—or any naked skin, for that matter—were fair game to the scurriers scavenging down here. She'd treated many prisoners for bites and wounds caused by the vicious little carnivores. A draft of air brought with it the stench of unwashed bodies, which almost overpowered her. She coughed and lifted a sleeve to cover her nose.

"You know none of the others will come down here." The old healer's tone held censure for her surliness.

If Annika were honest, the physical conditions of the dungeon weren't the real reason for her reluctance. It was the mumbling voices of prisoners: some babbled, driven mad by circumstance, some cried piteously, others wailed in despair. The sound of their helplessness was heartbreaking and she could do little but try to ease their pain.

Hesia shot her an arch look. "'Sides, you're the only one the demons will let into the Pit."

Her face heated. Her half-blood status was a boon and a curse. While even the lowest caste of the *Na'Reish* outranked her, their fear of her father was the only thing stopping the guards from refusing her access.

"Who's imprisoned there now?" she asked.

"Rumor has it that *Na'Hord* scouts captured a warrior during a slave raid in the Outer Provinces." A thread of excitement colored the old woman's voice. "He refuses even to give his name."

Hope fired deep inside her and she glanced sharply at Hesia. "A Light Blade?"

"Yes."

Annika bit her lip as hope surged from deep within her. *Lady's Blessing*, this could be the opportunity she'd been waiting for, the chance to escape.

Hesia's wrinkled face peered up at her, her blue eyes somber. "He was the only survivor. You know what the *Na'Hord* do with any warriors they capture."

Annika clenched her fists, empathy quickly replacing her hope. As a child she'd been forced to watch the *Na'Hord* kill human warriors many, many times. Her heart went out to the survivor.

Hesia's steps slowed then faltered as they neared the Pit. She turned and gripped her forearm with gnarled fingers. "Be careful, Annika, *Na'Reisha* Tal is on duty."

Despite the flash of anger that warmed her cheeks, the warning sent a shiver of fear along her spine. "I thought that lower-caste scum had been relieved," she whispered.

The last time she'd treated prisoners in the dungeon, he'd locked her in a cell without Hesia, then told the prisoners who she was. If it hadn't been for another guard interceding she'd have suffered far worse than a few bruises and a head wound.

"Your father's inspecting a new wagonload of female slaves that arrived this morning." Hesia kept her voice quiet. "You know once his attention is diverted elsewhere, things go back to the way they were."

Glancing ahead, Annika saw Tal's burly form and another guarding the top of the stairway leading down into the Pit. The small cobblestoned chamber reminded her of a sunken arena. The demons tortured slaves or prisoners within it while others watched from the raised ledge above.

"Tal suffered the brunt of your father's displeasure for his error." Hesia gripped her arm tighter. "He's looking for any excuse to exact revenge."

Standing nearly seven feet in height, Tal was an imposing figure: all muscle and brawn, renowned among the *Na'Reish* for his great physical strength, but the full suit of leather armor tempered his physical dominance. Slave prisoners just weren't dangerous enough to warrant such caution but a Light Blade warrior possessed the kinetic power to kill through any weapon, the skill a Gift from the *Lady*, their human deity. Having faced such warriors in battle before, Tal's precaution was warranted.

Had the prisoner made an attempt on his life? The idea brought a small smile to Annika's lips. She hoped the Light Blade had given the *Na'Reisha* a lot of trouble.

Tal turned at the sound of their footsteps, his violet eyes glowing in the ambient light of the smoking braziers. His gaze met hers, his narrow-eyed stare colder than the icy prison. Annika schooled herself not to react, not to hesitate in her stride, not to give him the satisfaction of knowing she feared him. It was bad enough he thought her existence an abomination without inflaming his need to dominate by appearing weak.

The shadows darkened the spotted pattern of demon markings running down the sides of his face. No matter how many times she'd listened to *Na'Reish* females of all castes whisper behind their hands about how handsome his markings were, to her, and in this light, they compounded his ruthlessness.

The smile he gave her revealed pointed teeth sharp enough to puncture human skin. Hers crawled at the thought of him touching her—not that he'd be attracted to one such as her, thank the *Lady*. There were few benefits to being a half-breed, but this was surely one of them.

"What do you want, *Na'Chi*?" His usual derogatory drawl accompanied the name.

"I'm here to heal the prisoner, my lord."

"You waste precious resources on this human. He lives only until he tells us who he is and about the leader of his people. Another session spent under my lash should see to that."

His attitude made Annika even more determined. The human warrior represented the chance of a new life free from her father and other tormentors, if she could help him escape. "Has he been condemned to death?"

The other guard shifted from one foot to the other, his boots scraping on the stone floor. "There's been no such order given."

"If he dies without revealing that information, our leader, *Na'Rei* Savyr, will want to know who refused the human access to a healer. You must allow me to treat him."

The leather of Tal's gloves creaked as he curled his hands into fists. "You don't give the orders down here." He leaned closer, his voice dropping to a harsh whisper. "I do." His violet eyes flashed and darkened. "Do you want to find yourself in a cell again? Alone with humans? You remember what happened last time, don't you?"

She shuddered, the memory too near, too fresh to control her reaction. Tal's lips curled. She wished she could control her reactions more successfully, hating that he took pleasure in provoking her fear.

Swallowing hard, she met his gaze. "You'd risk the wrath of my father a second time?"

Tal's eyelid flickered. He gripped her upper arm in a hold so tight she knew her skin would yield bruises by morning. She held still, unwilling to give him further reason to hurt her.

"The blood in your veins barely gives you the right to breathe! Why the *Na'Rei* continues to let you live is a mystery," he hissed. "The entertainment value of watching you cower and suffer under his belt must provide him with more amusement than it would me."

He released her suddenly, as if he couldn't bear to touch her a second longer, and she stumbled back toward Hesia. The elderly woman caught her before she fell.

"One day the *Na'Rei* will die and the leadership will pass to someone who believes purity of the bloodlines should take precedence over petty revenge." He stabbed a gloved finger at her. "You'd do well to remember that, *Na'Chi*."

Annika dropped her gaze. Pushing Tal too far would destroy her chances of meeting the human warrior who might be able to save her from that fate. Showing him submission grated, but if it meant he'd give her permission to enter the Pit she'd do it.

"Tal, let her treat the human with her herbal remedies." The second guard wore an uneasy frown. "I don't fancy being the scapegoat of the *Na'Rei* if the Light Blade dies while under your command. Besides, if she enters the Pit to heal him, who says he won't try to kill her? He's tried often enough with us."

After several tense heartbeats, Tal grunted then began to chuckle. The sound wasn't pleasant. He motioned toward the Pit. "You have half an hour, *Na'Chi*."

With a soft sigh of relief, Annika descended the steps and glanced toward the center of the Pit, eager to see the prisoner. She winced at the silent pain the human male was surely forced to endure as a part of his captivity.

Chains suspended from the ceiling spread his arms wide, while more shackled him to the floor in a kneeling position. There was no leeway to sit or stand; the chains pulling at his arms were taut. Raw, chafe marks encircled his wrists, undeniable signs of a struggle to escape torment.

She murmured a soft entreaty to the *Lady* for help. Her whisper must have carried, for the male lifted his head, his long, jet-black hair parting to reveal a battered face. Her breath caught.

Lady of Mercy, she had not expected him to be so comely.

The bruises, cuts, and dried blood did little to hide an attractive face. Strong, fierce, captivating, yet his eyes commanded most of her attention. They were an intense, dark green that almost seemed to glow, bright with intelligence and power. His gaze reached deep into her, sparking an unfamiliar excitement that made her stomach flutter. A feeling so alien to her she almost forgot why she was there.

"I never expected him to be so handsome." Hesia's hushed comment turned her head. The old healer stood close behind her.

"Handsome? If he had the markings, he'd pass as one of the *Na'Reish*."

Did he possess the same arrogance and air of superiority the lordlings exhibited, the same traits that she despised because of their belief that it gave them the right to flaunt it over others?

The older woman raised an eyebrow. "You do realize the upper-caste lords would be insulted to be compared to a human? But I wholeheartedly agree with you." Hesia's comment steered Annika's thoughts in an entirely new direction. Annika blushed as her friend chuckled. "What? I may be old but I'm not blind."

"We're here to heal him. Not stare at him."

"Then go heal him."

The Lady of Light has finally granted me a peaceful death, Kalan Tayn thought. He wasn't afraid but he'd expected to die at the end of some demon's sword in battle, a death more honorable than having his life cut short in the depths of a dungeon.

He listened to the Handmaiden speaking nearby. Closing his eyes, he shut out the less-than-ideal surroundings and concentrated on her voice. It was soft, sensual, well suited for the task of easing a man into the Light. It wound its way deep inside him, touching his soul, fortifying the ragged remnants of his strength. He recognized the *Lady*'s power emanating from her; warm, gentle, and soothing. Her touch would ease the abuse his body had suffered in the last sennight.

He parted battered lips and sighed in relief. "Handmaiden, the *Lady* is truly merciful. I welcome your guidance as I pass over."

His one regret was leaving his sister, Kymora, the unenviable task of taking up his position on the Blade Council. His death would bring chaos at a time they could least afford turmoil; there were too few Light Blade warriors left to defend their territory from the growing demon horde.

"What?" The second voice was older. "What's he saying?"

Lighthearted laughter teased his ears. "You're mistaken, warrior. You don't stand at death's door." The alluring voice whispered to another. "He thinks we're Handmaidens from the *Lady*."

"Then who are you?" Although his eyelids were heavy and reluctant to obey, the temptation to see the woman with the captivating voice was too strong to resist.

"My name is Annika."

In the flickering torchlight, long, thick, honey-colored hair fell to her waist, acting as a veil over her face and shoulders, shielding her from his gaze as she knelt to one side of him. A pale, flowing dress clothed her slender form but she was all woman: rounded breasts, a narrow waist, and curved hips. She was everything he'd imagined a Handmaiden of the *Lady* to be.

A wry smile twisted his lips at the heat stirring in his gut. Deriving enjoyment from looking at her was strange considering his predicament, but it was better than the memories of the last few days. He'd take pleasure over pain any day.

Delicate, graceful hands untied a pouch and removed several jars and pots. They gave no clue as to the identity of the woman but the clean, fresh scent of herbs and oils told him she was a healer.

"You waste your time." His voice was hoarse. Kalan tried to swallow but his mouth was dry. "I thank you for your concern but there's little you can do for me that won't be undone by 'morrow-eve. Save your salves and potions for another who would benefit from them more."

The woman raised her head, a gentle smile curving her lips. All pleasure fled as his gaze met hers.

Lady's Breath, she had demon eyes.

Adrenaline burned through him. He sucked in a shocked breath. They weren't quite the same shade of violet as the *Na'Reish* but lighter, flecked with pale yellow highlights.

She wasn't human.

He jerked back from her, hissing at the pain that shot through his manacled wrists. "Keep your hands off me!"

She flinched at the anger in his voice and turned away. A cold shiver worked its way along his spine. Perhaps the flickering torchlight affected his sight, or maybe there'd been one too many blows to his head. He scanned her face again. The swirling design on her skin, the pigment paler than any he'd seen on the *Na'Reish*, trailed down the side of her face and neck then disappeared beneath the neckline of her dress.

The enemy in the guise of a healer? Shame pricked and burned beneath his skin at his body's earlier response and the attraction he'd felt for her. How could he have felt anything but horror and disgust for a cold-blooded killer? *Lady's Breath*, he'd need every shred of strength to resist whatever torture this demon was here to inflict.

An old woman knelt on the other side of him. She was human. The small pale blue tattoo on her wrinkled cheek, a crescent moon in design, was the mark of a slave. Snow-white hair was pulled into a tight bun at the back of her neck. "You have nothing to fear from Annika. She's a healer. Let her help you."

"I want no help from the *Na'Reish*!"

Her brown eyes narrowed and flashed with anger. "She's no more *Na'Reish* than you or I. Surely you can feel the *Lady*'s Gift burning within her?"

"Hesia, it's all right." The younger woman's rebuke was soft.

"No, Annika, he's judged you too quickly. Perhaps I was wrong in my assessment. A Light Blade would never do that. They're more intelligent."

The old woman was insulting *him*? Kalan glanced between the two of them, tempted to laugh but the heat of anger curling tight inside his stomach stayed the impulse. Was he dreaming? Had he passed out during the last beating and now drifted in some sort of surreal world?

"His intolerance is unacceptable." The old woman leaned in close, her gaze burning. "Warrior, listen carefully. Do you want your freedom?"

Of course he did. What warrior wouldn't wish for escape from the torment inflicted by the *Na'Reish*? He resented the flash of hope her question sparked. Was this another of their tricks?

"I don't know either of you. Are you blood-slaves?"

The old woman snorted. "You're a fool!"

The *Na'Reish* placed a gentle hand on the old woman's arm. "He's cautious, Hesia, as I would be if I were in his place. Roll up your sleeves and show him your wrists."

Her skin was unmarked, scarless. Neither was enthralled to a master or mistress. The younger woman's eerie gaze linked with his. "We're not blood-slaves."

"Why would you help me?"

The demon woman glanced toward the guards and lowered her voice to a whisper. "I can get you out of here, but I'll need your assistance."

"You need my help to escape?"

"No, I've already planned our escape. It's afterward . . ."

Her words made no sense but the offer of freedom burned in his heart. Kalan glanced to the guards standing on the lip of the Pit, gut seething with renewed anger. Was this a new tactic to get him to talk? The *Na'Reish* commander couldn't be the mastermind behind this plan. The hulking leather-clad bastard enjoyed inflicting pain too much. Fourteen days of torment and not once had he answered their questions.

And a *Na'Reish* healer treating a human prisoner? No demon would condescend to aiding an enemy. Her story about wanting her freedom had to be false.

But *Lady's Breath*, if she could help him he'd be a fool not to take her up on her endeavor. Even overlooking the fact she wasn't human, the odds of escaping the demon's realm were slim. But could he trust her? A demon?

"I don't understand why you'd want this."

Frustration colored her voice. "What is there to understand? You want to escape. I want my freedom. We need each other."

He snorted. "Why should I trust you?"

"You should." The old woman's whisper was fierce.

How could a *Na'Reish* earn such loyalty from a human without forming a blood-bond? "I'm sworn to kill you."

The younger woman's abrupt laugh was bitter. "My death would be a cause for celebration among the *Na'Reish*, Light Blade. Do you think they welcome one such as myself among their ranks?"

The power of her Gift nudged his senses, warm and strong. The heavy, cloying evil he usually associated with the demons was notice-ably absent.

"How can that be?" He frowned, recalling something he'd heard earlier. "The guard called you *Na'Chi*. What's that mean?"

For the briefest moment, vulnerability flashed in her gaze, the colored flecks in her eyes changed to orange, and then she glanced away. Her reply was barely audible. "Half-blood." He sucked in a shocked breath. "Now do you understand why I want to help you escape from here?"

"Demons pride themselves on the purity of their bloodlines. How did you survive beyond birth?"

"Does it really matter? All you need to decide is whether you can trust me enough to help you escape."

He peered at the markings on her face more closely. They weren't as dark or as prominent as the *Na'Reisha* commanders, and the violet coloring of her eyes was lighter. Her stature didn't seem as heavily boned, either. He couldn't refute what he was seeing but a half-human, half-demon hybrid?

Mother of Mercy, stories of their existence had been around for centuries, figments of the imagination used as campfire tales to scare children. Evidence to refute that belief knelt beside him. Considering the *Na'Reish*'s intolerance for bloodline contamination, how had this woman survived into adulthood?

"What do you want in return?" he asked.

For the barest heartbeat, excitement flickered across her face. "I can get you out of the fortress, make sure we aren't recaptured within *Na'Reish* territory but after that I need your help. I have very little knowledge of your land or your people."

"You want to leave *Na'Reish* territory? And you want my protection?"

"I know it's a lot to ask . . ." Her voice shook as it trailed off and she glanced toward the old woman, biting her lip.

She was scared. The revelation burned through him. Did she fear him or her own plan?

Her head lifted and her shoulders straightened. The flecks in her eyes went from yellow to a dark green color. "I doubt I'd survive long outside the valley. I have no way of hiding what I am."

"Annika . . ." There was a wealth of love and pain in the old woman's voice.

"They won't know me like you do, Hesia. The warrior's reaction proved that."

Her fingers pleated the material of her dress. When she realized he was watching her, she met his gaze, proud and unflinching, but her anxious action didn't stop. Unusual. Vulnerability was considered a weakness among the *Na'Reish*.

Was it another ploy?

"Kalan," he said.

A startled expression flitted across her face. "What?"

He'd go along with her plan, for the moment. If she could unshackle him, he could fight. Even bare-handed, he stood a better chance at escape than he did now. Should he fail . . . well, he'd make certain he wasn't recaptured alive.

"My name is Kalan. If we're going to escape together, then you need to know my name."

And by the *Lady of Light*, if she were deceiving him, he'd make sure she never drew breath again either.

Chapter 2

ANNIKA stared at the warrior, her mouth slackening in shock. *Dear Lady*, he'd agreed to her plan. So used to rejection, she'd been so sure he'd rebuff it outright after seeing the hatred in his eyes for what she was but hope had spurred her to try.

Wariness replaced his anger, which he wore like a cloak. His long limbs were tense, as if bracing himself for a blow he knew would come, expecting her to tell him she'd merely been taunting him with freedom. That he was as uncertain as her about their tentative alliance was an oddly reassuring realization.

"Which guard has the keys to your shackles?" she whispered. "We must leave tonight. I may not be given another chance to visit you again."

"The one on the right."

Dread's cold fingers clawed her stomach. Tal wore the key on his belt. "Figures," she muttered and turned back to him.

In his present condition, the scabbed and weeping whip weals and raw burns on his body would slow him down. If she healed him and they began their escape, would he take advantage of his newfound strength and attack her? It was a risk but one she had to take.

"You can't run in your present condition." She had little choice if they were to succeed. "Your wounds need healing. Will you let me help you?"

His eyes narrowed. "How? Your salves and potions will take days to help me."

"As it stands, I doubt you'd be able to walk out of the Pit." And she didn't think he'd let her carry him. She took a deep breath. "You use your Gift as a tool to rid the world of demons, I use mine to heal."

He didn't need to know she used her special skill as an act of secret rebellion against her father and the *Na'Reish*, to help others caught in a life as helpless as her own.

"Who taught you this skill?"

"We don't have time for this conversation."

One dark eyebrow arched upward. "Make the time."

He was stubborn like a *Na'Reish* lord.

Hesia's hand touched her shoulder. "Tell him."

She sighed. "No one. I inherited it from my mother."

"Your mother? She's human?"

She nodded. "A Light Blade warrior. She died after birthing me."

"Why weren't you killed, too?"

She shared a look with Hesia. Her friend nodded encouragingly but answering that question would only delay them further. "Please, Kalan, I'll tell you whatever you want to know later. Just let me heal you."

Suspicion tightened the lines on his face.

She touched her fingertips to her breast then lips, sealing her promise. "By the *Lady*, I swear to answer your questions."

"You honor *Her*?"

Her chin lifted at the skeptical tone in his voice. "How could I not after being blessed with *Her* Gift?"

Hesia's response was somber. "No other *Na'Chi* has ever been able to do what she has, Light Blade."

Long heartbeats passed before he finally nodded. "All right."

Annika smiled and moved in front of him, covering her actions from the guards with her body. She gently touched the center of his chest, avoiding the worst of the lash marks. Beneath her fingertips, his skin was warm. His fine linen shirt had been slashed repeatedly until the front was barely more than a collection of bloody, threadbare rags. His muscular chest and abdomen were covered in weal marks, some deep enough to have broken the skin. She hated to think of the agony he'd endured.

Closing her eyes, she focused her thoughts and felt the soothing warmth of her Gift deep within her gaining strength. She concentrated on directing it down along her arm then into Kalan through the touch they shared. As she breathed in, his pain eased; as she exhaled, his body accepted the energy she was giving him and began the healing process.

She stopped only when she knew all the whip marks had healed over. She withdrew slowly, leaving a lingering warmth in his muscles. Once unfettered, he needed to be able to move unhindered, free from stiffness or soreness.

Opening her eyes, she found the warrior staring at her. His dark green-eyed scrutiny, so strong and compelling up close made her flinch. What did he see when he looked at her? Did he see her as an ally or enemy? Nothing was reflected on his face to betray his thoughts; they were well hidden. She pulled her hand away from his chest.

"Thank you."

His quiet comment caught her by surprise. Very few had ever expressed their gratitude before. She nodded and rose to her feet. "I'll be back in a moment."

Kalan stretched, testing his muscles, and found no pain. She'd healed him completely. He'd never heard of any healer with such a skill. None of Master Healer Candra's apprentices in the hospice back at Sacred Lake exhibited a skill similar to this. Her Gift was truly unique.

Uncertainty ate at his gut as he watched Annika walk to the stairs, her stride strong, determined. Was the compassion she'd just showed him genuine or just a calculated move to ensure his compliance? His mouth twisted.

So far, the demon was doing exactly as she promised she would. As long as she continued to help him escape he'd trust her—at least until he was free of the dungeon. Perhaps then he'd see her true nature, her true plan.

The old woman, Hesia, swiftly repacked the healing pouch and slung it over her shoulder.

"What's she doing?" he whispered.

Her somber brown eyes met his gaze. "Getting the key to free you."

"But those demons are twice her size."

"You should already know size doesn't matter." Hesia glanced once toward Annika then back at him, resolve shining clearly in her eyes. "Annika has many strengths, and you'd do well to discover them when you escape from here. Keep an open mind when you talk to her. Listen. Growing up as *Na'Chi* hasn't been easy. If you can see past the marks on her body and the color of her eyes, she will be your strongest, most loyal ally. Remember this because the days ahead will not be easy for either of you."

The wealth of emotion in the elderly woman's voice made him frown. "You won't be coming with us when we escape?"

"No. The path you take goes where these old bones won't." She glanced toward the stairway. "Annika is about to kill for the first time using her Gift. She does it to free you. To free herself. I only hope whatever future you take her to is worth it."

Her words pricked his pride. "I'll keep my end of this bargain, old woman, and I'm not so closed-minded as you seem to think I am. The *Lady* has a purpose for our meeting. What, I don't know yet, but if it eases your mind, I promise not to harm her unless she attacks me."

Her shoulders sagged. "Then I know she will be safe with you."

Hesia placed a lot of faith in the young woman. He peered up to where Annika stood facing the two demon guards, her hand resting on the shorter one's arm in entreaty. The man abruptly dropped to the ground. She swayed on her feet as a roar came from the second, taller guard; the *Na'Reisha* commander who'd taken great pleasure in torturing him.

"I'll kill you!" the demon howled.

She reached out a hand toward him and he backhanded her, hard. The sound of him striking her cheek echoed around the chamber. She stumbled to one knee under the force of the blow. The demon bent down to grasp her around the throat with his gloved hands. Hesia gasped. Annika's fingers wrapped around the bare skin exposed at his wrists. Abruptly, the second demon collapsed.

"It's done." The old woman's whisper reached Kalan.

Annika turned her back on them all and hunched over. Kalan heard the unmistakable sounds of retching. Whatever skill she possessed left him in no doubt that this healer could look after herself.

Two full-grown *Na'Reish* warriors had died at the touch of her hand. Such power. What had he got himself into? This woman would be a formidable adversary. Was bargaining with her for his freedom a wise decision?

"If she's never killed before, then how'd she know she could do it now?" he asked.

Hesia's reply was tinged with sadness. "You know how to use a sword and what it's capable of doing but it doesn't mean you have to use it, does it? The *Lady* gave Annika great power. She chose to heal others rather than take life—until now."

He remembered the first time he'd taken a demon's life and the loss of innocence that had been sacrificed with it. She would never feel the same again. Keys clattered to the floor and skidded to a stop in front of him. He peered upward. Annika stood on the lip of the Pit, staring down at them, her face pale, her arms wrapped tightly around her waist.

"Free the Light Blade." Her voice was hoarse. "I'll finish with the guards."

The elderly woman scooped up the keys; for the first time in a sennight, Kalan felt the stirrings of excitement as she inserted one in the shackle at his wrist. He was free in moments. Rubbing his arms, he followed Hesia up the stairway, snatching a torch from its brazier along the way.

At the top, he found both demons impaled with their own swords. Annika waited for them farther along the corridor. Her gaze was shadowed, haunted, the flecks in her eyes now a faint red. Her mouth was pulled taut.

Hesia answered his unspoken question. "When the guards are discovered, the Na'Reish must believe you escaped on your own. They can't know she can kill with her Gift or they'll use it against her. Come, we must hurry."

They didn't know about Annika's skills? Kalan reined in his uncertainty. Getting answers could wait until later; for now, he needed to focus on escape.

Hesia took his hand and pulled him along after Annika. The only sound they made came from his bare feet slapping on the stone pathway and the rustling of their skirts. He had no way of knowing if the path they led him on was one to freedom. He'd entered the dungeon barely conscious. For now he would have to rely on them, and while every instinct rebelled at the idea, he had little choice.

They hurried along a corridor, going left when it split at an intersection. The intervals between torch-braziers grew longer as if this part of the dungeon was rarely used. Stone lined the corridor instead of wooden cell doors. Underfoot became wetter and their pace slowed. He drew in a deep breath. The air smelt fresher.

At another intersection, Hesia drew him to a halt. "This is where I must leave you."

Annika saw Kalan nod. Once their escape became known, her father would interrogate Hesia. Her heart raced at the thought. They'd been companions too long for him not to suspect the old woman might know something. While Hesia could handle her father, and had before, Annika still feared for her friend. She embraced the old woman. "Please, come with us."

Hesia patted her back. "You know I won't make it. I'm far too old to run." The woman released her and placed the healer's pouch on her shoulder. Gnarled fingers gently traced her face. "May the *Lady* bless your path." Her gaze met his. "Both of you. Go swiftly now, and don't look back."

A gentle push started Annika on her way but at the last corner in the corridor, her steps slowed. What was she doing? She placed a hand on the cold, stone wall, her fingernails digging into the grimy surface.

An ache started deep within her chest and spread outward, expanding to include her lungs. She labored to suck each breath in, and hot tears stung in her eyes and made her throat ache. She was leaving the woman who'd been more her mentor, protector, and best friend, the closest thing she'd had to a mother since her own had died giving birth to her twenty-five years ago. And here she was leaving behind the only person who'd ever loved and cared for her. For a half-blood outcast.

Annika swallowed hard and fought the urge to look back. It took everything within her to fulfill Hesia's request. Her heart felt like it was being torn from her chest. She gripped the leather strap of the healer's pouch until it cut into the skin of her hands, and forced herself to focus on the man walking beside her.

Merciful Mother, she'd entrusted her life to a warrior sworn to kill demons. Her mouth dried. Despite his compliance so far, would he see past her demon side as Hesia had? Would he give her a chance to prove she meant him no harm?

The plan she'd spent many seasons mulling over suddenly seemed foolish. She trusted a human who'd just spent weeks being tortured by demons. Wouldn't he want revenge? Once free of the dungeon she'd be alone with him. Alone to face reprisal and retribution. The very things she was trying to escape.

Annika stumbled to a halt, panting, her stomach churning. She wanted to be sick again. The temptation to turn back pulsed as rapidly as her heart.

"Annika?" Kalan's deep voice was tinged with urgency. The warrior grasped her shoulder. She flinched. "What's wrong?"

She kept her head bent, away from his searching gaze. "Nothing." Her voice wavered. *Lady* forgive her for that lie. She licked dry lips and tried to control her fear.

His voice was quiet, terse. "We can't stop now. You know that. Killing the guards and freeing me sealed your fate. There is no going back."

She clenched her teeth so hard her jaw ached. As much as it galled her to acknowledge it, he was right. She would never be safe. Then again, she never had been. Leaving was the only thing to do. They had to get out of the catacombs and be into the forest before dawn.

She flushed, embarrassed by her weakness and forced herself onward. "This way."

Kalan followed her. The torch in his hand spluttered. A draft of fresh air brushed past her face as the sound of rushing water echoed through the tunnel. They were close to the grate that was the final barrier to freedom. Hurrying forward she grasped the shiny black bars and pushed hard. Nothing. No movement.

"No!" She couldn't stop her outcry. "This grate should be rusted, more corroded. It's been repaired."

The underground river that supplied the castle with water surfaced within the catacombs of the dungeon and joined its tributary outside the grate. Beyond it she could hear the sounds of the forest: a night owl hooting as it hunted for prey, the rustle of leaves as a breeze passed through the trees.

She hadn't returned to check the grate, afraid the *Na'Reish* guards would see her and question her motives for visiting the catacombs. She pressed her forehead against the cold metal, panic eating at the edges of her fragile control.

They were so close to freedom. Turning back meant death. Her father would never pardon her for helping a Light Blade warrior, and even if by some miracle he did, the death of two *Na'Reish* was unforgivable. The skin on her back ached with past memories. All his tormenting and past abuse would be nothing compared to what he'd do when he discovered her most recent actions.

Kalan crouched beside her. "Is there any other way out?"

His tone was neutral, his gaze intent but calm. The condemnation she'd expected to see on his face for her failure was nonexistent. It helped rein in her fear. She shoved the bars again, this time in frustration.

"Nothing that wouldn't be considered sheer suicide. . . ." She broke off, her gaze going to the water running through the grate. Leaning over the lip of the pathway, she tried to see underwater. "Wait . . . there might be . . ." The water was too dark. She scrambled to her feet and stripped off her cloak. "Undress. Hurry."

The warrior's face lit up in surprise. "What?"

She toed off her boots and unlaced the front of her dress. "The grate shouldn't extend much farther below the water. There should be a gap to let debris through."

He caught her arm. "Are you sure? It's winter. The water will be freezing."

"You want to go back?" She peered up at him as he grimaced. "I didn't think so. We're going to need dry clothes when we get out. I'll take our things to the bank once you pass them through. Then you'll only have to make one trip. Can you swim?"

"Yes."

"Will you make it?"

As his gaze flickered to the grate and beyond, her stomach churned. No male had ever seen her without clothing before. Her cheeks burned at the thought of him seeing her body. He'd likely find her repugnant.

Why that thought bothered her she didn't know. She tried to focus on the task ahead. The temperature of the water and his condition should concern her more. He had to be weary from his imprisonment and the cold water would likely drain what strength she'd given him when she'd healed the worst of his wounds. His gaze met hers again, lips thinning.

"I'll make it." He pulled off his shirt. "Going back isn't an option."

She finished unlacing her dress, her hands clenching a moment in the folds before letting it drop to the cobblestoned floor. Kalan's sharp intake of breath brought another flush to her face. She'd been ridiculed too many times by the *Na'Reish* for her paler skin markings to be comfortable with nudity. She crouched on the edge of the pathway, and let her long hair hide as much of her body as it could.

Kalan couldn't take his eyes off Annika. Swirling patterns marked the sides of her face, trailed over her shoulders down either side of the slender length of her back, then curled over the curves of her hips and along the backs of her legs.

The wavy strands of her hair brushed the top of her buttocks and he caught the pale flash of a curved breast as she perched on the edge of the waterway wall. Desire mixed with shame slammed in his gut. How could the sight of a naked demon stir him?

He sucked in a ragged breath, fighting his body's heated response to the sight of her. Was this some bastardized version of her power? She could heal him with a touch. Could she make a man's body feel things his head told him were dangerous?

"I apologize if the sight of me offends you." Annika's shoulders hunched, her words stilted, softly spoken.

Growing up as Na'Chi hasn't been easy. Hesia's words echoed in Kalan's head. How could she not know she was beautiful? Annika slipped into the water before he could reply. Her startled gasp as the water closed over her echoed around the chamber. He shoved the torch up against the wall and knelt on the edge, ready to offer a hand if she needed to get out.

She swam to the grate and grasped the bars. He heard her take several deep breaths before she disappeared under the water. Long seconds passed, then her head reappeared beyond the grate on the other side.

"The hole is an arm's length below the water's surface." Her teeth were chattering hard. "Roll up our clothes and put them into my pouch."

He fought his body and gained control as he stripped from his breeches and stuffed his clothes along with hers into the pouch. The less time she spent in the water the better. He pushed the tightly strapped pouch through the bars into her outstretched hand.

She peered up at him. "Wait until I return."

He chafed at the warning, listening as she swam to the bank, disappearing into the darkness of the night, but her words were prudent. She knew his limitations as well as he did. He shivered, shifting from leg to leg, rubbing his bare arms then glanced toward the grate. The cold night air chilling his skin would be nothing compared to the water.

On her return, Annika grasped the bars again, gasping in deep, shuddering breaths. The sound of her chattering teeth echoed back off the tunnel walls, and in the flickering torchlight her face seemed even paler. For some reason her vulnerability concerned him.

"Are you all right?" he asked. She nodded and motioned for him to hurry. He doused the torch and let it wash away, then slid into the water. The cold shocked the breath right out of him. It felt like a thousand icy needles were piercing his skin, and his nerves screamed in protest. Resisting the urge to scramble out, he grasped the bars of the grate.

"*Lady's Breath!*" It was all he could manage as he searched with his feet for the gap. There was a current pushing at his legs. Something slimy brushed the back of his thigh and he tried not to think about what it might be.

"Perhaps if you move faster you'll warm up some." Her soft taunt distracted him from the cold.

He shot her a frown that probably looked more like a grimace and she laughed, the sound light, engaging. With a prayer to the *Lady* for help, he took a deep breath and ducked under the water.

Keeping his eyes closed, he used his hands to feel his way through the hole in the grate and surfaced as soon as he could. Even that brief submersion sapped the strength from his limbs. He shook his hair from his eyes, gasping in air. His breath frosted in front of him as he fought to curl his fingers around the bar. They were already numb from the cold.

Annika pressed up against his back, one arm curling around his chest from behind, the other hooking in the grate, supporting them both as the warmth of her body seeped into him. "I've got you." The feel of her soft curves against him made him thankful the water was so cold.

Her strength surprised him. Supporting a full-grown man twice her weight and a head taller shouldn't have been so easy. *Na'Chi* blood;

demon strength. Her slender stature hid it well. The reminder quelled his desire as quickly as water doused a flame.

The nape of his neck prickled. In battle, he'd seen *Na'Reish* warriors break limbs like they were sticks and once decapitate another with his bare hands. Was she as strong as them? Best he remember she wasn't human and that she could kill with a touch.

"Let's keep moving, warrior." Her voice sounded strained. "The longer we wait, the colder we'll get."

Kalan nodded. She swam only an arm's length away from him as they made their way across the river. His chest felt tight and the aches he feared would hamper him in a swim were superseded by the numbing cold invading his body.

He made it to the bank under his own power but only just. Stumbling from the water, he collapsed onto the grassy verge, sucking in desperate breaths. Once down, his limbs shook uncontrollably. He couldn't even feel the ground beneath his buttocks.

"Here, wrap yourself in this." Her cloak settled over him and she tucked it close in against his body, her hands rubbing his back. He would have pulled away from her to do it himself but his limbs wouldn't obey.

After several minutes though, he felt a rapid warmth seeping through his limbs. He sensed the familiar tingle of power emanating from her. The heat invading his body came from her hands and wherever she touched him. Yet another variation of the healing skill he'd never heard of before tonight. His shuddering slowly eased, replaced with a good dose of caution. She was still a demon and now he knew with complete surety to be wary of her strength.

In the faint moonlight, he saw an enticing flash of naked female skin as Annika crouched beside him. He clutched a fistful of blanket. Why hadn't she taken the time to dress? Her brow furrowed in concentration, and she kept glancing up at the fortress wall and along the bank. He cursed softly as he realized that she was keeping watch.

His brain must have frozen right along with other parts of his anatomy to forget the danger they were still in this close to the fortress.

She looked at him as the power and the warmth she'd created faded. He averted his gaze from her lush body and looked only at her face, startled to see that the flecks in her eyes now glowed a bright red color.

He frowned. "Your eyes . . ."

She hesitated in reaching for the pouch at her feet. "What about them?"

"Why do they keep changing color?"

She unlaced the pouch and thrust his clothes at him then turned her back on him to pull her dress over her head. Was she ignoring his question?

"The color changes with what I'm feeling. This trait belongs only to the *Na'Chi*."

"Your eyes are red now. What does that mean?" He laid aside the sodden cloak and slid into his breeches, lacing them up swiftly. They were torn and ragged but better than no protection against the cold night air. He paused, his shirt in his hands, as the silence between them lengthened again. "Annika?"

"You've made it quite clear you don't trust me." She fiddled with the flap of the pouch. "What's to stop you from killing me if you don't like some of my answers?"

"There's always that chance," he conceded as he pulled on his shirt. He doubted he had the strength for a sustained fight, though she didn't need to know that. Instilling fear into an opponent didn't always require a blade.

Yet he owed her his life. He was out of the dungeon and now he'd have a fighting chance to escape the *Na'Reish* and live. "But Hesia advised me to listen to you with an open mind, and that's what I'll do."

She glanced at him then away, something he noticed she did a lot. "Perhaps we can talk as we keep moving."

A stalling tactic. The reluctance in her voice was a dead giveaway. He motioned her to lead the way, willing to let her get away with it but determined to get some answers.

A half-moon provided enough light to see by. The grassy bank gave way to a rocky roadway, which they crossed quickly. His patience ended as they reached the edge of a densely wooded forest but before he could prompt her, she spoke.

"I've used a lot of energy tonight. Red means I'm hungry."

"Hungry?" He halted by a thick tree trunk, the shadowed darkness beyond it less daunting than the fear that skittered along his spine. "For what?"

"For blood."

His scalp crawled, shock and anger twisting within him. *Lady's Breath!* Hadn't he been trained never to let his guard down? A half-demon, even a pretty one, was still a demon. With a curse, he jerked away from her, reaching for a sword no longer belted around his waist. "You drink blood?"

Adrenaline raced through him when he realized he was unarmed. Unarmed against a woman powerful enough to kill with a touch. He fisted his hands.

"That's why you helped me escape? Why you need me with you?" The image of her latched on to him, feeding, flashed through his mind. "I'm a convenient food source?"

How many Light Blade warriors had he seen fall in battle? How many had he heard scream in agony as demon teeth ripped into their throats or wrists so they could be drained?

Nausea choked him. Too many.

Kalan dropped into a crouch, teeth bared. "Come one step closer and I will kill you."

Chapter 3

HESIA hurried along the dark corridor, her thoughts centered on Annika and Kalan rather than the rough, wet stone underfoot. She inhaled a shaky breath and swallowed hard against the tightness in her throat. Had she made the right decision sending Annika away with the Light Blade?

After so many years of watching Savyr's attempts to break Annika's spirit, and knowing time worked against her efforts to save Annika, Kalan's capture and imprisonment had certainly been the answer to her prayers. She had to have faith that the *Lady* would provide Annika with a better future, that Kalan would keep his word to her, and that *She* would keep them both safe.

"I can't believe you entrusted the life of someone you love like a daughter to a Light Blade warrior."

The deep-voiced, softly spoken reprimand came from the shadows of a bisecting tunnel. Hesia jerked in surprise, her hand clutching at her throat in fright as a figure dressed in black moved to block her path. The tall, lean, muscled body moved with fluid grace. Powerful and dangerous.

The nearest torch threw enough light so she could see his face. Glowing violet eyes ringed with green met her gaze. The pounding of her heart eased. He was more than capable of killing her, had learned that skill at a very young age, but she knew he'd never harm her.

"Varian, you've taken a great risk coming here."

"None greater than any you've chanced over the last thirty years, old woman."

She smiled at the undertone of affection in his voice. He'd called her that from the first time she'd found him, a young child of five scavenging in the fortress rubbish pile for food, half wild and belligerent.

The young *Na'Chi* came closer, his tread silent. "He'll kill Annika the first chance he gets. His kind won't see the difference between us and the *Na'Reish*."

"His honor binds him. He's promised to help her."

"Annika should have been told about us." His somber tone made her grimace.

"Do you think I liked keeping that secret from her? Her knowing of your existence would've put you all at risk."

"She believes we were all killed as young children."

"And the *Lady* forgive me for lying to her all these years." Her gaze sharpened. "But you know why it was necessary."

His sigh was heavy. "Do you really think the Light Blade will help her?"

"He gave his word. He'll learn to trust. When he does, he'll realize that to be *Na'Chi* is not the same as *Na'Reish*." She prayed with all her heart the path she'd helped prepare was one the *Lady* approved of. Nothing would provide more peace and comfort than knowing the *Na'Chi* were safe and able to live happy lives. "If she's accepted by him, this will pave the way for you. The *Lady* will guide them both."

He reached out an arm to help her around a rut in the tunnel floor. "You put too much faith in *Her*."

"And you not enough." Her words were sharper than she intended. Hesia squeezed his hand in apology.

He gave a derisive grunt. "What faith can I put in a deity who allows us to suffer as we have?"

"Varian! The prejudice and fears of humans and demons alike cause the suffering you speak of, not the *Lady*." They'd had this argument many times before. Going over old ground wouldn't solve anything. "Are you and the others ready?"

"We've moved to the old ruins by the river."

"No one saw you?"

The ghost of a smile shaped his lips. "Avoiding *Na'Reish* patrols is second nature to us. Years of learning to hide from them have ensured that. We'll use the same skills to avoid the humans."

She grasped his hands tightly and peered up at him, her own smile tinged with sadness. "Then I've done all I can to help you."

She cherished the next couple of moments as Varian hugged her tightly. She smoothed his long, wavy black hair, and lovingly traced the dark markings that dotted the sides of his face and the jagged scar that ran from the corner of his eye to the bottom of his square jaw. He flinched but tolerated her touch.

The wound was one he'd received when he'd killed one of the dungeon guards after he'd followed her to where he and the other *Na'Chi* lived outside the fortress. He'd once worn it like a badge of honor until others had seen it as a disfigurement, a flaw in what was otherwise a handsome face. Some *Na'Reish* prejudices influenced the *Na'Chi*. The memories of the child he had been and the man he was now merged. Despite his bitterness and cynicism, he cared for and protected the other *Na'Chi*. She was proud of the warrior he'd become. She sighed softly. It would likely be the last time she saw him. There would be a price to pay for helping Annika and the *Na'Chi* escape. Savyr would question her, and with her refusal to speak, he'd kill her. If it meant Annika and the *Na'Chi* would all get the chance at a new life, one free from the *Na'Reish*, then she would accept her destiny. In her heart she knew that the *Lady* would comfort her as she crossed over. Soon she'd be reunited with her own children.

"I'll continue to pray for you, for Annika, for all *Na'Chi*," she promised. "Once your journey begins, your future lies in the hands of the *Lady*."

"I put my faith in you, Hesia, mother of my heart." His whispered words brought tears to her eyes. "We all do."

He pressed a kiss to her forehead then released her. She lifted a trembling hand to her lips as he returned to the tunnel from which he'd emerged. He halted, barely a shadow in the darkness, only his violet eyes visible.

"You've saved us all, no matter what the future brings."

Then he was gone.

Hesia closed her eyes, her heart aching as fiercely as it had when she'd farewelled Annika. She could only hope that the *Lady* would protect the *Na'Chi* now; trust and believe that all she'd done would save their lives as she'd been unable to do for her own half-blood children so many years ago.

"YOU drink blood, just like the *Na'Reish*?"

Annika flinched at the hatred in Kalan's voice. His emerald-colored gaze narrowed and his hand flexed. He'd have drawn a weapon had it been sheathed at his waist. The distance between them across the clearing seemed far too small. She tensed, preparing to flee if he lunged at her.

"No, not just like the *Na'Reish*." She hated how her voice wavered. "I eat food just like you, but I need blood, too. I won't survive if I don't drink it." Disgust flashed across his face. "Do you think I like it? I'd stop if I could. I've tried, believe me."

The face of a human boy rose like a specter in her mind, his mouth stretched wide in a silent scream. He'd had such vivid blue eyes, like the color of the sky on a sunny winter morning. Shuddering, she wrapped her arms around her waist.

"I haven't drunk human blood since I was a child."

She blinked and the image changed. The same beautiful eyes, no longer so vivid but glassy in death, his skin pale and waxy, one cheek smeared with a rivulet of blood. Saliva flooded her mouth.

Annika swallowed hard and shoved the memory back into the darkness where it belonged. Twice she cleared her throat before she was able to speak. "The *Na'Reish* took great pleasure in locking me in a room with a human to watch me feed when hunger overwhelmed me. They thought it . . . amusing."

Disbelief and revulsion warred in the expression on Kalan's face. The hot rush of familiar embarrassment streaked through her.

"You promised to listen with an open mind." With her heart pounding in her chest, it took every shred of strength she had to stand and face him instead of running away. "Do you think I liked what they did to me? They turned me into an animal. I hated them for it and I hated myself for letting them do that to me."

Unable to remember a time when she hadn't had to justify her own existence, she avoided his gaze, too raw from the memories to let him see her humiliation, and laughed bitterly. "Their little game cured me for life. I swore never to drink human blood again. I abhor the practice."

"You don't look like you're starving."

His reply cut like a whip. Her temper flared. "That's because I drink animal blood." She'd been mocked for that, too. In the world of the *Na'Reish*, she was despised for drinking animal blood instead of human blood and the humans despised her for having to drink any blood at all. "I wouldn't take your vein, human, even if I were dying."

"You're part-demon." His tone was flat, unconvinced.

"So, you're saying that the nature of the beast can't be controlled?"

"You weren't able to stop yourself from attacking and feeding on a human."

"I was a child!" Her cheeks warmed even as she ordered herself not to react, not to show pain, or shame, or anger.

All the taunting, the name calling, and beatings paled to the horror and loathing she'd felt once she'd come down from her blood-high and discovered the lifeless body of the blue-eyed boy lying on the ground next to her, his throat shredded and torn out. With her tears mingling with the blood smeared around her mouth, she'd vowed never to drink human blood again, to die before letting herself become the animal she'd shown herself to be.

Her body trembled. How many times had she relived that savage attack? Too many, and not enough. Never enough to atone for her weakness.

"You can stay here if you want"—she forced the words past stiff lips—"but being caught by a Patrol is a certainty if you do."

Without waiting for a response, she turned on her heel and strode into the forest. Being born a half-blood wasn't her fault. Her throat tightened. Would she ever find a place in this world where she felt at peace? Where no one judged her for who or what she was?

Moonlight filtered through the thick canopy but even without it she'd have been able to find her way. Enhanced sight, inherited from her demon father. Yet another reason for Kalan to condemn and reject her.

Why was she letting his attitude affect her so much? Both human and *Na'Reish* despised her. She'd suffered their hatred and disgust all her life. Why had she expected this human to be different?

She blinked back tears. Perhaps because she had healed and then saved him. What did she have to do to make anyone value her beyond what her gifts could provide them?

Without her, this human would be dead. Annika lifted her chin. She wouldn't let him make her feel like the dirt under his feet. She was *Na'Chi*, and if he couldn't see past his own fear of the *Na'Reish* then his preconceptions were his problem.

The brisk night breeze whistled through the branches of the trees. She peered skyward to watch them sway and dance in the moonlight. Many in the fortress feared the forest, claiming it was too quiet, eerie in its stillness, but she loved it. She inhaled the pleasant, earthy odor of leaf litter carried on the night air, and allowed it to calm her frayed nerves. But with peace came the niggling of her conscience. Her steps slowed. She stopped in another clearing and closed her eyes.

What if Kalan decided to strike off on his own? He'd eventually find a trail out of the valley but he knew nothing about the *Na'Hord* Patrols. He was a warrior, but unarmed he'd stand little chance against a pair of hunting *Vorc*. Free of their restraints and unleashed the vicious animals would kill a human on sight.

Behind her a branch snapped, the sound crisp and sharp. Her nostrils flared. An earthy, spicy scent, heavy with salty sweat and the dampness of river water filled her lungs. A familiar bitter tinge of controlled fear underscored it.

The human.

"So red means you're hungry." Kalan's deep, low-pitched voice came from one side of the clearing. "What does yellow mean?"

The comment was an opening, even though he couldn't quite manage a neutral tone, if she wanted to take it. He stood in the shadows of one of the trees, his arms folded, his stance wide, still wary.

She mimicked his pose. "Why would I want to expose myself to your arrogant, narrow-minded attitude again?"

The muscles along his shoulders bunched. His lips thinned along with his gaze. He took a deep breath, then another before inclining his head. "I deserved that."

The words were stilted, bitten off, grudgingly given but as close to an apology as she was going to get.

"We need each other, *Na'Chi*." His admission came from between clenched teeth.

The idea of relying on someone who could barely stand her presence had her temper flaring again. She cast a quick glance at the forest. Three steps, that's all it would take. Three steps and the darkness would conceal her. Without the benefit of night-sight, he wouldn't be able to follow her, not with any speed.

But what was she going to do once she left him? She couldn't return to the fortress. She couldn't enter human territory without his protection. That only left hiding in the forest. Surviving off the land was possible, but years of unending loneliness stretched before her. What sort of life would that be?

Annika fixed her gaze on the Light Blade warrior once more. She wasn't willing to concede anything yet. "Out here you need me, human."

A muscle in his cheek twitched. "And once we reach human territory, you'll need me." One eyebrow lifted. "Do we keep arguing until a Patrol hears us and the problem is resolved or will we begin cooperating as your friend Hesia encouraged us to do?"

Just like that, he resurrected her long-sought-after dream.

"Your eyes still have yellow flecks." His reminder lacked subtlety. The last thing she wanted to do was to give him an advantage over her by answering him. He shrugged. "Have it your way," he said and pivoted on his heel. "I'll make it to the border without your help."

He was leaving her? As he reached the edge of the clearing he showed no signs of slowing. She licked dry lips and took a breath.

"Yellow is fear."

He stopped. Her heart thudded so hard she could feel it against her ribs. When he turned back to her, his expression was slack with surprise. "You're afraid of me?"

"You're the first Light Blade warrior I've met. You kill demons. How do you think I'd feel? If you'd had your sword a moment ago, would you have drawn it?"

"You said you were hungry."

"There's a lot of difference between hungry and starving."

"The *Na'Reish* aren't known for curbing their impulses when they're hungering for blood."

"I'm *Na'Chi*, not *Na'Reish*!" She bit back her anger, unable to refute the truth in his statement. Their conversation was rapidly deteriorating. Again. She wished Hesia were with her. She'd have handled this situation much better.

Annika's legs trembled as Kalan walked toward her and halted an arm's length away.

"Let's stop bluffing one another." Weariness leeched into the tone of his voice. "You're the first *Na'Chi* I've met. With five hundred years of conflict between the *Na'Reish* and us, can you fault me for being wary of someone who has inherited their penchant for blood?"

He had a point.

"I'll give you the same promise I gave your friend. I won't harm you, if you don't attack me."

Annika peered up at his shadowed face, looking for a flicker of deception. His scent remained the same but caution urged her to make sure. "Swear it by the *Lady*."

He frowned. "My word is my oath."

Hesia had always told her Light Blades would honor any oath they made but he'd already turned on her once. "Swear it by *Her* name. Now."

He stiffened as if offended. Too bad.

"By the *Lady* I swear I won't harm you if you don't attack me." Again his words were uttered from between clenched teeth. "Satisfied?"

She gave a curt nod. "It'll do."

"You mentioned *Na'Hord* Patrols earlier. We need to avoid them. Your night vision is better than mine. I almost broke my ankle following you in here." His jaw flexed. "If you'd lead me through this forest I'd appreciate your help."

Kalan extended a large hand. She stared at it. Was this some trick? His expression was tight, angry, and he made no move to hide it from her even as the silence between them grew. She chewed her bottom lip.

Trust has to start somewhere. Hesia's wisdom echoed in her head.

Taking a deep breath, she placed her hand in his. Her palm tingled as his warm skin touched hers. For the first time since fleeing the fortress, she felt hope and something more. He unsettled her in a way no other man or demon ever had.

"There are some caves just ahead of us," she said. "We can hide in them during the day when the Patrols or any other people from the fortress frequent the forest."

"How long will it take us to get there?"

"An hour, perhaps a little more given the dark."

"Then lead on . . ."

For the moment he seemed willing to trust her. The idea warmed her more than it should have. She pursed her lips. Perhaps *tolerate* was a better, safer word to use. The memory of too many years of being betrayed hovered at the back of her mind. And they still had to get out of *Na'Reish* territory unscathed.

Would he abandon her once they reached the safety of the border? Hand her over to the humans at Whitewater Crossing? Kill her? Annika rolled her tense shoulders as she led the way through the trees. For now, they were allies. She'd guide them both to freedom. For now she'd trust him, but if he thought she'd be an easy mark later on, he'd discover his error soon enough.

KALAN couldn't recall how many times he stubbed his toes on tree roots or trod on rocks hidden beneath the debris littering the trail in the journey that followed but exhaustion dogged his every step. Time narrowed to putting one foot ahead of the other.

The cold no longer mattered but the days spent in the dungeon had waged an exacting toll on his body. His muscles ached, despite Annika's healing, yet he was determined not to complain. They needed to get away from the fortress. A day, maybe two, in his weakened state would see him at the boundary between *Na'Reish* and human territory.

"There's a log ahead of us." Her soft voice drew him from his thoughts.

He felt a change in their grip as he heard the quiet scrape of her dress brush over something rough. He'd given up straining his eyes trying to see his surroundings. The world had narrowed to shadowed forms and whatever his other senses could decipher. About waist height in front of him, he touched smooth bark.

"If you sit down you'll be able to swing your legs over more easily."

Being dependent on someone else was a humbling experience. He'd expected Annika to take advantage of his blindness, to punish him for his earlier attitude, but she hadn't. And that went against everything he knew about her paternal heritage.

Was that because of Hesia's influence? Or was she planning something more devious?

"Rest here." She released her hold on his hand and, for a moment, he regretted the loss of her touch. There was a soft rasping sound as if she was looking in her pouch. "I see the river over to our right." He heard the rushing sound of water over rocks. "I have a flask in here somewhere. I'll be back in a moment."

Kalan sighed wearily, content to rest on the log as she headed for the river. The night air was cold and still around him. The trek had left him warm but he knew they didn't dare rest for too long. As she returned, Annika's tread was deliberately heavy.

"Here, drink this." She pressed a wet flask into his hand. The cool water tasted sweet. Despite the temptation, he only drank half then offered it to her. "Keep it. I drank at the river."

"Thank you." He drank again then recapped it. "The ground is steadily rising. We're headed up an incline. How much farther to the caves?"

"Perhaps a quarter-hour." She touched his arm. His skin tingled. "I know you're tired. Would you let me . . . help you?"

"What do you mean?"

"A part of my Gift is being able to feel energy levels. It's how I know when to stop healing someone." She paused again. "I can pass some of my energy on to you, if you would permit it."

He could feel the *Lady*'s power inside her through the touch they shared, the resonance so similar to his own. He knew of no other healer capable of doing what she claimed she could. It wasn't unheard of, the *Lady*'s power being passed from one generation of Light Blade warriors to the next. It was rare but possible. Her mother must have been exceptionally talented.

Annika was *Na'Chi*, an anomaly. Not that he'd voice that thought aloud. But having already experienced her healing touch, Kalan inclined his head. "All right."

His arm grew warm as the power of her Gift increased. It poured into his body, gently at first, like waves lapping against a bank, but then steadily grew in strength, sweeping away his exhaustion. With it he could feel his senses sharpening, becoming more alert. As the power faded, she withdrew her hand. It left him feeling refreshed and warm once again.

"Thank you." Although her face was shadowed, he saw her duck her head as if uncomfortable with his gratitude. "Why do you do that?"

She was silent a moment then her gaze met his, level, steady. The flecks within her eyes glowed a burnt crimson. The skin between his shoulder blades crawled. She was hungry again.

"Very few want me to touch them once they know what I am. And those who do allow me are often too afraid to remember."

Her reply gave him pause. He couldn't imagine living without belonging, without approval, without a loving family. With all the suffering she'd experienced, why did she continue to help those who rejected her? He didn't know if he'd be so noble. "Then why do you keep healing?"

"Because I can't imagine doing anything else." She jumped off the log. "We'd better keep moving. Dawn isn't far away."

Kalan grunted and pushed to his feet. She held out her hand and he took it. They followed the edge of the river using an animal trail. Underfoot the ground was smoother, compacted by hooves and paw prints, and the moonlit sections were more frequent, much to his relief. It gave him some independence.

"How do you know about these caves?" he whispered.

"I found them by accident while out foraging for herbs. I needed shelter from a summer storm. Most of the caves are too small for anything but animals, but the one I found is large enough to shelter in. I've used it for overnight stays before. No one else knows about it." Annika spared him a glance over her shoulder and he heard her take a deeper breath. "It's my safe haven. A place where I can find peace and forget about who and what I am." Her gaze held his a moment longer then dropped away, as if she expected some ridiculing remark.

The stark loneliness of her life struck Kalan low in his gut. Anyone else would have sought out the company of friends. She'd found solace in a cold, empty cave. Was she expecting him to respond? Should he? In the end, he couldn't think of anything to say. Her truth was something he just had to accept.

Passing through another clearing he peered upward. The stars were no longer bright pinpricks of light in a curtain of black. Grey tinged the eastern sky. Ahead he could see the silhouetted shape of a small, rocky hill covered in bushes.

Annika's arm suddenly slapped against his midriff. "Stop!" she hissed and glanced to her right.

He could see nothing but shadows along the opposite bank of the river. "What?"

He heard her inhale. "Can't you smell that?"

The pungent odor of mud from the river and the scent of his own sweat filled his lungs as he took a deep breath. Whatever she sensed eluded him.

A howl shattered the quiet of the forest.

"*Vorc!*"

The word sent a cold shiver skittering down his spine. The predatory animals were used by the *Na'Reish* to hunt humans. It was how he'd been captured. They'd been used to sniff out humans who'd run from the raiding party and hidden within the woods. If the beasts hadn't been muzzled and controlled by their trainers, he and the half-dozen villagers hiding with him would have been torn to shreds.

Had his absence from the Pit already been discovered? The snapping and cracking of branches sounded in the distance. Something large and heavy was racing toward them. Annika's hand squeezed his.

"They've scented us." In the moonlight, her face was pinched with fear, the flecks in her eyes glowed yellow. "Run!"

Chapter 4

DESPERATION and anxiety drove Kymora from her bed and to the *Lady*'s temple. While the hour was late, well past the new morning watch, she half expected to find a fellow Handmaiden or Manservant keeping vigil at the altar.

Without sight, she tilted her head to one side, relying on her other senses to tell her what she couldn't see and listened for the murmur of prayers, the sound of breathing or footsteps, and heard only blessed silence. The empty blankness at the edge of her mind assured her that no Servant occupied the temple. Had her appearance startled them she'd have sensed the flare of surprise in their aura.

Her shoulders sagged in relief. She needed this time alone to search her heart and organize her thoughts. The previous evening's meeting with the Blade Council, coupled with the news of Kalan's disappearance and suspected capture by the *Na'Reish*, had left her in turmoil and she needed the *Lady*'s guidance.

Her temper warmed her with the memory of several scathing comments some of the Councilors had leveled at Kalan's decision to visit the border village. Rather than embracing his policy of being a warrior who remained accessible to his people, a quality they needed now more than ever, they'd criticized his approach and urged him to remain within the walls of Sacred Lake.

She shivered, more from the emotions welling within her than the cold night air upon her skin. Clutching her thick woolen temple robe around her, she made her way carefully down the center aisle, counting her strides, her staff sweeping from side to side, its taps echoing back off the high stone ceiling. When she found the stone altar, she knelt and placed her staff within arm's reach. It took a few moments to find the incense sticks.

Her hands shook as she struck a flame-tip to light the stick. Kalan's absence was not yet common knowledge, and until a successor for his position was found it wouldn't be announced. The Blade Council wanted her to temporarily take his place. Their request implied they thought him dead, which she refused to believe as true.

She sighed. The sweet scent of the incense usually calmed her but tonight her worries weighed too heavily on her mind for it to help.

"*Lady*, forgive me, I know I promised to serve you with all my heart, mind, and soul . . . but Kalan is the only family I have left," she whispered, her throat too tight to voice her thoughts any louder.

She reached for the flat metal amulet hanging between her breasts and drew it out from under her robe. Trying to focus her thoughts, she ran her fingertips over the indented circle etched into it then followed each wavy line radiating out from it. The sun: a reassuring symbol of strength and life.

A gentle breeze brushed her cheek. The scent of new-fallen rain and fresh flowers overrode the odor of incense. Kymora's heart leapt as she sensed the familiar buildup of energy around her. It was soothing, all-powerful. A heartbeat later, she felt the warmth of someone standing beside her and the flutter of silky cloth brush her cheek.

"HANDMAIDEN, I HEAR YOUR PRAYER."

"You bless me with your presence, *Lady*."

A hand touched her head. "I FEEL THE ACHE IN YOUR HEART . . . THE WORRY IN YOUR MIND FOR YOUR BROTHER."

"Please forgive my selfish thoughts, *Lady*."

"HE WAS YOUR BROTHER FIRST BEFORE HE CHOSE TO SERVE ME, KYMORA. THERE'S NO SHAME IN THINKING AS YOU DO."

Kymora bowed her head and closed her sightless eyes as they burned with tears at the wealth of compassion and love that flowed through her. "*Lady*, I beg you to keep him safe . . ."

"HIS JOURNEY HAS ENDED."

Her breath caught. The impulse to issue an immediate denial rose on her lips. Guilt at her selfish reaction kept her silent. Whatever happened to Kalan was a part of *Her* plan, *Her* journey path for him to traverse. As hard as it was to accept *Her* words, to question *Her* will was akin to paramount disrespect.

"BE AT EASE, HANDMAIDEN. YOU KNOW THAT WE TRAVEL MANY PATHS WITHIN OUR OWN LIVES. YOUR BROTHER'S FIRST JOURNEY HAS ENDED; ANOTHER BEGINS."

"He's still alive?" Relief forced the question.

"HE DOES NOT COMPLETE THE FINAL JOURNEY BUT THE PATH HE WALKS NOW WILL NOT BE EASY. MANY WILL OPPOSE HIS CHOICE, ESPECIALLY THOSE WHO HAVE DONE SO IN THE PAST."

Was *She* referring to the Blade Council? Kymora bit her lip, forcing herself to listen, to ignore the myriad of questions hammering through her mind. Discipline and patience would serve her better.

An aura of approval brushed her mind. "ANOTHER JOURNEYS WITH HIM. HER PRESENCE IS NECESSARY. SHE THREATENS ALL WE KNOW BUT MUST BE WELCOMED.

AS DO THOSE WHO COME AFTER HER. MY CHILDREN MUST SURVIVE."

"Survive?" She blurted that without thought. "Your pardon, *Lady*."

"YOUR STRENGTH AND LEADERSHIP WILL BE NEEDED IN THE COMING DAYS. DECISIONS MADE IN THE PAST MUST BE REVEALED AS THEY WILL DEFINE US AND SET THE PATH WE MUST TAKE TOWARD THE FUTURE. HEED MY WORDS."

Kymora had long ago accepted the mysteries *She* revealed when *She* spoke to one of *Her* Servants. Unraveling the puzzle and understanding what was asked of them would come with time. "I'll speak your words to the Council and your Servants, *Lady*."

She sensed *Her* hesitation and resisted the urge to lift her head.

"HANDMAIDEN, YOUR FOURTH JOURNEY BEGINS SOON. DON'T BE AFRAID TO TAKE THE PATH I'VE CHOSEN FOR YOU."

Surprise tingled through her. The *Lady* rarely allowed the one *She* spoke with to know her future. What was coming that *She* felt it necessary to warn her? "I rely on your strength and wisdom to make the right decision, *Merciful Mother*."

"YOUR DEDICATION WILL NOT GO UNREWARDED."

The hand on her head lifted. *Her* warmth and power slowly faded and the scent of incense filled Kymora's lungs once again. She remained kneeling, thinking, long after *Her* presence had retreated.

The patter of footsteps on the flagstones behind her made her stir. She reached for her staff.

"Your knees have frozen to the prayer stone again, haven't they, Kymora?"

The age-worn voice and lighthearted question brought a smile to her lips. "Good morning, Nemtar." She heard a rusty squeak and listened to the temple's oldest Manservant set his lantern on a temple bench. "Is the sun shining this morning?"

"Yes, but you wouldn't guess it. There's a layer of ice coating the courtyard." His robes whispered against the stone floor as he headed for the dais where they kept the temple's supply of candles. "Nor by the temperature in here. You haven't been here all night, have you?"

"No." Kymora used her staff to help her rise. "I'll light the candles, Nemtar. Would you ring the temple chime, please?"

The old man's footsteps halted. "*She's* spoken to you?"

"Yes. I have a message the Blade Council must hear."

As Nemtar hurried off to ring the chime, she inhaled a deep breath. She allowed herself a moment to rejoice in the fact that Kalan had survived the *Na'Hord* attack and hoped he was safe, wherever he was. In her heart she knew he'd do everything in his power to return home.

Her step was lighter as she tapped her way to the dais and retrieved the morning prayer candles. The fresh odor of lemon-scented wax filled her lungs. Her duties as the *Lady*'s Handmaiden would take only a few moments, then she could focus on the coming meeting. She had the feeling she would need all her wits, as the *Lady*'s words were likely to cause a stir.

ANNIKA threw the strap of her healer's pouch over Kalan's shoulder as they reached the base of the rocky outcrop. There was enough moonlight to make out hand- and footholds in the faces of the rocks. She heard the splashing of one, then two heavy bodies in the river not more than a stone's throw behind them. Adrenaline spurted through her, quickened her breathing.

"*Vorc* can't climb," she gasped. It was almost their only weakness. "See that bent tree about halfway up? The cave entrance is behind it. Don't stop, no matter what you hear, do you understand?"

Kalan turned toward her. "What are you—?"

"No time!" she hissed and pushed him toward the rocks. "Up!"

She watched only to make sure he'd begun the climb, then pivoted on her heel. Swallowing hard against a dry throat, she sent a swift prayer to the *Lady* for help then stepped forward to meet the two *Vorc* racing up the slope.

The incline barely slowed their powerful, barrel-like bodies. Their claws churned up the soft dirt underfoot, and pointed snouts with long, sharp fangs were low to the ground as they raced along the animal trail, tracking Kalan's human scent. Prodigious hunters, they could track for days and through most weather.

Moonlight glinted off metal chain amongst the fur at the ruff of their necks. Annika inhaled a relieved breath. While their Masters' saddles were absent, they wore the collars of trained *Vorc*. That meant they were out hunting alone rather than on patrol with any of the *Na'Hord*. It gave her and Kalan a chance of remaining undetected—if she could deal with them. The musky odor of the oil in their shaggy coats sharpened as they drew closer.

When they saw her, they split up and approached from two sides, their small slitted, luminescent green eyes glowing with feral intelligence. The larger one, the alpha male standing eye to eye with her in height was the one she watched.

"*Shavesh ka ris!*" It took all of her courage to issue that command, clear and loud.

From the corner of her gaze she saw the ears of the smaller, female *Vorc* lift from its skull. Her stalking stopped as she followed the order, transforming from predatory to command alert. The male kept coming.

She swallowed dryly. "*Shavesh ka ris!*"

The alpha's nostrils flared and his upper lip curled back as he caught her scent. He hesitated, narrow head tilting to one side. Sharp, dagger-length fangs gleamed in the moonlight. Blood stained his whiskery jaw. They'd already hunted and fed. She shivered. Once sated *Vorc* often wounded new prey and chose to play with it until it died from exhaustion or shock.

"*Shavesh ka vaag!*" Heart pounding, she enforced the command with a descending hand signal. The female *Vorc* lowered herself to the ground.

The male snorted and huffed as he caught her scent again. He glanced to the female then back at her. His saliva-covered lip dropped and his nose twitched again. Slowly, he lowered himself as well, still poised, his muscled body tensed. For once her blood was a blessing. She smelled *Na'Reish* enough for the *Vorc* to believe she was one of them. The male had acknowledged her command but her hold on him was tenuous.

Annika moved closer and to one side of the male, very aware that she was now within striking range of his unsheathed claws. His lip trembled as a rumble came from deep within his chest.

"*Kula veh*, be calm, *kula veh* . . ." She kept her actions slow, her words soft and soothing, keeping her gaze on the spurs on the back of his claws. They glinted wetly, coated in a deadly poison the males used to paralyze their prey. During training, and while on patrol, they were usually capped to avoid accidental poisoning of Master or human prey.

Placing her hand on the alpha male's hide, she gently stroked the coarse pelt. The pungent, musky odor coming from his fur was almost overwhelming. She kept her breathing shallow as she smoothed her hand along his side. The bristles on his neck lowered the longer she petted and murmured reassurance. She focused her thoughts on that rather than the pounding of her heart.

She'd never imagined having to use the commands employed by the *Na'Hord* Masters in charge of training the *Vorc*. The many hours spent in the pens treating the warriors for injuries sustained during obedience lessons now seemed fortuitous.

Hoping the *Lady* would forgive her, she honed in on the beast's life energy beneath her hand. Like all wild animals, the energy was pulsing and raw, hard to link with.

"I'm sorry," Annika murmured and aimed one, focused burst of energy straight into his heart, just as she had done with the guards, and stopped it. Her power surged through her, burning like the flames of a fire, but necessary to end the *Vorc*'s life instantly. She bore the pain as the huge body jerked, then dropped to the ground.

An earsplitting howl shattered the night air. She barely turned to face the female when she was knocked from her feet. The massive weight on top of her drove the breath from her lungs.

"Annika?" Kalan's shout broke through the *Vorc*'s incensed snarls. Annika twisted her fingers in the fur at the animal's neck as her claws ripped through her dress. Hot pain scored her side. She twisted, trying to avoid being shredded completely. Needle-sharp teeth sank deep into her forearm; agonizing tendrils of fire lanced every nerve and muscle. She screamed.

"Annika!" Boots scrambled on rock. Glancing up, Annika saw Kalan descending the cliff.

"No!" Her warning came out as a hoarse whisper.

The *Vorc* released her arm and went for Annika's face. Annika locked her hands around the straining neck and jerked her head aside. The female's jaw snapped so close to her ear, she felt the hot, moist breath on the skin of her neck. The *Vorc* lunged again. Agony tore through her shoulder as her teeth pierced skin and muscle then grated on bone.

Desperate, and knowing the *Vorc* would kill Kalan once he made it to the ground, she drove a second burst of energy into the female. The animal howled in pain then collapsed, her life energy quickly fading from the fatal blast.

Nausea washed through Annika, closely followed by throbbing pain. Sucking in deep breaths, she pushed the female's corpse to one side and rolled to her knees. Something warm and wet ran down her arm. She sat back on her heels. With a shaking hand, she touched her shoulder then stared at the blood covering her fingertips.

"Annika? Are you all right?" Kalan's bootsteps crunched on the pebbled ground. He appeared at her side, peering from her to the lifeless *Vorc*.

"I'm fine."

Kalan's gaze narrowed at how hoarse and strained her voice sounded. Shadows and darkness hadn't let him see much of her struggle with the *Vorc* but he recognized the metallic scent of blood.

Annika swayed as she pushed to her feet. "I told you to stay in the cave!"

Ignoring her reprimand, he caught her arm and felt a hot stickiness soaking the sleeve of her dress. "How badly are you hurt?"

"The *Vorc* need to be disposed of . . . can't leave them to rot." She pushed against him. "Their Masters will search for them when they don't return . . . the river will wash them downstream . . ." Her slurred speech made his decision easy.

"I'll take care of them." He urged her toward the ledge behind them. "Sit. Before you fall down. Tell me where you're wounded."

"Shoulder . . . forearm."

Kalan tore strips from the bottom of her dress, wadded them and, using his fingers to feel along her arm, he pressed and tied the makeshift pads against the puncture wounds. Not exactly pretty but it would have to do for now.

"Rest. I'll get rid of the carcasses." She didn't argue. Kalan worked as quickly as he could.

The sky was beginning to glow yellow by the time he'd dragged the *Vorc* to the riverbank. The swift-moving water would carry them well downriver before they snagged or were seen by anyone. Scattering leaf litter to cover the drag marks ate away more precious time.

Annika was slumped against the cliff face, cradling her hurt arm against her body when he returned. Her eyes were closed but they opened as he approached. The irises glowed a dull red.

"Your scent . . ." Her voice was thin, reedy.

"Too late to worry about that now. How are we going to get you up to the cave?"

Inhaling deeply, she slid off the ledge and peered upward. "I'll manage."

The climb was going to require both of her arms. Kalan eyed the distance she was going to have to cover. "Are you sure you can do this?"

Her mouth flattened and an inky blackness flashed through the red in her eyes. "I'll make it."

He matched his pace to hers as they climbed; saying nothing more but watching to make sure she secured each grip and hold before pushing up. The light from the impending dawn was bright enough for him to see the taut, pain-filled expression on her face but beneath it he recognized the stubborn flex of her jaw. Her determination sparked his grudging admiration. Her attitude was one he expected in a seasoned warrior, not a healer.

Annika's breathing was harsh and ragged as they neared the top. The visible tremors in her limbs warned him she'd reached the limits of her strength. Covering the remaining distance quickly, Kalan scrambled over the final ledge and leant back over. "Take my hands."

Grasping her wrists he hauled her over the lip. She issued a muffled cry and slumped against him. Half sprawled on top of him, and even through two layers of clothes he felt just how cold she was. She started to shiver. All the symptoms warned him she'd lost too much blood. He shifted into a sitting position and reached for her healer's pouch.

"There's *fer-moss* in the inner pocket. Pack it into the wound. It'll stop the bleeding." Her words were slurred, thick, as if she was struggling to focus on forming every word. "The jar tied with red string. I need to sip the liquid . . ." She slumped against him.

Cursing under his breath, Kalan eased her to the ground. With the dawn light he could see fresh blood seeping from the puncture wounds in her forearm and shoulder. Little remained of her sleeve, and four long tears shredded her dress just below her left breast.

"Annika?" He tapped her cheek and frowned when she didn't respond.

One-handed he riffled through her pouch, looking for the *fer-moss* and jar she'd mentioned. Placing both beside him, he packed the soft, springy moss into each wound, making sure the delicate fibers began to swell with the congealing blood before retying the bandages. Then he picked up the jar and pulled the cork with his teeth.

A heavy, minty odor filled the air, one he'd smelled many times in the healing halls and on the field after battle. *Vaa'jahn*. Every warrior knew the benefits of this broad-leafed plant. The roots were dried and ground up into a powder then brewed into a thick liquid that could be applied directly to a wound or swallowed to aid in the fight against infection. He placed the edge of the jar against Annika's lips. She swallowed reflexively as he dribbled a small amount into her mouth.

That done, he moved her into the cave, surprised to find it well provisioned, lending credence to her earlier claim she'd used it before. Blankets lay folded on a flat-topped rock and wood had been neatly stacked near a shallow depression dug into the floor of the cave. As much as he knew they both needed the warmth of a fire, he decided against starting one. He had no idea how far they'd traveled from the fortress, and he couldn't risk the scent of smoke giving away their position.

Spreading out one of the blankets, he laid Annika on it, shook out another to cover her, then hesitated. Blood coated her upper body and soaked the material of her bodice. He should check the claw marks along her ribs. All his efforts so far could be wasted if he didn't see to those wounds.

Kalan paused, his fingers tangled in the laces on the front of her dress. Usually the sight of a naked woman didn't bother him but the memory of her disrobing earlier during their escape from the underground prison had aroused and unsettled him.

He smoothed a long strand of hair away from her pale face. Fighting his aversion to the skin markings, he lightly traced those trailing down the side of her face. Other than in battle, this was the first time he'd seen the demon markings up close.

Annika's were less prominent than those he'd seen on *Na'Reish* warriors, darker than freckles and smooth to the touch. Curious, he nudged her top lip up a fraction. She hadn't inherited her father's pointed teeth; hers were as square and white as Kalan's.

The Blade Council's archives contained accounts of demons siring children with human-slaves but they'd been based on rumor and speculation, not fact. She was living proof that those rumors were true. Hesia and Annika had hinted at the existence of other *Na'Chi* and both had mentioned the *Na'Reish's* intolerance for her heritage.

Kalan ran a hand over his face. *Lady of Light*, her existence would shock many, including those on the Blade Council. No, shock was too mild a word. History and centuries of beliefs would be *challenged*, maybe even threatened, by her existence.

Her actions of the last few hours had left him feeling confused and unsure, a state he'd rarely allowed himself to fall prey to and one he disliked intensely. Her compassion and her Gift from the *Lady* were traits he'd never expected a demon to possess.

Kalan grimaced and ran a hand through his hair. Her motives in helping him were self-serving, but assisting others seemed to be an innate part of her nature. There was more to her than there appeared on first glance.

How had she survived past childhood? That she had survived hinted at an independence bolstered by an incredibly strong will, one developed from a very young age. Logic told him her father had to be *Na'Reish*, a demon lord. The whim of raising a child of mixed blood belonged to the upper caste, not underlings.

How much of an influence had her father had on her? How *Na'Reish* was she? And there lay the problem. How would her presence affect his people? By bringing her back to Sacred Lake, he could be risking not only the safety of his people but the stability of their culture, too.

He sighed. The unknown was too much right now for his tired mind to grapple with. Perhaps if he was more sure of her, trusted her more, the future wouldn't seem as uncertain. But he wasn't sure if he could learn to trust someone like her.

She healed you, helped you escape. She is *Na'Chi*, not *Na'Reish*. He shivered, the difference not as reassuring as he'd hoped it would be. *Mother of Mercy*, he'd drive himself insane trying to solve this now. Perhaps after some sleep he'd think more clearly, but first he had to deal with Annika's wounds.

Inhaling, he plucked at the knot in the laces of her dress. Getting it over her head wasn't an option, not without reopening her shoulder wounds, but with the top of it torn he'd be able to slide it off her body and down her legs.

He tried to keep his gaze averted as he tugged the dress downward over her shoulders but he couldn't avoid touching her when the fabric stuck. Even though his fingertips barely grazed her breasts, he knew they were soft and full, and from the corner of his eye he could see dusky nipples puckering and hardening in the cold morning air. His groin started to ache and throb. He had no control over his body's response, and that confused him.

Careful not to touch her more than was necessary, he eased the material over her abdomen and hips. He couldn't stop himself looking at her. The pale glow of dawn lightened bare flesh at the junction of her thighs and her skin took on a tawny hue. She had curves in all the right places, undeniably a woman, but her limbs were lean like a female warrior's. There was strength in her well-toned muscles, even while relaxed. He swallowed dryly as his arousal increased, and tried to fight it.

Merciful Mother, give me strength. Sucking a breath in through his teeth, he forced his thoughts back to the task in hand. He'd treated female warriors on the field of battle, stripped them to tend wounds. Not once had he had this sort of instant physical reaction. Now should be no different.

Checking the claw marks scoring her ribs, he saw that they were red raw but not bleeding. *Thank the Lady.* She couldn't afford to lose any more blood. Rolling her onto her side, he checked her back, and was surprised to see a myriad of pale scars marking her skin, mingling among the twin trails of her body markings; old ones and none of them claw marks.

Back in the tunnel there hadn't been enough light to see them. He traced one of the longer ones with his finger. It had been made by something thin and straight, perhaps a cane or very thin belt. She'd been beaten. Disturbing.

Quickly cleaning the blood off her body he spread a little *vaa'jahn* over the scratches to ward off infection. Her skin was smooth, silky, and as soft as it looked. And ice cold.

"Fool of a warrior," he hissed under his breath. Here he was staring at her while she froze. His arousal tempered by his thoughtlessness, he jammed the cork back into the jar and quickly drew the second blanket over her.

Wrapping another blanket around himself, he sat against the cave wall and leaned his head back. Old bruises throbbed and his limbs were beginning to ache. He longed to lie down and sleep but, in unknown territory, instinct warned him to keep watch.

Kalan pulled Annika's healing pouch closer. The leather was soft but well crafted. He ran his fingertips over the sun etched into the flap. The symbol was a familiar one. It belonged to the *Lady*, an image used to remind believers of *Her* power and goodness.

Again the incongruence of the situation caught him off guard. The symbol was a reminder that a demon believed in *Her*. He had no doubt *She* had preordained Annika's healing Gift and faith, but who had encouraged and guided her? The old healer, Hesia? Other human-slaves?

The *Na'Reish* certainly wouldn't have encouraged her. They ridiculed the *Lady* and desecrated any temple they found, murdering and obscenely displaying the bodies of any Handmaiden or Manservant discovered within.

Kalan flipped open the pouch flap and peered inside. It was well stocked. He sifted through and examined various bags, jars, vials, bandages, and small instruments.

"The tools of a healer," he murmured, setting them on the ground beside him.

Spotting a small pocket sewn into the side of the pouch, he felt inside, eyebrows lifting as his fingers brushed against something cold. It felt like a necklace. The feeble morning light caught on a small sun charm dangling from the silver chain. It was a Light Blade amulet, similar to the one that hung around his neck.

Smoothing his thumb over the etching, he wondered at the woman who'd worn it. Had she been taken in battle? Annika was young, perhaps in her early to mid-twenties, several years younger than he, so that gave him a rough idea of when her mother had lived. The Council had records going back half a millennium of all the Light Blades killed or lost in battle against the *Na'Reish*. He had little doubt the warrior would be listed among them.

Should he make it back home, Annika's presence there would certainly cause uproar, but worrying about his people's reaction to her should be the least of his qualms. They'd yet to get safely away from the fortress. He should be more concerned with how long it would be before she was ready to travel and whether they'd remain undetected in the cave until then. Staying in one place increased the chance of being discovered.

He placed the amulet back in the pocket, repacked the pouch, then checked on Annika. She seemed to be resting peacefully. Her skin felt much warmer. A jaw-splitting yawn caught him by surprise. Exhaustion dogged him now that the adrenaline of their flight had worn off. He rubbed his burning eyes. Sleep was something he'd had little of in the last fourteen days.

Bowing to the inevitable, he settled down beside Annika and arranged his blanket over both of them. With a short prayer to the *Lady* to keep them safe during the coming daylight hours, he let sleep claim him.

Chapter 5

ANNIKA roused, driven from sleep by a sharp hunger. Saliva filled her mouth as she scented a human close by. Knowing the need would only get worse the longer she went without feeding, she fought the encroaching signs of blood-fever.

In the past she'd always been careful to feed well before they appeared. Her reputation among the human-slaves was dubious enough without fuelling their fears by turning feral as she treated them.

She moved closer to the warmth pressed along her side, hoping the pangs would ease. Pain lanced through her wounded shoulder, dulling the pangs until only a lingering nausea remained. Grateful for the reprieve she opened her eyes.

Her breath caught in her throat. Curled up beside her, a blanket covering them both, Kalan was the source of the warmth. She held still, not wanting to wake him, unsure of how he'd react when he realized he slept so close to her.

Asleep he no longer seemed as fierce or intense. Up close, his expression was relaxed yet captivating. Dark locks of hair fell over one half of his face. Without thought, she reached out to brush them behind his ear. The strands were soft and smooth beneath her fingertips.

Full and expressive, his lips were parted slightly as he breathed evenly, oblivious to her scrutiny. Several days of stubble shadowed his strong jaw and high cheekbones. A pale, razor-thin scar ran across the lower edge of his jaw, from his chin to his ear, but in no way did it mar his masculine beauty. She smiled, liking what she saw. All that was missing were the distinctive markings and he'd have passed as a *Na'Reish* lord.

But he wasn't. He was human, a Light Blade warrior. Her smile faded. Hesia had regaled her with tales about the legendary human warriors, of their dedication to the *Lady* and sacred oath to protect and defend those who needed their help. Her friend's faith in their reputation was unswerving.

Annika chewed her bottom lip. Had she been fully human, trusting them wouldn't have been an issue. With cursed blood running through her veins, Kalan's recent actions had only strengthened her doubt. For the moment they shared a common goal and a temporary truce, but how long that would last remained uncertain.

Blinking, she found herself staring at his throat, at the pulse throbbing just beneath his skin. The hunger stirred inside her. This time her stomach cramped. It took several heartbeats for them to subside.

She had to feed, and soon. As reluctant as she was to wake Kalan, they had to move on. It would be dangerous traveling in daylight but no more so than her ignoring the warning signs of blood-fever.

Shuddering, she placed a hand on his shoulder. "Kalan?" She gasped in surprise as his eyes opened, instantly alert, a warrior trait.

"Annika?" The sleep-roughened voice was deep. His head rolled toward her. She averted her gaze as he sat up. The blanket slipped from her shoulder. "What's wrong?"

She flushed, and clutched the blanket to her as she realized she lay naked beneath it. "Where are my clothes?"

"I had to treat your wounds."

Her cheeks burned with the thought of him examining her despite knowing she'd have done the same for him. He rolled to his feet and fetched her dress where it lay on her pouch, then helped her to a sitting position. Dropping it over her head, he supported her until she tugged it into place under the blanket. Her shoulder throbbed.

"You've lost color." He pulled the blanket over her again, made sure it was tucked securely around her. The gesture touched her. "You should rest."

Sleep would aid her healing but Annika shook her head and peered toward the cave mouth. The slant of the sun told her it was late afternoon. Gritting her teeth, she flung the blanket aside and reached for her boots. They stood beside her healer's pouch. "We need to move on. If we follow the river out of the valley, we might reach Whitewater Crossing by morning."

"Why now? It'll be dark in a couple of hours. There'll be less chance of being seen if we wait until then."

Shadows were filling the cave and the temperature was dropping. She fumbled with the bootlaces. "It's too dangerous to stay. There'll be Patrols combing the forest tonight. We have to get farther away."

She could hear her own heartbeat in the silence that followed. Her laces finally tied, she quickly refolded the blankets and reached for her pouch.

"I don't think it's the *Na'Hord* Patrols you're worried about." Kalan crouched beside her, his head tilting to peer at her. "Let me see your eyes."

Lady's Breath, he was perceptive. Annika tensed, steeling herself for his reaction as she lifted her gaze. Dark green eyes locked with hers.

"They're bloodred," he said. His gaze narrowed. "You're hungry?"

Just how hungry was she? She ducked her head, almost able to hear his unspoken question as she returned to her task of securing the blankets onto her pouch. "I need to hunt. I can do that as we travel."

"You're in no condition to travel—"

"I've no choice."

He motioned at her bandaged shoulder. "Your wounds need time to heal."

"We don't have time." She rose, slinging the pouch over her good shoulder. A frown marred his brow. It looked like he was ready to argue with her. His stubbornness sparked a bitter anger. She strode to the mouth of the cave. "Your safety is forfeited if I don't feed soon. I'm still strong enough to overpower you. I'll drink until I'm sated. Do you want to risk that?"

Even though it had been years since she'd last tasted human blood, the memory of the hot sweetness of it in her mouth was immediate. The urge to grab Kalan and pin him to the ground so she could feed filled her mouth with more saliva. She shuddered.

Breaking the addiction to human blood as a child had almost killed her. Only through carefully weaning herself off human blood and onto animal blood, and the resilience of her youth, had saved her. Hiding her transition hadn't been easy. It'd taken nearly four months, using the excuse of foraging for herbs in the forest to cover her need to hunt, but for once her father's disdain and the *Na'Reish's* contempt for her presence among them had proved beneficial.

Instinct warned Annika not to risk addicting herself to human blood again. Hunting now rather than later was her only option.

Kalan appeared beside her and she fought not to flinch under his scrutiny. Staring out into the shadowed forest, she waited for some cutting remark or epithet.

"How will you get down from the cave?" he asked.

His calm response startled her, delayed her answering for several heartbeats. "The same way I got up here."

"Then give me the bag." He took her healer's pouch. "You'll have enough to worry about without that hampering you. I'll go first."

A quarter hour passed as Kalan scouted the area. When he gave her the all-clear, she took her time descending, testing the strength and flexibility in her arm.

Concentrating on secure hand- and footholds helped keep her mind off her hunger but by the time she reached the ground she was shaking with fatigue. Her wounds burned and throbbed in time with her pulse. She placed her cheek against the cold rockface until she recovered, her breathing ragged. Would she be able to reach the river-trader village in her present condition?

"We need to follow the river awhile," she said. "I'll fill the canteen . . ."

Kalan caught her arm before she could move off. "I saw no signs of a Patrol or other *Vorc*." He placed her pouch on the ground beside a bush. "Rest while I hunt."

Alarm raced through her. "Your scent—"

"I'll leave one whether I hunt or travel to Whitewater Crossing." His argument made sense but it would also take time she wasn't sure they could afford. "You've already admitted you're a threat to my safety. How can I watch for Patrols if I'm worrying about you attacking me to feed?"

Annika nodded, albeit reluctantly. "Be careful."

She watched Kalan take an animal trail into the forest then made her way toward the river. It felt strange having him head off on a task she'd fully expected to do herself. For so long she'd had to do everything on her own, no matter how tired or ill she'd been. She knelt on the bank of the river and started to fill the canteen, pausing a moment as a frisson of unease skittered along her back.

Would Kalan use the hunt as an excuse to leave her behind and head for Whitewater Crossing on his own? He was experienced enough to realize she was a liability. It might take him a little while to negotiate the darkness once the sun set but all he had to do was follow the river.

Her hand shook as she capped the water flask and peered along the trail he'd taken. Deep shadows obscured it where the forest thickened. She listened for footsteps, a branch breaking. All she could hear were the intermittent squawks and flapping of feathered wings as birds settled in the upper canopy. Sunset was barely an hour away.

Fear curled in the pit of her stomach. She placed the canteen into her pouch and wiped her hands on one of the blankets. From the outset Kalan had shown a reluctance to trust her. She had all the supplies, her medicines, the blankets, her cloak but the idea that he would leave her behind was still a possibility.

Following him once she regained her strength wouldn't be an option. Her tracking skills just weren't that good. Going back to the fortress would be foolhardy. Her compassion for humans was well known.

She bit her lip. Not all humans were likely to accept her. A demon alone was fair game. It was why she'd bargained with Kalan for his protection. For time to prove she was no threat. For the chance to find sanctuary among the Handmaidens and Manservants dedicated to serving the *Lady*.

Hesia had often spoken about their tolerance for all who came seeking help. If she could find one who would aid her, perhaps she could lead the new life she'd dreamed of for so long.

Overhead, a cool breeze rustled the leaves of the trees. Annika shivered, pulled her cloak out of her pack, and wrapped it around herself. She took shelter beside a bush. Her stomach clenched with hunger. Should she hunt for herself or trust Kalan would return?

For the moment, the only decision she could make was to rest. She'd expended a lot of energy climbing down from the cave. She tried to shake the uneasiness eating away at her but the longer she waited the heavier the sinking feeling in her gut grew.

Half an hour passed. A full hour. Late afternoon became purple-tinged twilight, then full darkness.

She buried her head against her up-drawn knees, fighting a combination of disappointment, fear, and hunger. Until Hesia had found the Light Blade warrior in the dungeon, her dream of freedom had been as unattainable as finding acceptance among the *Na'Reish*. She'd dared to anticipate a new life among humans but now it looked like she was going to have to survive on her own after all.

Hot tears prickled in her eyes. Clenching her jaw, she swallowed hard. Crying wouldn't solve anything.

If Kalan had left her, she hoped he made it out of *Na'Reish* territory safely but while she could understand his motives, being abandoned still hurt.

Chapter 6

A BREATHLESS curse left Kalan's lips as he stumbled over yet another unseen obstacle in the growing darkness. The heavy weight of the long-whiskered tree-climber on his back canted to one side, throwing him off balance. He tightened his grip on it and braced himself against the nearest tree, then sucked in several weary breaths.

It'd taken him longer than anticipated to find a well-used animal trail and set up a snare. Trapping the nocturnal animal so early in the evening was a boon. Usually it only ventured down from its nest to hunt in the late night hours. Hopefully the carcass would have enough blood to sate Annika's hunger.

Her warning that she would attack him if she didn't hunt was so un-*Na'Reish* like. His brow furrowed. He still didn't like the idea of her drinking blood. Logic dictated that without drinking the blood she'd be weaker, less of a threat. Could he take what she said as truth? But why would she lie?

He couldn't take the risk of not letting Annika feed. For now, he'd take her word. Being *Na'Chi*, would she heal as quickly as the *Na'Reish*?

He'd seen *Na'Reish* warriors with minor wounds heal in less than an hour after drinking human blood. Hers were more severe.

It was something he'd find out once he made it back to where he'd left her. Jostling the carcass into a more comfortable position on his back, he moved on. Staying close to the river had been wise. Without the sound of running water he'd never have been able to find his way back in the dark.

Moonlight dappled the undergrowth as he skirted another bush. The forest seemed thinner up ahead. To the left he saw a familiar silhouetted rockface. Scanning the riverbank, he saw a dark shape huddled beside a bush. Relieved, he picked up the pace.

"Annika?"

The figure moved then he saw her glowing red eyes as she peered up at him, a startled expression on her face. "Kalan?" Her husky voice held a note of disbelief. "You're back."

He sank down onto the leaf-littered bank, grunting as he dumped the small carnivore on the ground between them. "It took me longer than I thought to catch something . . ." She swiped a sleeve across her face and he heard her inhale a shaky breath. He frowned. "You didn't think I'd return?"

She shrugged. "I'd given you directions to Whitewater Crossing—"

"So you thought I'd strike out on my own?"

Avoiding her gaze, Kalan poked at the leaf litter with the toe of his boot. He had thought about abandoning her, more than once during the hunt. The darkness provided cover from easy detection, and with the knowledge of how to get to Whitewater Crossing the lure to leave had been tempting.

The shallower water near the trading village was considered neutral territory, the safest place for *Na'Reish* and human Patrols to cross—the former to bring slaves back from raids, the latter while rescuing them.

During the hunt, he'd mulled over all sorts of arguments to justify leaving Annika behind even though she'd been the instigator of his chance at escape.

His sister needed him. His people needed him. Annika's weakness was a liability. Staying to help her meant the risk of being recaptured was greater. All valid reasons. No one could have faulted him for taking the journey to freedom.

Except his conscience. And curiosity. He wasn't sure which took precedence over the other but Annika deserved an answer.

"I returned because I gave you my word I'd help." He gave her a partial truth. She flinched and her gaze swerved away from his. "Once given, it's as binding as my faith to the *Lady*."

Her fist clenched around the edge of her cloak. "Hesia always said a Light Blade's honor was as important to you as your faith. I shouldn't have . . . doubted you."

She stumbled over the second half of the sentence and he wondered at her reaction. Did she care about what he thought of her?

"I'm sorry." Her voice was pitched so low he barely heard her. "It's not an excuse, I know, but I'm not used to people keeping their promises to me."

He rubbed a hand over his jaw. What sort of life had she lived to expect that sort of behavior? He wanted to question her further but the tension between them didn't lend for confidence sharing.

He motioned to the animal. "What do you want done with it?"

She drew her pack closer and pulled out two objects: a wooden cup and a small knife. "Cut its throat. I'll collect the blood as it drains."

A chill rippled through Kalan, her request triggering the memory of watching Light Blades butchered and drained by the *Na'Reish* at the time of his capture.

"I've seen *Na'Reish* drink straight from the source." Tension made his voice hoarse.

She stiffened, pausing in the act of passing the knife to him. "I'm not *Na'Reish*." The reminder did little to banish the raw images in his head. "If you'd rather, I can do this by myself."

His gaze locked with hers as he reached for the blade. Several long heartbeats passed before she relinquished the weapon.

"If you attack me, I'll defend myself, Light Blade." Her voice shook. The flecks in her eyes went from yellow to green and the familiar hum of her Gift teased his senses. "All I want to do is drink."

Kalan tightened his grip on the hilt of the blade and sliced the throat of the tree-climber. The rich, metallic odor of blood filled his nostrils. Annika placed the cup under the dark liquid flowing from the wound. It filled quickly. Her hand shook as she lifted it to her lips. She hesitated. The sharp pinch of hunger was there in her face as her gaze met his over the rim of the cup. She drank.

Nausea curled in his stomach at the thought of what she was doing. He had to look away. The screams of his comrades in arms as they were murdered echoed in his mind. He could still hear the laughter and taunts of the *Na'Reish* guards and feel the painful grip as they'd restrained him from going to their aid. His warriors had died slowly. Cursing under his breath, he fought to hold the tree-climber steady.

"I take no satisfaction in this." The bitterness in Annika's voice made him look back at her. She was watching him as the cup filled again. "I do it to survive."

When he said nothing, her gaze dropped but not before he saw her eyes change from red to orange. The emotion behind her actions became clear. The *Na'Reish* took pleasure in flaunting their feeding habits. She was ashamed of what she was doing, but her hunger gave her no other choice. The idea gave him pause.

How much easier for her would it have been to give in and feed from a slave? Instead she'd chosen to resist her demon instincts, defy her heritage, and subsist by hunting and feeding from animals. The resolve involved in such a decision spoke of a strong person, one incredibly determined and disciplined.

Annika continued to avoid his gaze as she finished the last cup then took it to the river to wash. He cleaned the small knife and disposed of the carcass. It was a pity to waste the meat but they couldn't risk a fire to cook it.

She was waiting for him when he returned, her pouch slung over her shoulder. "Let's move." She motioned with her chin the direction they should head.

"Annika." He reached out and caught her shoulder. She stiffened. "You're not *Na'Reish*. I'm sorry I implied otherwise."

The apology didn't come easily but she hadn't deserved his anger.

"I'm a demon." She shrugged, as if it didn't matter. But it did, he knew that now.

"Half-demon." She remained silent, her stance still tense. He was surprised that her being uncomfortable around him bothered him so much. "You haven't attacked or hurt me and you've done everything to warn me about your nature. The *Na'Reish* would never do that."

"You trust me?" While her expression gave away nothing her voice held hope.

"Not yet. But I can't deny the truth of your actions."

After a long heartbeat she exhaled a shaky breath and nodded. "I can accept that."

And so could he, for now. It didn't mean he'd let his guard down around her, and only the *Lady* knew where it was going to lead, but for now he'd trust *Her* to guide him.

"Ready to go?" Her quiet question reminded him they still had a long night ahead of them. With a nod he let her lead and they began to follow the river.

ANNIKA tilted her head to one side and glanced back over her shoulder. The tall trees lining both sides of the rutted cart track they were walking along weren't thick enough to block the morning sunlight. Pale sunbeams danced with shadows on the leaf-littered roadway all the way back to the last undulating rise.

A pretty scene, had it not been for the uneasy feeling eating away at her stomach. Trusting her instincts, she reached out to touch Kalan's forearm.

"Do you hear that?" she murmured.

He halted. "Hear what?"

"Exactly." She swept her gaze over the forest around them. "Birds should be calling this time of morning."

His expression tightened, his eyes narrowed. "How far are we from Whitewater Crossing?"

"It's just around the next bend." Before she could speak again she spotted movement on the roadway behind them. Six dark forms, two on *Vorc*-back, topped the last rise. One knelt to examine the ground. Her heart began to pound.

"A Patrol?" Kalan's question was terse.

She nodded and pushed him into the bushes. "Use whatever cover you can. Run."

He followed her instruction without hesitation. There was little doubt the *Vorc* had already picked up his scent and they'd probably left tracks for the *Na'Reish* scout to find on the trail. Using the road-way had been a risk but a necessary one to reach the river-trader village in good time.

A cry shattered the air, loud enough to drown out the sounds of their rapid footsteps.

Kalan glanced back. "They've reached the place where we left the road."

"Keep going."

On the uneven ground, they risked turned ankles if either of them tripped between the twisted tree roots but it would be just as difficult for the Patrol. The *Vorc*-riders would have to force a path through the undergrowth or follow the roadway and wait for the scouts to capture them. Either way, the Patrol would be divided. It increased their chances for escape.

Kalan drew to an abrupt halt as they broke through the treeline onto a cleared paddock. Annika bent over to gasp in deep breaths as she sent a silent prayer of thanks heavenward.

On the other side of the fallow ground a small village of ramshackle wooden huts sat perched on a bend in the river while below on the pebbled scree a flat platform ferry was anchored to a wooden dock.

Squeals of laughter drew her gaze to the rocky shore. She recognized the half-dozen children pitching stones into the water. While the younger ones hadn't been allowed near her during her previous visits to the village, she'd seen them from a distance, as curious about them as they were about her.

"Cross this field," she panted and pointed toward the dock. "There's the ferry. We need to find Vash, the ferry-master."

A shrill whistle came from the dock house the moment they began traversing the cleared field. The children on the riverbank dropped their stones and ran for the buildings. They didn't even bother to look around. The tallest sprinted along the main thoroughfare shouting a warning.

A hoarse yell behind them told Annika the Patrol had spotted them through the trees. She stumbled on the raised sod, and Kalan caught her arm to stop her from falling. His grip jerked her half-healed shoulder. She grimaced but bore the pain as he urged her on.

A high-pitched howl came from behind them. Another echoed it. She risked a glance. Her blood ran cold. Following them at a ground-eating lope were the four *Na'Hord* scouts, their weapons drawn, while bearing down on them at full gallop were the two *Vorc*-riders, covering the distance twice as fast as they could run. The riders split, urging their beasts on, one to the left, the other to the right. She could hear the deep, raspy breathing of the animals as they drew level with them.

"They're trying to cut us off." Adrenaline burned through her but her tired muscles refused to move any faster. "We're not going to make it!"

"I won't be captured again!"

She gasped in surprise as Kalan veered to his right and launched himself at the *Vorc*-rider. He grasped the rider's shoulder and his weight pulled him from the saddle. As they fell he wrenched the demon's dagger from his belt. She felt a familiar surge of power a moment before he drove the blade into the guard's neck.

It was all she saw before a heavy body collided with her. The impact sent her tumbling and drove the breath from her lungs. Her pouch ripped from her shoulder as she rolled. Her wound throbbed.

Dizzy and disorientated, she ended up facedown on the ground. She spat dirt from her mouth. The overpowering odor of musk filled her lungs. Instinct urged her to move. With her head spinning, though, all she could manage was a crawl.

She heard the *Vorc* grunt. It planted its sheathed claws in the soil in front of her, blocking her escape. Its musky scent filled her lungs as she inhaled a gasping breath. A pair of large boots thudded barely an arm's length away. Brawny, muscled thighs in dark leather breeches flexed, stepped closer.

"Who'd have guessed I'd find you out here, *Na'Chi*, and in the company of our escaped prisoner?" drawled a deep voice.

She peered up into the *Na'Reish*'s broad, angular face, noting the dark markings mottling the side of his jaw. He belonged to the *Na'Reishu*, the demon middle class, and was probably the captain of the Patrol. She didn't recognize him but the cruel twist of a smile on his lips was familiar.

"You deserve death for helping this human. It's a pity that pleasure belongs to your father."

His boot struck her side like a steel bar. The force drove her onto her back, choking for breath. The demon straddled her, pinned her to the ground with his weight. Drawing on her Gift, she grabbed for his wrists.

A balled fist struck her cheek. Pain exploded in her head. Another blow caught her mouth. Her cheek. More pain. Her vision dimmed. The iron tang of blood coated her tongue. Cries split the air. She was wrenched off the ground a moment, then the demon's heavy weight was gone.

Thuds and grunts sounded nearby. Glancing up, she flinched. The blows to her head had doubled her vision because there were too many blurred figures fighting nearby for the number of *Na'Reish* she remembered. Desperate to flee, Annika crawled in the opposite direction.

"Stop her, she's getting away!" a gravelly voice bellowed.

Running footsteps came toward her. Her heart pounded. Her hand touched something cold and hard. She curled her fingers around the rock. Her head was yanked back by the hair as she swung the rock at her assailant. A hard, muscled arm blocked her. Her wrist was caught, squeezed, and her numbed fingers released the weapon. She was slammed to the ground on her back and held there once again.

Blinking furiously to see her opponent, she gripped the bare flesh of his arm, sensed the strong thudding of his heart, his life energy, and summoned her Gift. The sound of a blade being drawn from a sheath chilled her. Its cold edge bit into the skin of her throat.

"Stop!" Kalan's hoarse voice came from close by.

"She's one of them!" The deep voice was filled with contempt.

"She isn't part of the Patrol. She helped me escape."

Annika's heart pounded. She dared not move. She could hear the harsh rasp of her assailant's breath. Abruptly, the blade was withdrawn. She released the man's wrist and blinked once more, relieved as her sight returned and she stared up at one of Vash's sons, not the *Na'Hord* guard she feared he had been.

She recognized the young man as Maren, Vash's youngest son. She'd seen him on several of her visits to the village to buy herbs from the traders. He was built stocky, like his father, with the same broad facial features and straw-colored blond hair, the wavy strands tied back in a long braid. His deep blue gaze bore into her, hard, severe, and older than the twenty years she knew him to be. Barely contained savagery burned in their depths.

Kalan appeared behind him, disheveled, a cut bleeding on his cheek. He laid a hand on the youth's shoulder. "Let her go."

Something darker than reluctance seethed beneath the ferocity but the man complied. Had Kalan not intervened, she doubted anyone else would have stopped Maren. She sat up, unable to hide her trembling. She'd come too close to death.

Kalan crouched beside her. While he didn't touch her, she could feel his gaze moving over her. "Your brow is split."

She pressed a hand to her forehead. It came away bloody. The side of her face felt hot and swollen. Her newly healed shoulder ached. "I'll live." She'd suffered worse. Licking her lips, she kept her voice low. "Why didn't you let him kill me?"

A frown creased Kalan's brow. His confusion surprised her. She raised her chin in Maren's direction.

"In half a heartbeat I would have been dead and you'd have been free of me . . . our bargain."

His emerald gaze widened as the hand resting on his thigh curled into a fist. "You question my honor again?" His lips compressed into a thin line. "If I wanted you dead I'd kill you myself, not rely on someone else."

Never doubt a Light Blade's word, Annika. Hesia's admonishment whispered in her mind. *Their oath is as binding as their faith.* Heat burned Annika's cheeks. She should have trusted in her friend's assurances but before she could apologize Kalan spoke.

"Do you know these people?"

Her gaze drifted over his shoulder then widened when she saw the bodies of the *Na'Reish* and two *Vorc* sprawled on the ground behind him. Three other human males stood with Maren. She eyed their bloody weapons, then glanced up at the eldest.

"That's Vash," she murmured, nodding toward the man with silver streaking his blond hair. Years of hauling the ferry across the river accounted for the muscled shoulders bulging beneath his coarse-woven long-sleeved shirt. Worn leather trews fit his brawny thighs like a second skin and were tucked into scuffed work boots. "Next to him are his sons, Maren, Carne, and Riccalo."

Kalan held out his hand and helped her to her feet. "Who's Vash?"

"He and his wife, Gerla, own the tavern." She gestured to the largest building closest to the dock. Smoke curled from its stone chimney. "He also owns the ferry and trades supplies with the *Na'Reish* in this end of the valley. Not by choice, though. As long as he provides the goods they need, they leave the village alone."

"You keep unusual company, Light Blade." The bearded man's gravelly voice carried over the distance between them.

Kalan pinned the man with a level stare. "Do you always help strangers being pursued by a *Na'Hord* Patrol?"

"Only if they're human." He cocked his head to one side. "Do others follow you?"

"I doubt they're the only ones searching for me."

Vash gave a quick hand signal and his sons headed for the battle scene. As unofficial leader of Whitewater Crossing, he'd ensure the dead bodies of the guards and *Vorc* disappeared. To leave them there would court the wrath of the next Patrol. One of the traders scooped up her pouch and threw it to her. Her hands still shook as she drew the strap over her head.

"Thank you," Kalan said solemnly. "We couldn't have escaped the Patrol without your help."

Vash inclined his head and signaled them to move toward the village. Annika's gaze traveled to Whitewater Crossing. Several people watched from the edge of the village. The idea of them helping escapees didn't surprise her. The families made a living from ferrying the men, women, and children taken during border raids by the *Na'Hord* Patrols, saving the demons from having to man the crossing.

These humans had seen their kind abused and used as bloodslaves. And while her father traded with them, his Patrols also ransacked and plundered their homes and businesses whenever it struck their fancy. There was certainly no love lost between the two groups.

"Annika tells me you own the ferry. We need passage across the river."

Vash's pale blue eyes surveyed Kalan then her. "Does she go with you?"

"Yes."

His lip curled. "What business do you have traveling with her?"

"What concern is that of yours?"

"If another Patrol learns that she was here, especially in your company, it becomes my concern." Vash halted their trek to the village and folded his brawny arms. "I don't want the wrath of the *Na'Rei* brought down on my family."

Dread surged through Annika, gripping her heart in its iron fingers and squeezing. *Lady of Mercy*, she hadn't anticipated this. She should have.

Frowning, Kalan glanced between her and Vash. "Why would the demon leader be troubled by her disappearance?"

"She's his daughter."

Annika's insides shriveled with his damning words. Shock flitted across Kalan's face. The muscles in his jaw flexed, hardened. The pupils of his eyes dilated then shrank as his gaze fixed on her. "You're Savyr's *daughter*?"

She pressed a hand to her chest, hardly able to draw breath to answer him. "Yes."

Kalan took a slow step toward her, his right hand flexing then fisting, every line in his body taut. Annika wanted to run but a sulfuric odor underscored by an earthen heaviness emanated from him. It possessed the same sharp intensity her father's scent had seconds before he lashed out at her. She tensed, anticipating, expecting a blow from his fist but the physical strike never came.

Kalan's emerald eyes glittered. "The half-blood daughter of the demon leader." His clipped tone was as cold as the ice that lined the riverbank.

She flinched. Her pulse leapt with fear until she could hear it pounding in her ears. She should have told him earlier when Hesia had encouraged her to share her story with him back in the dungeon.

Would he give her a chance to explain?

Lip curling, Kalan moved away as if he couldn't stand to be anywhere near her, his thunderous expression unforgiving. A hollow ache writhed in her chest. Any explanation now would be seen as an excuse. Too convenient, too late. What little trust they'd established was gone thanks to her stupidity.

After a quick glance around, she knew there'd be no escape. Goose bumps prickled her skin. The villagers surrounded her, their gazes as cold as Kalan's boring into her back. Would they now kill her? Her mouth dried. She clutched her pouch closer to her chest, fragile protection against danger.

Fear urged her to run.

Chapter 7

KALAN shook with raw fury even as a chill raced through him. Annika's birth and survival to womanhood took on new meaning and her evasiveness back in the dungeon now made sense.

The demon leader had a *Na'Chi* child, one he'd kept alive. His reasons for doing so remained unknown but Kalan had no doubt that once her disappearance became known she would be hunted down like him, for different reasons, but hunted all the same. They were in greater danger than he'd ever suspected. His stomach twisted and knotted.

Why hadn't she told him who she was? Fresh anger raced through his veins. Because she knew she'd deliberately taken advantage of his desperation.

"Leave the *Na'Chi* with us." Vash gripped his wide leather belt. "She'll only bring trouble. We'll take care of her."

As a Light Blade warrior, his first tenet was to protect his people from danger. Fleeing across the border with Annika would increase the threat of *Na'Reish* Patrols invading human territory.

Tempting as it was, the bargain he'd struck with her stood in the way of accepting the trader's offer. To break his oath now would be dishonorable.

His shook his head. Damned if he kept his word, damned if he didn't. And to think he'd been afraid for her when he'd seen Maren place his blade at her throat. His gaze slashed to her. She stiffened. Her eyes were yellow; the brightest he'd seen since meeting her.

"You'd let them kill me?" Her voice shook. Terror and indignation sparkled in her gaze as she glared at him. "I saved your life, Light Blade."

Vash's thick eyebrows lifted. "Is that true?"

"Yes." Kalan couldn't deny her claim as much as he wanted to. *Lady's Breath*, what a mess. Everything inside him rejected the only solution to the problem. He forced the words through clenched teeth. "She stays with me. How long before we can cross?"

A long silence followed and for a moment he believed Vash would refuse them passage. The river-trader finally shrugged. "We can go now."

"Good." Kalan caught Annika's arm in a tight grip, disliking the contact but there was no way he was giving her a chance to escape. Not before she answered his questions. Questions he'd delayed far too long in asking.

She gasped but made no move to jerk free. Ignoring the trembling in her muscles, he focused on getting them to the dock and the thought that in another half hour he'd be safe on the other side of the river.

"Go on board." Vash issued several more orders that sent his men hurrying to untie the ferry, then joined the pair on the deck. Satisfied all was in order he turned toward them, jutting his chin in Annika's direction. "What do I tell the *Na'Reish* when they come searching for her?"

"Nothing." Guilt flared in Kalan's gut. Annika wasn't the only one hiding their identity. "We all have our secrets. . . ." His decision didn't sit well with him, but, *Lady* forgive him his hypocrisy, he had no right to endanger himself more than he already had. Others depended on him. He'd deal with the consequences later. "I'm sure our passing this way is something you'll want to keep to yourself."

Vash shook his head. "You tread a dangerous path, Light Blade."

Once they were aboard, Kalan left Annika by a stack of empty crates and retreated to the side, needing to distance himself from her. Leaning on the wooden railing, he closed his eyes and rubbed his hands over his face.

Merciful Mother, he was tired. He kneaded the shoulder that had taken the brunt of the fall when he'd dragged the *Na'Reish* guard off his mount then shivered as the morning breeze picked up strength. The cold made his whole body ache. He wished he dared stop for a bath, a solid night's sleep, and a good meal, but until he made it across the river and out of *Na'Reish* territory, he wasn't safe.

Around him, the river-traders called out to each other as they prepared to cast off. The ferry jerked then began to rock as it hit the rapids that gave the crossing its name. Rope hissed through the metal rings on the guide rails as the workers hauled on them. That sound and undulating motion as the ferry was buffeted were soothing.

"Traveling with her is a huge risk." Vash's statement was just loud enough to be heard over the rushing water. He leaned on the rail next to Kalan. "You said it yourself—she's the half-blood daughter of the demon leader. Why take her with you? You'd be better off going on alone."

Kalan grimaced and scrubbed a hand over his face. "In exchange for her help getting out of the fortress, I promised to take her to Sacred Lake and protect her."

"An honor debt." Vash grunted. "Perhaps you could turn this to your advantage then. Hand her over to the Blade Council. Being who she is, who knows what sort of information she might have about *Na'Reish* warrior numbers and the like."

The Blade Council knew next to nothing about the *Na'Rei*'s defenses. They were going to need every advantage available if they had any hope of stopping Patrols from raiding across the border.

He peered over his shoulder. Annika sat by the small shelter, leaning back against the wooden wall, her arms clasped around her drawn-up knees, looking as tired as he felt.

And alone.

Don't be fooled by her looks. She'd used him. She didn't deserve his empathy. Did she?

"Here." Vash's gravelly voice broke into his thoughts. The older man handed him a small pile of faded clothes, worn but in better condition than Kalan's garb. "They're not much but they're clean and certainly warmer than what you have on. Change in the all-weather cabin."

Nodding his thanks, Kalan took them and glanced at Annika again. She'd placed her head on her knees. A vulnerable pose. Deceptively so. He shook his head. She had a strength of will most men lacked. That, coupled with her skill when it came to killing demons, or humans, proved she was as accomplished as any Light Blade warrior.

Something he'd better never forget.

"I'll watch her."

Nodding his thanks to Vash, Kalan headed for the small cabin. Changing would only take a few minutes, then Annika was going to need that inner strength. It was time she answered his questions.

Annika drew in a slow, deep breath to ease the thumping of her heart as Kalan's footsteps retreated to the all-weather cabin. Over the sound of the ferry disembarking, she'd caught parts of his conversation with Vash. What were his plans for her? He'd neither confirmed nor denied any suggestion made by the river-trader.

"Sometimes Light Blade warriors take their honor too seriously when it would benefit them more to bend a little." Vash's voice sounded closer than before. Annika glanced up to find him, Maren, and another walking toward her. "But I have no problem dealing with rock-scum like you."

The pungent scent of their hostility raised the hairs on the back of Annika's neck. A rush of adrenaline cleared away her fatigue.

"I don't care why you helped this Light Blade escape from Savyr's fortress but I do care that your father will come looking for you. We both know he won't be happy." Vash's grey eyes narrowed. "What I need to know is how many Patrols will he send to my village looking for you?"

So that was to be the way of it. Kalan had left Vash to question her, unable to stomach doing it himself? Annika scrambled to her feet, unwilling to face them all while sitting down.

Maren seized her injured arm, his fingers clamping directly over the newly healed wound. Gritting her teeth, she tried to pull away only to find her other arm caught. Both Maren and the other man hauled her back toward the wall of the all-weather cabin and slammed her against it. The impact drove the breath from her lungs.

"I noticed you favoring this arm earlier," Maren hissed. His fingers dug into her shoulder. Pain shot through it, numbing every muscle along the length of her arm. "How many Patrols track you?"

"I don't know."

He scolded her with a tongue clucking noise. "Wrong answer, *Na'Chi.*"

He twisted her arm until every muscle, tendon, and ligament screamed in protest. Nausea flooded her belly. She bit the inside of her cheek, her temper flaring at Maren's brutal tactics.

"Think carefully, demon, and answer my father with the truth. Claim you don't know again and I'll break your arm." The whispered threat increased her anger. Compared to her father, Maren's technique was amateur.

"What are you doing?" Kalan's sudden question saved her from answering. She couldn't turn her head without putting more pressure on her wrenched arm but she heard his rapid approach. "Release her."

Maren and the other man made no move to obey until Vash nodded. Sensation rushed back into her arm. Light-headed, she slumped against the wall, and bit back a groan.

"I thought you'd appreciate a few answers." Vash folded his arms. "Her kind don't tend to tell the truth without a little persuasion."

"I'll ask my own questions, river-trader." Kalan's voice was clipped, short. "I don't need your . . . help."

Disappointment speared through Annika. So much for Light Blade honor.

Vash grunted then signaled his men to return to work. "Suit yourself." He retreated to stern.

She glanced warily at Kalan. Was his anger for Vash or her? She straightened, unwilling to cower like she'd been forced to do with her father as he'd punished her for some infraction; defenseless, too vulnerable.

Kalan turned his stormy gaze on her. "Why'd you lie to me?"

Her mouth dried. The muscles across his broad shoulders were bunched, tight, and his knuckles had whitened where they grasped his folded arms as if he was restraining himself from grabbing her.

Fear clawed in her gut. Would he pick up where Vash had left off if she refused to answer him?

"I didn't lie to you." To her shame, her voice trembled. "I neglected to tell you something important."

"You used deflection and deception." His accusation cut like a whip. She flinched. "When were you going to tell me who you were?"

"Would you have helped me had you known who I was?" she demanded. His silence answered for him. "Hesia might have had faith in your reputation as a Light Blade but I didn't, not when my life hung in the balance."

His face darkened with her reckless tone. "Your life? Your lineage ensured your status among the *Na'Reish*."

Blood drained from her face. She sucked in a ragged breath. "You think that gave me an advantage?" Her voice rose and cracked. "My father barely tolerated me."

"Then why did he let you live?"

"Revenge." She bit out the word even before she had the chance to think.

Kalan blinked then a slow frown marred his brow. *Merciful Mother,* surely he didn't imagine her father *cared* for her? Her temper soared higher.

"Savyr's firstborn son was killed by a Light Blade warrior." Trembling, she ground out the facts past stiff lips. "He wanted the human responsible dead, but that was before he learned the warrior had offspring of his own. A *daughter.* So, he captured her instead then raped her until she fell pregnant."

Chills raced along her arms. The memory of watching her father's dark lips peel back over his fangs in a malicious smile terrified her even now. He'd taken such pleasure in telling her how her mother had screamed and fought him. Even knowing how sadistic and malicious he could be, the thought of him forcing her mother, time after time, made her sick to her soul.

While raping slaves wasn't condoned by the *Na'Reish*, it was a practice rarely spoken about. Especially considering bloodline purity played such a prominent role in their culture. Many talked about Savyr's obsession for revenge but few were naïve enough to question him about it in his presence.

Annika clenched her hands. "He made sure she couldn't kill herself or injure the baby inside her so that she'd lose it. For nearly eleven months, he'd kept her chained to a bed in his private chambers, her every move observed by loyal blood-slaves."

Kalan still watched her, his gaze intense, his expression shuttered. Unlike the other humans in her father's household, he hadn't flinched or grimaced with the details of her mother's story. Did he believe her? It shocked her to realize she wanted him to, badly. Blood pounded in her head. Had it been a mistake to tell him anything? She couldn't hold his gaze and stared at the wooden boards beneath her boots. When would she learn not to care about what others thought?

Her fingernails bit into the skin on the palms of her hands. He was going to hear the rest of the story whether he believed her or not.

"Once I was born, Savyr intended sending us back to her father. The disgrace of returning with a *Na'Chi* child would've satisfied my father's need for revenge, but the birthing was difficult. It took too long. My mother died. If I believe his version of events, she did it just to spite him. Sending me back to my grandfather alone served no purpose. There was no proof of my bloodline. So, he kept me and has reminded me daily of why I existed."

His blood runs through your veins. Savyr's angry mantra echoed in her head. *Breaking you is the only satisfaction I have left.*

Defying him had brought her a great amount of satisfaction. She wanted to believe her endurance and strength were traits inherited from her mother.

The smile that stretched her lips felt brittle, crooked. "Someone had to pay for the death of his son."

Her past was distasteful, yet worse was the hope and assumption that Kalan might accept her. The expressionless mask on his face gave away nothing but his recent actions proved he was just like everyone else. He didn't care.

Annika buried her disappointment and hurt deep but couldn't stop trembling. She'd made a mistake thinking her life could be anything different. Hesia's love was a blessing and she'd abandoned her to follow a *haze*-induced dream.

She met Kalan's eyes, her gaze steady but inside she felt as frozen as the water rushing beneath the ferry. Her next words, forced from between numb lips, felt like shards of ice slicing her throat. "Tell me, Light Blade, what privileges do you think I inherited being *bred* as a tool of retribution?"

Kalan stood silently, reeling from shock as the rawness of Annika's emotions washed over him. Hesia had warned him but he'd never realized the full extent of what she'd meant. Until now.

While instinct cautioned him not to believe her, he suspected Annika wasn't lying. Savyr's brutality was legendary. In the last five years alone he'd slaughtered every member of two *Na'Reish* clans who'd dared raid across the border without his sanction. To use a child, someone so innocent and vulnerable, to satisfy a blood-debt was unthinkable. Immoral. Her tale left an acrid taste in his mouth.

Annika turned her back on him and walked to the other side of the ferry. Kalan tried to hold on to his anger but the revelations of the last few minutes and her hunched shoulders projected such aching loneliness and despair that maintaining it was impossible.

Mother of Mercy, how had Annika dealt with being told every day of her life that she was only a means to an end? She had as much reason to despise her father as he did. He very much doubted anyone could fake the stark loathing he'd heard in her voice as she'd recounted her story. The shadows in her gaze hinted at more, at a dark self-hatred only a lifetime of abuse could cause.

The memory of stripping her naked in the cave was vivid. The scars on her back came from being beaten. And there were too many marking her skin for it to have happened only once. Savyr's behavior would've encouraged others to treat her in much the same fashion. What additional horrors had she endured at the hands of her father? The other *Na'Reish*? The human-slaves?

How could he have accused her of living a privileged existence?

She was an outcast. Ostracized by all except the old healer. *Lady of Light*, it was a miracle she hadn't become as embittered and vengeful as her father. Instead, she healed others and dreamed of freedom.

Annika had deceived him, but *Lady* forgive him, she hadn't deserved his anger, especially considering the secret he hadn't shared with her.

Kalan sighed roughly and moved toward Annika. She tensed. The flecks in her eyes were black as her gaze slashed up to meet his.

"So, do you now slide a knife between my ribs and slip my body overboard to save everyone the trouble of what to do with me?"

Her tone was biting, caustic. Unsurprising considering how he'd treated her but the remark wasn't aimed at provoking him. He recognized it for what it was. Armor.

She'd lashed out at him to keep from being hurt again. And he had hurt her. Unforgivably. He'd blamed her for his own weakness and desperation to escape. Her actions were a convenient scapegoat for him to hang his guilt. The injustice of what he'd done ate at him.

Honor demanded he make amends. The path the *Lady* encouraged him to walk was undeniably a challenging one.

"I should have listened to my own instincts back in the dungeon, when I believed you were evading my questions. The responsibility of what I chose to do then lies with me, not you. Implying otherwise was wrong. Hesia tried to warn me your life among the *Na'Reish* hadn't been easy. I should have listened to her. I'm sorry."

Her involuntary start reminded him she rarely expected apologies. She remained silent, her breathing uneven as she fought for control of her emotions. Her pain was very much his fault.

"Are you going to hand me over to your Council?" Astonishment must have shown on his face because one side of her mouth curled upward into a cynical smile. "*Na'Chi* have excellent hearing, Light Blade. Did you forget that?"

He had. "Despite what's happened, our bargain stands."

"I misled you." Her chin lifted. "I don't expect you to honor it."

A convenient out, if he wanted it. His estimation of her grew. Few men could have made a decision like that; most would have begged to renegotiate. Somehow he doubted Annika had ever pleaded for anything. It just wasn't her way.

Deep inside, he rejected the idea of taking the coward's way out. Curiosity prompted his next question. "What would you do if we part ways?"

She shrugged. "There's always the need for a healer somewhere."

Too general an answer for his satisfaction but he didn't press her. "And if Savyr finds you?"

"My sympathy for humans is well known. He'll assume I helped you escape."

"Which means what exactly?"

"He'll kill me."

There it was again: that hint of helplessness and dark desolation in her voice that pulled at him.

"You're giving up?" he asked.

The yellow in her eyes flashed to black. "I should have known living among my mother's people wouldn't work."

The white lines of tension bracketing the corners of her mouth indicated she really believed what she was saying.

"You'd abandon your dream of freedom?"

"Dreams are for fools! It was stupid to think I could ever fit into your world."

Her vehement denial prodded his guilt. He didn't like that he'd played a part in crushing her dreams. He shifted from one foot to the other.

Again he wondered at the purpose of the journey the *Lady* had set him on. Was he destined to take Annika back to Sacred Lake? Despite the upheaval that would cause, *She*'d thrown them together for a reason.

He wasn't afraid of a challenge. *Mother of Light*, he wouldn't be where he was in the ranks of the Light Blades if he hadn't overcome many already. It was just the potential ramifications and the effect it would have on others besides himself.

Did he dare presume everything would work out in the end? Would it? What path did *She* want him to take? Which direction was the right one?

Kalan ran a hand through his hair. Perhaps the choice should be Annika's. The journey was as much hers as it was his. Even as he thought it, a sense of rightness settled close to his heart.

"Only the *Lady* knows for sure if you'll find a home among us," he refuted. "You dream, you plan, you adapt." Her closed expression firmed his decision. "If you really want to strike out on your own when we dock, then I won't stop you."

Her gaze flickered behind him to where he knew Vash and the others stood. "What about them?" she asked.

"They won't stop you either." Her gaze followed his hand as he touched the amulet on his chest. He'd trust in the *Lady* to guide them both. "You have my word. The decision is yours."

It took every ounce of resolve to turn away from her then and leave her to her thoughts. He prayed he'd made the right choice of leaving the decision in her hands.

Only time would tell.

Chapter 8

ANNIKA could feel Maren watching her from where he stood on the riverbank waiting for Kalan to finish talking to Vash. His gaze was intense, almost predatory, as he tracked her every move. Other river-traders stood near him but he made no effort to join their quiet conversation as they anchored the ferry. His silent scrutiny stroked the nerves in her stomach.

Trying to ignore him, she settled her pouch over her shoulder then followed a set of wheel tracks to the top of the bank. They disappeared into a thick forest. One she'd only ever seen from a distance. She'd never been farther than Whitewater Crossing. Never dared.

This side of the river was human territory, a place no demon went without a Patrol or two as an escort. She glanced back at the river. How it had come to be the natural division between *Na'Reish* and human territory she wasn't sure. Learning any sort of knowledge or history belonged to the *Na'Reish*, the privileged upper caste.

But the map on the wall of her father's chamber had given her some insight. She knew the humans lived on the eastern side of the river, all the way into the mountains and beyond them to the plains that bordered a huge sea. They lived in cities and towns and villages as well as crofts and isolated huts. That much she knew from listening to the *Na'Hord* scouts talking among the ranks.

The *Na'Reish* were broken into a dozen clan provinces, with most living within the confines of a keep rather than spread across the land like the humans, even though as a race they patrolled an area similar in size. Annika couldn't recall how many times she'd heard her father stress that strength in numbers and purity of bloodlines would ensure the survival of the *Na'Reish*. The *Na'Reish* had been bound by those beliefs for the last five hundred years.

Annika's gaze returned to the ferry and Kalan. He would expect a decision from her shortly about whether she continued traveling with him or went her own way. That he'd given her the choice surprised her. Was this a way of getting back at her? Elicit her response then refuse? If not, then what had changed between him discovering her identity and now?

Despite her brave words about making it on her own, Annika knew she'd be lucky to survive a week alone on *either* side of the river if she went on without help. Perhaps Kalan knew this and letting her decide her own fate would keep his conscience clear and honor intact.

Her throat tightened. Should she remain with him or gamble on finding a safe place on her own? What was the right thing to do? She drew her cloak closer around her, wishing Hesia were with her. She missed her so much. The old woman's advice always managed to calm her when things didn't go to plan.

Trust in the Lady. She *will guide you.* Hesia's age-worn voice whispered the familiar words in her mind. How many times had she heard her say them? They brought her a modicum of comfort.

Hesia claimed their first meeting had been *Lady* ordained. Annika remembered the incident, not because it had been the start of a lifelong friendship, but because she'd been a scared seven-year-old hiding from a *Na'Reish* lordling intent on giving her something worse than a bloody nose. Walking through the snickleway on her way to a slave-birthing, Hesia had heard her crying behind a water barrel.

With a lot of coaxing and gentle words, the healer had treated her bloody nose as well as several other scrapes she'd gained in her flight from the lordling. A simple act of kindness but one that impacted Annika in the days and weeks that followed.

Some of her earliest memories were of tagging along behind Hesia on her rounds through the fortress. There'd been no reprimands or curses, just more softly spoken comments and, once she'd gathered enough courage to join Hesia by her side, explanations of what she was doing to heal her patients. With the knowledge of the humans' letters and words a skill she'd been forbidden to learn by her father, Annika had memorized every scrap of information.

Then there were the prayers to the *Lady* for guidance and assistance. At first Annika believed Hesia and the human-slaves had been talking about an actual person, but the more she'd listened she'd discovered that *She* was a deity who offered them wisdom and comfort while guiding them in their journey through life.

To a child raised on rejection and disdain, *Her* compassion and love fulfilled a need she'd never known existed until then. *She* was also a part of her mother's world, something Annika had always craved to learn more about.

The *Na'Reish* refused to acknowledge a deity of any sort. They believed only in the power of might, enslaving those who submitted, killing those who resisted.

Compassion belongs to the weak, love an illusion for fools. The scathing words of a father who'd showed her neither one.

Annika dug into her pouch and drew out her mother's Light Blade amulet. A familiar warmth filled her as she allowed herself to think about her dream of living and learning more about her mother. She smoothed her thumb over the small sun symbol etched into the metal disk. She knew nothing about the woman who'd worn it but had tried to imagine many times what she might have been like.

Strong. Compassionate. Loyal. All qualities a Light Blade warrior possessed. Physically, she knew the woman had blond hair. Annika hadn't inherited Savyr's dark locks. Loving? Probably, given the right situation. Most humans loved someone.

Would her mother have loved her? Annika peered into the distance, not really seeing the forest or the mountains. Deep down she knew what she wanted the answer to be but hovering just behind it was what she suspected to be the truth.

Having attended the births of several *Na'Chi* babies with Hesia, she'd seen the loathing and revulsion on the faces of their human mothers. They'd begged Hesia to kill their children. It didn't matter that it was innocent of any of the crimes of the father. The babies had disappeared and when questioned, the old healer had refused to explain. Annika had never pushed her, fearing the worst.

Had her mother begged the healer to kill her after she'd been born? It was too late to ask Hesia but if she continued on to Sacred Lake, surely someone would know more about her mother and be able to answer the questions she'd wondered about for nearly twenty years.

The crunch of gravel under boots drew Annika from her thoughts. She turned, dreading her visitor would be one of the river-traders. She didn't think she had the strength to deal with their suspicion and dislike right now.

The sight of Kalan striding up the slope to join her filled her with relief. Her breath caught in the back of her throat at his striking appearance. River-trader clothes looked good on him.

A strange heat burned within her as she began at the scuffed leather boots and worked her gaze upward. The faded breeches clung to him like a second skin. She could see each muscle in his legs flex as he walked but the material was still supple enough to give him freedom of movement.

The dagger taken from the *Na'Reish* rider hung on his belt, sheathed and strapped to his right thigh. A long-sleeved shirt fit his broad shoulders perfectly. The laces at its neck remained untied, allowing her a tantalizing glimpse of the tanned skin of his chest.

His hair fell in haphazard waves around his face, softening the harsh look that came with the shadow of stubble on his jaw. He exuded such confidence and self-assurance. Once again, she found herself captivated by him.

Her face flamed at the memory of him sprawled naked on the bank of the river after they'd escaped from the tunnel. Muscular yet lean. She focused on the bare skin peeking through the laces of his shirt. She swallowed at the thought of the warmth of his skin, the steel hard strength of the muscles beneath it. What would it be like to have him touch her? Like a lover?

Desire burned through her so swift and strong she was unable to move. For the first time in her life she wanted to be intimate with someone. Annika blinked, shocked at the direction of her thoughts. Inwardly she cringed as she remembered the expression on Kalan's face back in the pit, and then when he'd found out who she was. What was she thinking?

Looking at him made her wish for things that never could be. She was neither demon nor human. He hadn't wanted her anywhere near him, and she doubted he'd welcome her touch now that he knew who she was. While he claimed to be open-minded about her being *Na'Chi*, his recent actions had revealed his true feelings.

"Have you made your decision yet?" Kalan asked.

Annika refused to look at him as he drew level with her. Her emotions were nowhere near under control and she didn't want him questioning the color of her eyes.

"Yes." She squared her shoulders and, even though she was tired, reached deep for the well of strength she knew existed inside her. "The *Lady* guides us in mysterious ways, doesn't *She*? Although this time I think *She*'s made *Her* will quite clear. I travel with you." She glanced at him. Relief flickered across his face. So his offer of a choice had been genuine. "My decision surprises you?"

His smile made her heart lurch and her innards burn once more. "I wasn't sure if my arguments had swayed you."

"They didn't." His smile lost strength with her blunt words. She'd never hidden from the truth. "If I'm to survive, what other choice do I have?" There was no going back. Tucking her mother's amulet back into the pouch, she drew in a deep breath. "I'll be tolerated in your world, just as I was in mine. It's the best I can hope for."

VARIAN crouched to examine the faint scuff marks pressed into the moss on the boulder-strewn ridge. Placing his hand beside the indentation, he noted the size of it and knew it belonged to the heel of a boot. Someone short, light in weight. A partial footprint was impressed into the moss beside it. The depth indicated the second person was taller, heavier, and by the width of the print, definitely male.

He scanned the ground ahead. Small boulders protruded from the leaf litter as the moss gave way to rocky ground. There was little soil on this stretch of the trail, so it made looking for tracks more difficult. His lips curled upward as he spotted an overturned rock just ahead, as if something had caught its edge.

He followed the faint signs along the trail, his senses attuned to every scent carried on the gentle breeze, every leaf flutter in the trees above him and the sounds of animals in the undergrowth around him.

A flicker of movement to his left among the trees caught his eye. Crouching low, he curled his hand around the hilt of his dagger. A young man, his dark hair twisted into multiple braids and dressed in brown, stepped out from behind a tree. Violet eyes met his—hard, knowledgeable, older than his seventeen years of age.

Varian relaxed and rose to his full height. "What are you doing here, Zaune?"

The youth was one of his best scouts, a fierce fighter and a loner, like himself, which probably accounted for why he liked the youth so much.

"Lisella sent me. She's called a halt."

He grunted. "She did, did she?"

"You've been pushing the group hard, Varian. It's difficult for them to travel quietly and at the pace you've set. They've managed but they're worn out."

Varian raked a hand through his hair and tamped down his frustration. "The Light Blade's escape has been discovered. I've spotted three Patrols in the last two hours. We need to get across the river into human territory."

"Tired people make mistakes."

He rubbed his jaw, felt the hard ridge of flesh where his scar intersected it. "How many?"

"Seven, all children."

Zaune also looked drawn, although he doubted the *Na'Chi* would admit to any weakness. They'd all learned to be tough, had to, in order to survive.

He motioned to the tracks on the ground. "They're only a day ahead of us. We can't afford to fall any farther behind, not when we have to travel downstream in order to cross safely where the river narrows."

He wasn't telling the scout anything he didn't already know. Zaune waited patiently for his orders.

"Pull five of our scouts off duty. Get them and two other adults within the group to carry the children. We need a few hours' distance between us and that last Patrol before we stop for the night."

Zaune nodded. "Lisella won't like it."

"She's not in charge." His gaze narrowed. "Remind her of that, and if she doesn't like it, tell her to take it up with me tonight. Get the group moving."

He was pleased at how quickly the scout blended in with the dappled shadows of the forest and was gone. His thoughts turned to Lisella. The safety of forty-seven individuals weighed heavily enough on him and those he'd trained as scouts without her countermanding his orders. Headstrong and stubborn, he wondered if the young *Na'Chi* woman realized the danger she was placing them all in.

Zaune would make sure the group moved on. His lips thinned. Lisella needed to realize that this journey wasn't going to be like living at the compound. Debating every decision wasn't an option. For the moment their survival depended on everyone following his orders, no questions asked.

ANNIKA stood by the open doorway of the small barn, the hood of her cloak pulled well over her head as Kalan negotiated with the farmer for a night's shelter and food. The man glanced over his shoulder at the young, pregnant woman watching them from near the small hut where she was sitting, mending clothes. Dressed simply, both reminded her of the farmers who visited Whitewater Crossing in the harvest season to trade with Vash.

"With Lessie's time due I could use a hand with a few chores." The farmer waved a calloused hand toward the hut. "The shutters on the windows need fixin' afore the summer storms, 'n I ain't had the chance to water the stock this evenin'. Lessie makes a good stew but we don't have much, Light Blade . . ."

Kalan gripped the man's upper arm. "Whatever you can spare is appreciated."

Sighing softly, Annika placed her pouch on the ground at her feet, and gently rotated her healing shoulder, easing stiff muscles. They'd traveled hard and fast most of the day, avoiding the well-used trail from the ferry, knowing any *Na'Reish* Patrol would use it if they crossed the river in search of them. Instead Kalan had led her into the thick forest and they'd forged their own path along gullies and over hills.

"I'll get the hammer 'n nails for you . . ." The man pointed to the well over by the stockyards. "The bucket's over there 'n there's hay in the barn."

She waited until he'd started toward the hut before closing the distance between her and Kalan. "I'll take care of the animals," she murmured, expecting him to protest, astonished when he didn't. She tested his scent, puzzled by the absence of acrid overtones that should have projected his suspicion and distrust. "I'll wait in the barn when I'm finished."

He nodded. "It shouldn't take too long to repair the shutters."

By the time she'd finished feeding and watering the animals, the sun was sinking behind the mountains. With the onset of evening came a cool breeze. Drawing a final bucket of water from the well, Annika took it and her pouch with her as she retreated inside the barn.

There was enough light to see as she looked around the interior. Clean straw covered the floor of the half-dozen stalls and the loft above. After placing the bucket on the ground, she headed for the middle one. Straw was an improvement to spending the night on the cold floor of a cave. It took a moment to spread out the blankets.

Grimacing at the grime on her hands, she unclasped her cloak as she returned to the bucket to wash her hands and face. The water was ice cold but it felt good to be clean.

"Hello?" The female voice was hesitant. "Are you in here?"

Annika's stomach lurched. Soft footfalls sounded behind her. Snatching up her cloak, she put it on, tugging the hood forward to conceal her face. Heart pounding, she scrambled to her feet as the farmer's wife appeared inside the entryway of the barn, holding a lantern and carrying a bag over one shoulder.

The woman lifted the lantern higher, throwing the light farther into the barn. "Hello?"

"I'm here."

"I'm sorry iffen I startled you." She offered a small smile as she hung the lantern on a hook by the stall where she'd set up their blankets. "I'm Lessie 'n I've brought you some dinner."

Annika stepped backward into the shadows. Thankfully the woman's attention was on opening her bag. She set a lidded tureen, a hunk of bread, and a water flask down in the middle of the floor.

"It's not much . . ."

The scent of an herb-laden stew filled the air.

"It smells delicious. *Lady* bless you and your husband for your kindness."

The woman pushed back a handful of long, dark hair as she straightened. Surprise flitted across her face as she registered her location but she said nothing. "I overheard the Light Blade telling Stevar you helped him escape the demon's fortress. 'Tis rare to hear of anyone doing that . . ."

"It wasn't easy but, by the grace of the *Lady*, here we are."

"Iffen I'm pryin' jus' tell me, but the only people I heard live there, 'sides the *Na'Reish*, are their slaves." Lessie cocked her head to one side. "How is it you came to be in the fortress?"

"I was there to help heal Kalan." What exactly had he told them? "The opportunity to escape arose, so we took it."

"You're a healer?" A hopeful smile broke over the woman's face and she took a step closer. Annika tensed. "Would you have experience with birthin'?"

"Yes." While she didn't want the woman to see her, Annika couldn't refuse to assist her. "Do you need my help?"

"Stevar took me to a healer a few months ago. Everything's going well." She gave a half shrug. "It's jus' my back aches almost every day . . ."

"How far along are you?"

"Eight months."

"No bleeding or contractions? Are you on your feet a lot?"

"No, but Stevar needs my help 'round the farm." A worried frown creased her brow. "Is there a problem?"

"I don't think so." There was only one way to make certain everything was all right. "May I touch you?"

"Go ahead."

Keeping her gaze downcast, Annika stepped into the light. She moved behind the young woman and placed a hand on her lower back. Focusing her thoughts, she felt the familiar warmth of her Gift flow through her. Lessie's pain was a nagging ache. A smile curved Annika's lips as she also sensed the life-force of the baby. He was healthy and happy.

"Just as I suspected." Annika rotated her hand gently, massaging the sore area. "You have muscle strain. Feel how I'm pressing my hand against you? Get Stevar to do this every morning and evening. It'll bring relief to your back muscles." She stepped around Lessie to find her pouch. Kneeling, she rifled through it and brought out a small bag. "A pinch of these herbs steeped as a tea will help ease the pain during the day."

"I don't have nothin' to trade for them—"

"I'm not expecting payment." Annika pressed the bag into the woman's hands and closed her fingers around it. "You've shown kindness to complete strangers. Thank you."

After a moment's hesitation the young woman nodded and tucked the bag into her dress pocket. "Will you tell me your name?"

"Annika."

"It's been a while since I had 'nuther woman to talk to, Annika. P'haps after dinner you might like to sit awhile with me?"

Annika fisted a hand in her cloak. There was such longing in Lessie's tone of voice, but the woman thought she was human. If Lessie ever discovered exactly what Annika was, she'd be appalled by her assumption. Following that would come the revulsion and denial of any offered friendship.

Chewing on her bottom lip, Annika glanced toward the barn doorway. Where was Kalan?

"Is there somethin' wrong?"

Annika hesitated. "No. I'm just . . . not used to this sort of situation."

"What situation?"

"Slaves were punished for talking."

"Did the *Na'Reish* also make you wear the cloak?"

"I have . . . marks . . . on my face I'd rather others didn't see." She didn't want to lie to the woman. "My looks offended the *Na'Reish*." A partial truth; *Lady* forgive her.

Lessie bit her lip. "I'm sorry iffen I made you uncomfortable."

A familiar, broad shouldered figure appeared in the doorway.

"Annika?"

Kalan's deep voice sent a wave of relief washing through her. She sighed. His brows dipped low as his dark green eyes flickered from Lessie to her, direct, measuring. The irony of preferring his company as opposed to Lessie's didn't escape her.

"We were just talking." Her reassurance eased the intensity of his gaze but the tightness around his mouth didn't lessen. Did he think she'd hurt a pregnant woman? Annika closed her pouch and stood. "I appreciate the invitation, Lessie, but I'm tired from our traveling. Thank you again for the food."

The young woman ran a hand over her rounded stomach, a disappointed smile on her face. "I guess Stevar'll be wantin' his dinner now that the chores are done." She patted her pocket. "Thank you for the herbs. I'll leave you the lantern. Sleep well."

Kalan shut the door after she'd left. "I didn't realize she'd headed over here to deliver the meal. Are you all right?"

She fumbled with the tie on her pouch and shot him a sideways glance. He'd been worried about her? Odd behavior considering his cold response to her at Whitewater Crossing. A flash of astonished pleasure raced through her anyway. She dipped her head to cover her confusion.

"I'm fine." Discarding the cloak, she lifted the lid on the tureen. Her mouth watered with the appetizing odor wafting out from underneath it. "Lessie believes I'm a slave from the fortress."

"I warned Stevar about the possibility of *Na'Hord* Patrols hunting for us this side of the border." He snatched a rag hanging in one of the stalls and crouched by the bucket. "Start eating while the meal is hot. I'll wash up."

He pulled off his shirt and set it aside. Annika froze, unprepared for the sight of his ridged abdomen and the play of muscles rippling across his naked chest. Sharp prickles of awareness stabbed the pit of her stomach. He was all solid muscle, lean and hard.

The urge to reach out and touch the hard plane of his shoulders, to smooth away the droplets of water sparkling there was so strong Annika had to clamp her fingers around the lid of the tureen to stop herself from doing just that.

A shiver rippled along her spine. He was off-limits to someone like her. She was something no one in his world could ever love. The bitter truth writhed inside her and constricted around her heart. She dropped her gaze, disappointment aching in her chest, but couldn't stop watching him from the corner of her eye.

Na'Reish control their emotions. Savyr's harsh voice echoed deep in her mind. *Your mother's blood betrays your weakness time and again.* Shame burned her cheeks. She pushed it back, angry at her ingrained response.

How many times had she endured a beating for revealing her

emotions? Her back twinged with the memories. She counted every time he'd given up whipping her as a victory, every scar as a testament to just how strong she was, despite his belief to the contrary.

Suppressing the vivid encounters, she cleared her throat. "Do you think a Patrol will come this far into human territory?"

"They have before." Kalan's muscles flexed as he used the rag to dry himself. He raked a wet hand through his hair then slipped his shirt on. Disappointment of a different kind elicited a soft sigh from her. He inhaled deeply. "Whatever Lessie made smells good."

Tearing the bread, she handed him half as he joined her on the ground beside the tureen. They ate the small but simple meal in silence, scooping up the stew with chunks of bread and sharing the flask of water. Annika was glad for the silence as it gave her the opportunity to restrain her unruly emotions and bury her desires deep.

A wry smile twitched the corners of her lips. Her father's lessons in discipline and control had finally proven valuable.

Chapter 9

O N this side of the river, the forest grew right to the edge, only
a narrow graveled scree peppered with boulders defined the
shore. Varian clambered up onto one of the boulders and scanned
the treelined bank. The tall, needle-laden boughs were thick enough
to obscure the late afternoon sunlight and the temperature was cooler
than the sunlit shore on the *Na'Reish* side of the river. Not ideal
conditions for wet boots and breeches, especially with the cold breeze
and the onset of evening.

He glanced over his shoulder and was relieved to see the last of
their party emerging from the knee-deep water. Zaune brought up
the rear. He carried a child in his arms and staggered onto the scree.
One of the women took the child from him and deposited her in the
middle of the closest group huddling behind a boulder for protection,
out of the breeze. The young scout bent over at the waist, hands
propped on his knees.

Varian ran a cold hand over his face. The crossing, even at this
shallow part of the river had exhausted everyone's energy reserves.

The way they sat together, many of the youngest children dull-eyed and listless, warned him they needed shelter and rest very soon.

The tall, lithe form of one of the women caught his attention. Her back was to him but he recognized the long dark braid of hair trailing down her back. Lisella always seemed to find energy from somewhere, no matter how tired she was.

She flitted from group to group, checking on and speaking to everyone. Whatever she said brought a smile to weary faces. The ease with which she dealt with so many different personalities, the compassion she showed, was a trait he admired and valued.

Sometimes though, she was too giving, too generous. Others often took what she gave without returning in kind. Once he'd questioned her about it. She'd just smiled and said she was willing to help others in this way, that one day it would all be returned to her tenfold. A teaching from the *Lady*, something she constantly badgered him to try.

The ghost of a grin curved his lips, and he wondered what the *Lady* would say about her acerbic tone as she berated him over the issue. He watched as she bent over one of the children, her hand smoothing the crown of the child's head. Seeing her in the pair of form-fitting breeches was a rare sight, considering she preferred the comfort of a dress.

When he'd suggested all the females wear breeches for their journey he'd been surprised she'd sided with him against those who'd complained. Practicality won out and she'd been the first to trade her dress in for a pair of breeches and an anorak, similar to the ones the scouts wore.

Lisella turned as if sensing his appraisal and her light violet gaze found his. She propped her hands on her hips then swept one arm outward, motioning to the people around her, her meaning more than clear. He nodded in silent acknowledgment and called out to Zaune and a couple of the other scouts.

"We need to find shelter, preferably a cave." He slid off the boulder and met them on the ground. "You two head upstream. Zaune, we'll go down." Varian glanced at Lisella as she joined them. "The sun sets in an hour. Be back in half that time."

Two of the scouts headed off on their assigned task.

Lisella stepped closer. "We need fire to dry our clothes." Her quiet voice held a thread of steel. "The children also need a hot meal."

"If we find a suitable camp where the light and smoke can be hidden, then you'll get your wish," he promised her.

Her lips pursed and he thought she might argue with him; instead she nodded. "I'll organize the gathering of some wood."

"We're in human territory now. Don't let the children wander from the scree."

The young woman's brows pulled down into a deep frown, hurt flashing in her gaze. "I'm aware of the dangers, Varian."

He regretted the gruffness of his words, knew he could've phrased them better. Tiredness had finally caught up with him. He usually didn't speak so rudely. He softened his tone. "We'll be back soon."

"Be careful."

A small smile curved his lips. He made sure she saw it. "Have you ever known me not to be?"

She just folded her arms in a typical Lisella pose. With a nod to her, he and Zaune set off downstream. Tonight they'd all rest. Traveling through *Na'Reish* territory had been tough, but moving through human territory would require every skill and ounce of strength they possessed.

It wasn't going to be easy but it was a challenge he looked forward to. Once he'd had a few hours' sleep.

STOMACH pleasantly full, Kalan wondered at the distracted expression on Annika's face. She'd barely spoken during the meal. Now she placed the tureen lid on its dish and capped the empty water flask with quiet efficiency. He supposed tiredness and hunger could account for that, he could certainly relate to both, but it didn't explain why she was avoiding his gaze.

"Lessie's appearance must have been disconcerting."

Annika's amber-flecked gaze lifted to meet his then veered away. "It was unexpected but . . . manageable." She reached for her healer's pouch and fished through it. "I believe my answers satisfied her curiosity."

He recognized the jar she pulled out. "Are your wounds troubling you?" The familiar minty odor of *vaa'jahn* permeated the air. "I thought they'd healed."

She rubbed a little of the gel into the pink scar on her forearm. "Healed over, yes, but it will be another day or so before I can move my arm like I used to."

Maren's earlier assault flashed through Kalan's mind. On top of that, they'd traveled over some rough terrain during the day, some of it involving climbing or traversing rocky ground. Then she'd taken on half the chores.

"Why didn't you say something earlier?"

"What good would it have done?" Her tone was guarded, tense. "Besides, I can take care of myself."

Annika had an inner strength that continued to amaze him but the loneliness haunting her gaze tugged at him. She was so unused to trusting people and, for some reason he wanted her to trust him.

He grunted, caught off guard with the realization but unable to deny there was more to Annika than the simple label *demon* could define. When she glanced at him, a questioning frown on her face, he covered by moving closer and peering at her wounds.

He grimaced. They were healed but bruises discolored her skin. The ones on her shoulder, where the *Vorc*'s teeth had sunk into the muscle, were the darkest.

He held out his hand for the jar. "Let me help."

"I can manage."

"I swear all healers are mixed in the same pot." Ignoring her protest he took it from her. "Push the sleeve off your shoulder."

He rubbed his hands together to warm them while waiting for her to follow his instruction. Annika hesitated then turned her back to slip the dress off her shoulder. Her movements were stiff, awkward as she held it against her breasts. Was that due to her injuries or his nearness?

The way the lantern light reflected off her tawny skin reminded Kalan of the time when he'd stripped her to treat her wounds in the cave. Burned into his brain were the memories of curves and softness and a hunger that made a man instantly hard. The sudden spear of need in his groin shouldn't have been a surprise considering his earlier reactions to her, but the intensity of it bordered on pain. He bit back a groan.

"What's wrong?" Annika's question made him realize he'd been staring at her too long, lost in thought.

"Nothing." He moved closer, shifting to alleviate the tightness of his breeches if not the fierce need inside him. His lack of control over his body's responses bothered him almost as much as his attraction to her. Neither were logical.

Exhaling slowly through his teeth, Kalan spread the gel on her shoulder then gently rubbed it in. Her skin was as smooth and soft as he remembered it. Giving in to temptation, he trailed his fingers over the markings running down her back, no longer avoiding them, curious more than repelled. They looked like strange tattoos, dark and oddly shaped.

He took care smoothing the gel over her skin where the bruises were the worst, kneading her muscles a little deeper where they were absent. Her flesh heated as the unguent began to work. She relaxed after several minutes. Her dress slipped farther down her back to reveal another bruise, only this one curled around her ribs just under her breast. Frowning, he touched the edge of the dark discoloration with his fingertips. Her breath caught and she shuddered.

"Sorry." He withdrew his touch. "Did I hurt you?"

"No." Her voice was barely a whisper.

"That wasn't there last time. How did you get it?"

"One of the *Na'Reish* kicked me during the fight near White-water Crossing."

Anger spiked through him. She'd been knocked to the ground by one of the mounted *Na'Reish* and hadn't been given the chance to get to her feet. That much he recalled, but she'd been kicked while defenseless on the ground?

He gripped the *vaa'jahn* jar hard. It was a good thing all the demons were dead or he might have been tempted to go back and hunt them down. His ministrations slowed. It was his duty to protect her but why such an intense reaction?

Frowning, he scooped more gel out of the jar. "Lower your dress farther . . ."

When Annika hesitated, he regretted the gruffness of his tone. He intended to look away, give her some privacy, but the graceful movement of her fingers plucking and drawing the laces free of the bodice enthralled him.

It would be a mistake to touch her. The thought went right out of his head as her dress slid off her shoulder. The curve of one breast was revealed and he caught a glimpse of her nipple, a delicate, dusky colored nub of flesh that peaked in the cool air before she covered it with her hand. His body heated, hardened further as he swallowed another groan.

All he had to do was move his hand upward a fraction and the back of his fingers would graze the side of her breast. He could easily imagine the fullness of her flesh fitting into the palm of his hand. Would her skin be warm? Soft?

He wanted to stroke his thumb over her nipple and watch it grow rosy and hard beneath his touch. Would her breath hitch or would she cry out in passion as he played with her? His hand shook as he applied a final smear of gel close to the underside of her breast.

Mouth dry, Kalan forced his gaze upward to her face. "Your cheek and eye need some of this, too."

Eyes downcast, Annika tilted her head toward him. He swept her hair behind her ear and realized she was trembling. Her cheeks were flushed, her breathing shallow and fast.

"Annika?" *Lady's Light*, was he scaring her? "Look at me." Her fist tightened around the crumpled bodice of her dress and she shook her head. He had to know. "Please . . ."

The longest minute passed then slowly her dark lashes lifted. Her eyes were a vibrant turquoise blue, like the color of a glacial lake. Beautiful. Stunning.

He sucked in a sudden breath. "You're aroused."

She flinched and orange infused the brilliant turquoise of her eyes. He'd seen the same change occur in them just before she'd drunk the tree-climber's blood and when she'd told him about her birth. *Shame.*

He opened his mouth to confess to his own arousal, to ease her embarrassment. There was no denying what he felt. He frowned. Was he insane? She was half human, half demon, the antithesis of everything he believed in. The knowledge tore through him, sent a wave of unease prickling along his skin. He pressed his lips shut and shook his head. To admit to anything would change the way things were between them.

The way things *should* be between them.

An almost inaudible whimper snapped his attention back to her. The tormented sound pricked his heart like a shard of glass. Didn't the *Lady* teach that to allow another to suffer would only compound your own?

The rip and pull of his thoughts left him bewildered.

"Annika . . ." He had to touch her.

Beneath his fingertips, she tensed. Her gaze locked with his, her nostrils flared as she drew in a deep breath. Her tongue skated across her lips. A soft hiss escaped him with the innocent action. Ignoring common sense, he leaned closer. He couldn't help it.

Annika jerked away from him with a gasp. She scrambled to her feet. "What are you doing?"

Her shocked words hit him like a dash of ice water and he reared back. Long seconds stretched silently between them as he stared at her, disbelief spearing his chest. *Merciful Mother*, what *was* he doing trying to kiss her?

"You're a demon."

Annika flinched like he'd struck her. Her cheeks drained of all color, shadowed pain flashed in her eyes, and Kalan realized too late he'd spoken aloud.

"Don't forget the words *tainted* and *cursed half-blood bastard*, Light Blade." Her fists clenched tight in the dress she held against her chest. "They're always a popular accompaniment with that label."

The lack of any sort of emotion in her voice betrayed just what it cost her to utter those words.

A flush stained his cheeks. "Annika . . ."

She cut him off with a hollow, brittle laugh. "Just get me to Sacred City and the *Lady*'s temple." Her voice was hoarse, gravelly, painful to listen to. "The sooner you fulfill your oath, the sooner you'll be rid of me."

With that, she headed for the sleeping pallet in the stall. A short pause by the lantern to blow it out plunged the barn into darkness. Straw rustled, then silence.

Kalan sat there staring into the inky blackness, his face still hot, confusion and mortification raking him with razor-sharp claws. He didn't understand the effect she had on him, but *Lady of Light*, he hadn't meant to hurt her. Nor had he intended to kiss her. It'd just happened.

He grimaced; *almost* happened. For someone who prided himself on self-control, a careless slip of the tongue had flayed her to her soul and he'd proven himself as cruel as her father.

The *Lady's* teachings absolved no one of bad behavior. He couldn't undo what had happened but he could try to make it right. Acknowledging Annika was *Na'Chi*, not a demon, would be a start, though he doubted anything he tried to say to her now would be believed. Perhaps the morning would bring calmer circumstances.

And somehow he had to combat the attraction he felt for her. Denying it existed would be reckless, and giving in would only complicate an already difficult situation.

Kalan raked a hand through his hair. *Merciful Light*, the journey *She* had tasked him with seemed filled with hazards and pitfalls. Was he destined to stumble over every one of them?

In the past he'd accepted *Her* will, eventually, knowing *She*'d never test him beyond his endurance but this time he wondered if he would survive the experience.

Chapter 10

THE scent of spring flowers gave away Lisella's presence a moment
before she appeared in the mouth of the cave. Varian remained
motionless in the shadow of the boulder where he kept watch. She
wore a hooded cloak but her lithe form was one he'd recognize anywhere. Her posture seemed stiffer than normal and he sensed an aura
of tension. She spent a few moments peering out into the darkness,
searching. He suspected it was for him, not Barvi, the other scout on
watch duty.

With the moon yet to rise the shadows were thick, hard even for
Na'Chi eyes to pierce. She'd see very little other than the outline of
rocks and the stunted shrubs that grew among them and beyond that
the forest.

"Varian?" At least she kept her voice low.

"Over here," he replied.

She turned in his direction and came toward him. He admired
the confident, graceful way she walked. The ghost of a grin shaped
his lips. She looked nothing like the skinny-limbed, gangly girl he

remembered from their childhood. Her clumsiness had provided a source of amusement to other girls her age and so she'd taken to hanging around with him and an older group of *Na'Chi* youths.

He understood the need not to draw attention, especially after the *Na'Reish* guard had marked his face. The small differences in them both had set them apart. He'd earned respect by standing up to anyone who'd dared disparage him because of his scar, and Lisella's tenacity to master her coltish body during scout training finally won the others over.

"Everyone's asleep." Her soft voice brought him back to the present. She sat on a rock beside him, the hem of her cloak brushing his boots with a soft rasp as she arranged it around her. "The children almost fell asleep during the meal."

"You should join them," he murmured. This close, he could see the weariness darkening the skin beneath her eyes. "Tomorrow will be another hard day."

"Varian, we all need more than a night's rest. Even you." She turned her head and he saw the faint glow of her eyes. Violet ringed with green. A very familiar reaction from the past he'd just been remembering. "Four days of hard traveling has taken its toll on all of us, particularly the children."

"We can't fall any farther behind." Her lips thinned. He sighed, his breath frosting in front of him in a white cloud. "A day's rest. It's all we can afford."

"We need three, minimum." Her words were pitched low, her voice as hard as rocks they sat on. He shook his head in silent disagreement. "Have you even looked at your scouts' eyes this evening? The children? They're bloodred. We've used all our energy reserves escaping *Na'Reish* territory. We need to hunt, feed, and sleep."

"If we lose Annika's trail then we lose hope of finding the human city."

"If we keep going as exhausted as we are then you can guarantee the humans will notice us. We'll make a mistake when we can least afford it; it might even be you."

A tremor of genuine fear underlay her words. Her blunt truth wasn't one he wanted to hear but he could always rely on Lisella to tell it like it was. Another trait he admired in her.

"Do you think we'll remain undetected in human territory if we stay in one place that long? They're more vigilant than the *Na'Reish*."

She shrugged. "Then we move every day." Her gaze met his. "Send out a scout to track Annika, have them leave markers." Her tone was hard, determined. "We'll follow once everyone's recovered enough to travel."

He peered toward the cave mouth and heard only the breeze rustling the leaves of the bushes around him. The sweet odor of wood smoke wafted to him on the next puff of air. There was no quiet murmur of voices or soft singing to lull the most reluctant child to sleep. Exhaustion had been persuasion enough.

He inclined his head. "All right. We'll hunt and rest but not for long."

"See how our people recover first."

He nodded once and in his mind sorted through the names of the scouts asleep in the cave. "Let Zaune sleep through the night. At first light I'll send him out to find and mark a trail. He'll need a hearty breakfast and a pack of supplies."

She nodded. "Thank you, Varian."

The tension he sensed in her when she'd come looking for him eased. He scrubbed a hand over his face and rolled his shoulders to loosen muscles that had remained motionless in the cold for too long.

"I didn't mean to make things more difficult earlier today. I'm sorry." Her apology came out of nowhere. He knew he'd revealed his surprise when she smiled. She reached out to place a gloved hand on his forearm. "We're all scared. There's talk about turning back."

Varian frowned, already suspecting the identities of the doubters.

"We can't do that. They'd prefer to live half-lives back in the compound, hiding and scavenging, living in constant fear of being discovered by the *Na'Reish*?"

"They're scared. It's natural to want the security of the familiar, even when it's dangerous. The uncertainty of our new future is frightening them."

"Hesia warned us it wasn't going to be easy."

"I know." Lisella smiled sadly. He knew what she was thinking: the old healer should have come with them instead of staying behind but Hesia had known she'd have only slowed them down. "She saved each of us. I keep reminding everyone that we have to trust what she told us and keep going. You rarely spend time with the others so I thought you should know what was going on."

He was appreciative of what she'd done to avert a potential problem. He'd been so caught up in keeping them safe he'd never even noticed the unrest she'd spoken of.

Lisella laid a hand on his forearm and squeezed. "You don't have to shoulder the responsibility of this all on your own, Varian. Share your plans, talk to us. We're all capable, even the young ones. You've trained us for this venture for years."

She read him well. Her quiet words struck deep. Slowly he nodded. "I just want us to succeed."

"*Lady* willing, we will."

He envied the complete faith he heard in her voice and wished he could feel certain that things would go well. So much hinged on Annika, and she didn't even realize they existed.

Lisella squeezed his arm again. "A day at a time, Varian." He lifted an eyebrow at the familiar saying, one they bandied around as children. "I recognize that blank-faced expression. You worry too much."

He grunted. "You care too much."

"It's what I do best." She pushed to her feet. "Good night."

"'Night." She deserved something better than a generic send-off. "Lisella, thank you. I couldn't do this without your help."

Her smile was wide and he felt the warmth of it deep down in his soul. No wonder people responded so well to her. She nodded and entered the cave. Her reminder was timely. For the moment, their survival relied on them getting through one day at a time.

He would do well to remember that in the future.

THE winter sun was barely an hour old when Annika followed Kalan from the farmer's croft to begin another day of traveling. Heavy frost crunched underfoot and the forest around them held an anticipatory stillness broken only by the occasional birdcall. The air was fresh enough to help shake the vestiges of sleep from her head.

Securing the hood of the cloak over her head, she sent a prayer heavenward, thanking the *Lady* for a peaceful start to the day. Other than a brief greeting from Kalan morning conversation was non-existent. Not that she minded after what had happened the night before.

Her cheeks flamed at the memory. *Mother of Light*, the enticing odor of dark spiciness and heated male still clung to her nostrils. With her knowledge as a healer she could categorize hundreds of scents, all important when diagnosing an illness but Kalan's arousal had been beyond her realm of experience. She hadn't been able to identify it at first. Until he'd leaned in to kiss her.

Her stomach knotted hard. Why had he done that? Her mind came up blank. She didn't understand how he could go from hating her to wanting to kiss her to conveying shock as if he hadn't antici-pated his own actions, to insulting her. She had been so careful to hide her attraction to him but somehow she'd betrayed herself and he'd used it against her. Why else would he have tried to kiss her?

Chills shivered over her skin. Did it really matter now? He was just like Savyr, taunting her, playing on her weakness. but for what purpose?

Back at the ferry, Vash had suggested Kalan hand her over to the Blade Council for information. Did he think by toying with her emotions he could control her? Having an unresisting captive would make the journey to Sacred Lake easier for him.

Why did he feel it necessary to manipulate her? After revealing her sordid history, couldn't he see she held no allegiance to the *Na'Reish*?

The knot in her stomach twisted. Annika stroked the leather shoulder strap of her healer's pouch and considered ingesting a little *vaa'jahn* to ease the feeling. If only.

Whatever his reasons for the previous night's actions, now that she understood what his scent meant she could preempt him if anything like last night were to happen again. Adapting to circumstances was one thing she could claim experience with. He wouldn't catch her off guard again.

"We'll use the traders' road." Kalan's voice drew her back to their surroundings. The air frosted in front of his mouth as he wrapped one of their blankets around his shoulders. He waited until she drew level with him before starting along the compacted trail.

"What about *Na'Hord* Patrols?" she asked. "If they cross the river they'll spot our tracks."

Ahead of them fog ghosted the ground and battled for dominance with the pale beams of sunlight beginning to dapple the trail.

"The risk is offset by the advantage of speed. We can cover quite a distance today using the road. By midday I want to be in the foothills."

"The Lower Crags," she murmured.

"You know of them?"

"My father has a map on the wall of his chambers. I've only seen it a few times but I know scouts add information to it after every foray into human territory."

Kalan said nothing further for the next half hour, seemingly content to walk beside her on the trail. Had he engaged in conversation just to be friendly? Given her earlier thoughts, pumping her for more information about what she knew of human territory would fit with his plan.

Useful for the knowledge she could provide his precious Blade Council. If that was his strategy, it was the more likely scenario. The idea left her heavyhearted. It shouldn't. She'd been disappointed so many times in the past that once more shouldn't make a difference. Hesia was the only person she considered a friend. The old healer had never betrayed her or offered false promises.

She didn't need Kalan's friendship. She'd survive without it. Even as she thought the words, Annika knew she was fooling herself. Shooting a furtive glance in Kalan's direction, she couldn't ignore that the tall warrior walking beside her was coming to mean something to her. She shied away from exactly what, not willing to go there just yet. It was unsettling enough to know she couldn't control her emotions around him.

"Who taught you the skills of the trail?"

His sudden question drew her back to the present. "What?"

"You're deep in thought yet you just skirted that puddle to avoid breaking the ice and marking your trail." He waved a hand at the trail behind them. "You're trail savvy."

She cast a brief look back at the puddle then shrugged one shoulder. There was little harm in telling him. "As a child, I watched the *Na'Reish* instructors teaching the trainees. It helped fill in my day. The skills came in handy when I didn't want to be found by my father or his friends."

A grimace flickered across his face. "You say that so matter-of-factly."

"So?"

"Hiding from a father is not something a child usually does."

She met his eyes, her gaze level. "You do if you want to survive." Her childhood was as far from normal as he could probably imagine.

"A friend and I used to slip away from the training barracks to go to the night market."

She blinked, amazed Kalan hadn't delved into her past by asking more questions. She shot him a glance. He caught her inquisitive look. A smile played around the corners of his mouth.

"The taboo of the night market was irresistible," he elaborated. "Learning how to scale trees without the use of a rope helped us get over the compound wall."

"What's a night market?"

"A select quarter of the city that caters to after-dark entertainment . . . pleasures of the flesh and other interests."

"Oh." Her cheeks flushed with heat.

"I preferred the alehouses." Laughter tinged his words. The lighthearted expression on his face filled her with warmth.

"Were you ever caught?"

"Many times." His smile widened. "Arek and I spent a lot of our free time cleaning out the animal stalls."

"That was considered punishment?" At Kalan's nod, Annika grunted. "*Na'Reish* warriors were flogged if they were caught disobeying their instructors' rules. I treated those punished for infractions." Stepping off the trail, she halted beside a small, dark-leafed bush. The clusters of brown berries hanging from it made her mouth water. She broke off a couple of branches and gave him one. "Who's Arek?"

He popped a couple of the tart-tasting fruit into his mouth before replying. "My second-in-command. We grew up and trained together as Light Blade warriors."

She hesitated before asking her next question. "Was he with you when you were captured by the *Na'Reish*?"

"No, thank the *Lady*. I'd left him to attend a meeting of the Blade Council in my stead."

Annika finished her impromptu breakfast mulling over the snippets of his life. She longed to ask him more about it but didn't want to fall into the trap of becoming too comfortable with him.

Know your enemy. Savyr's much-uttered warning came to mind. Perhaps she could play Kalan at his own game, if that's what he was doing with her.

"Ask your questions, Annika, I don't mind answering them."

Her head jerked up in astonishment. "How did you know—?"

He motioned to the branch in her hand. "You've been snapping pieces of it off. It's the same habit I use when thinking."

Glancing down, she saw what was left of the branch. Shaking her head, she tossed it to the side of the trail. Out of the corner of her eye she could see him waiting for her to respond. He seemed so . . . comfortable . . . conversing with her, not at all calculating.

"Aren't you worried I'll use this information against you?" she blurted.

Fool! Savyr's derisive tone rang in her head. *Never give away your intentions.*

Kalan's brow creased with a frown. "What are you talking about?"

"I can't believe you're so ignorant of what could happen." She gestured between them. "Isn't this what the conversation is all about? Engage in friendly chatter, swap some innocuous tidbits then get me to tell you any *Na'Reish* secrets I might happen to know? The situation can be manipulated both ways, Light Blade."

Kalan halted in the middle of the pathway and pivoted on his boot heel. "This isn't about eliciting secrets from you." He stared at her for several long heartbeats, a stunned look on his face. "You can't believe I'd do something like that."

"Considering your past actions, why wouldn't I?"

He grimaced as if he'd tasted something unpleasant. "*Mother of Mercy*, this is such a convoluted situation." He strode several steps down the track away from her then paced back, raking a hand through his hair. "I'm truly sorry this is the result of everything that's happened."

The light citrus odor emanating from him stopped her from rejecting his apology outright. She inhaled again. There was no mistaking it. His response was genuine, and scents didn't lie.

"Annika, *Lady* knows my behavior toward you has been disgraceful." The ruddy color in his cheeks darkened but his gaze never wavered. "I've done little to inspire your trust in me but can't we put aside our differences? I want to get to know you better, and not for any underhanded reason." The muscle along his jaw tightened. "Just because I'm willing to talk about my life doesn't mean I expect you to reciprocate in any way. I'm prepared for this to be a one-way arrangement if that's what it takes to prove I'm sincere."

To leave a wrong undone against another is to disrespect the Lady's teachings. The words came from Annika's childhood, from a conversation she'd had with Hesia, though at the time she hadn't understood their meaning. Recalling it now, when she sorely needed her friend's advice most made it seem like the old healer was right there beside her.

A dream of the heart is one worth any sacrifice, Annika. She could almost feel Hesia's work-roughened fingers trailing over her cheek. She would urge her to trust Kalan. The old woman had grown up respecting the Light Blade warriors and their reputations. Annika hadn't.

Will you let fear destroy your dream? Annika bit her lip. She'd planned and worked too hard to give up now. If Kalan was sincere in his intentions, there was only one way to find out.

"Hesia spoke of the Blade Council." Where to start? Perhaps with information she could verify, to see if he was candid with his responses. "Your people are ruled by them, aren't they?"

Kalan nodded, his expression bemused, as if he'd expected a very different question than the one she voiced. "The Council is made up of the *Lady's Chosen* and five Councilors, all retired warriors. The Councilors represent different provinces within our territory."

She nodded, more to herself than to acknowledge his answer. "What is the *Lady*'s *Chosen*?" Again, another fact she could confirm.

"A Light Blade selected by the *Lady* to lead the Council."

Her jaw slackened. "*She* chooses? You don't base leadership on bloodlines or strength?"

"Blood relatives can be elevated to the position temporarily until the *Lady* approves the Council's choice or indicates *Her* own. Unlike the *Na'Reish*, the strongest warrior doesn't necessarily have the greatest potential to lead our people."

"I assumed you had one ruler." Her breath caught. A female deity *and* multiple leaders. Details Hesia had probably taken for granted but never shared with her. "And is your *Chosen* male or female?"

"We've had both in the past." His gaze flickered to the forest. He motioned for them to resume their trek along the track. "The current *Chosen* is male."

Something about his tone caught her attention. "You don't like him?"

He cleared his throat as a wry grin shaped his lips. "Depends what mood he's in," he said. "For the most part he's well liked." Again she sensed something odd in his comments but he continued speaking before she could inquire about it. "The village Councils listen to what their people want, they pass that on to the Councilors. The Blade Council then tries to make the best decision possible."

"Everyone gets a say in what happens?"

"Yes. Everyone might not eventually agree that the decision made suits them, but they've had the chance to make their views known."

She whistled softly. He was sharing information as he'd promised. While he wasn't expecting her to reveal anything in return, the disparity in their cultures was too startling not to.

"Only the most powerful *Na'Reish* families benefit from any decision made by my father. In return for their loyalty he'd sometimes award special dispensations: extra blood-slaves, a rank among the

Na'Hord, a family alliance." She frowned. "If your Council spends all its time talking about what everyone wants, how do they get anything done?"

Kalan's laugh made her start. He didn't just chuckle or snort. He stopped in the middle of the trail and clasped his ribs as the sound rumbled up from deep in his chest.

She stared at him, captivated by the way his green eyes lit up and sparkled, fascinated with the wrinkles that appeared at the corners of his eyes and mouth. She hadn't meant her comment to be amusing and wondered what had caused such humor. She waited until it finally abated.

"Some would agree with you. There are times when it seems all the Council does is talk." Another grin creased his face. "Or argue. Around and around and around." He chuckled, and then offered her an apology. "If you ever get the chance to sit in on a meeting, you'll understand. Despite my irreverent humor, all that talking is the fairest way to make a decision that best suits most of the people."

Annika tried to imagine Savyr and the *Na'Reish* debating a decision and couldn't. He always did what he wanted, even if it meant ignoring more logical suggestions.

Kalan started walking again. "Occasionally the *Temple Elect* contributes, bringing the words of the *Lady* to the meetings."

"Hesia told me the Temple Servants receive visitations, that they are truly blessed. Do you have more than one temple in Sacred Lake?"

"Yes, although the main one everyone tends to visit is in the Light Blade compound."

Her breath caught. "Would it be possible to visit it?" He didn't answer her immediately. A shiver skittered down her spine. Perhaps demons weren't allowed in human temples. "If I've offended you, I'm sorry."

"You haven't," he assured her, his lips twisting in a lopsided smile. "Your faith in *Her* keeps catching me off guard."

"Does the *Lady* make distinctions between who *She* calls to believe?"

"Humans have been the only ones to acknowledge *Her* existence."

"The *Na'Reish* acknowledge *Her* existence," she countered. "They ban human-slaves from worshipping *Her*. Anyone caught is executed. I've heard the guards talk about the temples they destroyed when they ventured into human territory. They mightn't believe in *Her*, but they know *She's* the source of your strength."

The astonished look on his face was enough encouragement to keep going.

"The *Na'Hord* whisper in the training courtyards." She mimicked some of the voices she'd overheard. *"When that Light Blade fought Lenac I felt the explosion of power when he died. It was like they burnt his soul . . ."* She changed to a deeper voice. *"If you listen to the commanders' talk you'd think humans were weak. There's little danger from the average human but you need to face a trained Light Blade to understand their potential. Their power makes them more than a match for us . . ."* Annika spread her hands wide. "They sense the power *She's* given you in battle and they fear the Gifts *She* bestows upon you to wield it."

A long silence followed. Had she said too much?

"I've never considered it from that perspective before," Kalan murmured. "We've always seen the *Na'Reish's* physical strength as a daunting factor when engaging them in battle, but the thought of them being afraid of our Gifts evens out that advantage, doesn't it?"

"You seemed pretty confident taking on that *Na'Hord Vorc-Master*."

He tilted his head in acknowledgment of her compliment. "Training sessions are tough. It takes years of practice to wield our Gifts through our weapons, so learning to fight, and fight hard helps us overcome that." He gave her a sideways look. "Your Gift feels similar to ours. If you'd like, I could teach you a few basic moves to go with it. They might be useful next time you engage a *Na'Reish* guard."

His offer was so unexpected Annika missed seeing the small patch of ice on the ground in front of her. Her boot slipped. Kalan's hand shot out to steady her. She caught his arm and her balance.

"You'd teach me?" she asked, her eyes widening.

"Why not? You did say you wanted to know more about your mother. Training was a large part of her life. This would give you more insight into what it meant to be a Light Blade warrior."

Her throat tightened. Did he realize the gift he'd just given her? She smiled. "I'd like that very much."

Chapter 11

KALAN jerked back, barely avoiding Annika's sweeping kick. Even in a hitched-up dress she was fast. He feigned a body blow that turned into a grab as she threw up an arm to counter block. She twisted, just as he'd taught her, but this time instead of letting her break free, he used her momentum to pull her in against him.

"Stop!" he called. Annika froze, her breath coming in rapid gasps, as she stood trapped against him, both her arms pinned between them. "I haven't taught you how to get out of this hold yet. What could you do?"

She flicked a wayward strand of hair from her eyes. "I have the physical strength to break free."

"What if you were wounded or exhausted?"

"Certainly more problematic." A frown marred her brow a moment before her violet eyes met his. The flecks within them were a dark green; a color he'd seen a lot of in this first training session. He'd labeled the characteristic as determination. "Taking into account your wide-legged stance, I'd try to disable you with a knee to the groin."

He grimaced and conceded her suggestion with a nod. "Good thing I halted this sparring session when I did then." Her husky laughter had him joining in. "I'll talk you through one more move then we'll finish up."

Disappointment flashed across her face. "All right. What do I do?"

Kalan's respect for her grew. Most novice warriors pushed beyond their limits when they began training, ignoring their instructors' orders. Annika had followed every instruction and listened to his advice, constructive or positive, without comment. That, coupled with how quickly she'd retained what he'd taught her, impressed him.

"Without your hands, what do you have left to fight with?" he asked.

"My head, legs, and teeth."

He grinned. She was also a more creative thinker than most. "Wind one leg around mine and plant it firmly on the ground. Good. Now push me backward."

As she threw her weight against him he released her to use his arms to break his fall. A thick carpet of dead leaf litter helped cushion the impact. The late afternoon sun lit the delighted smile on her face as she stood over him.

"Use your opponent's body weight and size against him." Kalan propped himself up on one arm and used the other to wipe sweat from his brow. "It's a move that gives you more options than you had pinned against me. You can now attack or run."

"With surprise on my side, now would be a good time to use my Gift." She held out a hand to help him rise. He dusted off his breeches. "Healing and killing someone aren't that dissimilar. When I touch you with my Gift I sense the organs and vessels inside you as easily as I feel your life force. I can repair wounds or I can stop organs from working with a burst of power. It's how I killed the *Vorc* and the guards."

The small insight into her Gift was unexpected. Kalan wondered what had prompted her to offer it so freely and kept his tone casual. He wanted to hear anything she had to say.

"I understand now what Hesia meant when she said the *Na'Reish* couldn't find out about your skill. When did you first realize you could heal with your *Gift*?"

"A couple of years after Hesia started teaching me about healing. We were called to an accident in the pens . . . a young slave-boy had been attacked by a *Vorc*, he'd ventured too close to its cage. Hesia couldn't stop the bleeding fast enough. I felt her urgency, her worry and just touched the boy's hand and willed him to get better. Hesia must've suspected something because she was able to treat and save him but she never said anything in front of the *Na'Reish* guards. Once we were alone though, she questioned me and worked out what happened. She helped me harness the Gift."

They gathered their meager belongings from the base of a tree. "Did the *Na'Reish* ever become aware of your healing Gift?"

"Other than that one time, I never used it in front of them. Slaves talked, but little credence was given to what many believed were rumors." She fiddled with the tie on her pouch a moment and her voice was soft as she continued speaking. "I was thirteen when my father summoned me to his chamber. He'd heard the rumors. He wanted to know if I could do what the slaves had been telling him, if I could manipulate the injuries; heal them or inflict pain.

"I denied having the skill." Her face lost some of its color and a muscle flexed in her jaw. "He had a human child brought to him. He whipped and beat her. I had to listen to her screams, unable to do anything because he had two of his guards hold me when I tried to help her. They laughed as they made me watch."

The hoarseness in her voice was as raw as the nausea churning in his stomach. Annika's firsthand accounts of Savyr's brutality only reinforced what Kalan knew about the demon king.

Jaw rigid, she stared out at the forest, her gaze fixed. He doubted she saw the wooded forest or rocky trail wending its way through the clearing where they'd stopped to train.

"Annika, don't," he murmured and reached for her hand. He held it tightly, brushing his thumb over her cold fingers. "You don't have to tell me any more."

"Yes, I do." Her smile was bitter and brittle. The gaze she turned toward him was so haunted it tore at his heart. "My father whipped her unconscious. When the guards released me, he ordered me to save her, to show him my skill. She'd lost so much blood . . . I knew he'd use me to hurt others if I showed him what I could do with my Gift. His goal was always about being more powerful than the next *Na'Reish*.

"But I couldn't let her die. I thought I could save her. I wanted to . . ." Her voice dropped to a whisper. "But I'd underestimated the injuries done to her. I hadn't developed enough skill in my Gift to save her. She died." She inhaled a shuddering breath. "At least my father dismissed the rumors of my Gift as being untrue. He never forced me again to prove what I could do. Small consolation though."

Kalan searched for words of comfort but there weren't any he could offer. The grief or the guilt of being unable to save lives was a familiar pain, one that couldn't be dismissed with blithe words.

"I've also held friends in my arms and watched them die." His voice reverberated with remembered anguish and sorrow, but he spoke steadily and clearly. Her violet eyes reflected equal amounts of wariness and uncertain hope as she searched his gaze to confirm the truth. "I've sent warriors into battle against the *Na'Reish* knowing that the next time I saw them they would be dead. Worse still is that the warriors also knew it."

She gasped. "They didn't object?"

He shook his head, somber. "We all understand the risks of what we do. It doesn't make it easier to deal with the pain of loss or the memories that haunt me, but I've learned to accept them. It's either that or let them destroy me. I've seen too many warriors take that path to want to follow them."

He drew in a slow breath, gently rubbing the back of her hand with his thumb to ease the sting he knew his next words would deliver.

"It's tragic the girl died but that misfortune saved countless others, Annika. You either believe that or run from the memories and let them cripple you."

She pulled her hand from his. Kalan let her go, regretting having to be so blunt. There was a connection forming between them yet he didn't want to force it. He watched her walk ahead of him and wrap her arms around herself.

"You'll find I understand more about you than you realize," he stated softly.

The look she shot him over her shoulder was guarded, almost fearful. He'd pushed her as far as he could. For now.

Changing his tone, he kept it light and pointed to the trail ahead. "Up ahead, a jagged ridgeline spreads to the east of the trail. You'll find some caves, naturally weathered rock steps, and hot springs. Set up camp there and get a fire started."

She frowned, suspicion tightening her features. "Where are you going?"

He held back a sigh. Their connection was weaver-web thin. Not that he blamed her for doubting his actions.

"Hunting." He tossed her his cloak-blanket. "We deserve a hot meal tonight. There's a half-hour of daylight left. I'll be back as soon as I can."

Heading into the forest, he searched for signs of animal tracks. Convincing Annika to trust him was proving to be a worthy challenge and, astonishingly, one he was starting to enjoy.

FINDING the location Kalan described proved easy. The forest thinned out along the ridge in favor of hardy bushes. They clung to the stony landscape with thick, twisted roots that looked like gnarled fingers wending their way into cracks and holes in the rock.

Pushing past a thicket, Annika detected a faint bubbling sound accompanied by a fetid odor that belonged to a hot spring. Rounding a large boulder, she found herself standing on bare rock flanked by a number of low, shallow caves. She was unprepared for the natural beauty spread out before her.

Like a giant stairway, tiers of grey rock stepped its way down the side of the ridge. Hot water pools, each ringed by a pale yellow residue, dotted each level. Delicate tendrils of steam writhed and twirled in the evening breeze above some, while others wore a thick layer on their surface, the stark whiteness broken by the odd bubble of air escaping from the boiling water. The brilliant turquoise-colored water was so clear she could see to the bottom where the bubbles originated.

"*Lady of Light!*" she murmured and stepped closer to the edge. "Incredible."

The largest pool on this level flowed over the rock-lip and into another below, creating a small, steaming waterfall. Crouching beside the pool, she cautiously dipped her hand in. The tepid temperature made her smile.

Putting her pouch inside one of the caves, she made short work of gathering enough wood to last the night and starting the fire Kalan would need to cook whatever he brought back from hunting. Then, kicking off her boots and picking up a blanket, she walked around the large pool to its shallowest edge, pleasantly surprised that the rock beneath her feet was warm.

Shedding her dress she slid into the pool, sighing as the warm water engulfed her. The strong odor was unpleasant but she was willing to put up with it in order to feel clean. Using the fine sand on the bottom of the pool she scrubbed away the dirt and grime then washed her hair. Her sore muscles ached for a good, long soak but Kalan's imminent appearance dissuaded her.

She stopped scrubbing as her thoughts turned to the warrior, and she let the grains of sand sift through her fingers to drift to the bottom of the pool. Hesia had taught her the value of friendship; finding another friend as steadfast and accepting as the old woman was something Annika had dreamed about but never truly believed could happen.

She'd never told anyone about the death of the little girl—not even Hesia—yet instead of being repulsed and horrified by what she'd done Kalan had listened to every word, showing no horror, no revulsion, no condemnation. Instead he'd revealed memories of his own that troubled him.

Annika lifted the hand he'd held, watching the water run in rivulets along her skin. It tingled where he'd smoothed his fingers over the back of her hand. Such a simple gesture of comfort, one that had wrapped itself around her heart and squeezed.

Caring about what Kalan thought of her was becoming more and more important. She'd used her past to shock him, testing his earlier promise, preferring another rejection sooner rather than later. It hadn't come. Her heart leapt, although whether it was in hope or fear she wasn't certain.

Annika sighed, and hit the surface of the water, sending a wave splashing over the edge of the rockface. Perhaps she needed to leave her worry in the care of the *Lady*.

Raking a hand through her wet hair, she climbed out of the pool and wrapped herself in the blanket. In the cool night air, steam curled from her skin as she gave the pool one last, lingering glance before heading for the fire.

An evening breeze rustled the undergrowth and hurried her along in getting dried. Wrinkling her nose at having to get back into her worse-for-wear dress, she pulled it on wondering what she'd do for clothes once she reached Kalan's home. With a shake of her head, she fed another piece of wood into the fire then began combing the tangles out of her hair with her fingers. Worrying about something she had no control over was a waste of time.

"I see you've taken advantage of the hot springs." Kalan's deep voice came from the semi-darkness outside the circle of light thrown by the fire.

She heard his soft footsteps a moment before he appeared along the same trail she'd walked. In one hand he carried a small carcass, already skinned and gutted.

"I could have stayed in that pool all night." She gave up trying to comb her hair and watched as he knelt by the fire and sifted through the pile of wood. He set up a spit over the flames. "I might smell of rotten eggs but at least I'm clean."

He gave a hearty chuckle. "With that recommendation, I think I'll join you." He held up his bloodstained hands. "Ground-burrower might smell slightly rancid come the morning whereas rotten eggs will fade."

He toed off his boots and set them aside. She handed him the blanket she'd used as a towel. "I'll make sure dinner doesn't burn."

Kalan padded past her, unlacing the neck of his shirt. She heard the slide of cloth over skin as he stripped it over his head then shed his breeches. Out of the corner of her eye she saw his powerfully built form silhouetted against the purple-hued twilight.

Knowing his back was to her, Annika stared in open appreciation, a twinge of guilt prodding her conscience at watching him without his consent but it wasn't enough to make her look away.

The firelight gave his skin a warm, golden tan. She forgot to breathe as the flickering shadows delineated every masculine dip and hollow from his broad shoulders to his lean hips, tight buttocks, and long, muscular legs.

Reaching up to untie his hair, he shook it free and the dark strands fell to lie between broad shoulders. Light-headed from the lack of air, Annika inhaled deeply as he slid into the pool. His groan of pleasure sparked a smoldering heat that curled in her belly.

"Pass me a pillow, I've found my bed for the night."

His drawled words made her smile. He turned and she averted her gaze, unwilling to let him know she'd been observing him.

"You'll end up looking like a wrinkled old man, Light Blade."

"At least I'll be a warm, wrinkled old man. I bet you thought twice about curling up in here." He laughed as her silence spoke for her. There was more splashing as he washed. "You're partial to a hot bath. I'll have to remember that, shouldn't be too hard seeing as we have that in common."

His banter was as warm as the heat coming from the fire.

"It might be a good thing if you stay there the night then." She patted the bundle that lay on the ground next to the fire. "There's only one dry blanket to sleep under tonight."

His dry chuckle sent a thrill rippling along her spine. "What? Sick of my company already?"

Hardly. But she didn't say that out loud.

Leaning forward, she rotated the carcass on the spit, the scent of cooking flesh making her mouth water, delighted to discover she enjoyed his gentle teasing. She glanced toward the pool. It lay beyond the light of the fire but with her enhanced sight she could see Kalan's face clearly in the darkness. He was grinning.

Her breath caught and, for the smallest second, Annika let herself forget the tension of the last few days. Just once she wanted to indulge in the pleasure of the moment.

Tilting her head to one side, and keeping her expression bland, she pretended to consider his question. "You're tolerable, I suppose, for a human."

"Tolerable?" Her smile broke free at his mock, outraged tone. He swam to the side of the pool closest to her and hooked a wet arm over the edge. One dark eyebrow arched as his gaze locked with hers. "That's not what your eyes are telling me, *Na'Chi*."

Chapter 12

*H*ER *eyes.* Annika stiffened. Her smile froze then faded. Kalan didn't need enhanced sight, just the flickering flames of the fire to see the color of her eyes.

Bracing his hands on the rocky edge, he surged from the pool, the movement graceful. Long, lean limbs and hard, toned muscles glistened wetly. Water sheeted off him as he walked to where he'd left the blanket, and retrieved it.

Her heart began to pound. She tried to look away but couldn't stop herself from staring. He had the sleek, powerful body of a warrior in his prime. All raw, masculine strength. The steam curling off every inch of his smooth skin gave new meaning to the word *hot.*

Kalan took his time drying, so comfortable with his nudity it made her envious. As if aware of her scrutiny, he turned, his gaze locked with hers. The connection, the hunger of arousal glittering in his eyes sent fire racing through her.

"The blue in your eyes right now reminds me of glacial ice on a cold winter's day." He tossed the wet blanket over a boulder to dry and bent to retrieve his clothes. He pulled on his breeches. "Beautiful."

An automatic rejection rose in her throat but instead she breathed deep, seeking his scent, needing more than just visual clues to ascertain the truth. The fragrance of heated male drifted across the distance separating them, earth and spice, the same one she'd detected in the barn the night before.

Like a *haze* addict she inhaled again, biting her lip as it settled heavily in her lungs. The herbal plant was used by the *Na'Reish* to lower new blood-slaves' resistance to servitude. Burning the leaves induced a euphoric daze. The longer it was inhaled, the more they required next time to reach that state.

Kalan's scent proved just as alluring. If he smelled this good, what would it be like to actually taste him? The image of her running her tongue along the skin of his throat formed in her mind and the heat in her cheeks spread much lower.

Annika squirmed where she sat, fighting the sensation. Hadn't she learned her lesson last night? Nothing could come from being attracted to a human. She looked away.

"Annika, don't be ashamed of what you feel."

His soft admonishment caused her cheeks to flame afresh.

Her gaze snapped up, snagged his. He'd shrugged on his shirt. "Have you any idea how many times I've wished that my eyes were just one color?" She hated that she never seemed to be able to control her emotions around him.

"You see them as a flaw?"

His incredulous tone wrenched a derisive laugh from her. "How can I not? Once the *Na'Hord* or human-slaves could interpret the colors what do you think they did, Light Blade?"

"I won't use that knowledge to hurt you."

"So you say now."

A muscle flexed in his jaw and the emerald color in his eyes darkened. "If my honor isn't enough to reassure you, perhaps my words will be."

An air of tension radiated from him but it wasn't anger. On bare feet he padded around the fire to crouch in front of her. His tongue swept across his bottom lip and his brow dipped a little as if he was debating telling her something.

"What you're feeling . . . I'm experiencing it, too . . ." He exhaled an unsteady breath. "It brings me pleasure knowing that you enjoy looking at me."

She wanted to deny his words but the hunger in his gaze intensified, and with him so close she knew his scent had altered, strengthened, spice mingled with light citrus with just the faintest tinge of smoky surprise intertwined with trepidation. No heavy, putrid odor of repulsion.

She searched his face for any sign of deceit. The human part of her couldn't credit he'd admitted to being attracted to her, her demon half insisted she trust her instincts. Which should she trust—her heart or her senses?

Kalan watched the flecks in Annika's eyes change from black to pale bronze. She looked as astonished by his admission as he felt.

"I'm a demon . . ."

Her whispered words, an echo of his own the evening before, pierced his gut. Her pain challenged him.

"You're *Na'Chi*," he refuted.

"You think I'm tainted . . ."

Less than three days ago he'd have agreed with her. Three days ago, if they met anywhere but in that dungeon below Savyr's keep, he'd have driven his blade into her heart and used his Gift to kill her. But she'd saved his life, given him his freedom, and called into question everything he believed to be true about demons.

"Annika, I don't understand the attraction between us any more than you do."

"You continue to toy with me. Why?"

If the situation wasn't so tenuous Kalan would have laughed. Her suspicion and distrust grated against his pride.

He shook his head. "I'm not toying with you. I have no ulterior motive."

"You claim you're attracted to me, yet last night you were repulsed by the idea that you almost kissed me." Her accusation was shadowed with pain. "Am I to believe you've had a change of heart in less than a day?"

Her disbelief was justified. He ran a hand through his damp hair. "Annika, I don't know what else I can say—"

"Prove it."

"What?"

She swallowed convulsively. "Kiss me." Her chin tilted. Flecked with green, her eyes sparkled in silent challenge.

His pulse began to race, his body grew hot, and *Lady's Breath*, he was getting hard, turned on by her dare. Closing the distance between them to place his lips on hers took little effort to imagine. A single heartbeat and he'd finally discover what she tasted like.

None of what he was experiencing was making any sense and until it did, kissing her wouldn't be a good idea.

Her lip curled the longer he hesitated. "Your scent might reek of desire but you're still disgusted by the fact you're attracted to a demon."

"Not disgusted, *Na'Chi*," he denied, and deep inside that was the truth. It was frustrating that she continued to see him in such a negative light. "Try confused."

With that, he dipped his head and slanted his mouth over hers. For the barest moment Annika stiffened, and then placed her hand against his chest to grip his shirt and hold on. He buried his fingers into the soft strands of her hair at the back of her neck to steady her.

Merciful Mother, her lips were soft, silky, and sweeter than any fruit he'd ever consumed. Kalan traced them with his tongue, allowing himself to enjoy their texture and taste, feasting on and teasing himself with the scintillating combination. He sucked on the fullest part of her bottom lip, grazing it with his teeth.

The small voice in the back of his head warning him to stop, that kissing her was a mistake, was drowned out by the blood pounding inside his head. Every heartbeat spent tasting her wasn't enough to satiate the need building in him.

He groaned; the wild, untamed sound wrenched from deep within his chest. Dropping his other hand to her waist, he pulled her up against him.

Annika twisted away from him, her breath coming in small gasps. In the firelight, her lips shone wet from their kiss. Her eyes glowed a pale ice blue, almost silver. "Kalan . . . I can't . . ."

The waver in her voice drew him back from the edge, checked his desire. *Lady's Breath*, he'd never intended to lose control so quickly. He dropped to his knees, his own breath ragged, and gripped his thighs hard to stop himself trembling.

"I didn't mean to scare you."

"You didn't." Her shudder indicated otherwise. Her head dropped. Guilt dampened his arousal. Her voice fell to a whisper. "I've never done that before."

"What? Kissed?"

"Yes." She gave a half-shrug before meeting his gaze head-on, the obstinate tilt to her chin back. How could such vulnerability and incredible inner strength coexist in this woman? "Human or demon. I didn't think you'd do it . . ."

She didn't know how to kiss? The thought of teaching her sent a thrill racing through him and was enough to rouse his hunger back to life. Now wasn't the time though. She had to understand something first.

Heat curled in the pit of Annika's belly at the flare of hunger in

Kalan's eyes. Was he remembering their kiss? She laced her fingers
together, resisting the urge to touch her mouth.

His scent saturated the air, heavy, drugging her senses, tempting
her as nothing ever had before. *Lady of Light*, it made her burn,
ache. Her lips tingled, felt swollen, and the spicy flavor of him lingered on her tongue. She'd give anything to taste him again.

She tensed as he lifted his hand and reached out to her. The backs
of his fingers trailed along her cheek, then he cupped her cheek in
the palm of his hand.

"Annika, I liked kissing you."

She shook her head. "You're a Light Blade warrior—"

He placed a finger across her lips to stop her speaking. "I'm a man
who enjoyed kissing a woman." His deep voice slid through her, its
husky tone caressing the length of her spine.

The meaning of his words sank in. She stilled, hating how sincere
he sounded, but even more she loathed how her heart leapt in hope at
his declaration.

"You lie . . ." Her words were hoarse, harsh, unforgiving.

She lifted her gaze to meet his as the silence spun out. The barest
hint of a smile tilted the corners of his mouth, promising so much,
and the impact of it hit her low in the stomach.

When Kalan spoke his tone was gentle. "Kiss me this time. See
for yourself how much I enjoyed our first encounter."

Her eyes widened. What he suggested was madness. What did
he expect to come of this?

One dark eyebrow inched upward. "Afraid?"

The softly delivered dare sparked her temper. She planted a hand
against his chest, fisted it in his shirt then hesitated as his smile grew.
She didn't know whether to push him away or pull him closer. His
scent teased her nostrils. Aroused male. Her nerves sizzled.

Human weakness tempted her with the need to know what it
would be like to kiss him again, only this time fully aware of his

intentions and free to give rein to the desire burning within her. To know that what she felt was reciprocated in him.

"You want to, Annika. I can see it in your face."

The blatant hunger in his gaze raked against her, as tangible as fingers against her skin. She tightened her grip, her lips so close to his she could feel the moist warmth of his breath against her skin. He didn't force her closer or cover the remaining distance himself. He waited, his green eyes darkening, heating.

That she aroused him was irrationally satisfying but she had no business feeling this way.

"You're trembling." Kalan's whisper stroked sensitive nerves. "Does it help to know, so am I?"

Lady's Breath, yes.

Annika closed her eyes. He made her *feel* more than any other person had. He made her *want* what existed in her imagination but had never believed possible.

Until now.

The shudder that raced through her was one of hot excitement. She shoved indecision and doubt to the back of her mind and pressed her lips against his.

She tasted his desire. It was fierce and spicy, just like his scent, igniting a burn that started at the tip of her tongue and wove its way rapidly south. She kept her touch feather light on his chest, unsure of his reaction. Even through his shirt she could feel the heat in the heavy curves of muscle stretching the width of his shoulders and down into his corded arms, male flesh, solid and hard beneath the palms of her hands. A first for her outside the healer's domain.

She heard the soft rasp of his hand sliding over her dress as he cupped the curve of her hip, his grip firm, sure as he pulled her in against the hard length of his body. His heat engulfed her. Every sensation pushed her to the edge of reason.

The experience of kissing someone scared her yet the pressure of

Kalan's mouth on hers, the warm slide of his tongue between her lips and the gentle strength of his hands tunneling through her hair made her feel . . . safe.

Annika broke the kiss and drew back, panting softly, and stared up at him. Desire had darkened his cheeks a ruddy hue, his lips were still wet from their kiss, but his smile was tender.

"Well?" he asked.

She shook her head, overwhelmed by potential of what accepting the truth of his earlier claim would mean. "This isn't possible . . ."

Kalan's gaze gleamed. "Then what just happened?"

"You know what I mean!" She scrambled to her feet. "This isn't right."

He rose but made no move to step closer. His arms folded across his chest. "If I'm willing to try and accept whatever's happening between us, why can't you?"

Any other time she'd have admired him for his blunt honesty but he seemed intent on ignoring the obvious. "Where can it possibly lead, Light Blade?"

"That's something I'll trust the *Lady* to reveal in *Her* own time." His confidence was unwavering, his scent true. "Do you think I expected something like this to happen? I thought to spend all of my life serving *Her* and protecting my people. I never planned to be captured by the *Na'Reish*. My life changed the moment that happened. And only *She* knows the outcome of taking you back to Sacred Lake, but this is the Journey *She*'s chosen for me. For us. It's clear *She*'s demanding that I adapt."

"You make accepting *Her* plan for your life sound so easy!"

He barked a laugh and shook his head. "Accepting *Her* will has never been easy. Once you get to know who I am, you'll realize that." His smile turned rueful. "I've no doubt I'm going to face problems on this Journey. All I can do is trust that *She* will guide me in the decisions I make."

Kalan doubted Annika realized just how much of her inner struggle was reflected on her face. Her skepticism and vulnerability would ease in time, especially given her faith in the *Lady*. She'd adjust, just as he had to do. Of the few times she'd shared snippets of her life with him, he knew she'd honed that skill to an incredible degree.

What made his chest ache was the fear he sensed behind those emotions. Dealing with derision and hatred wouldn't be her greatest challenge as she entered his world. She'd spent a lifetime developing the strength to combat the rejection that came with being *Na'Chi*. Believing someone could accept her unconditionally would be her new journey. She wasn't ready to face that yet.

"The decision to pursue the attraction we share is yours to make," he promised her. Her tense stance eased. "But I'm here if you need me, Annika. You're not alone."

The sense of rightness that filled Kalan once he'd made that offer was reassuring but it was time to back off. He retreated to the other side of the fire and sat down.

He motioned to the carcass still roasting over the flames. "This looks ready to eat. Care to join me?"

He felt her scrutiny as he took the spit off the fire and divvied up the carcass. Returning to the fire, she accepted the portion he held out to her. Their meal passed in silence.

She tossed the bones into the flames, her expression pensive. "I'm sorry," she murmured.

His gaze met hers over the flickering flames. "For what?"

"For doubting you again." She wet her bottom lip. "I'm just not used to someone keeping their promise. The *Na'Reish* might have a code of honor but it never exists beyond their caste. So trusting isn't something I do well."

"I haven't made it easy for you to trust me." His conscience wouldn't let her accept all the blame. Throwing the remnants of his meal into the fire, he leaned back on his hands, attentive, hoping his relaxed pose would encourage her to continue talking.

"Kalan, is the *Lady's Chosen* a fair-minded man?"

He hid his grimace. Of all the topics he'd expected her to pick, this was not one he wanted to delve into. Not yet. But to ignore her request would damage the progress they'd made. Sending a swift prayer heavenward for guidance, he responded. "He tries to be."

"Will he listen to what you have to say? Will I be allowed to speak?"

"He believes it's important to know all the facts so he'll listen to what everyone has to say." A wry twist curved his lips. "Much to the Blade Council's annoyance."

"They don't like him?"

He paused to pick up a twig. Snapping pieces off it, he threw them into the fire. "There's always going to be some who disagree with the decisions or opinions of the *Lady's Chosen*. Personalities get in the way. I believe that some of the Councilors are used to a different style of leadership. The *Lady's Chosen's* predecessor was a lot older and more . . . conservative and rigid in his style."

Annika frowned. "This wasn't a good thing for your people?"

"It depends on your point of view." He leant forward. "The last *Lady's Chosen* led for almost fifty years. When the new *Chosen* ascended we'd reached five hundred years of conflict with the *Na'Reish*. The times demanded a conservative leader. But it bred a form of elitism among the Light Blades. They and the Council lost sight of what our purpose was, that we were there to protect and serve everyone."

"They didn't do this?"

"At first they did but as our losses grew the decision was made for the Light Blades to withdraw from the outer areas of our territory in order to protect the provinces of the Councilors and Sacred Lake."

Her eyes widened. "So, if you didn't live in those areas you were unprotected?"

"Essentially, yes." Here he grimaced. "It made the Blade Council very unpopular. When the current *Chosen* took over, he wanted to restore the reputation of the Light Blades. It hasn't been easy and his more liberal attitude has often been in direct conflict with the older Councilors."

"What has he done that they disagree with?"

"The Light Blades patrol all our territory now, even though our numbers are less than half of what they used to be fifty years ago. He visits the outlying villages to meet with leaders and talks with them about their concerns. He accepts everyone into the Light Blade academy regardless of what province they come from."

"So, he's made himself and the ranks of the Light Blades welcoming to everyone. Surely that's a good thing if you need to increase the number of warriors protecting your territory?"

"It's not easy balancing the politics and there are times he's frustrated by the Council. Attitudes take time to change, but he has faith that the *Lady* will guide us all."

She bit her lip. "Do you think he'll grant me sanctuary?"

Uneasiness curled in Kalan's gut. He really didn't want to take the conversation in this direction. "Your arrival will herald change," he said slowly, carefully. "Our history books and teachings tell us the *Na'Chi* are a myth. Your existence will challenge a lifetime of beliefs."

She shivered but met his gaze head-on. "You haven't answered my question."

He rose and took his time creating their makeshift bed for the night. As much as he wanted to answer her question honestly, there were other factors to consider. Others to protect. The conversation had to end now.

"Granting you sanctuary should be discussed between him and the Blade Council. The ultimate decision is his but it helps if the Council agrees, too." He banked the fire then crawled under the blanket. "We've a long day ahead of us. We should get some sleep."

With that, he closed his eyes. In the silence that followed he could feel her confusion, her uncertainty. There wasn't anything he could do to rectify it, not until they reached Sacred Lake.

Several minutes later, Annika joined him under the blanket. He heard her sigh softly. It was a long while before either of them managed to sleep.

Chapter 13

"ANNIKA, we're here. Look!"

Kalan's soft call jerked Annika from the steady rhythm of placing one boot in front of the other. Exhaustion made her clumsy as she stumbled to a halt. It took a moment for his words to penetrate her tired mind.

Traveling from daybreak to early evening, pausing only for a meal, Kalan had expressed his desire to push on rather than make camp. Eager to see Sacred Lake, she'd agreed but had lost track of their progress somewhere between dusk and moonrise, succumbing to the exhaustion and the numbing cold of the night.

Blinking blearily, her last memory of their surroundings had been a thickly wooded forest on a hillside. Now she stood on a roadway that followed a river and wound its way across a bare plateau.

"Where are we?" She rubbed a hand over her face in an effort to wake up. The chill on the night breeze did a much better job as it fluttered the folds of her cloak, sneaking beneath it to stroke her skin. She shivered as Kalan gestured along the way. Peering past him, a soft gasp escaped her lips and adrenaline cleared the last of her tiredness away.

The moon was nearly full, heading for the jagged horizon of a mountain range. Its light shimmered off a large lake below the snow-capped peaks—but that wasn't what caught her attention.

Sitting right on the lip of the narrow plateau, at the edge of the lake, nestled against the mountains was a huge city surrounded by a stone wall that seemed to glow in the moonlight. The road led straight to a set of massive double wooden gates. Like giant sentinels both the wall and gates stood almost five men tall, intimidating, awesome. This close they dominated the landscape.

A grin creased the weariness on Kalan's face. "Welcome to Sacred Lake."

Eyes wide, she barely glanced at him. "I've heard others talk about it but never envisaged this."

Another shiver passed through her. Her mother had lived here; trained daily as a warrior, prayed in the temple, walked the city streets. Beyond the great gateway lay her identity and an uncertain future. Her dream.

A wave of longing hit her hard: to hear Hesia's age-worn voice, for the small room she called her own inside her father's chambers, for the scent of fresh herbs from her garden, for the feelings of peace and reassurance as she dried them, for her collection of bowls, bottles, and jars she used to store her remedies. She didn't have much in the way of possessions or friends but she missed them all. Her throat tightened.

"Annika." Kalan's voice was a soft murmur, gentle. His hand stretched toward her.

I'm here if you need me. You're not alone. His words from the night before.

The need to feel the warmth of his touch ate at Annika like a ravenous animal. She tried to stay strong—she didn't need his pity— but found herself reaching for his hand. She wrapped her fingers around his then let him slowly pull her in against his chest. He slid his free arm around her. The gentle action of cradling her against him cut straight to her heart.

She shuddered. *Mother of Mercy*, she didn't know what scared her more—the incredible peace she felt cradled against his chest listening to the steady *thump, thump, thump* of his heart beneath her ear, or the pain of realizing she no longer had the strength to stand alone.

"You make me feel safe." Her admission came out as a hoarse whisper. Kalan's arm tightened around her. "I'm a fool for needing your comfort, your friendship."

"Annika, you're one of the most courageous people I've met." She leaned closer to him, craving more of the sincerity she heard in his voice. "There's nothing wrong with wanting, with feeling the way you do."

Don't believe him . . .

She squashed the voice of reason and inhaled a ragged breath. "It'd be a whole lot simpler if I could ignore it and not get tangled up with feelings. Too many times I've been human enough to hope someone would care enough not to hurt me."

Inwardly she flinched. How many times had her father ridiculed her for that?

"*We're born alone and we die alone. In between we take as much as we can using our own strength and others to get it. Show them your feelings and you give them the power to cripple you.*" Kalan's arm tightened around her as she recited her father's words. "I was too human to meet *Na'Reish* standards and too *Na'Reish* for any human to want me near them." Tears stung her eyes, fierce and hot. "How do I fight a lifetime of being taught that I'm worth nothing?"

Heat burned her cheeks as she kept her gaze downcast, bracing herself for his reaction, anticipating rejection.

Kalan grimaced at the hoarseness of her voice. It sounded like shards of glass shredding her throat. "Annika, you're not worthless."

He heard her sharp intake of breath then she started to pull away from him. "Just listen to me a moment. Please."

She stilled, her breathing ragged against his chest, her body so tense she felt like steel in his arms. It didn't matter just as long as she didn't move away. Away from him she'd erect a barrier he had no chance of breeching. He rubbed her back slowly, soothingly.

Lady help him find the right words to ease her pain. "Hesia doesn't see you as nothing. Neither do I."

He kept his voice soft, calm, doing everything he could to leash the raw anger he felt for her father. He wanted to kill Savyr. The abuse meted out to Annika went against his every belief that a child, human or demon, should be loved and cherished.

"I can't take away your past, or make the things done to you hurt less but I can tell you what Hesia sees in you because I've witnessed it, too." He pressed his cheek to the top of her head. "We see a strong, determined woman who refuses to believe everything her father told her. Defying a parent and daring to stand against abuse designed to break you, that takes courage.

"You became a healer with your special Gift. Instead of hiding or using it to elevate your status among the *Na'Reish* you chose to help the human-slaves in your father's keep. You aided them and suffered because of it, but it didn't stop you. That shows incredible compassion. Your intelligence and bravery has saved countless lives, mine included.

"The *Lady* has given you these qualities and the courage to fight what you've been taught. How else do you explain Hesia's friendship with you? Or my desire to want the same for us?"

Annika slowly lifted her head. While her expression remained pinched with fear and her violet eyes were still flecked with yellow, he saw a faint stirring of hope deep within her gaze.

"I want to trust you." She swallowed hard. "But wanting to and being able to are two different things."

"Meet me halfway. Please."

Her chin dipped in a jerky nod. Relief and excitement made his pulse race in relief.

"*Lady's Breath*, this isn't going to be easy . . ." She stiffened in his arms. "What will your family or friends say?"

Unease gnawed at his innards but he pushed it aside. There was no doubt there'd be opposition. He was probably a fool for ignoring the issue, for not considering the implications but he just wanted to deal with what was happening between him and Annika.

"Let tomorrow worry about itself, Annika." With *Her* help they'd get through whatever trials lay ahead.

Kalan cupped her cheek with his hand. She stared at him solemnly for several long heartbeats, her expression so vulnerable it made his heart hurt. Then, her eyelashes flickered closed and she leaned into his touch. That small show of trust made him want to shout in triumph.

"Soon we'll be in my home, where we can bathe then sleep what's left of the night." He smoothed his thumb over the curve of her cheek and her bottom lip before dropping his hand. "Let that be enough for now."

"All right." Her reply was husky, tired.

"Thank you," he murmured, and tugged lightly on their joined hands. "Come on, let's finish this journey."

They covered the remaining distance to the city in less than a quarter hour. Annika tugged up her hood to cover her face as Kalan hailed the watchmen standing on the wall. As he announced his name a commotion broke out within the watchtower. A heartbeat later a metallic winching sound came from behind the huge double gates and they cracked open.

As they entered the city, they were surrounded by a number of men and women wearing leather armor with the *Lady*'s sun etched into their chestplates, all quite vocal in their greetings. Kalan acknowledged each of them with a grin and an arm clasp.

Even without the identifying Light Blade symbol on their armor, Annika sensed *Her* Gift within each of them, some more strongly than others.

She moved back as a barrel-chested man, much older than the others, pushed his way toward them. He brandished a lantern in one hand, while the other rested on the hilt of the sword at his waist. His face was as weathered and brown as a nut, a striking contrast to his silver grey hair. His gaze swept over her then Kalan, bushy eyebrows rising swiftly.

"Commander?"

"Yevni!" Kalan's grin widened. "It's good to see you!"

The man shoved the lantern into the hands of a younger warrior then embraced Kalan, laughing and slapping his back hard. She peered around at the circle of grinning faces and wondered at the friendship the two men shared. Neither looked enough alike to be blood-related; perhaps the man was an instructor.

The old warrior held him at arm's length and looked him over. "The Blade Council made an announcement about the *Na'Reish* attack on Durrat over a sennight ago. We thought you dead!"

"I would have been if it hadn't been for Annika." Kalan turned and motioned her closer. "She helped me escape the *Na'Reish* fortress."

"Then you are most welcome within our walls." The warmth in the warrior's voice left her feeling uneasy. Ducking her head, she nodded in thanks, hoping he wouldn't question the hood. "How is it you helped him escape?"

Kalan broke in before she could answer. "The story is long and complicated but rest assured, Yevni, you'll hear it. Right now we're both tired."

The tall warrior grunted. "What are your orders?"

"Send a messenger to Councilor Benth's quarters. Let him know I've returned. I'll meet tomorrow with the Council."

Yevni nodded to one of the warriors. She raced off down a wide cobblestoned street, her bootsteps echoing loudly off the buildings on either side.

"Oskan, accompany Kalan and his friend to his apartment." Yevni grasped his forearm tightly. "Your return will bring back hope among our ranks, Commander."

"Thank you." He motioned her to follow the young man holding the lantern.

Annika looked left and right, curious about the buildings around her. Most were two-story structures made of stone with double doors spaced at intervals. They reminded her of the storage rooms in the fortress, only they were much bigger. No light came from the few that possessed windows: they were dark and quiet.

She longed to ask Kalan questions about the city as they walked its streets but was reluctant to reveal her ignorance with a stranger listening in. The stone buildings changed to smaller wooden ones. These were poorly constructed and none were taller than a single story. Very few were made entirely of the same material and bits seemed stuck or added on over time. The ramshackle houses were similar to the human-slaves' quarters within the fortress.

As they moved deeper into this area, a rank odor intensified with every step. Her nose wrinkled in recognition: rotting garbage and human filth.

Several times they passed what she thought were three or four individual houses but it looked as if they'd been joined together so that they became one long row of connected buildings. Some had small overhanging rooves and benches or chairs had been placed on the ground beneath them. A few had lines of washing strung up.

She moved closer to Kalan. "People live here?"

"The workers in the city," he replied softly. "It's known as Coppertown. They're paid copper chits when they hire on as labor. Most are good, decent people but, unfortunately, it's also where the vagabonds like to live. This area by far is the largest within the city and easiest to escape notice or get lost in."

Annika remembered the first time Hesia had mentioned the human custom of money. The idea of swapping colored pieces of metal for supplies had seemed absurd, especially when the *Na'Reish* levied tithes within their Clans and took what they needed from the lower-caste craftsmen. For those wanting to curry favor, owning human-slaves with particular skills was a way of settling a debt or gaining an advantage.

Coppertown gave way to more stone buildings, only these ones had well-constructed awnings, most made of shingles or tiles. Small pieces of bright-colored cloth cut in the shape of triangles hung on lines tied around the support poles. Whatever they signified they'd certainly be attractive and eye-catching on a breezy day. Large, thick shutters covered windows and empty stalls stood pushed against the walls.

"This is Bartertown, where all the guilds sell their crafters' wares." Kalan pointed to one of the buildings. "See the signs above the doors? This one sells carpentry tools."

Annika peered at the swirling designs carved into the lintel. She'd mistaken the etchings as patterns. Some had small painted pictures accompanying them. The next one had a person sitting in front of a loom, perhaps a weaver's or clothmaker's stall.

"How many live within the walls?" she whispered.

"Almost ten thousand," he replied. "There are several districts within the city. Coppertown, Northgate, and Lakeview are all housing areas. The Business District includes places like Waterside Dock, where the fishing boats come in from the lake, the factories we passed behind us are in Eastgate, and Bartertown belongs to the guilds and their crafters sell their wares from their holds. Then we have places like the Salesyards and the People's Market. The traders and farmers from outside the city come in at the beginning of each week, on market day, to sell their animals and produce.

"The Entertainment District backs onto Guild Square. That's where many come to find work. We're headed for the *Lady*'s compound. We have about a thousand Light Blades living there."

"You only have a thousand warriors?"

"On duty, yes. Another five thousand live in the city or out on farms in the countryside. The Barracks work on a three-monthly rotation. If we had to, we could call them all in but to have them living here full-time isn't fair to their families and it puts a strain on the city's resources."

Still, six thousand warriors weren't a lot.

"Kalan, the *Na'Hord* number almost fifteen thousand." She kept her voice low so only he could hear her. "If my father ordered every *Na'Reish* male young and old to bear arms that number could easily be increased to twenty-five thousand."

His jaw tightened. "We knew their *Na'Hord* outnumbered us but it seems we've underestimated their strength. That information needs to be passed on to the Council." His gaze met hers. "Thank you."

Annika nodded as they entered a large, cobblestoned court. Guild Square. From behind the southern line of buildings, drifting on the evening breeze, she heard the faint strains of music, the only sign of life other than the watch in the sleeping city.

She shot a swift glance at Kalan. He walked head held high even though dark shadows ringed his eyes. He was home, safe, in familiar territory. She tugged at her hood, more aware than ever of the stark differences in their worlds.

Sacred Lake had watchmen. No Patrols or *Vorc* enforcing a nightly curfew. The slave quarters within the *Na'Reish* fortress were locked from sunset to sunrise and any blood-slaves kept within Clan homes were chained to the hearth so they couldn't escape. Here, people were free to walk the streets.

"This is the *Lady*'s Gate." Kalan's soft statement drew her from her thoughts. "We've reached the Light Blade compound."

Their escort spoke to the warrior on duty and they passed with a minimum of fuss. A series of buildings were scattered around the compound, all built in a similar style to the stone structures within the Business District. They crossed an open parade ground.

Peering at a thin building to their left, Annika wondered why it was the only one where some of the windows glowed with light. Shadows of people passed the windows. She was on the verge of asking Kalan what that place was but then bit her lip. There would be time for questions later.

"I'll take my leave here, Commander." The young warrior halted at the edge of the parade ground. He handed over the lantern. "Sleep well."

Kalan nodded and the man headed back toward the gate. "Your eyes are a deep violet, Annika," he murmured as he steered her along a wide pathway bordered with a garden on one side and a formal arrangement of monoliths that stood at even intervals on the other.

"I'm curious." She waved a hand at the standing stones. "This is so different to the fortress. You have stone gardens inside your keep. Plants grow in boxes on the sills of some of the buildings. There was even a forest of trees on one of the streets with a small statue sitting in a pool of water. There's nothing like this in the *Na'Reish* fortress."

His soft chuckle carried on the night air. "There's more, but if I begin telling you we'll be up for the remaining hours of the night."

"I'm sorry." The garden pathway led them to a three-story building. He motioned her through an open doorway. "My questions can wait until morning."

They walked through long corridors and climbed flights of stairs until they reached the third level. Annika smothered a jaw-popping yawn as they reached the end of yet another corridor.

"We're nearly there." A weary smile curved Kalan's lips. He stopped in front of another door, pushed it open, then ushered her into a large room reminiscent of her father's inner chamber. But that was where the similarity ended. While her father preferred lavish surroundings, the best of everything to remind others of his status, this chamber was decorated simply.

Kalan left her by the door as he went around lighting braziers on the walls of the chamber and a stand full of candles, each as thick as her arm. Light filled the room and her eyes widened when she saw the intricate rug beneath her feet. Geometric circles in shades of blue patterned the weave. She stepped off it, afraid she'd mark it with the dirt on her boots.

"You live here?" she asked as Kalan lit the wood stacked in the great fireplace to her left. The crackling of tinder and scent of burning wood was soothing.

"Most of the time." He dusted his hands. "During the warmer months I tend to spend more time on the training grounds with my warriors than here."

"Do all Light Blades live in chambers like this? Is that why there are so many buildings in the compound?"

Shields and weapons hung on the walls, a variety of chests were pushed up against the walls, and a large table with high-backed chairs sat in the middle of the room.

"Most live in the Barracks. Being the . . . commander comes with certain privileges." His hesitation made her wonder why he'd faltered mid-statement. He gestured at two smaller wooden doorways on the wall opposite her. "My bedroom is on the left. The other used to be my sister's, until she became a Handmaiden at the Temple. I don't think she'd mind it being yours for a while."

Annika edged her way around the rug to stand in front of the fire, sighing as she felt the warming air. An open archway on the last wall of the room showed her smaller chamber shrouded in darkness. She was tempted to wander over and look in but she hadn't been invited yet.

"It's a bathing room."

She jerked in surprise and discovered Kalan watching her, a grin curving his lips. She pushed back the hood of her cloak. "I didn't mean to pry."

He motioned to a third door. "That opens onto a balcony over-looking the gardens." Grimacing, he ran a hand through his hair. "Annika, I don't want to leave you alone. We need to talk. There's something very important I have to tell you that I couldn't before, but I'd like to visit my sister. She'll have worried during my absence."

"Then go." She raised an eyebrow as Kalan hesitated. The deep frown and uncertain expression he wore made her wonder what would take precedence over reuniting with his sister. "We can talk later. I promise not to leave the room on one condition." She glanced long-ingly toward the archway. "May I bathe?"

Kalan's somber expression lightened. He pointed to a chest near the archway. "Bath cloths and cleansing sand are in there." He disap-peared into his room a moment then came out holding a small bun-dle of linen. "Wear one of my shirts. I'll ask Kymora to bring some clothes tomorrow. Are you sure you'll be all right here by yourself?"

With a smile, Annika took the bundle off him. "Once in that bathing room, I'll hardly know you're gone."

"Hedonist," he accused her with a chuckle as he headed for the door.

Despite her reassurances, she felt his absence immediately. Her smile faded. The hollow sensation inside her went heart-deep. Unwill-ing to dwell on the problem, she focused on collecting what she needed for her bath.

After lighting more braziers within the room, she turned and her jaw dropped. She'd expected a wooden tub or maybe a basin and jug—not a tiled pool big enough to fit four people and deep enough that it would submerge most of her when she sat down. It was already filled with steaming water. Bending down to examine the mosaic on the bottom of it, she watched the water ripple and undulate and heard the faint sound of it splashing into something beneath the floor.

Her eyes widened. It was piped through the buildings? Not even her father had such luxury. Kalan hadn't been joking when he'd said he liked to bathe.

Eager to try it out, Annika stripped and slid into the water, groaning as its warmth touched her skin. She was tempted to lie back and float but a series of eye-watering yawns dissuaded that idea. More likely than not she'd probably fall asleep mid-float.

Reaching for the jar of cleansing sand she washed quickly, starting with her hair and working her way down her body. She enjoyed its creamy texture as she smoothed it over her skin. As the foaming sand heated its fresh, light scent filled the room. With the water constantly circulating, it had little chance to cloud or get dirty.

Too soon she was finished. Reluctantly, she left the pool. The sensation of being clean for the first time in days was a pleasure she'd not forget anytime soon.

A hollow, wooden thud, much like the sound of a door being flung open in the outer chamber made her start. Snatching up the shirt, she slid into it, fingers fumbling with the laces.

"Kalan!"

Annika froze. The deep voice was unfamiliar. Bootsteps clicked on the flagstone floor, heading toward the bathing room.

"Kalan? It's me . . . Arek. Are you in there?" A tall man about the same age as Kalan appeared in the archway. "Yevni told me—"

The man drew to a halt, surprise flitting across his clean-shaven face as he spotted her standing beside the pool. The armor covering his chest bore the sun symbol of the *Lady*. Did *She* bless all her warriors with such striking looks?

At first glance, the warrior's hair was dark blond but when she looked closer it was made of a number of colors; light yellow, red, brown, even a few strands of pale gold. It was brushed back from his chiseled facial features and tied at the nape of his neck. His eyes were a deep blue, much like the sky as twilight approached, but there was nothing soft about them.

A cold sliver of fear sliced through Annika. *Lady of Mercy*, her cloak lay underneath the pile of dirty clothes. His eyes darkened. He'd seen her body markings.

"*Na'Reish!*" His snarl lifted the hairs on her neck. His gaze bore into her, hard and merciless. Dangerous. Lethal. With a cry, he leapt across the distance separating them.

Heart pounding, Annika flung the jar of cleansing sand in the warrior's direction. The granules sprayed through the air, blinding him and giving her enough time to dart around to the other side of the pool. She heard the jar shatter against the floor as she ran through the archway.

If she could just make it to Kalan's room and close the door . . . his hand grasped her shoulder. She cried out in frustration and fright as she was swung around. A forearm slammed against her chest and pinned her against the wall. Instinct brought her knee up in a move she'd practiced with Kalan but the man twisted, his hard muscled, leather-clad thigh taking the blow. He grimaced.

Candlelight flashed off metal. A blade pressed against her throat. She sensed a sudden rush of power. Dark satisfaction burned in the man's blue-eyed gaze.

"Now you die!"

Chapter 14

*S*IX *Light Blade warriors.*

Varian heard Lisella suck in a sharp breath as Zaune's hand signals alerted them to what lay just over the ridge. A stone's throw away, the young scout lay flat on his stomach, barely noticeable, in the shadows of a bush perched on the rock ledge.

His hands gestured again. *Coming west.*

Toward the line of *Na'Chi* traversing the slope behind them.

Breath hissed out from between Varian's teeth. Why had he insisted on traveling before dark? Because they'd fallen behind Annika and he'd wanted to make up time. What a stupid, stupid decision. Risking all their lives should never have taken precedence over their safety.

He scanned the steep hillside. A few bushes. A half-dozen stunted trees. Even fewer boulders. He grimaced at the lack of cover to hide behind as the warriors went by. Backtracking was an option but he doubted they'd have time to erase their tracks. The Light Blades would top the ridge in less than a quarter hour.

"What are we going to do?" Lisella's whisper barely reached his ears. "There's nowhere to hide."

"Get the group to crouch low and keep the children quiet." He caught Zaune's eye and motioned the scout back. "I need Barvi and Leanna."

Fear flashed across her face. "You're not going to kill the humans?"

"No." Her hasty assumption made him smile. "Something even better." His smile widened into a grin. "How good do you think humans are at running?"

Lisella stared at him as if he'd lost his mind, then her eyes flickered with comprehension. She slithered down the hillside to fetch the two scouts he'd requested. He waited with Zaune until they'd returned and quickly outlined his plan to them.

"Lisella, stay with the others." He was expecting her frown.

"I'm just as fast as you."

"If something goes wrong, you'll be in charge of leading this group to the city and to Annika." Her mouth tightened but she gave a nod. "Once we lead the Light Blades away, head for Zaune's last marker. Push hard and you'll close the gap to a day behind Annika. If we don't meet you there in two hours, go on without us."

"Be careful."

"Always." With that, he and the other scouts followed the ridge-line. The late afternoon sun was at their backs and they kept below the edge until they were well away from the group. With only the scent of the humans to guide them, they worked their way along the ridge until they reached a ravine that intersected the well-worn trail.

Zaune crawled up the short slope, peered along the trail then dropped back down. His fingers moved swiftly. *Four males, two females. Still advancing.*

Varian glanced at each of them. *They must follow us. Ready?* He received three nods. *Now!*

They all scrambled from the ravine onto the path. Varian almost laughed as the humans came face-to-face with him and his scouts. Their astonished expressions were remarkable. For the longest moment they all stood watching one another, barely a stone's throw apart then he threw back his head and uttered a *Na'Hord* war cry.

"They're *Na'Reish*!"

Adrenaline surged through him as the Light Blade warriors charged. Two even drew their weapons. Several heartbeats later he gave a sharp nod to the others and they all took off running.

Varian split off from the trail and headed downhill. Behind him, he heard boots scrambling over rocks. He swerved around a tree and caught sight of two warriors pursuing him. Another leap and he was into the shadow thrown by the hill. Sunset was minutes away.

Farther along the trail, he heard several cries then Zaune's voice shouting at his pursuers.

Darkness would be their ally.

KALAN heard Annika's cry when he was halfway along the corridor. The distressed sound ripped through him like a blade and he sprinted the remaining distance. The door to his quarters was wide open. Heart pounding, he took in the scene before him.

He recognized the blond warrior who had Annika pinned against the wall of his chamber, his dagger digging into her throat. Her fingers clamped so tightly around Arek's wrist they were bloodless. Every muscle in her body strained as she tried to stop him from slicing open her throat.

"Stand down, Arek!"

The warrior's head jerked around to stare at him. "Kalan?"

"Annika has my protection!"

Shock flickered across his friend's face. His lip curled. "She's *Na'Reish*!"

"She saved my life!" It was a relief Arek was even listening. He tended to act first and think later, especially where anything *Na'Reish* was concerned. "Let her go."

Disbelief flashed across Arek's face. He glanced back at Annika, a frown creasing his brow. For the longest moment all Kalan could hear was the blood pounding in his head and the harsh rasp of all their breathing. He waited, hoping Annika wouldn't panic or try to move, ready to surge forward if the blade pressed any deeper into her neck.

Abruptly, Arek stepped back, but he placed himself directly between Kalan and Annika, shielding his comrade.

Kalan let out a quiet sigh and placed a hand on his friend's tense shoulder. "Thank you." His fingers bit into thick muscle as he squeezed. "What are you doing here in my apartment?"

"I ran into Yevni as I was coming off perimeter watch."

Annika remained motionless against the wall, held still by the very real threat of the dagger clutched in Arek's hand and the fact he hadn't taken his eyes off her. She was trembling. Vivid yellow flecked the violet depths of her gaze.

"Annika, I need to speak with Arek." The thin red line of blood on her neck stirred Kalan's temper but he remained calm. "Go into my room and close the door."

Her nod brought a wince of pain. "I need my pouch. It's on the table."

Arek scooped it up before she could move. He riffled through it, withdrew the small knife she used for cutting herbs, and tucked it into his belt. Then he tossed her the pouch. Annika took it without comment and retreated.

Arek pivoted as the door closed and Kalan found himself in a backbreaking hug. "*Lady of Mercy*, Kalan, don't you ever leave me sitting in that damned Council chamber in your stead when I should be at your side protecting you. You never would've been captured if I'd been with you on that visit to Durrat."

His friend's anger was genuine but Kalan chuckled as he returned the hug. "It's good to see you, too."

The man pinned him with a savage glare. If he'd been any other person, that look would have chilled him to his innards.

"I'm still waiting to hear why you stopped me from killing that demon." His hand flexed around the hilt of his dagger.

Kalan sobered, knowing just how close Annika had come to death. If he'd arrived a minute later . . . he sighed softly and waved the warrior to the table. He wasn't surprised when Arek sat in the closest chair facing his bedroom door and placed his dagger on the edge of the table.

"I'm really tired, so I'm going to keep this short. Long explanations can wait until tomorrow. For now, you need to heed me and spread the word around the compound. Annika has my protection. Anyone who harms her will answer to me. She saved my life getting me out of that fortress. Twice."

"Why would a *Na'Reish* do that?"

"She's *Na'Chi*, not *Na'Reish*."

"A half-blood?" His brows pulled down low. "They're a myth."

"Not anymore. She carries a Light Blade amulet. Her mother was one of us."

Arek listened as Kalan shared Annika's story. When he finished, he leaned back in his chair and gave his friend time to absorb the facts. The only sound in the room was the crackling of the fire.

"She drinks blood. She has the strength of a *Na'Reish* warrior. She's the *Na'Rei*'s daughter." Arek ticked off the facts on his fingers. "She's still a threat."

Kalan held back a sigh and rubbed tired eyes. He'd hoped for some understanding from Arek but wasn't surprised by his lack of sympathy. Having lost both parents to the *Na'Reish* as a young baby, he harbored a deep, abiding hatred for demons. Being raised by his maternal grandfather, a man embittered by the tragedies, hadn't helped.

"Do you think I'd bring her into the heart of our city if she was such a risk?" he asked.

"Their nature has been proven time and again on the battlefield."

"You judge too swiftly, my friend."

A muscle ticked in Arek's cheek. "I also find it hard to believe the *Lady* would share a rare healer's Gift with a demon."

Kalan ground his teeth together. Challenging his decisions or risking his anger was part of the warrior's job. That he would do it despite the close friendship they shared was what made Arek such a valuable Second. But his stubbornness tested Kalan's patience.

"Annika," he called. Arek stiffened as the door to Kalan's room cracked open. "Could you come out here, please?"

Reaching across the table, Kalan claimed the dagger and sliced open the skin on his forearm. The wound was shallow but it began to ooze blood. His gaze met hers.

"Would you please demonstrate your Gift?"

"The *Lady* frowns upon this sort of display. *Her* Gifts aren't for show."

"I think *She*'ll excuse us just this once."

She shot Arek a narrow-eyed look. "Are you going to attack me if I approach Kalan? I have to touch him so the healing can work."

Her challenge earned her a deadly glare. Her chin lifted as she met the glare head-on. Kalan admired her grit and determination.

"It's all right, Annika," he assured her. "He's just going to watch."

She came over and placed her hands above and below the cut. Taking a deep breath, she closed her eyes. Through the touch they shared, he felt the familiar surge of raw power as she drew on her Gift.

A warm tingling began around the site of the wound then spread deeper. The bleeding stopped, the skin healed over. In less than a minute there was no evidence of the cut.

"Thank you." He looked at his friend and lifted an eyebrow. "You felt it."

His statement was met with a sharp nod and folded arms. "Ever since the *Na'Reish* started taking humans as blood-slaves, rumors about half-blood children have existed." The corners of Arek's mouth pulled downward. "Why haven't any records confirmed their existence?"

Kalan shrugged. "I don't know. Maybe there are some annals we aren't aware of."

"Secret records?" He shook his head then snorted. "That would mean years of hiding the truth."

"Do you think the historians or the Blade Council would reveal something like this to our people voluntarily? Rumors can be dismissed, facts cannot."

"Even from the *Chosen*?"

"Perhaps. Depending on who they were." He shared a pointed look with Arek. "It's certainly worth investigating, don't you agree?"

"I'll have Jole begin searching the library tomorrow." The warrior scrubbed a hand over his face. "Whatever the case, her presence will cause chaos."

"I'll handle it," Kalan promised. "Just remember, Annika has my protection. Make sure no one dishonors that agreement."

The blond warrior's brow dipped. "I won't compromise my responsibilities."

"I don't expect you to, but Annika isn't a threat." Kalan hardened his tone of voice. "Do you doubt my word?"

Arek did little to hide the fact he wasn't happy. "No, but there's more here at stake than just your word." Suspicion and doubt shadowed Arek's gaze as he glanced at Annika. His lips thinned. "She has your protection . . . but I shall remain vigilant."

"I expect nothing less, my friend." Kalan relaxed, knowing that like any Light Blade warrior, Arek never gave his word lightly. "Thank you."

"I'd feel better if she slept elsewhere. I can arrange guest quart—"

"No. She stays here." Kalan rose from his seat, went to the door of his apartment, and held out the dagger. "I'll see you in the morning."

Arek collected the blade from his friend, his fist curling so hard around the hilt his knuckles whitened. "Will you at least let me post a guard outside your door?"

"Good night, Arek." Kalan closed the door behind him. He raked a hand through his hair as he turned. "I'm sorry. I didn't expect any of my warriors to learn of my return until tomorrow."

"He's your friend." Annika's quiet reply held no condemnation. "I was frightened by him, but he was only doing what he thought was right. His concern was for you."

She deserved some sort of explanation. "Arek lost both parents when he was young. The *Na'Reish* captured his mother. His father couldn't reconcile her loss."

"I suspect many warriors have lost someone close to them. Being angry over those losses is only natural. And finding me here had to have been a huge shock."

"You handled this situation far better than I'd have, Annika." His gaze slid slowly over her and for the first time he noticed what she was wearing. "My shirt looks good on you."

Clearly not expecting such a comment, her cheeks flushed with color. He wasn't about to tell her that standing in front of the fireplace made the material sheer enough to see the outline of her body. He grew instantly hard as he realized that she wore absolutely nothing beneath it.

Sucking in a sharp breath at the pleasurable sight of her rounded curves and sleek limbs, it didn't take much to imagine untying the laces of the shirt and slipping his hands inside to cradle and caress her warm breasts. She was a passionate woman but would that quality extend to intimate relationships? The idea of being the first to find out made his entire body burn.

Annika's nostrils flared and her startled gaze lifted to meet his. The scent of his arousal had to be strong for her to pick it up across the room.

"Bath, bed, sleep," he muttered. A frown creased Annika's brow. "It's what I should do. Right now." It was difficult to focus on the present when he wanted to strip his shirt from her body and touch and taste the tawny skin beneath. He headed for the bathing room. "We're going to need rest before meeting with the Blade Council."

Tomorrow was going to be hard enough on her without losing what little sleep she could get now. He knew the Councilors and what to expect from them. She didn't.

Pausing in the archway, he glanced back over his shoulder, unable to resist a final look at her. The shirt barely covered her to mid-thigh. She fiddled with the hem, the slightest tinge of blue in her eyes. An encouraging sign but one that tested his resolve.

Smothering a groan, he turned away. "I'll see you in the morning, Annika. Sleep well."

Chapter 15

"WHAT are you doing out here? It's barely an hour past dawn and cold enough to freeze the horns of a furry-bleater."

Kalan's sleep-roughened voice came from behind Annika. She jerked in surprise, so totally absorbed in watching the people in the garden below she'd missed hearing the balcony door open.

She had to take a deep breath at the picture he presented standing in the doorway. In the pale dawn light, the cloak wrapped around him had been hastily tied. As he adjusted it she saw plenty of bare skin and partly laced breeches riding low over his ridged abdomen. Some of his hair had pulled free of its tie during the night and her fingers itched to smooth it back off his face.

Seated on the wall, wrapped in her cloak, she gave a shrug. "I couldn't sleep."

There was something very appealing about a man just roused from sleep. She looked away, over the compound, not willing to let her eyes betray her thoughts.

"Why not?"

She heard a smothered yawn, and the sound of the door closing. "Strange place, unfamiliar people."

His boots crunched on the thick layer of frost on the stone balcony a moment before he appeared beside her. He blew on his hands, and his breath steamed into the cold morning air, dissipating slowly.

"Instead of waking you with my restlessness, I headed out here."

Kalan leaned right beside where she sat on the balcony ledge, his shoulder pressing against her. His presence was peaceful, comforting, something she'd only ever felt around Hesia. Something she could easily let herself become used to with him.

"What are you watching?"

"The people down there." She pointed with her chin, fascinated by the sleek, dapple-furred animal that followed them. "They've been walking a *lira* around the garden." It was smaller than those she'd seen stalking prey in the forest. "I never thought something so wild could be led on a leash."

"If you raise one from a kit it'll learn that the family is its new pack."

A tamed carnivore. She shook her head and watched the man walking it. He actually talked to it and the small predator's pointy ears flickered as if it was listening to him. Its graceful gait slowed so that it could arch and rub its body against the man's leg.

"So, do you always perch on balcony ledges?"

"Not always." She shot Kalan a sideways glance. The pale mauve sky silhouetted his strong profile. "Usually I sit on the pitch of a roof."

His eyebrows rose and the changing expression on his face said he was trying to work out if she was joking. She wasn't. He was curious but she knew he'd never question her, not unless she continued the conversation. He gave her the choice to share her past with him. Another thing she was coming to like about him.

With her fingernail, Annika scraped a design into the frost coating the stone beside her. "I was chased up into one of the fortress towers by some *Na'Reish* children once. I think I was eight or nine at the time. They were several years older than me and considered it sport to try and catch me. The winner got first-rites." She smiled crookedly as his brows dipped. "They got to hit me first before the others joined in."

He issued a soft, vehement curse. "Did that happen often?"

"Two or three times a week."

In her mind's eye, Annika could see her father's angry face as she'd dared complain the first time it happened. Inwardly she cringed remembering the sharp sound of the blow as he backhanded her, the pain just becoming the freshest ache in her body.

You deserve whatever you get! Maybe it'll teach you to run faster, think smarter.

She stopped scratching the ice and took a deep breath. "Getting caught in the tower, hearing them charge up the stairs and knowing what awaited me if I didn't escape forced me out the window. My limbs shook so badly as I pulled myself over the eave I thought I'd fall before I reached the pitch of the roof," she said softly. "After that I learned every hidey-hole, every dark corner, and possible escape route around the keep." She pointed to several places around the compound. "I've counted six good places here already."

She sensed his gaze on her and tried to remain unaffected by it, but the intensity increased the longer the silence went on between them.

"You're safe here, Annika."

She trembled at the deep tone of his voice. "Am I? I know last night Arek was acting on instinct but what if it happens again, with someone else?"

"I think I'd better explain something to you," he said. "My protection means you've been given sanctuary and the protection of my house. You're free to go anywhere, do anything I would, without fear of being harmed.

"Arek mightn't like my decision but he'll ensure everyone's told.

Offering sanctuary and protection are traditions we hold dear. Anyone who breaks with them risks death."

This time Annika stared at Kalan, searching his gaze for any hint of untruth. She was so used to doubting everything said to her. Her cheeks heated as his eyebrows arched high, as if he sensed her disbelief. He deserved better.

"What's wrong?"

She bit her lip. "Why would you stand against your own kind to protect me?"

"Isn't that what you asked for back in the dungeon?"

She blinked then shook her head. "I thought you might help me show them I'm not a danger. I don't expect you to kill anyone for me!"

"You saved my life. Twice."

"So you feel like you owe me?"

"Earlier I would have. Now? No, not at all." His mild response was at odds with the sincere look in his eyes. "Why would I do anything less than what you did for me?"

Annika swung her legs around to sit on the ledge facing inward, her gaze fixed on him as she tried to sort out the tangle of emotions his words evoked. He was treating her as if she were human, and making it easy for her to forget the fact that she wasn't.

She shouldn't like that but she did. She clenched her hand around the edge of her cloak. His recent behavior was making it safe to share things she'd never have thought to reveal to anyone else. He didn't criticize her, didn't laugh at her ignorance, hadn't taken advantage of her weaknesses. Other than Hesia, no one had ever kept their promises to her.

He treated her like a friend.

Annika started to shake. Not in fear, but with the strength of an unknown emotion filling her heart. With every beat, the warmth of it spread through her. He stood close enough that she could feel the heat of his body, even through two cloaks. She lifted her hand toward him then hesitated.

Touching Kalan, exposing her need for him, lifted the hairs on her neck. She hated being vulnerable. But she wanted to show him the same amount of trust he'd finally given her.

Mouth dry, she cupped his cheek then trailed her fingers along his stubbled jaw and shuddered, liking the rough sensation of it beneath the palm of her hand. Her gaze dropped to his lips. They looked soft, unlike the rest of his lean body. She wanted to kiss him but wasn't sure if she had the courage. The scent of his arousal filled her lungs.

"I don't bite." The corners of his mouth turned upward ever so slightly. "Not unless you want me to."

The subtle challenge was like throwing a striker-light into tinder. Annika slid her fingers into his hair, loving the silky feel of it caressing her fingers, its color matching the night heavens, so dark it absorbed the morning sunlight. The sleek strands felt like the gentlest of caresses against her skin. She stroked his hair, again and again, liking the sensation. It was enough to set her blood pounding in her veins.

Winding the long strands around her fingers, she tugged him forward until his lips touched hers. Heat exploded in her belly. She moaned as his tongue stroked hers, as she tasted his scent, on his lips, in his mouth. Rich and raw. Addictive.

Kalan moved toward her without breaking their kiss, his body nudging her legs apart so that he could stand between them. His hands skimmed the sides of her legs, before cradling her hips, a move that parted his cloak.

She gasped, unintentionally breaking their kiss as he brought her flush up against his body. Hard curves of muscle, from his shoulders to his hips, pressed against her softness. Every breath he took gently caressed her breasts. Her nipples peaked and the tingling sensation shot straight from them to the knotted heat burning between her legs.

"Wrap your legs around me." His voice had dropped, deepened with desire.

With very little thought, Annika complied, burying her face against his neck as he lifted her effortlessly, his arms linking behind her rear in support. Then he carried her back inside the apartment, to his room, and carefully laid her on his bed.

Here his scent hit her much more strongly. It was in the blankets underneath her, the cloak he discarded over a chest, the pillow she lay her head on. Each held the unique spiciness that was him.

"Your eyes are so blue." A smile kicked up the corner of his mouth. He toed off his boots then tugged at hers, rubbing each of her feet with strokes of his strong fingers before coming to lay on his side next to her. He toyed with the hem of the shirt, stroking it as if he was caressing skin. His scent intensified. "I want to kiss you again."

He sat there watching her, as if waiting for her to give him permission, the hunger on his face enough to send goose bumps rippling down the length of her body. It felt surreal knowing Kalan desired her enough to want to be intimate with her. Annika half expected to wake up in the next room and realize what was happening was the product of a tired but active imagination.

Hoping it wasn't a dream, she gave a small nod, her breath catching in her throat as his green gaze blazed brighter, in triumph and raw need. The ache between her legs became a throb. How could just a look excite her so swiftly?

Kalan plucked at the ties of her cloak and pushed the fabric from her shoulders, keeping his movements slow, unhurried. The blue flecks in Annika's eyes had the slightest tinge of yellow.

"Do you realize how much pleasure I feel knowing you want me to kiss you?" He caressed the shell of her ear as he tucked a lock of hair away from her face. He hid his smile as she trembled and trailed his fingertips along her jaw to rest just under her chin. "I want to slide my tongue across your lips and tease myself with the sweet taste of them. After I've done that I'm going to enjoy the honey of your mouth, taking as much of it as I can before I run out of breath . . ."

The blue in her eyes intensified, changed to a pale mercurial color. The yellow was gone. Her lips parted in unconscious invitation. He leaned down and placed his mouth on hers, softly nibbling at the fullness of her bottom lip, teasing her with feather-light nips and licks, working his way from one side to the other and back again. He savored the small groan that came from the back of her throat.

"Kalan . . ." Her breath was hot against the skin of his cheek.

He slanted his mouth over hers, muting her cry, holding her still for his kiss with the pressure of his fingers beneath her chin. He swept his tongue along the length of her lip, sampling her sweetness, then he allowed himself the briefest of forays, past her lips, delving into the deeper, hotter part of her mouth. He delighted in her taste and gave a groan of his own.

Her body undulated against his and he felt the softness of her breast pressing into his ribs. He cupped it with his hand through the material of the shirt. Even through the layer separating them, he could feel how hot she was. Her body arched into his touch, encouraged him. Her nipple grew taut as he caressed it.

The small cries she made at the back of her throat drove the flames inside him higher. His body tightened with need but he fought it. He was poised on the edge, so tempted to devour her, to let their desire burn them from the inside out. But rushing this wasn't a part of his plan. He wanted her to experience the subtleties involved, the variation of pleasure that could be given and taken with the sharing of lips, of touching one another. He drew back.

Annika's eyes were half closed, her cheeks flushed, her lips slick and moist from his kisses. Beneath her breast her heart beat a rapid tattoo.

"This time open your mouth, take me in, taste me," Kalan whispered against her lips then claimed them again. He thrust his tongue into her mouth, relishing her flavor like a thirsty man savors water. His whole body tensed when her tongue curled around his, the slow slide tentative, unsure. He encouraged her with a groan.

Her fingernails scored his chest, a sweet pain that surged southward, then she skimmed her hand over his torso, inching it lower, lighting a trail of need wherever she touched him. He hissed in surprise and jerked back.

Annika stared up at him, expression dazed, uncertainty dulling the mercurial blue color in her eyes. "I did something wrong."

"No. I wasn't expecting that . . ."

"I just . . . it felt like the right thing to do."

"Touch me, Annika. It feels very good."

"That's too dull a description." She placed her hand on her abdomen. A small frown crinkled her brow. "This kissing and touching makes me—burn."

Kalan watched as her fingers stroked the nap of the shirt, so close to the juncture of her thighs.

"It's a strange experience." Her voice was soft, almost shy. "I mean, as a healer I know the physical signs, I've seen what arousal can do to a man but for a woman it's not so obvious. I didn't understand, until now." She touched her lips. "When you were kissing me . . . everything you did with your tongue I felt down here . . ." Her hand slid to her abdomen.

Kalan hardened to the point of pain. *Mother of Mercy . . .* "Annika . . ." His voice was hoarse.

Whatever she saw in his gaze widened hers. He watched the blue flecks shimmer and expand until they almost concealed the violet striations. Her tongue snaked out to wet her lips. It was too much. He closed the distance between them.

The passion, the intensity of the kiss burned him. There was little gentleness or tenderness, just hot, ferocious, unadulterated need that demanded satisfaction, culmination.

He growled fiercely as his tongue explored every part of her mouth. She buried her hands in his hair and her body writhed against him, her soft little mews pushing him to greater heights. She was so close to release, and all from his kisses.

"That's it, Annika, just feel," he whispered against her mouth. "Let yourself go."

He slid his hand from her breast to the gentle swell of her mound. Tugging the fabric upward, he nipped at her bottom lip with his teeth then massaged the heel of his hand against her softness. The pads of his fingers smoothed over the bare mound of her sex. She was swollen, wet. The scent of her arousal was wild honey and musk.

He groaned, the sound wrenched deep from in his chest, and pressed his fingers into her slick folds, stroked once, twice, felt her muscles contract. On the third stroke her body arched and she shuddered. Another sharp gasp and her warmth coated his fingers, her thighs clamped tightly around his hand.

"*Kalan!*" she cried out, the pleasure on her face beautiful to watch.

He swallowed her cry in another kiss, continuing to work her, prolonging her pleasure for as long as she could stand it, easing up only when she relaxed against him.

Gathering her close, he listened to her uneven breathing, felt the heat of it grazing his skin. He wasn't sure whose heart he heard pounding in his ears. His body throbbed and ached with unrelieved need. It hurt but the pain was sweet to bear.

Annika had trusted him enough to cede control of her pleasure. Wrapping an arm around her and smoothing a hand over her hip, he pulled her closer and pressed a kiss against her flushed cheek. He couldn't help the satisfied grin that curved his lips.

"Kalan?"

Annika started at the sound of a female voice out in the other room. He ran a reassuring hand over her back. "It's all right. That's just Kymora, my sister."

"Doesn't anyone knock around here?"

Her disgruntled reply widened his grin. "I'm sure she did. We were probably just too . . . busy to notice."

A delicate pink hue stained her cheeks. She reached for her cloak and wrapped it around her. The tender moment broken, he sighed, wishing they'd had more time to share together before having to face the day. He wanted to make sure Annika felt secure about what they'd done.

"Kalan?" Kymora's voice came from right outside his door. "I've brought breakfast and clothes for Annika."

"We'll be out in a moment." He snatched up a shirt from the chest at the end of his bed and put it on then held out a hand to Annika. "Come, meet my sister."

"Kalan, I'm half dressed!" Annika kept her voice to a furious whisper.

"Don't worry, she won't mind." She shot him an incredulous look. He grinned. "Kymora's blind."

Chapter 16

THE outer room of the Blade Council chambers was filled with warriors. An equal amount of men and women, all dressed in the *Lady*'s armor, sat on benches scattered around the room; others stood in groups on the mosaic-tiled floor. There were so many Annika could only guess what number occupied the room or lined the corridor that led to the Inner Chamber where their leaders met.

Heads turned and conversations tapered off as the closest became aware of their arrival. Kalan and Kymora walked on either side of her, the Handmaiden using Annika's arm as a guide instead of her walking staff.

During breakfast, Annika had sensed the strength of the *Lady*'s Gift within Kymora and been awed by it. So pervasive had the sensation been, she'd felt it pulsing in the air around them. Having never met a *Lady*'s servant before, it'd come as a surprise to see such incredible power offset by humility and gentleness. Kymora's welcome and natural warmth quickly put her at ease and Annika had the sneaking suspicion that Kalan had enjoyed watching her reaction to their meeting.

The reactions of the Light Blade warriors told a different story. The chamber was heated. Annika could hear flames crackling in a fireplace to her left but there was little warmth in the sea of faces. The whispers began and hands strayed to weapon hilts and belts, their unease and hatred hitting her like a wave.

Wishing now she hadn't left her cloak behind in the apartment, Annika fisted her hands in the soft folds of her new dress and tried not to cringe. The gathering was a stark reminder of the times her father had insisted she attend the *Na'Reish* banquets. Never one to pass up a chance to humiliate her in front of his peers, he'd actually encourage them to taunt and abuse her for her half-blood status. To be the center of attention now sent chills racing down her spine.

Kalan's hand came to rest in the middle of her back, his touch light but encouraging. "Just remember how I acted when I first met you, Annika." His murmur carried no farther than their ears. "They've yet to understand the difference between a *Na'Chi* and the *Na'Reish.*"

"They know the *Lady* supports you." Kymora's soft but strong voice added her reassurance. "Have faith and all will be well."

Annika slanted a sideways glance at the woman, still astounded by the revelation that the *Lady* had spoken to Kymora of her arrival. Kalan's sister shared his height and coloring, although in a more slender, graceful form. With the same black hair and green eyes, only the length and her inability to see differed. Annika had quickly learned, however, that her lack of sight in no way debilitated her.

"These warriors respect my brother's leadership skills." Kymora turned her head in her direction, a smile hovering at the corners of her mouth. "Many of them are also his friends. In time, they'll understand why he has included you among them."

Swallowing hard, Annika squared her shoulders and lifted her chin, and tried to emulate Kymora's air of confidence. The Handmaiden squeezed her elbow in silent encouragement.

Halfway across the floor, Annika's pace slowed again. The warriors around them parted to clear a path and as they did so, all went down on one knee, their heads bowed. They remained so until Kalan acknowledged them.

"What's going on?" she whispered, leaning closer to him.

Kalan was the only one in the room not dressed in armor or leather. Instead he wore a matching set of black breeches and a long, loose-sleeved shirt with a dark green over-tunic belted at the waist. The breeches were tucked into knee-length boots and he'd tied his hair back into a simple ponytail. He was also the only one without weapons of any sort on his belt or peeking from the top of his boots. That fact didn't detract from his aura of strength or authority.

"Kalan?" she prompted.

The strangest look of discomfort flickered across his face, but before he could answer a familiar blond-haired warrior stepped forward to meet them.

"The Council awaits you in the Inner Chamber." Arek was the only one in the vicinity who remained standing as he addressed Kalan. He lowered his voice. "Dayn and Jole are already in the Great Library searching our annals."

Kalan nodded. "Keep me informed. If they find something, I want to know immediately."

The warrior raised an eyebrow. "I have your permission to interrupt the meeting?"

"After your last performance in chambers, I have serious doubts about whether they'll want to let you in again." Kalan's dry tone made both Kymora and Arek chuckle. Annika glanced among the trio, feeling like she'd walked in halfway through a conversation. "But for something as important as this, yes, you can interrupt."

The Handmaiden must have sensed her confusion. "Arek managed to insult four of the five Councilors in a past meeting. He was asked to leave."

The statement didn't surprise Annika. He was a man of strong emotion and it was logical that they would influence his attitudes and opinions.

"They were tolerant enough of me when Kalan went missing." The Second's drawled reply made several of the warriors close by grin.

"I just bet they were," Kalan muttered. Again, Annika felt like she was missing an important part of the conversation but this time no one provided an explanation. "Just don't give the Councilors—especially your grandfather—any excuse to refuse your right to speak."

"They're like two peas in a pod, as stubborn as one another," Kymora murmured. Arek's head jerked in her direction. Annika wondered if she'd meant her words to be overheard. "He lives to frustrate Davyn."

"Every chance I get, *Temple Elect*," he drawled, a gleam in his eye.

"I'm surprised the Council hasn't had you stripped of your title, *Second*."

His lip curled. "They're welcome to it if they want to take it. I won't miss attending meetings or official functions in your brother's stead."

Kymora laughed lightly. "Ahh, but while your little performances have alleviated the boredom of endless discussions on policy and administration, I think he'd miss you by his side. You just need to learn a little tact. Model yourself after Benth. He manages to repri-mand the others without insulting them."

"You want me to use diplomacy? Pfft!" A grimace passed over his face. "I'll leave that to you, Handmaiden. You manage that quite well."

Their banter fascinated Annika. While there was an implied ten-sion between the two of them, there was very little true animosity. Kalan seemed relaxed, quite tolerant of, and somewhat amused by their verbal sparring.

Her father wouldn't have allowed such levity. Meetings among the *Na'Reish* consisted of him giving orders and everyone listening and obeying. Arguing with or contradicting him resulted in execution on the spot.

Kalan cleared his throat. "If you're finished sniping at one another, we have several Councilors waiting for our arrival."

Arek bowed, an impudent grin on his face. "Then by your leave, Commander, I'll go help the others in the library. Enjoy your meeting."

Kalan motioned them to continue. They entered a short corridor and left the crowd of warriors behind. They passed a small atrium filled with green plants and flowers. Annika glanced skyward, wondering at the source of light filling the small garden and discovered the entire roof was made of glass.

"Ahh, the sweet scent of Mothers' Tears." Kymora sighed. The strong odor of the delicate winter flower hung heavily in this part of the corridor.

Two young Light Blade warriors stood to either side of a set of double doors that looked like mini-replicas of Eastgate, the entrance they'd used into Sacred Lake. The *Lady*'s sun symbol had been carved in intricate detail into the wooden panels. Kalan drew them to a halt just before they reached them.

His sister tilted her head to one side. "Kalan?"

Annika glanced up at him as he took one of her hands in his. He wore the same troubled expression of a few minutes ago and his thumb rubbed over her knuckles repeatedly, as if searching for the right words to say.

When his eyes lifted to meet hers she saw doubt and worry shadowing his gaze. "Before we go in, and no matter what happens today remember that you're not alone in this journey. I stand with you." Fear flickered across his face, gone as swiftly as it had appeared. His hand tightened around hers. "I also ask for your understanding and forgiveness, Annika."

His words made no sense. She glanced at Kymora but the Hand-maiden seemed as confused by them as she was. With no further explanation, Kalan released her hand and nodded to the two warriors guarding the Council Chamber. The double doors opened inward and the guard on the right stepped inside.

"Honored Councilors!" the young woman called. Annika peered past her, curiosity and dread flooding her in equal amounts as she saw five older men and women, all dressed in finery similar to Kalan's, sitting at a round table in the middle of the room. "May I present Kymora, the *Temple Elect* and Kalan, the *Lady's Chosen*."

Chapter 17

ONE road in, one road out, and open ground between the foot-hills and the city. Varian stared at the makeshift map of Sacred Lake made of rocks and scratched markings inside the circle of his scouts. There was nothing drawn inside the circle that represented the city.

Barvi tapped his stick and marked the ground at several points on the edge of the circle. "There are watchtowers over the gates, and another in between each pair. Four humans man them and two patrol the battlement walkways."

Lisella quietly handed the stocky, dark-haired scout a water flask. He nodded his thanks and drank deeply before splashing some on his face then gave it back.

"We couldn't see anything beyond the walls." Zaune shook his sweat-dampened braids out of his eyes. "They were just too high. Had we gone any closer we risked being seen by the watch in the towers."

Both *Na'Chi* sounded as exhausted as they looked. Their faces were pale and drawn, the lines deeply etched around their mouths and eyes. The flecks in their eyes glowed red in the firelight, but neither deigned to show any discomfort.

They'd pushed themselves hard over two days to get what little information they could about Sacred Lake back to them. Varian made a note to send out one of the others to hunt for them. They needed to drink before morning if they wanted to avoid the symptoms of blood-fever.

"Following that Light Blade patrol was still a good idea, Varian," Lisella said, softly, taking a seat beside him in the circle. "They led us straight to the city."

Zaune snorted. "You should have heard the humans, Varian. By the time they reached the valley plateau our fleeing party of four had grown to a full *Na'Hord*."

"How else are they going to explain they couldn't capture one of us?" Barvi asked, a gleam in his eyes.

Varian joined in the laughter. Lisella hushed them, a tolerant smile on her face. "Keep the noise down. We've only just managed to get the last of the children to sleep."

He glanced over his shoulder toward the blanket-wrapped bodies huddled in shallow caves they'd found less than a day ago. Other members of the group also slept although a few sat near the fire talking quietly amongst themselves.

Their camp overlooked the main roadway leading toward the city. There was enough shrubbery along the ridge and around the caves they'd found to obscure any activity from the casual observer and, if they were careful, it was the ideal spot to live while they decided what the next move would be.

"That Patrol is likely to cause us problems." Zaune's low-toned comment drew his attention back to the circle. "If they report the sighting of four *Na'Reish* soldiers the humans are going to respond by increasing their Patrols."

"We're going to have to lay in supplies in case we're unable to forage if a Patrol comes too close." Barvi's statement drew a few comments.

"I think it'd be wise to instigate the old rules we had living near the fortress," Lisella added, her gaze sweeping the circle. Several heads nodded.

"Lisella, can you organize the camp?" Varian knew she'd keep any naysayers too busy to worry about the danger in the coming days. As he gained her assent, he glanced to another of his scouts. "Jinnae, you're in charge of setting the watch. If we're discovered we need time to escape. I want an inner and outer perimeter established. Everyone from the age of twelve and up can share the responsibility. Set up snares and anything else you think would slow an intruder."

A wicked smile curved the young *Na'Chi*'s mouth. "I can do that." She shared a look with Lisella. "I'll get Fannis and Rystin to help."

The two mentioned were the most vocal about turning back.

"Varian, there's something else you need to know." Zaune shared a look with Barvi. The older scout nodded. "We noticed an increase in the amount of people and animals on the road as we returned. I managed to get close enough to one of the wagons camped on the side of the road last night. The humans were farmers who spoke of traveling to market within the city."

"How does this information help?" someone asked.

"Perhaps we need to think about it overnight." Varian saw others nod in agreement. "If there's nothing more I suggest we all get some sleep. Good job, Barvi, Zaune."

After arranging for the two scouts to be fed, the circle broke up. Varian remained where he was, watching his people disperse. It didn't take long for silence to settle over the camp.

The map drew his attention again. The blank circle bothered him more than he'd let on. They might have found the way to the city but what use was that when they had no idea where Annika was within it? He ran a hand through his hair. They needed to know what lay inside the walls.

Varian slowly straightened. How many humans went to this market? The increased number on the road suggested more than a few. Depending on vigilance of the guards on the gates, a crowd of farmers, their carts, herds of animals, crates of supplies could provide a potential distraction and be a way in. A *Na'Chi* with a cloak and a prayer might just pass as human and get inside unnoticed. Blending in with the city would be as easy as hiding in a forest. The kernel of a plan brought a smile to his lips.

Now, all he had to figure out was how to find Annika.

THE Inner Chamber was brightly lit and a number of lanterns and candles were ensconced around the four walls. A large wooden table sat in the middle of the room, a few steps away from a fireplace. The chamber was windowless and the stark grey of the stone walls was broken up by a tall shelf of books and several large tapestries.

Any other time Annika would have been fascinated by the brightly colored, detailed weavings as they depicted activities from daily life—historic battles, Light Blades engaged in training, portraits of various humans—but she barely noticed them as she sat stiffly on the edge of her seat, clutching her pouch on her lap.

The bag provided her with an anchor even though the muscles between her shoulder blades protested the knot of stress forming there. It took everything she had to keep a neutral expression on her face.

Her gaze strayed to where Kalan was seating his sister on the opposite side of the table then sat in the one beside her. Annika's chest ached with a combination of disappointment and anger but what cut more deeply was her sense of betrayal.

May I present to you . . . Kalan, the Lady's Chosen.

Her jaw clenched so hard she could hear the pounding of blood between her ears. His words outside the chamber now made sense. Reaching back into her memory she realized that the pieces of the puzzle of who he was had been there all the time.

The refusal to give his name to the *Na'Hord* when captured, his knowledge of a man she'd believed to be someone else, his hesitancy to answer some of her questions, his commanding presence and air of authority he projected and the respect given him by the other warriors in the Outer Chamber.

Leather creaked in protest as she squeezed the strap of her pouch. Kalan had deliberately withheld his identity while berating her for concealing hers. Heat exploded low in her gut and surged upward. The hypocrisy of his actions scored deeply. She closed her eyes, feeling hot and feverish one moment, light-headed the next.

Never show weakness to anyone. Disguise it, purge it, cut it from your heart. Savyr's voice hissed in her head. *If you can't, then squeeze your mind around it and control it until you can.*

"Councilors, I would like you to meet Annika, the *Na'Chi* who helped me escape the *Na'Reish* fortress and saved my life."

Her eyes snapped open and she discovered Kalan watching her with wary concern. He'd built their friendship on lies. She dropped her gaze, and drew on every shred of strength she had to get through the meeting. The only way she was going to get through this was if she ignored him.

Her father had subjected her to years of torment; she could survive a few hours of this without falling apart. Even as she thought it, Annika knew she'd have to deal with the terrible ache surrounding her heart eventually. But not here. She shoved it to the back of her mind and focused on the five pairs of eyes that turned to scrutinize her.

"The *Lady's Chosen* tells us you're that demon, Savyr's get." The gaunt-faced man addressing her was seated directly to her left. Long, silver hair framed his wrinkled face as he pinned her with his brown-eyed stare.

Annika's gaze narrowed. So, that was going to be the way of it.

"Councilor Yance, we forget our manners," Kymora interrupted smoothly, her face turned in the old warrior's direction. "I'd like to start this meeting with a prayer of thanks. The *Lady* has remained true to *Her* word and returned Kalan safely to us. Then, perhaps a few introductions would be appropriate before we begin our discussion?"

Yance snorted, an action that earned him a censuring glare from Kalan. "I mean no disrespect, *Temple Elect*. We're all unsettled by the situation."

"I understand your concern." Kymora offered him a small smile. "Shall we pray?"

Annika bowed her head, heard someone gasp and ignored the startled whispers coming from her right.

"*Lady*, we thank you for the truth of your words. They bring us strength in our time of need—" Kymora spoke confidently but with humble grace as she prayed.

Annika thought of Hesia as Kymora thanked *Her* for blessing them with Kalan's safe return. She sent her own petition for Hesia's continued safety among the *Na'Reish*. How she would have liked to meet Kymora, a woman with a faith as dedicated as her own.

Kalan introduced each of the Councilors at the end of the prayer and Annika memorized each name and face.

"In answer to your statement, Councilor Yance, I'm Savyr's daughter." She was relieved her voice held steady. "What else would you like to know?"

"You'd answer our questions freely?" Candra, the woman who spoke, seemed genuinely surprised. Like many of the Councilors around the table, her dark hair was sprinkled liberally with grey, but she was the youngest barring Kymora and Kalan.

"Why wouldn't I?" Annika met her eyes, her gaze direct. "I bear

no allegiance to my father or the *Na'Reish*. By coming here I expected
to answer many questions."

"Then answer me this . . ." The growled words came from across
the table, from the man sitting next to Kymora. Blue eyes, the color
of a winter sky at midday, raked over her. "What proof do you have
that you're *Na'Chi*?"

The raw hostility of his hatred was oppressive, suffocating, and
eerily reminiscent of her father's. Annika's mouth dried.

This was Davyn, Arek's grandfather. Kalan had warned her about
him at breakfast. His darkly tanned face was creased with age, a
warrior past his prime but still strong if the thickness and width of
his shoulders was any indication. She imagined Arek would look like
him in another thirty years.

Candra rapped the table with her knuckles, drawing Davyn's
attention away from her. "Are you blind?" She waved a hand in her
direction. "The differences are obvious. Her eyes change color, the
pigment in the markings on her body are paler and the patterning is
more irregular. She doesn't have the larger skeleton or musculature
of the demons." The corner of her mouth quirked upward as did one
eyebrow. "Nor has she leapt across this table to slit the hearts' vessel
in your throat."

Annika stared at the woman as chuckles erupted around the table.

"Candra is the Master Healer here, Annika." Kymora's explanation was accompanied by a smile. "Hence the detailed description of
your physical attributes."

The women's easy chatter eased the tension somewhat, although
Davyn certainly didn't share in the humor of the situation. His
expression remained cold and unmoved and when he glanced back
at her, something dark flickered behind his eyes. It sent an icy finger
of fear down her spine.

"Annika's mother was a Light Blade." Kalan's deep voice held a
steely edge. "She has her amulet."

Annika dug into her pouch and laid it on the table. The Councilor to her right examined it and passed it on.

Davyn's eyes narrowed, the light in his eyes particularly bright. "Who was she?"

"I don't know. Savyr never allowed me to discover her name."

"Surely, at some time, he let something slip."

"No, nothing."

Davyn shared a look with Yance. Annika shifted uncomfortably in her seat. Her scalp tingled and she became aware of a faint, malevolent scent in the air. She inhaled deeply, trying to pinpoint its origin. Davyn was the obvious choice but there were others at the table whose expression mirrored his.

"There's no doubt Annika's mother was a Light Blade, Councilors. We all know *Her* power needs one parent to come from our ranks to produce a Gifted child," Kalan stated. "Annika has the Gift of healing. Show them your pouch."

Annika placed it on the table. His lip curling back from his teeth, Davyn reached forward but Candra beat him to it. The older woman displayed everything on the table, her eyebrows lifting as she examined the tools and made interested sounds as she sniffed the contents of the bags and jars.

"Where's your journal?" she asked. "I don't see it here."

"Journal?"

"Yes, the one for the recipes of your remedies?"

"I don't understand."

"When you apprenticed, didn't your mentor make you write all your learning in a book for later reference?"

"A book." The smirk on Davyn's face caught her attention. It grew as he rose from his seat. Crossing to the tall shelf behind him he pulled a thick, leather-bound tome from it. "You do know what a book is, don't you?"

"Your rudeness is uncalled for, Davyn." Kalan's voice held an underlying thread of steel. "Annika saved my life. Twice. And is due the respect you would give any warrior."

"My apology, *Chosen*." Davyn sounded far from contrite. His dark gaze locked on her. "Well, *Na'Reish*?"

Annika's temper sparked. "I'm *Na'Chi*. And, of course I know what a book is." She'd seen them in her father's chamber, in the homes of the *Na'Reish*. She focused on the Master Healer. "But I've never needed to keep a journal."

Yance huffed and issued a protest, which was supported by three other Councilors. She drew back, startled by their outburst, and glanced around the table. Their supercilious expressions as they stared down their noses at her reminded her of the *Na'Reish* lords who'd visit her father. Uneasiness ate at the pit of her stomach.

"Caring for the sick holds great responsibility," Candra commented, her gaze thoughtful. "All our healers have to know how to read and write. How else does one learn the hundreds of potions, gels, and treatments?"

As if sensing her unease, Davyn came around the table, like a *lira* after its prey. The book thumped onto the table in front of her. A dry, dusty odor tickled her nostrils. Her heart thudded just as loudly in her chest as he flipped it open to a section near the middle and waved a hand at the page.

"Perhaps you'd care to show us an example of your learning and read aloud the recipe used by a healer to treat . . . say . . . Blackroot-fever."

Annika's mouth dried as she stared at the pages of laboriously handwritten markings and beautiful pictures. She ran her fingertips over the colors, awed by the incredible craftsmanship of the scribe then delicately traced the wafer-thin edge of the page. A familiar longing burned in her chest as she scanned the spidery symbols she had no idea how to interpret.

"Well, *healer*?" Davyn returned to his seat and folded his arms.

"Enough, Davyn." Kalan's voice was hard.

Heat filled Annika's cheeks; first with frustration because she lacked the knowledge Davyn demanded she show them, and secondly with self-directed anger because she so desperately wanted to prove herself to them all.

"I said I'd answer your questions." With a trembling hand, Annika gently closed the book and pushed it away from her. "I don't keep a journal, Councilor Candra, because I don't know your letters and words. I was never allowed to learn them."

Davyn grunted loudly. "Illiterate and a liar."

Annika flinched, shocked by the utter derision in his tone, but a heartbeat later heat exploded throughout her body.

"You go too far!" Kalan leapt to his feet. "You're dismissed from this meeting."

Kymora reached for his arm with unerring accuracy. "In the name of the *Lady* let wisdom and peace guide us, warriors. Not anger or blind hatred."

Neither man seemed to be listening. Annika rose from her seat, the slow scraping of her chair capturing everyone's attention. Trembling, she fisted her hands, aware that her admission had damaged their impression of her.

"For what it's worth, Councilor Candra, I don't need a journal to remember what I was taught." Her voice wavered but she kept her head held high, drawing the shreds of her pride around her like a cloak. "My teachings are all up here." She tapped her forehead and ignored the few who snorted. "Hesia, the human woman who taught me, told me many stories about the courtesy and tolerance of humans compared to the *Na'Reish*. She held the Council in high regard and spoke of you as respected leaders. She said with your faith in the *Lady* you could be relied upon to be open-minded and fair. But you're not the Blade Council she spoke of."

Her glance strayed to Kalan. He stood silent, his face an implacable mask, his gaze hooded. What was he thinking? Did he support her or not? Her anger faltered. Perhaps she'd overstepped the mark. It was too late to take back her words.

Why she was even bothering to care about what he thought of her she didn't know. She turned her attention back to the other people in the room and raked her gaze over each of the Councilors, unable to stomach their prejudice alone or hide her contempt.

"If you measure a person's worth by a single set of standards, and dismiss them because they don't meet them, then I don't know if you live up to mine."

She turned on her boot heel and left the chamber.

Chapter 18

"ARE you hurt?"

Annika stiffened at the hesitant concern in the voice at her back. She turned slowly, scrubbing tears from her cheeks, unaware that she'd made any noise to alert someone to her distress. She'd learnt never to cry aloud.

A pair of deep brown eyes stared at her through the bushes. The eyes belonged to a freckle-faced girl no more than ten years old. She was crouched on the other side of the garden bed, dressed only in a pair of green colored breeches and shirt, her cheeks ruddy with the cold.

"I can get Healer Danna from the hospice iffen you need her." A worried frown creased her brow, her lilting voice filled with earnest sincerity. "I'm not full-trained yet but I can feel you hurtin' bad."

The child crawled through the hedge to the hidden niche Annika had fled to after leaving the Blade Council chambers. It was the only place, away from prying eyes, she could find before her tears had started to fall. Her small visitor cursed as a branch snapped under her boot and she emerged from the hedge holding it in her hand.

"Ohh, *Mother of Mercy*, you won't tell Master Gardener Pel I did this will you? He spent months tending this gard—" The guilt-ridden expression on the girl's face froze then changed. Her eyes widened and she sucked in a shocked breath, and Annika knew she'd been recognized.

"I won't hurt you. Please don't scream."

Her freckled nose scrunched up. "Why would I scream? That's such a girly thing to do. I was jus' wonderin' if they hurt."

"What?"

A small finger pointed at her face. "Them. Some of the folk over at the hospice have sores on their skin like your spots. They're always complainin' they hurt."

The child was asking about her *Na'Chi* markings? "No, they don't hurt. I was born with them."

"Can I touch 'em?" More than a little bewildered by the child's lack of fear of her Annika nodded. A grin broke over the girl's face and she jumped up to join her on the stone bench, her dark, curly hair bouncing with her exuberant energy. "My name's Rissa, but my friends call me Bit on account that I'm so small. One day, though, I'm gonna be tall 'n strong 'cause my feet are big for my age.

"I don't have no parents so's I'm not sure whether they were tall but Animal Master Gorlas says big feet are a sign for growin' tall." She rubbed her hands together. "One of the tricks of the healin' trade. Gotta warm your hands afore you touch your patient. Not that you're my patient, but you get what I mean, eh?"

The child's rambling, one-sided conversation brought a small smile to Annika's face. "I appreciate it. My name's Annika."

"Yeah, I heard 'bout you this mornin' at breakfast. The whole Barracks was talkin'." Rissa's touch was gentle as she trailed her fingertips down the side of her face, her brow furrowed in concentration. She made a sound at the back of her throat, very similar to the one Councilor Candra had made when examining her pouch. "You're the first demon granted sanctuary ever!"

Rissa sounded excited rather than terrified and that confused her. Where was the wariness and distrust she'd come to know and expect? Her elders certainly made no secret of their feelings for her.

"Rissa, why aren't you afraid of me?"

Solemn brown eyes met hers. "Afore I was brought here to train, I used to live on the streets. You get to trust your feelin's about people, and learn real quick to avoid the one you know might hurt you. I don't feel that with you, 'sides, the *Lady's Chosen* would never have brought that sort of person here."

Annika closed her eyes briefly, touched by Rissa's simple honesty and her belief in the truth as she saw it.

"Rinnel's another pot of salve, though. He's jus' a big bully 'n one day someone's gonna pop him good for pickin' on the young'uns—" She suddenly stopped talking and gave her a lopsided grin. "Healer Danna says I chatter too much." A small, cold hand covered hers. "You never did tell me iffen you needed help." The girl's voice dropped to a whisper. "I still feel you hurtin'."

"It's not something a healer can fix, Rissa," Annika admitted. It was the second time the girl had made the odd comment. "So, how do you know I'm hurting anyway?"

"The *Lady* Gifted me with the skill to sense others' pain." The child shrugged. "I'm still learnin' to use it prop'ly. Bein' able to tell the diff'rence between a body pain and soul pain takes years of trainin'. So, yours is soul pain, huh? Who hurt you?"

There was such a warm innocence about the human child that Annika didn't feel threatened by her blunt questions. She sighed and stared up at the pale blue sky. Beyond the quiet sanctuary of the niche she could hear the muted goings-on of the compound and wondered if anyone was searching for her yet. Was Kalan looking for her?

"No one person hurt me, Rissa," she finally said, looking down at the child. "It was their attitude and beliefs that upset me."

"What's that mean?"

"You said you're training to be a healer?" She nodded. "I'm a healer, too, but my mentor wasn't allowed to teach me how to read and write. The people who hurt me think just because I don't have these skills I'm worthless."

"They teased you 'cause you didn't know?" Rissa's dark eyes flashed. "I was seven when I was brought here to be trained. That's late to be found with a Gift. The other children teased me 'cause my readin' and writin' wasn't as good as theirs so I know what that feels like." She tilted her head. "How did you learn everythin' to become a healer if you couldn't write it down?"

"I listened hard, repeated everything told to me over and over in my mind many times, watched closely, and remembered it." Annika met her gaze. "Do you recall everything you've said to me since you crawled through that bush?"

Rissa's brow furrowed a moment then she shook her head. Annika recited their entire conversation word for word.

The girl grinned and clapped. "*Mother of Mercy*, with a memory like that you'd learn to read 'n write in no time!" She jumped off the bench, waving the broken branch. "I could teach you the letters 'n sounds right now, if you like."

With her boot, she cleared small rocks and debris from a spot on the ground then scraped the stick over the dirt making a curve and a line that joined. Annika craned her neck to see what she wrote.

Propping a hand on one skinny hip she pointed with the stick. "That's the letter *a* and it makes two sounds . . . *ah* and *ay*."

Annika's heart leapt as she recognized the symbol from the writing in the book Davyn demanded she'd read. Excitement curled in the pit of her stomach.

"Show me more," she said and shared a smile with her small companion.

Rissa, trainee healer and destroyer of gardens, took to her task with enthusiasm. Her lack of guile soothed away the residual ache left behind in Annika's heart after the Council meeting.

Annika knelt on the ground to copy the symbols, a fiery determination to master them as quickly as possible growing with every passing heartbeat.

"KALAN, none of the Light Blades say she's on any of the rooves in the compound. Where else could she have gone?"

Kymora's voice drifted out from his apartment to where Kalan stood on the balcony after searching the apartment. Her staff tapped on the floor as she came toward him. He peered down into the garden. Relief rushed through him when he saw a familiar blond head of hair seated next to a small child in the secluded niche below.

"*Lady of Light*, thank you," he murmured, hours of searching and worry eased.

"Kalan?"

"Shh, it's all right, Kymora. I've found her."

His sister reached the balcony wall and her head tilted to one side. A breeze carried Annika's voice toward them. "Who's she with?"

"I think it's one of the children from the Barracks. A girl, maybe eight or nine years old, dark, curly hair, dressed in healer's colors."

"Sounds like Rissa." A slow smile curved his sister's lips. "If I'm not mistaken they're learning sounds and letters."

From his elevated position Kalan could see a number of symbols carved into the ground. They listened as Annika recited each name and letter as Rissa pointed to it. When she finished their delighted laughter drifted up to them.

"Her memory and recall is amazing," Kymora murmured. "She wasn't exaggerating when she told the Council she had all her learning inside her head."

He grit his teeth at her reference to the debacle of a meeting that had occurred that morning. "They never even gave her a chance. Never intended to."

His sister reached out to touch his arm. "The *Lady* said her arrival would bring opposition." Her hand slid to cover his. "Candra listened. The contents of Annika's pouch impressed her. I heard her speaking to Benth and Corvas after you ejected Davyn from the chamber."

"Their intolerance hurt Annika."

Davyn's heartless act of exposing Annika's illiteracy twisted inside him like a knife blade. She'd stared at the page with undisguised longing and hunger. Her eyes had changed color, from pale green to orange then black. The anger in her gaze had not just been for the Councilors.

"I know. I could hear it in her voice as she stood up to them." Kymora's warm hand tightened on his. "You didn't mention their hatred."

Kalan sighed heavily and raked a hand through his hair. "Annika expected that. Hatred is something she's lived with all her life. Sadly she's used to it."

"It certainly gives new meaning to the *Lady*'s words . . . *draw strength from life's experiences.*" Kymora gave a dry chuckle. "And she was strong this morning, older brother."

Annika's fierce independence was one of her greatest assets, and one of the many characteristics that attracted him to her. A reluctant smile lifted the corners of his mouth as he remembered her parting statement to the Council. The truth of her words had been punctuated with such fire as she'd stood up to their attempt to humiliate her.

He inhaled a ragged breath. "She's one of the most resilient, courageous women I know, Kym," he admitted.

"Annika didn't know you were the *Lady's Chosen*, did she?"

"I wanted to tell her . . ."

"But if the *Na'Reish* had found out, you wouldn't be standing here now."

"Initially, yes, that's why I didn't tell her." A muscle ticked in his jaw. "I was going to once we arrived safely here but the night we arrived I desperately wanted to see you. She insisted I go . . ."

Kymora made a tsking sound. "And on your return you found Arek trying to kill her . . . Oh, Kalan, you couldn't have predicted how events would turn out."

"One bad judgment call after another . . ." he whispered. "We both worked so hard to establish the measure of trust we had before today."

Below them Annika drew more letters in the dirt and he listened to her sound them out. Such single-minded determination made his heart swell.

"You care for her."

He stiffened with Kymora's quiet words. Slowly he turned to look at her. Her sightless gaze was fixed firmly on his face, her expression one of gentle acceptance.

"You should know by now how finely tuned my ears are to listening to people," she said, her words mildly censuring. "When you speak about Annika your tone softens. The timbre of your voice deepens. It's quite obvious really."

Kalan snorted. "Only you would claim something like that."

"Avoiding the issue isn't allowed, brother mine." She waggled a finger at him. "Ask yourself this. How would you feel tomorrow if she decided to leave and never come back?"

His growled protest arched Kymora's eyebrows. The strength of his reaction gave him pause. He sought out Annika in the garden below, needing to know she was safe. She was still there, crouched on the ground over the letters, her blond head close to Rissa's dark one.

"Are you questioning the path the *Lady* has chosen for you, Kalan?" Kymora asked.

"Surprisingly, not anymore." He grunted. "And that's a first for me."

"Then why so silent?"

"I was thinking how well Annika has handled everything with honor and dignity."

Every time he thought of her, of the way she touched him or spoke his name, his heart lightened. Annika had tangled herself in his thoughts, wrapped herself around his soul, and slid right in next to his heart. The realization filled him with the most incredible sense of peace.

He let out a slow, amazed breath. "She makes me happy."

"Sounds like you love her."

Kymora's blunt statement was like a blow to his gut. He opened his mouth to issue an immediate denial then altered his words at the last moment. "I can't love her, Kym."

"No? Why not? Because she's *Na'Chi*? If you'd believed her to be a danger to us, you would never have brought her here. You did, so you've accepted her. Are you afraid of what the Council will think?"

He fisted his hands. "Whatever our personal friendship might be it's none of their business."

"Your personal friendship with Annika will affect what happens next, Kalan, whether you like it or not." He hated that she was right. Kymora's brow creased. "The *Lady*'s guided you this far, Kalan. Don't doubt what you feel. You never have before."

"Your faith was always so much stronger than mine. You follow

Her path without question. I'm not like that, Kym." He shook his head. "It's too soon to know what I feel for Annika . . ."

"Figure it out, Kalan, because particular Councilors will take any hint of uncertainty and question your support for her. That will spread down through the ranks to their advocates." Kymora touched his shoulder. "Face the truth in your heart and embrace it. Then stand united before the Council."

"You know I don't like being forced into a decision before I'm ready."

"Do you think Davyn will wait for you to decide?" Her expression softened. "Just don't take too long." Her warning sent a shiver along his spine. She squeezed his shoulder. "Now that you know where Annika is, I'll leave you to think. I've temple duties to attend to."

He spoke as she reached the door to his room. "Kymora." She turned partway round. "Thank you for offering your advice, even though you knew I wouldn't like it."

A wry smile curved her lips. "Isn't that what sisters are for?"

He chuckled. "You also make a good *Temple Elect* advising your leader. You're right about the Council."

Her smile widened. "If it hadn't been for you and Arek helping me in my early days as *Temple Elect* I don't know how I would have accomplished half of what I did." She inclined her head in thanks. "I'm glad I can return the favor."

As the door closed behind her, Kalan's grin faded. The light-hearted moment disappeared as his thoughts returned to their conversation, or more rightly, the subject of their conversation.

Loving Annika.

He couldn't love her. But her compassion, determination, empathy, even her temper attracted him. Her capricious nature and fierceness certainly fired his blood. As did the way she responded to his touch. The memory of her finding release in his arms this morning was vivid. The anticipation he felt as he contemplated their next encounter was something he'd never experienced before.

Attraction? Definitely, but love? He grunted. It was a crazy thought but then how insane had the last week been? When would he have ever agreed to protect someone he'd first thought to be a demon in order to escape a *Na'Reish* dungeon? Or acknowledged the existence of a half-blood *Na'Chi*? Let alone kiss one?

He ran both hands through his hair, shaking his head. Kymora might be skilled in reading people's auras and emotions in their voices but how could she claim that he loved Annika when even he wasn't sure of what he felt for her?

Perhaps it was time he visited the temple and spent some time in prayer to the *Lady*. He could certainly use a few answers or barring that, any guidance *She* could provide him with in regards to Annika or the Council.

With a last look toward the balcony and a thought for the pair undergoing lessons carving letters into the ground, Kalan also decided he'd drop in to see a merchant in Bartertown to see about ordering some paper and books for Annika.

ANNIKA quietly closed the door to the apartment, steeling herself for the inevitable encounter with Kalan she'd tried to avoid all day. Spending most of it with Rissa learning the human's written language had helped but by late afternoon the girl had excused herself to undertake chores.

Turning, Annika surveyed the main room, listening for the sound of someone else in the other chambers. All she could hear was the crackling of the fire over in the grate and the faint murmur of voices outside in the corridor where Light Blade warriors now stood guarding the *Lady*'s *Chosen*.

Her nostrils flared at the mouthwatering scent of food. She hadn't eaten since breakfast. On the table platters, bowls, and plates for a meal had been set at one end. Delivered recently by the look of it. Steam rose through the holes. She hurried over, intending to sneak a look at what lay underneath the covers but a collection of objects at the other end made her detour.

"*Lady's Breath*," she murmured.

Piled carefully in one corner was a small pile of books, all different thicknesses, with gold letters on their front covers. Unable to resist, she picked up the top one and reverently thumbed through its pages.

Next to them lay a stack of paper tablets. Beside them, a stylus, a blank paged journal tied with a leather buckle, bottles of ink. And propped against one of them was a single sheaf of paper. A word and a likeness of her face were drawn on it. Her breath caught.

The note was for her?

Chapter 19

DRAGGING out a chair, Annika set aside the book, and sat down. Her hand shook as she opened the note. Under her breath she tried to sound out the words written on it. Some she managed but many she couldn't. The very last word on the page took a heartbeat to decipher.

"*Kalan.*" She bit her lip.

"I thought the paper and books would last longer than letters etched into dirt."

Annika's heart leapt in her chest as Kalan's voice came quietly from behind her. She jerked around in the chair to find him standing in the doorway of his room.

"Rissa makes a good teacher," he said. The smile he offered her was oddly hesitant as if he was unsure of his welcome.

"You saw us in the garden?" She averted her gaze as her cheeks flooded with warmth.

"Annika, you have nothing to be ashamed of."

"I don't live up to your people's standards." The words tasted like ash in her mouth.

"I've faith you'll prove them wrong." His voice was strong and sure. "By week's end you'll be reading most of those books."

Her gaze strayed back to his gift to her. Unbidden, her hand ran over the leather-bound book, enjoying the feel of its smooth cover. She inhaled the dusty, dry smell deeply, pleasure filling her as she detected Kalan's scent underneath it, as if he'd held each item awhile before placing them on the table.

Such a precious gift. His kindness touched her on a level that erased some of the raw emotions from that morning. She stole a glance at him. His green gaze burned with hunger and also something else she couldn't identify but it had the power to take her breath away.

She swallowed hard. "No one's ever given me a gift before." Her fingers rasped softly over the letter in her hand. "I wish I could read this."

Half a dozen strides and the tall warrior knelt at her side. Kalan took the sheet and spread it on the table. The warmth of his body pressed against her thigh and a few, long strands of hair brushed the side of her arm as he bent to read the letter.

"It says, 'Blessed is the day I ended up in chains as a prisoner of the *Na'Reish*, for I met a woman who opened my eyes and captured my heart with her compassion, her strength, and her dream.'"

She gasped. He paused and glanced at her. The light in his eyes held a vulnerability she'd never seen before. He continued reading, his voice husky.

"'I should have told you who I was once we were safe out of *Na'Reish* territory. I know I've broken your trust again, and you're justified in any anger you may feel because of what I've done, but I never meant to hurt you. I was a fool.'"

Regret and pain shadowed his voice. It made it hard to maintain the sense of betrayal she'd felt for him not telling her who he was.

Annika thought herself prepared for an encounter of some sort over the revelations of the day. But not this.

His finger trailed under the last line of writing. "'I'm a fool who values your friendship, one who would help you build a future here with me.'"

His soft-spoken words hung between them, held there by the fragile thread of hope. She found herself wanting him to read them again but was afraid to ask. Someone took a ragged breath. And another. And another. Then she realized it was her.

How could a simple letter affect her so much? Throat hurting, she swallowed repeatedly. Where was the ugly sting of betrayal she'd felt most of the afternoon? She wanted to confront him. She wanted an explanation for his hypocrisy. But she didn't want to lose what they had between them in this moment. Never had she experienced something so precious. Berating him would destroy his words and the intent behind his gift.

"Kalan . . ." Her voice sounded rusty and hoarse, and on the verge of breaking. She clenched her jaw shut until it ached. She wasn't sure if she wanted to rage at him or just cry. She just knew she was weak enough to consider forgiving him despite her emotions.

He took her hand in his. Somber, green eyes lifted to lock with hers. "I know you're probably not ready for any of this, not after today. All I ask is that you think about what I've said."

Relief washed through her. She grasped at his offer and nodded.

Inhaling deeply, he rose and motioned to the other end of the table. "Will you eat with me?"

He helped her to her seat. She watched as he uncovered the platters then served them both. Such a normal courtesy, one reserved for the *Na'Reish*, not her. Until Kalan. He made her feel special. Cared for. *Human.*

Annika ate what he placed on her plate but never tasted the food. Her mind was reeling, replaying the words in the note she still clasped in one hand. She barely heard Kalan recounting the events of his afternoon, the trip he'd made to the merchant to purchase the supplies sitting on the other end of the table.

It wasn't until she lay in her bed, hours after the meal finished, staring up into the darkness, that she realized what he'd done.

He'd given her his friendship. He'd accepted her.

And by doing so, he'd laid his soul bare.

For her.

Fingers clenching in the covers, Annika sat up. The strange vulnerability on his face and in his eyes had been fear. The fear of being rejected.

She cringed. How could she not have recognized the emotion? He'd left himself vulnerable in the most terrible of ways. Why would he do such a thing?

Her skin heated then goose bumps broke out over her body. She wrapped her arms around her knees and rocked. Forcing her lungs to take a calming breath she dared think of what his friendship meant. *Acceptance.*

Should she believe Kalan?

Could she trust him?

What was the alternative? Even without conjuring details, her future appeared bleak but an offer of friendship made it seem less lonely.

She reached under the pillow where Kalan's letter lay. As her fingertips touched the parchment she heard his voice reciting the words contained on it. The emotions behind them stuck in her mind and from them sprang a warmth that spread rapidly through her.

It brought to life a dream she'd only ever dared think about in the dead of night when there'd been no one watching, no one to see the longing on her face or the color of her eyes.

The darkness and silence of her room made it too easy to be tempted. Reality tended to destroy dreams and beautiful words written on paper. Had done it so many times she'd lost count. But she felt like a moth drawn to a candle flame. Just this once she wanted to know what it would be like to push aside all doubt and fear.

Before her courage deserted her, Annika slid from her bed and padded on silent feet to Kalan's room. He'd left his door open and there was enough light from the dying fire in the outer chamber to see that he slept. He lay on his back, the blankets draped over his body, where they twisted and tangled around his legs, testament to the fact that he'd tossed and turned before falling asleep.

She took a deep breath at the image he made lying there. Wavering shadows threw his handsome face into sharp relief. Even a day's growth of beard couldn't suppress the compelling power and strength of his features.

Just looking at him filled her with such longing. Her shoulders slumped. She could no longer deny she wanted whatever he would give her. A friendship. A future. A life instead of a dream.

You're weak, just like your mother! Savyr's condemnation tore through her.

A small sound caught in the back of her throat. Kalan stirred, as if the soft noise had woken him. Long lashes flickered opened and he glanced toward the doorway.

"Annika?" His sleep-roughened voice hit her low in the gut. "Is something wrong?"

She couldn't speak. He sat up, his bare chest and an enticing patch of naked hip revealed as the covers slid to his lap. She tried to swallow and couldn't, her mouth suddenly dry. Every instinct screamed at her to go back to her room but she couldn't make her feet move.

"How can you give someone the power to hurt you?" she asked, hoarsely. "In that letter you gave me the perfect weapon. You knew I was angry at you for not telling me who you were, yet you did it anyway."

Kalan reached for the striker sitting next to a candle on the small table by his bedside. He lit it and she moved to the end of the bed, to where he could see her face in the small circle of light.

"You take a risk any time you tell someone you care for them." His voice was soft as he propped his arms up on raised knees. "But what's the alternative? Denying yourself friendship? Happiness? Something more?

"Yes, I gave you the perfect weapon for retribution against me. I'm frightened my actions have hurt you too much to forgive me, but I'm more afraid of denying myself the chance of knowing what might happen between us."

Her fingernails dug into the palms of her hands. She stared down at the foot of his bed only half seeing the intricately carved workmanship of the wooden posts as what he said resonated in her soul.

"I felt like such a fool in that Council chamber." Her voice quavered. "I kept asking myself how I missed seeing who you were. I thought of all those questions I'd asked you about the *Lady's Chosen*, of how I was going to beg him for sanctuary because I didn't think your word would be enough for him to see past the markings on my face . . . and all that time, I was already speaking to him . . ."

"I'm sorry, Annika." His soft apology snapped her head back. His gaze met hers, remorse shining in their depths. "It was hypocritical of me to accuse you of deception when I was doing the same thing."

She shook her head, the last of her anger dying with his misunderstanding. "I understand why you never told me who you were, Kalan. Had you been found out my father would've used you." Speaking that aloud brought goose bumps to her skin.

A frown creased his brow. "Then why . . . I don't understand—"

"*Merciful Mother,* I drank blood in front of you!" The words slipped from her before she could stop them. "You, of all people!" Shame writhed under her skin. She took a small step back into the shadows, too afraid of what he'd see in her face.

His gaze sharpened and she knew she'd moved too late.

"You saw me at my worst, too, Annika. I lied and also almost killed you." He issued a frustrated sigh and raked a hand through his hair. "As much as this might sound strange, I wouldn't change what happened out on the trail. It gave us the opportunity to get to know the real Annika and Kalan. An identity would have hidden all that."

How many times had she wished for anonymity treating the human-slaves in her father's fortress without the title of *Na'Chi* hanging over her head? As much as she still felt uncomfortable with past events, his words held the truth. She'd never have let herself get to know Kalan the man with a title in the way.

"Hesia was right. The real test of a person is whether they can see past the names and labels." His gaze was steady. "I've seen you. You laugh, you fear, you cry, you love. You're as *human* as me, *Na'Chi*."

Her heart jolted so hard she was sure he heard it as they stared at one another across the distance separating them. His words resurrected her midnight dream and breathed life into it. He made her feel like somebody of worth.

He truly was the flame, and she the moth. The soft fabric of the bedcovers brushed against her bare legs as she stepped back into the candlelight.

"I'm tired of being alone, of feeling cold and empty all the time." Inhaling a deep breath, Annika trusted him to understand. "I've always had to stand back and watch others live normal lives, sharing their love and wanting the same, yearning for it so hard that sometimes it felt like a knife in my gut . . ." She pressed a hand to her stomach, then locked her gaze with him so he would see the truth in her heart. "I don't want to be alone anymore."

Annika's courageous words sucked the breath right out of Kalan and shook him to the core. With the life she'd led, and facing an uncertain future, she forged through situations that would have broken a lesser person.

"My friendship is yours." An unhurried smile curved his lips. "I haven't changed my mind about that, Annika."

Her tongue darted out to wet her lips as her chin lifted. "And if I want more than that?"

Desire slammed through him so fast it took his breath away. He'd never have believed her inner strength could arouse him like that but beneath the covers he was already half hard.

He liked the way her eyes widened as she caught his scent. It was tempting to reach over and pull her onto the bed but he knew how important choice was to her. Slowly, he lay down on his side and propped his head on one hand.

"There's space here if you don't want to return to your room," he said, and patted the vacant half of the bed beside him.

She knelt on the edge of his mattress, her thighs barely covered by the shirt. Her hands clenched on her thighs as she stared down at him with one of the most vulnerable expressions on her face that he'd ever seen.

"I want to make love to you." Her gaze stayed level with his, the blue flecks in her eyes ringed with green. She wanted him, no doubt, no hesitation. She reached out to touch him, her fingertips brushing his lips. The sensation shot straight to his groin. "Show me how."

Chapter 20

ANNIKA'S demand had Kalan unable to breathe. She was surrendering herself to his care in the most intimate of ways and he marveled at the courage and strength it had to have taken to ask that of him. The level of trust it took to do that . . . something inside him softened, expanded.

"It would be my pleasure." He caught her fingers in his lips and nibbled them, enjoying the startled look on her face. Encircling her wrist, he turned it over and placed a kiss on the palm of her hand. Her fingers curved over his cheek and her lips parted slightly.

He was going to enjoy showing her the love capable between a man and woman. His thumb stroked the inside of her wrist as he let his gaze move slowly over her. "Anytime you want to stop, just tell me and I will."

"And give up my dream?" The flecks in her eyes were a solid green.

He tugged at the hem of her shirt, and her lips met his halfway as she bent down to kiss him. He nibbled along her bottom lip then traced it with his tongue. Her mouth parted eagerly, a soft, breathy moan coming from her as his tongue darted between them. He retreated before she could capture it with her own. Her fingers tangled in his hair and he smiled as she took control.

He was more than happy to let her dictate the pace. Over the next few minutes her confidence grew. She deepened the kiss, her tongue flickering against his, teasing, stroking, her lips sliding against his. His body was tight, held in check, when she finally drew back so they both could draw in some much needed air.

Kalan smoothed a hand along her leg, from knee to hip. "As much as I like you in my shirt, I'd rather see it on the floor." She blinked at his gently delivered statement. Her gaze dipped and she swallowed hard, and for half a heartbeat he thought she wouldn't do it. Then, slowly, she pulled it over her head and lay on her side facing him.

In the candlelight, her skin took on a tawny hue, her honey colored hair swayed and settled over her curves like a living cloak. Through the long strands, he caught a provocative glimpse of rounded breasts and nipples peaked in the cold then his gaze moved lower, past her lean waist to curved hips and the hairless curves of her feminine mound.

He inhaled deeply and a sweet, musky scent teased his nose. "I'm not *Na'Chi* but I know you're aroused. I wonder if you taste as good as you smell?"

Her fingers curled into fists, an endearing betrayal of her nervousness. "You make me burn." Her voice was husky. "You love someone with your words."

"It heightens the pleasure." He reached out to smooth her hair back from her face, flicking the silken lengths over her shoulder. Her breasts rose and fell in shallow breaths as his hand roamed from shoulder to hip and back again. "I love the feel of your skin, so smooth and silky. Firm here . . ." His fingers trailed across her abdomen. "Soft there . . ." He curled them around her breast, loving the warmth and weight of her flesh in his hand as he caressed her.

"That feels so good . . ." Annika moaned and her body arched into his touch as if seeking more. Her nipple seemed to burn a brand in the palm of his hand as he rubbed it lightly back and forth.

"It feels good to me, too." A wicked grin curved his lips as her gaze darted from his face then lower. Even though the blanket covered his hips it did little to hide his arousal. The delicate flush on her cheeks gave him pleasure. "Roll onto your stomach."

She trembled and closed her eyes. "Kalan . . . I don't think—"

"Trust me," he whispered, disliking the tremor in her voice, hating how such a confident woman had been made to feel ashamed of her body.

Annika hesitated a moment, then complied, pillowing her head on her hands. Her show of faith added to the fire burning in his blood. He sat up and pushed aside the blanket then straddled her hips, tucking his legs in either side of her. She lay tense and stiff beneath him. Something he hoped to remedy shortly.

Holding his weight on his hands, he leant over her, bringing his hips in contact with hers, holding back a groan as his arousal pressed against the gentle swell of her buttocks. His mouth brushed the curve of her ear. "Feel what you do to me, *Na'Chi*." He moved his hips gently against her. "I'm hard, and hot . . . just this with only a few kisses."

"Kalan . . ." Her head turned.

He tangled a hand in her hair to hold her still and placed light kisses along the side of her face, following the trail of skin markings over the curve of her neck, the muscle of her shoulder then took his time teasing and tasting the dips and hollows of her back, alternating between the two sides, loving her with every nip and caress of his lips.

"You taste so sweet, Annika." An intriguing dimple at the base of her spine earned his close attention. She squirmed beneath him. "I could spend all night loving you like this."

He smoothed his hands over her back, felt her muscles ripple with his touch, then stroked the firm flesh of her buttocks and thighs with his hands. The scent of her arousal was stronger, and she moved restlessly, no longer tense.

"More?" he asked, his fingers tracing the outline of each mark high on her thigh in teasing swirls.

"Yes . . ." The word was a long drawn-out moan.

He continued his gentle seduction, placing more kisses along the spotted trails, working his way down from her hips to her thighs then to the back of her legs. Her moans were louder by the time he reached her ankles where the markings faded.

"Roll over again." This time there was no hesitation and he sat back on his haunches. He nudged her legs apart with his knees. The sight of her spread out on his bed, her body flushed with arousal, her eyes that incredible blue, made his heart pound harder in his chest. "I have never seen anything so beautiful. You take my breath away."

Again Kalan took the weight of his body on his hands but this time he gradually lowered himself until he lay on top of her, so that her pebbled nipples pressed into his chest and he fit into the welcoming cradle of her hips. He hissed at the delicious friction of skin sliding on skin. Her hands threaded through his hair and she devoured him in a deep, tongue-thrusting kiss that sent him close to the edge.

Annika delighted in the feel of Kalan lying on top of her. She felt surrounded by him, cherished. Safe. The weight of him, the hard planes of his body pressed flush against her created a delicious ache that centered low in her body. His heavy, spicy scent saturated her lungs and it added to the flames licking her flesh as his hands caressed her. She rocked her hips against him, gasped as his erection rubbed against her core. Her body responded with a rush of delicious heat.

Kalan's groan came from deep inside his chest, his breath hot on her face as he broke their kiss. "You're so wet."

Another deliberate slide. This time she cried out, her fingers digging into the solid muscles of his shoulders. He made her burn, and it wasn't just physical. Kalan was sharing himself with her, hiding nothing. The look in his eyes, the way he caressed her, the kisses, his tender words. She knew he wanted her and the feeling was mutual. It shook her all the way to her soul.

Kalan's hand moved between their bodies, his fingers finding and carefully parting her flesh to explore her slick folds. Annika closed her eyes as he stroked her. Anticipation built with the slow slide of his mouth along the column of her throat. As his lips reached her breast and his tongue flickered out to tease her hardened nipple, the tip of his finger grazed her core. She cried out as exquisite pleasure drew tight inside her and threatened to erupt.

Not knowing what to do next, but needing something more than just this agonizing torment of heated kisses and fiery touches, she curved one leg around his flexing hip. "Kalan, please—"

"I don't want to hurt you." His voice was a guttural growl against her breast.

Opening her eyes, she placed her hands both sides of his head, liking the fire and need burning in his gaze. "I trust you."

She moaned as his mouth covered hers. The fierceness of his kiss stole her breath. He gripped her hips and the tip of his erection parted her slick folds. Instinctively, her hips tilted upward. His gaze locked with hers, dark and hungry, then he slid into her in one, deep thrust. She couldn't look away even as the sharp, burning sensation tore a cry from her, and for a moment it overrode the pleasure she felt being so closely joined with him.

Kalan paused, his arms trembling with the effort to hold still to give her time to get used to him rather than thrust into her again and again as his body was demanding. *"Mother of Mercy*, I'm sorry, Annika." He shuddered. "You're so tight and hot."

Her eyelids flickered, the blue in her gaze almost silver. She smoothed a hand over his cheek. "I'm a healer, Kalan, I knew to expect the pain."

She shifted beneath him, as if testing the new sensations. Her inner muscles flexed and rippled, gripping him in an intimate caress that he felt right to his bones. He shuddered. A ragged groan tore from his chest.

"Kalan?" She ran her hands up over his taut back and shoulders. "Shouldn't you be moving, or something?"

His breath left him in a rush and he buried his head against her throat. Her eagerness brought a smile curving his lips. "So much for patience," he murmured.

"You did this to me." Her indignant reply held a hint of laughter. She tightened around him again, this time deliberately. He hissed a curse, and her husky laughter broke free. The sound melted into his heart.

"You asked me to love you." He nipped the soft flesh of her throat with his teeth. She sucked in a harsh breath and he soothed the bite with his tongue. "And that's what I'll do for as long as I can make it last."

Slowly, he rocked against her. Her arms tightened around him and she moaned. As he felt her beginning to move, to meet his gentle thrusts, he gradually increased the pace. He liked her small sounds of wonder and pleasure combined.

"You feel good . . . inside me . . . and on top of me." Her husky words fanned the flames inside him. "Your scent is sharp and hot, like molten spice."

Kalan ground his hips against hers, heard her breath catch, heard his own grow ragged. Her inner muscles squeezed him to the point of pain and he knew she was close. He quickened his strokes, loving the look of raw passion on her face and controlled his own desire, wanting to see to her pleasure before his.

Her eyes opened wide, the blue striations flashed silver, her back arched, sending him deeper inside her. She cried out. Pure satisfaction filled him as she shuddered in release. The sweet pain of her nails raked his back and he let himself go, wanting his own moment of ecstasy. Closing his eyes, he moved even faster. Her warm softness clasped him tightly and his body exploded.

Kalan heard the pounding of Annika's heart beneath his ear as he regained his senses and realized he'd collapsed on top of her. While he doubted she had the breath to issue a protest, he knew his weight had to be crushing her and rolled to one side, taking her with him, his arms wrapped tightly around her. One-handed he pulled the blanket up over them, keeping the chill of the night from their heated bodies.

She snuggled in close to him. He smiled as he felt her lips brush his collarbone. That small, innocent action was enough to make him harden, but as her breathing evened out into sleep, he knew he'd have to wait to pleasure her again.

Having her in his bed wasn't as disconcerting as he thought it would be. Her warm presence pressed against him felt right. Tonight she'd given him her trust and the peace that brought touched him all the way to his soul.

ANNIKA awoke surrounded by warmth and with the scent of Kalan deep in her lungs. It was morning. The candle on the bedside table had burnt to a stub and gone out, but there was light coming from behind the shuttered window on the wall opposite her.

She remained relaxed as she used her senses to listen to her surroundings, a habit she'd cultivated over the years living within the fortress. Her head rested on a muscled shoulder while a heavy arm lay across her stomach. She could hear soft, deep breathing close to her ear but nothing else.

Her heart picked up speed as fragmented scenes from last night slowly linked and became the memory of making love to Kalan. Latent desire mixed with bittersweet pain.

Mother of Mercy, what had she done?

Slowly, Annika lifted her head. The sight of him sleeping, his handsome face relaxed, his jaw darkened by a night's growth of beard hit her hard. Something inside her swelled and burst, filled her with an incredible warmth and tenderness. How could she dismiss or regret the most incredible night of her life?

His gift filled her with awe, but even more than that, she felt connected to him in a way she'd never experienced with another person before, not even Hesia. The intensity of the emotion was frightening yet also extraordinarily serene.

The arm curled over her ribs tightened. "Your eyes are silver." Her desire rekindled at the sound of Kalan's deep, sleep-roughened voice. "You look well-loved."

Her cheeks warmed but she met his gaze boldly. She reached up to run her hand through his hair then cradled the curve of his cheek. "As do you."

His chuckle came from deep down inside his chest. In one, easy movement he pulled her over him until she lay on top, her legs straddling his hips. She gasped as his erection slid against her tender folds. The intimate caress sent heat coursing through her but before she could comment his lips caught hers in a long, lingering kiss that had her squirming against him before he drew back.

Kalan's hand smoothed over her back until his fingers caressed the curve of her hip. "Do you regret what's happened, *Na'Chi*?"

The provocative nuance in his voice gave the name new significance. One she definitely liked.

"When I woke, I wondered what I'd done," she murmured. He shuddered beneath her and that small sign of vulnerability pricked her heart. "But it was an instinctual reaction. If I'd had any doubts last night, Kalan, I'd never have slept with you." Rising above him, she liked how his breath hissed in through his teeth as she undulated her hips against him. She felt him harden and grow even larger. "Nor would I be wanting more of your loving right now."

His green gaze heated with renewed desire. His hands caressed the skin of her stomach before sliding over her ribs to cup her breasts. Her eyes fluttered closed as he plucked then rolled her nipples between his fingers, the sharp pleasure streaking straight to her core. When he trailed one hand down her body to caress the soft flesh between her legs, she grew wetter.

"I think you enjoy it when I play with you like that." Kalan's gentle teasing was nothing like she'd ever experienced before—another first.

Annika gasped as he shifted his hips and filled her unexpectedly. She dug her fingers into the muscles of his chest unable to stop the cry that burst from her throat. He was so long and hard inside her. Such a different sensation from last night.

His gaze glittered as he stared up at her, his mouth curving at the corners. "Take your pleasure. Love me this time."

Shock raced through her like lightning. He was giving her control of their lovemaking? So used to having others demand that she submit rather than cede control of the situation to her, his unexpected gesture touched her heart.

Biting her lip, Annika hesitated, not quite sure what to do next.

"Ride me." The hungry look on his face gave her confidence. He made her feel desirable. Sensual.

She rose up then lowered herself, moaning at the heat it created as he slid out of her then back in, filling her again. With his hands on her hips, he guided her into a gentle rhythm then, once she knew what to do, he continued caressing her breasts.

Annika tried to take her time, wanting to enjoy the wonder of him filling her so completely, wanting to gauge his reactions, wanting to give him as much pleasure as he was bringing her. But she was a slave to her body's demands.

Her pace increased. She writhed against him, overwhelmed with the burning sensation building inside her. Leaning forward over

Kalan, her long hair falling around their faces like a curtain, she shuddered. The new position trapped him hard inside her.

"*Lady's Breath!*" Her words were no more than a breathless whisper. A spasm of heat speared her womb. "Not yet—"

"Let it take you." A hard flex of his hips accompanied Kalan's low groan. "Let it burn us both!"

She ground against him, squeezing him tight, and reveled in his hoarse cry and the sharp pain of his fingers digging into her thighs. His spicy scent saturated the air around her. She savored the expression of raw need on his face as he stared up at her.

Kalan claimed her lips in a scorching kiss as heat surged through her. He thrust hard upward, gave a shout and spent himself inside her. The searing heat triggered her climax. Their kiss stifled her scream, her body convulsed and her senses exploded. She came in a maelstrom of fire and lightning.

Annika collapsed on his chest and they both lay there, skin sweat-soaked, panting. He held her until the last tremor shook her then just stroked her back, gently, as an almost surreal calmness descended.

"Kalan." Enjoying the moment, she buried her head under his chin, and kissed the damp skin of his neck where she could see his pulse pounding. His inarticulate mumble brought a sated smile to her lips. "Thank you."

"What for? Making love to you?"

"For that, but mostly for having the courage to see the real me. For making me understand that it's all right to care and dream."

Lifting her head, she pressed her hand against the center of his chest. She could feel the hard thump of his heart beneath her palm and took comfort in its steady beat. For the first time since crossing the river into human territory she looked forward to discovering what her future with Kalan would hold. She wet her lips, uncertain about sharing her thoughts with the man who was coming to mean so much to her.

"There's something else worrying you, isn't there?"

She hadn't wanted to spoil their time together. "While I don't regret the decision of making love to you, I'm worried about how our relationship will affect you."

"In what way?" Kalan's eyebrows rose high on his forehead.

"Your sister, your friends, the Council." Her voice dropped to a whisper. "What will they think when they find out—"

"We both know this Journey is going to be hard—" He cupped her face so that she looked at him and could see the truth in his gaze. "—but, with the *Lady*'s blessing, we'll figure it out as we go. All right?"

Annika nodded and melted against him as he claimed her lips in a warm kiss, amazed at how quickly his touch had become familiar and comforting. It was strange letting someone else lend her their strength to vanquish her fears but she realized that trust allowed her to do that.

She could easily learn to love this man.

Chapter 21

THE array of stalls, tents, and holding pens had Annika turning her head left and right as she walked through the People's Market. One of the first things she noticed about the gathering, other than the looks directed at her, was the noise. She'd heard the muted hum of voices even before she and Kalan had reached the north bank of the city where the market was held.

Now she was surrounded by hundreds of people, all engaged in conversations or bargaining. Hawkers extolled the benefits of their wares over their neighbors and, in the background, were the cackling, bleating, and bellowing of pens and crates of animals. Musicians entertained small crowds of people, a high proportion of them children. Their giggling and sounds of amusement was a music all its own. Very few of the slave-children at the fortress had ever laughed.

She caught sight of Kalan watching her and sighed to herself at the handsome sight he made dressed in his Light Blade uniform. "I'm sorry. I'm slowing you down but look at this place. There's no order to it. No rows of stalls or lines of tents. They've set up everywhere. How do you find what you're looking for?"

The tall warrior grinned. "The People's Market was originally a field where farmers used to bring their stock. Over the years it's gradually turned into this. As a child one of my fondest memories is coming down here with Kymora and my parents. The hubbub was exciting. Don't you think it adds to the atmosphere?"

Nodding, Annika lifted her head as the aroma of roasting meat carried to her on the breeze. She craned her neck to see where it was coming from.

"The food court tends to set up in the northeastern corner of the market." He motioned in that direction. "In another couple of hours this area will be deserted as everyone heads over there for a meal. If you're hungry, we could go now."

She shook her head. They'd eaten breakfast with Kymora again before parting ways. "Do you mind if I look at the wares?"

"Go ahead."

She was grateful for his presence as she wandered toward a stall displaying woven fabric and rugs. The holder stared at her silently, a scowl on his face, and she wondered if he'd have said something to her if Kalan hadn't been standing beside her. Several of the holder's customers moved away from her, their disdain obvious.

"Why would he let someone like her come here?"

"Bloodsucking animal!"

She flushed and glanced toward Kalan, hoping he hadn't heard their comments, glad when he didn't react. He'd been so eager to show her the market this morning that she hadn't the heart to refuse. Derogatory comments were a natural part of life for her but she doubted he'd let them slide.

"You have such a love for color." She ran her fingers over the nap of a rug, enjoying the rough surface. "Such bright hues and variety of textures. I've never seen anything like it in the homes of the *Na'Reish*. They favor more austere surroundings and decorate their walls with trophies of war. Weapons, shields, and the like."

"Annika! Annika!"

She turned at the excited, high-pitched voice calling her name and caught sight of a dark, curly-haired child pushing her way through the crowded market.

"Rissa. What are you doing here?"

Dressed in what looked like a matching set of dark green breeches, shirt, and boots, the girl skidded to a halt, a wide smile on her face. "I'm over at the healers' tent, helpin'." She bobbed her head at Kalan. "Mornin', Commander."

He returned the greeting as Annika peered through the crowd to see the tent she spoke of. "A healers' tent?"

"Every market day the healers and their trainees offer free treatment to those who need it." Kalan indicated they should head in that direction. "It was one of the first needs I saw when I was appointed as *Lady's Chosen*. Most of the poorer districts had little or no access to healers."

The young girl grabbed her hand and tugged her through the crowd. "One of the best things 'bout being a trainee is gettin' to go with the healers to market. You see all sorts of ailments 'n injuries. Why, jus' this mornin' I helped Healer Danna mix a gel for winter's rash. Pretty ugly case of it, let me tell you . . ." Her nose screwed up but there was an animated sparkle in her eyes. "There's lotsa learnin' to be done, but even better you get to practice your craft."

Kalan chuckled and shook his head. "Only a healer would get excited about boils and broken bones."

The young girl glanced up at him, her nose wrinkling again. "No offense, Commander, but you Light Blades are too healthy, 'n treating bruises 'n sprains taken in training can be a little . . . dull."

Annika shared a grin with Kalan, delighted by Rissa's honest observations as they reached the healers' tent. It was a large pavilion divided into two rooms. The flaps on the sides of the first room had been raised and the sick sat on benches inside being treated by a small swarm of people dressed in clothes similar to the ones Rissa wore. A line had formed of those waiting their turn to go inside.

Just outside the tent, a woman in forest green called out instructions to a small group of children about Rissa's age. They all wore serious expressions as they listened, some even took notes in their journals. As they were dismissed and scattered to do their chores, the woman turned and Annika's step faltered as she recognized Councilor Candra.

Candra's dark gaze lit up in surprise, and then she smiled. "Commander, Annika, I see you've found Danna's wayward pupil."

Rissa grimaced. "I'm sorry, Master Healer. I jus' saw 'em over the other side of the market 'n went to greet 'em."

"You have duties that need attending to. Perhaps you'd best return to them." After Rissa had said good-bye and they watched her disappear into the second room, Candra chuckled. "Why am I not surprised that she's already met you, Annika?"

Her tone was light, not quite what Annika was expecting considering the outcome of the last time they'd met. "I hope Rissa's not in any trouble."

"Not at all, although I daresay Danna will have a quiet word with her. She's an excellent trainee but easily distracted." The older healer stepped inside the tent. "Would you care to help treat some of our patients?"

Annika glanced uncertainly at Kalan. He raised an eyebrow, a small smile on his lips. "Annika?"

She glanced back at Candra. "You'd let me near them?"

"I'm not one for dancing around the floor," the woman said, her gaze direct. "What I saw in your pouch at the meeting impressed me. Only a fully trained healer could have made the salves and gels

I saw. Your mentor was thorough in her teaching, much better than some of mine. If you say you learned everything using your memory then I'm not going to be one to gainsay you.

"Sometimes the other Councilors forget that learning comes in many forms. I'll reserve my judgment until I see you in action." She waved a hand at the people around them. "You can watch as I do my rounds, or you're welcome to help. If you elect to help then I'll watch until I'm satisfied you are what you say you are: a healer."

Kalan's hand touched her elbow. "You'll find the Master Healer tends to be more open-minded and candid than many of her counterparts on the Council."

The woman snorted. "Your angry departure out the other day did us the world of good. Shook some of the stalwarts to their boots being told they weren't living up to their reputations. Thank goodness for you young ones who aren't afraid to voice an opinion and a few home truths.

"And it's a good thing I'm not the *Chosen*. I'd have reformed the Council and found some young blood to take the seats. Take Arek, for example. He might be impetuous at times but he's refreshingly straightforward. A man after my own heart."

"I'll let him know you said that, Candra." Kalan chuckled, easing Annika's uncertainty about the whole situation and she was left wondering if Rissa's honesty came from the Master Healer and was a trait encouraged by her.

"So, what's it to be, Annika?"

A little overwhelmed by the outspoken woman, she nodded. "I'd very much like to help, Councilor."

A finger wagged at her. "We dispense with formality outside the Council Chamber. You can either call me Master Healer or Candra."

"Commander!" An urgent shout came from outside the tent.

A Light Blade warrior Annika didn't recognize pushed his way through the line of people waiting to be treated. Kalan excused himself a moment to step outside. The younger warrior's face was flushed with exertion, as if he'd run a long distance, and he bent over at the waist as he delivered his message. A frown appeared on Kalan's face the longer the conversation went on then he nodded and strode back into the tent.

"I'm needed back at the compound," he said, expression grim.

"Bad news?" Candra inquired softly.

"A *Na'Reish* scouting party has been spotted less than a day from the city." He kept his voice low. "I need to meet with the Patrol that spotted them."

His news sent a cold shiver along Annika's spine. She never thought her father would go to such lengths to get her back. No Patrol had ever been ordered this far into human territory. She moved closer to Kalan. "We can go now."

He shook his head, giving her a rueful smile. "I'm sorry our tour of the city has been cut short, but there's no need for you to miss out on this. Stay with Candra. I'll go on to the compound. Likely as not, I'll be in a meeting when you return."

She bit her lip. "Are you sure?"

"You're in good hands here, Annika." His smile became a grin. "Besides, the look in your eyes says you want to stay, so stay."

She nodded, strangely relieved that she wouldn't have to miss out on the visit to the healers' tent. "Go to your meeting and I'll see you later."

"I'll make sure she gets home safely, Commander," Candra promised.

Kalan left, accompanied by the warrior who'd brought him the message.

"Well, let's get to work, Annika." The Master Healer clapped her hands and rubbed them together. "Time's a-wasting."

With a last glance at the crowd where Kalan had disappeared, Annika followed the healer into the tent, eager to learn and show what she knew.

"WHY wasn't a meeting called to inform the Blade Council about the threat at our gates?"

The booming voice of Councilor Davyn, and the angry sound of more than one pair of boot heels clicking on stone, came from behind the group gathered in the room.

Kalan slowly straightened from where he leant over a map with his Light Blade warriors and met Arek's gaze across the Council table. "How in *Lady*'s name did he find out about this?" he demanded, softly. "The news is barely two hours old."

His Second shrugged. "He might have retired as a Light Blade but that doesn't mean he's severed all ties with the Barracks."

Unimpressed, Kalan's gaze narrowed. "In the future, I want it made clear to the warriors that reports are not for general conversation."

"Yes, Commander."

Kalan turned as the small contingent of Councilors reached the table. A swift survey showed the group consisted of Davyn, Yance, and Corvas accompanied by a smattering of prominent Guild-leaders from the city. Benth and Candra, the remaining two Councilors, were conspicuously absent. Their exclusion didn't come as a surprise. In the past, they'd lent him support for many of the changes these people had opposed.

Bracing himself for the coming interrogation, he leant a hip against the edge of the table, obscuring Davyn's view of the map he was so keenly trying to see. "Councilors, Guild-members, what can I do for you?"

His polite question seemed to be a signal. The questions came, fast and furious.

"Is it true we have the *Na'Hord* camped outside our gates?" This came from the Weavers' Guild-leader. "Are we under siege?"

"How soon before they attack?" This from the portly Farmers' representative. "Do we have time to call in the crofters closest to the city?"

The head of the Business District raised her voice, "Are they here for the *Na'Chi* woman?"

He let them talk, waiting for them to run down, his gaze drifting over the gathered delegation to settle on Davyn. The older warrior asked nothing himself. An air of quiet anticipation seemed to surround him and he listened, a gleam in his eye as the panic of the Guild-leaders rose.

Interesting little power-play getting the others to take him on. When it became clear he wouldn't answer them, the furor died.

Kalan pinned each person with a look before speaking. "There is no threat to the city, Guild-members," he stated, calmly. "Nor is there likely to be. The *Na'Hord* are not camped outside our gates."

"But your patrol has spotted something, hasn't it?" Yance's gaunt face was creased with worry. "Scouts? A party of *Na'Reish*?"

"Once I know *all* the facts, Councilor, you will be informed."

"Are they here for the *Na'Chi* woman?" Corvas demanded, his cheeks ruddy.

"I don't know."

"So, there are demons this close to the city? Didn't I tell you the *Na'Chi* woman was a threat? I warned you at the last meeting she'd only bring trouble." As if addressing the room, Davyn turned rather than speaking to him. "If the *Na'Rei* wants her back then we should hand her over and be done with it."

That little speech set off the Guild-members again and sparked Kalan's temper. Behind him, Arek snorted then appeared at his side.

"Would you like me to remove this gaggle of *geefans* so that we can finish this meeting in peace?" the warrior asked in a low voice. "I'd be happy to start with my dear grandfather."

Kalan fixed the crowd with an icy stare as he shook his head. "Not yet."

A hush came over the clamoring crowd; anxious faces turned toward him as he pushed off the table and stepped toward them.

"Guild-members, in the past you've relied on our Councilors to inform you of any movements my warriors might take to head off a *Na'Reish* threat. Storming the Council Chamber like a riotous mob has achieved nothing but waste your time and mine.

"*If* a threat exists then be assured that the Councilors will be informed and you will be told the facts or of any decisions that might be made. Should you be unhappy with that arrangement then, by all means, express your concerns to the Councilor of your choice for inclusion at the next meeting and I'll abolish that system and instigate another. Perhaps one where you elect a representative to attend the meetings."

The Councilors present shared a look. Their unease filled Kalan with a certain amount of satisfaction. Yance, Corvas, and Davyn knew he wanted the Guilds represented on the Council and had opposed his proposals unanimously. If they wanted a power-play Kalan was more than happy to give them one; something they'd best take into account if they intended to make a habit of stirring up the city-folk.

"In the meantime, to avoid unnecessary worry and panic, think carefully about listening to gutter-gossip and half-truths, whatever their source. Now, if you'll let my warriors and I get back to what we do best."

He nodded to Arek and he and three other warriors began herding the group toward the chamber doors. With a glare at his closest escort, Davyn ignored the hint to leave and closed the distance between them.

"You refuse to acknowledge the danger of letting her stay," he hissed. "She threatens all our lives. It's in her nature to feed. She may claim to abstain from drinking human blood but the day will come when she won't be able to control herself. Will it take the death of an innocent to convince you, *Chosen*?

"And if that doesn't, then consider what would happen if we engaged the *Na'Hord* in a direct confrontation. By your own words they outnumber us four to one. They'll slaughter us!" His blue eyes flashed with aberrant fervor.

Disquiet stirred in Kalan's stomach. Davyn seemed agitated, more so than usual.

"The *Na'Rei* has been waiting for the chance to invade, now you've given him the excuse. You know he'll take it. Mark my words, once he crosses the border, he won't stop until every human—man, woman, and child—is enslaved or dead."

A silence fell over the room.

"Have a care, Davyn, that I don't consider your words concerning Annika another slur against her character." Kalan's gaze narrowed as he regarded the silver-haired warrior with barely concealed dislike. He kept his stance relaxed but his tone hardened. "I'll tolerate your ignorance once, but not twice."

The warrior's mouth pulled down at the corners. "I'm only expressing the opinions of many, *Chosen*."

"Now that you've expressed them, *leave*."

"Councilor, if you please." His Second took the man's arm.

Davyn shook himself free of the hold, his expression one of angry disgruntlement. "I expect a full briefing of this meeting before you retire tonight, Commander."

Kalan nodded sharply. "You'll get it."

Spinning on his heel, Davyn strode from the chamber. Arek made sure the doors were closed once the contingent was gone. He returned to the table.

"That was interesting," he drawled, an amused twinkle in his eyes.

The warriors gathered chuckled, and the tension of the last few minutes was relieved, but Kalan only grunted and turned back to the map. "Blood-kin or not, Arek, we deserve better. His hatred blinds him."

His friend took his place at the other side of the table, his expression sobering. "You know he has a point." Arek's eyes met his, his gaze steady. "And I'm not referring to Annika."

Briefly, Kalan closed his eyes and nodded. "I know we can't afford an invasion by the *Na'Hord*." *Mother of Mercy*, he hoped this was nothing that serious. He sighed. "We need more warriors."

"We could instigate another Search, bring in the potentials we identified during the last one."

"We'd be training children, Arek."

"If we engage in conflict with the *Na'Reish* it might come to that."

Kalan's gut churned at the somber statement. There had to be some other solution to the possible threat of attack. "No, we need to confirm that these four scouts are a part of an advanced group invading from *Na'Reish* territory. Until that's done, I want more frequent Patrols, and messengers sent to warn the Outposts."

He just prayed that the information the Patrol had given him was wrong. The uneasy feeling in his gut said differently.

Chapter 22

VARIAN allowed the ghost of a grin to curve his lips. Gaining access to the human city had proved easier than he thought. Timing it with the arrival of a large group of people, mid-afternoon, when the guards were at their least alert, and with everyone too busy herding animals along behind their carts, no one had noticed another figure cloaked against the cold weather slipping through the city gate with them.

After some careful scouting and patience he'd found the temple, the one place Lisella believed there would be someone who knew about Annika seeing as one of the *Lady*'s Light Blades had brought her here.

It was late. The last rays of sunlight had faded over an hour ago and most of the crowd drawn to the temple had gone with the light. From his vantage point between two buildings he watched the last visitor leave. Using the shadows, he slipped in through the wooden door before it closed. The familiar rush of adrenaline coursed through his veins as he scanned its interior.

Thankfully the temple was open in design, no side chapels or areas where someone could hide. And after an earlier foray he knew it had three ground exits and one from the chime tower if you were prepared to climb onto the roof and escape down the side of an adjacent building. Darkness would give him the advantage over any human pursuing him should he need to leave in a hurry.

The shadows were darkest where he stood. The smoky tang of extinguished candles lingered heavily in the cool air. The only ones still burning were those at the altar beneath the rectangular stained glass window. Surrounded by the tawny glow, a person knelt there in prayer.

On silent feet he skirted the rows of benches, his gaze fixed on the human. The charcoal colored robe, while simple in style, was belted at the waist and he knew from his discussions with Hesia that this was one of the *Lady*'s Servants.

The robe couldn't hide the feminine curves of a human woman. With her back to him all he could see was her long, wavy, black hair brushing the middle of her back and fine-boned wrists and hands as she held them together in prayer. Alongside her lay a wooden staff. His gaze sharpened noting the potential weapon.

With his time within the city limited, he needed to make the most of it to find out about Annika. Making sure the woman was the only one left in the temple, he avoided the last row of benches and came up behind her fast. Her head lifted sharply, as if she sensed him.

"Is someone there?" Her soft, melodic voice sent a strange chill through him. He'd never heard any woman who had a voice so inherently feminine.

Impressed by her skill in hearing his approach, Varian lengthened his stride and came alongside her just as she reached for the staff.

He placed a boot on it. "You won't need that, Handmaiden."

She jerked back from him. "You startled me. I didn't realize anyone was still here."

As her head turned toward him he realized two things; she was beautiful and, most astonishingly, that she was blind. Her incredible emerald green eyes stared sightlessly toward him, too far left. He stared at her.

The *Na'Reish* never let anyone with such an affliction live. There were no blind or injured among their ranks. Imperfection was seen as an aberration. This human woman not only lived but was also one of their most revered figureheads. If only he'd known she was blind he could've pretended to be human but he'd assumed all Servants would be able to see.

He hesitated the merest fraction of a heartbeat, then bent down to grasp her arm and pulled her to her feet before he backpedaled her toward the side of the temple where the shadows were deepest. She was tall, almost eye to eye with him but no match for his enhanced strength.

"What are you doing?" Alarm and fear mingled in her voice. Beneath his hands, she tensed and began to struggle. He pushed her against the wall and used his greater body mass to pin her there, then covered her mouth with his hand.

"Not a sound, Handmaiden," he murmured. "I won't hurt you."

She took no notice of him and heaved against him. Knowing his words weren't likely to calm her, he held her loosely as she struggled, letting her exhaust herself. Lush curves pressed into him and her scent filled his lungs. She smelt of honey and incense. His body tightened with need. He sucked in a deep breath shocked at the unsettling effect she had on him. Her struggling finally ceased and he felt her trembling. Beneath the forearm he had pressed against her chest her heart thudded erratically.

"I won't hurt you." Taking advantage of her and her fear of him didn't sit well. "Tell me your name."

He removed his hand from her mouth.

"You expect me to cooperate with someone who attacks me?" She might've been terrified but her words were scathing. Brave considering he could easily snap her neck.

"You cooperate, and I'll let you live."

Her eyebrows arched high. "Oh, that's a great incentive to cooperate." She never raised her voice, just berated him in that calm, melodic voice of hers. "Why don't you threaten to beat me while you're at it?"

"It's a dangerous practice annoying your attacker."

"You come into a place of peace and expect me to help you?" She shoved against him again then slumped against the wall, her expression anything but submissive. "Your attack is cowardly and low."

Varian couldn't help the smile twitching at his lips. Her courage and fiery nature appealed to him. "My apologies, but I had no choice but to approach you this way."

Her head cocked to one side. "You're not from the city. Good, I'll know to tell the Light Blades you're from the farmlands."

"Hush." He placed his hand over her mouth again. "Tell me about Annika, the *Na'Chi* woman. I know she's here within the city."

The Handmaiden stilled. He only lifted his hand far enough so he could hear her speak.

"I'll tell you nothing about her!" she hissed. "She's done nothing to harm anyone. I won't see her hurt because of your blind hatred and prejudice."

Shock coursed through Varian's veins. She believed he was here to harm Annika?

Kymora wondered at her attacker's sudden silence and while his hold never slackened, she thought her accusation had astonished him. For the first time she wished she could see.

All she knew about him was that he was tall and incredibly strong. She was held in close to a warm, hard-muscled body. Almost as tall as any man, she'd felt like a child struggling against him and there was an aura of power surrounding him. It was deadly. Dangerous.

Provoking him was foolhardy but she'd never liked being helpless and verbally attacking him had been the only option left to her.

This close to him she detected a combined scent of an earthy muskiness and cold winter's air, as if he spent a lot of time outside in the elements. The heat of his hands burned through her robe, and a tingling began in her skin where he touched her.

Her chin lifted. "Why do you want to know about Annika?"

"I ask the questions." His voice was rich and deep. It resonated with confidence.

"Then I won't answer." Now that her initial fright had subsided, Kymora wondered if his threats had been used only to ensure her compliance. He hadn't hurt her. Even when she'd struggled he hadn't harmed her. He hadn't touched her inappropriately and while he still restrained her, the hold wasn't painful. "It seems we're at an impasse."

"If I let you go, will you cooperate?"

She shook her head. "No."

He grunted. "At least you're honest."

Suddenly she was released. One moment he was hard up against her, the next he was gone. His sudden move to free her was stunning given the circumstances. Curiosity rather than fear kept her stationary.

"Is your staff a weapon?" His voice sounded farther away. She heard the slight scrape of wood on stone. She tilted her head toward the sound.

"I know how to use it as one."

There was a deliberate boot step then she felt the cool length of it pressed into her hands. "I trust you'll restrain from using it on me."

His tone was firm, slightly cold, as if warning her against the rash move of attacking him physically. A shiver ran down Kymora's spine. She had little doubt he could defend himself.

She curled her fingers around the smooth wood. "Are you hoping this will regain my trust?"

"Is it working?" Just a hint of amusement colored his tone.

Heart thumping, she drew herself up to her full height, incensed but perplexed by his gall. "Not in the least."

"I don't intend harm to Annika." His sigh was drawn out and she listened as he moved away from her then back again. Was he pacing? "I want to know if she's safe."

"What?" Of all the reasons she'd envisaged for his attack on her this hadn't been one of them.

"I need to know if she's safe."

"Why?" She couldn't hide her confusion.

Silence met her question. It lasted so long she began to worry he'd slipped away without her knowing.

"Because if someone like her has been given sanctuary then there's hope for me." His quiet reply was so close to her that she flinched. She hadn't heard or sensed him moving.

His warm hand took one of hers and brought it to the side of his face. Beneath her fingertips she felt the hard angle of his stubbled jaw, the soft caress of his hair against the back of her hand then the slightest of raised textures on his skin. She frowned and brushed her fingers back and forth over the small, irregular shapes. They ran up to his temple, then down the side of his neck and disappeared under his shirt collar.

Her breath caught.

"Do you understand now?" he asked.

"You're *Na'Chi*?" Kymora felt him nod. A frisson of shock raced through her. The *Lady*'s words now made so much more sense. "*Mother of Mercy*, how many more of you are there?"

He backed away from her so quickly her hand was left touching air. "I'm not telling you anything more until I know Annika is safe."

"She's fine. She's been granted sanctuary by the *Lady*'s *Chosen*." Kymora tapped her way toward the sound of his voice. "Who are you? Are there other *Na'Chi*?"

Again he remained silent. So many questions crowded her mind. How had he entered the city unnoticed? Why hadn't Annika mentioned the existence of other *Na'Chi*? Why had they come to Sacred Lake? She could feel his tension and knew he was a hairbreadth away from leaving. Not that she blamed him, the risk of discovery drove him, but approaching her in the way he had spoke of a need too great to be ignored.

"Before Annika arrived, the *Lady* spoke to me during a visitation. *She* said, *Her presence is necessary. She threatens all we know but must be welcomed. As do those who come after her. My children must survive.* Her words didn't make sense then, but now they do. *She* predicted your arrival." Her heart began beating twice as fast. "Our meeting isn't by chance. *She* also told me to be prepared for my fourth Journey. I've little doubt that it involves you."

"Fourth Journey?"

Kymora heard his confusion. "The decisions a person makes in their life determine the paths we take into the future. Everything you've done up until now has guided you to this meeting here. If I'm to help you, you need to claim sanctuary."

"Like Annika did with the Light Blade?" She nodded. "Will this protect me from death?"

"Unless you harm someone, it will."

Kymora heard a ragged, indrawn breath. "Then I ask for sanctuary."

"And I'll do everything I can to help you . . ." She smiled, liking the warmth that flowed through her. She doubted his trust had been easily given. "My name's Kymora."

Another short hesitation then, "And I'm Varian."

"You won't regret this, Varian."

"I hope not, because if there comes a time that I do, I'll kill you." She shivered, knowing he was a man of his word but the threat was delivered with such heavy reluctance she knew his regret was genuine.

"Where do we head from here then?" she asked softly. "I'll be guided by your needs, Varian."

There was another uneven inhalation. "I think it's time we talked more about the *Na'Chi* and a human slave called Hesia."

The name was one Annika had mentioned in conversation before. She inclined her head. "Shall we sit down? I've a feeling this might take some time."

As Varian took her arm to guide her to the nearest bench, a soft breeze brushed her cheek and the scent of new fallen rain and fresh flowers filled her lungs. The familiar buildup of energy around her widened her smile.

"MY CHILDREN HAVE ARRIVED, HANDMAIDEN." The gentle voice in her mind was filled with joy. "YOUR JOURNEY HAS BEGUN, KYMORA. THE FUTURE OF ALL MUST BE MADE SECURE. TREAD THIS PATH WISELY BUT CON-FIDENTLY."

Her presence faded. *Her* words gave Kymora hope and faith and assured her she'd made the right decision.

Chapter 23

"Y OU shoulda seen Rinnel's face when Master Healer Candra assigned him and me as your assistants!" Annika couldn't help but smile as Rissa danced around her, a grin as wide as the corridor on her face. "His skin went the color of parchment. He was as helpful as I've ever seen him when you were healin' those bad cases in the tent, and then when he saw the red color of your eyes . . . I swear he was gonna faint—"

"You shouldn't take pleasure in another's discomfort, Rissa," Annika chided her. "You heard me explain to him why my eyes changed color."

The young girl's smile faded. "You mightna been about to feed off him but it's jus' that it was the first time I've ever seen him afraid."

"I didn't frighten him on purpose, Rissa."

Ahead of them were the two Light Blades assigned to guard duty outside Kalan's apartment. Another warrior, with greying hair, stood in the corridor talking to them.

"Please don't feel bad." Rissa grasped her hand and squeezed. "I didn't mean it in that way."

"I know you didn't."

Her smile returned. "So, are you going to need to drink blood soon?"

Annika rolled her eyes at the sparkle in Rissa's eye, still astounded by the child's fascination with her *Na'Chi* characteristics. "If Master Healer Candra wants me to help again tomorrow then I'll have to feed in the next day or so."

The older warrior saw them approaching. He said something to the others then strode to meet them.

"Annika, I've a message from the Commander for you." His gaze flickered to Rissa then back to her. "He's been in a meeting all day and has another this evening. He's reporting to the Councilors his findings from the earlier meeting. He needs you to attend and asked that I take you there."

Annika tried to suppress the sick feeling in her stomach at this news. Another Council meeting? The first hadn't fared well and Kalan wanted her to go to a second one?

Rissa grimaced. "Guess our reading lesson might have to wait, eh?"

"Come with me." She smiled. "Perhaps it won't go long and we can still have our lesson. Is that all right?"

The Light Blade warrior shrugged. "I wasn't told how long it would go."

Their guide escorted them back out into the compound but instead of heading to the Blade Council Chamber he directed them to the Councilors' living quarters.

"Where are we going?" Annika asked, tugging her cloak more tightly around her as the evening breeze swirled around them.

"Councilor Davyn's apartment." The older warrior dipped his head to avoid the worst of the gust. "He's offered the use of his household for the meeting."

Since returning from the market just after sunset, the purple hued twilight had darkened to the full black of night. Lights glowed in many of the windows of the buildings around them. The compound was almost deserted and the various scents of cooking food in the air heralded it was mealtime for many.

As they covered the remaining distance to the apartments, Annika caught sight of two figures leaving the temple. Staff in hand, Kymora was talking to her taller companion. Wasn't she going to the meeting? With a hooded cloak Annika couldn't see who her companion was but they were walking toward the *Chosen*'s apartments.

"In here." The Light Blade warrior held open a door for them. She and Rissa preceded him. She wondered if the Councilor knew she was coming. The idea of being in the same room as him again was daunting but Kalan wouldn't have asked her to attend if it hadn't been important.

The sound of children's laughter echoed along the brazier-lit corridor but this stretch was empty of anyone. The man knocked on another door at the end of the corridor. They heard a muffled voice grant them permission to enter.

"Ah, Parnolli, I appreciate you escorting our *Na'Chi* guest here." Davyn's deep voice oozed insincere gratitude although the warrior did nothing other than nod his head. "Thank you, you may return to your duties."

A chill ran down Annika's spine as she surveyed the large open apartment. It was almost identical to Kalan's in structure but that was where the similarities ended. She eyed the collection of arms along Davyn's wall. It was a morbid display of *Na'Reish* weapons and armor; a trophy room of the warrior's past life.

The room was cold and shadowed. Only a few braziers had been lit and the fireplace remained dark. While the lack of light didn't bother Annika, the absence of warmth did.

"Where are the others?" Rissa whispered, and moved closer to her. "I thought they'd be here."

"How convenient." Davyn's tone was as precise and ice cold as his expressionless features. His pale gaze sliced from her to Rissa and his lips curved into a polished smile. "You've brought a friend along." The Councilor motioned to an adjoining door. "The others are in there, little healer. Why don't you both go through?"

Annika watched him warily as he rose from where he was seated at the large table in the room. Dressed all in black he presented an intimidating figure. As he stepped toward them a glint of silver at his waist caught her eye. The wavering light caught on the hilt of a sheathed dagger. It was the first time she'd seen a Councilor armed.

Keeping hold of Rissa's hand, Annika headed for the other room. As they passed the warrior, her nostrils flared at the dark scent emanating from him. It was the same one from before at the first Blade Council meeting. She saw something shadowy flicker through his gaze. Her skin crawled as Rissa dragged her into the room in her eagerness to be away from Davyn. The girl's uneasiness reassured her she wasn't the only one bothered by the warrior.

"There isn't anyone in here." The girl's soft statement held a thread of fear.

The room was empty save a weaving hanging on one wall but the angle was such Annika couldn't see what was on it. No furniture, no rugs, no shuttered window, only a lit candle on the floor in the middle of the room.

Goose bumps peppered her skin. A boot step sounded behind her. Annika half-turned, determined to demand an explanation when a clenched fist connected with her cheek. Searing, white pain flared through her head. Rissa screamed as Annika staggered under the force of it. She tasted the heavy saltiness of blood in her mouth.

"Annika!" The girl's cry came as her sight returned.

Davyn's enraged face filled her vision. His fist descended again. More pain exploded in her head as it connected with the same cheek.

Her knees buckled beneath her and she landed on all fours with a grunt.

"I won't have you threatening everything this Council has fought for, *Na'Chi!*" His hissed statement sounded close. Too close. "Nor shall I suffer your presence. You taint the memory of my daughter who died fighting your father."

His fist tangled in her hair. Annika gasped as her head was wrenched back. Candlelight flashed on metal. The dagger pierced her shoulder. She screamed, too late to deflect it as the blade sank deep into her flesh. Davyn jerked it free then kicked her backward onto the floor.

Rissa scrambled toward her, her face pale, her expression terrified. Davyn stood over them, his stance wide, his chest heaving, the bloody dagger clenched in his hand. His pale eyes seemed to glow with a fanatical light.

"No, Rissa, move." Every breath hurt as Annika tried to push the child behind her, afraid that Davyn would attack again. The wound ached fiercely as she pressed her hand against it.

The girl leapt to her feet. "Don't kill her!"

"I'm not going to kill her, child. That would defeat the purpose of this little exercise." His deep chuckle filled the room. "I need the *Na'Chi* alive and hungry."

Davyn's meaning sent a stab of fear into Annika's heart. She pushed harder against the wound, desperate to stem the flow of blood welling from it. Her healer's pouch lay on the floor at Davyn's feet. He saw the direction of her gaze, bent to pick it up and tossed it into the other room. The muffled sound of breaking jars and items scattering across the floor made her wince.

"Can't have you healing yourself." Madness tinged his laughter. "I see you understand your situation, *Na'Chi.* By the time either of you are missed, you'll have proven the very point I'm about to address at the Council meeting. Animals can't be trusted. Your nature won't allow you to be anything other than what you're born to be."

Davyn backed toward the door. Desperation drove Annika to her knees. "*Mother of Light*, I beg you, don't leave the child in here. She'll be defenseless."

"Grant the child mercy and feed from her now." The malevolent smile returned. "I look forward to witnessing your death, demon. Kalan will have no choice but to kill you once he sees what you've become."

Annika shuddered as the door thudded shut and a metal bolt slid home. Panic clawed at her throat.

"Councilor Davyn has an ugly blackness inside him." Rissa's quiet comment echoed in the empty room. "I could feel it. It was thick 'n vile." The girl turned and knelt beside her, untying her cloak. The expression on her face was grim as she tore the cloth in two, wadded one piece and slipped it under her bloody hand then tied the other tightly around her shoulder to hold it in place. "You've lost a lot of blood." Rissa's gaze lifted to meet hers. "Your eyes are bright red."

Annika swallowed hard. "You can't stay here. Check the door."

"He bolted it."

"Do it," she said through gritted teeth.

Rissa hurried over to the door. Annika slowly pushed to her feet, her anxiety increasing as her legs trembled with the effort. Even with both of them pushing, the thick wooden door remained unmoving.

Rissa thumped the door with her fist in frustration. "Healer Danna will wonder where I am in 'bout an hour."

"Will she search for you?" Annika slid to the floor, her thoughts as flighty as her pulse.

"She knows I'm tutorin' you 'n if the other trainees aren't muckin' around she might look for me around bedtime."

In less than an hour the first signs of blood-fever would assault her. While her wound was bandaged, the blood flow had only been slowed not staunched. Other than the Light Blade warrior who had escorted them to Davyn's room no one knew where to look for them. Any search would be a blind one.

"Was what Davyn said true? Are you gonna drink my blood, Annika?"

"No, I won't do that." *Lady* forgive her, Annika wasn't certain if that was a promise she'd be able to keep but Rissa didn't need to know that yet.

"But he said you'd do it . . ." Her voice dropped to a whisper. "He said you'd become an animal."

Annika closed her eyes, hating the hint of fear in her voice. "I won't lie to you, my hunger will grow the longer I go without feeding."

"Then why don't you drink some of my blood now? Won't that help?"

Icy fingers of fear inched along Annika's spine at her suggestion. She clenched her teeth against the image of another child lying dead at her feet, his eyes glazed over in a death stare, his neck and wrists torn open. "No. I'll fight the hunger and we'll wait for Kalan to find us."

The first hunger pangs twinged in her stomach. She sucked in a harsh breath at the nauseating sensation. Rissa's human scent sharpened as the need to feed enhanced her demon senses. Her mouth began to salivate.

"Rissa," she said calmly. "I'm going to move to the farthest corner of the room. No matter what happens, whatever you hear, or if I beg you to come to me, ignore me and promise me you'll stay here and keep quiet. The only time you can make a noise is if you hear someone in that outer room. Call for help. Do you understand?"

"Yes." Rissa's cold hand squeezed hers hard then let her go. "I'll keep quiet."

Annika struggled to her feet again and using the wall for support made her way around the edge of the room until she'd reached the darkest corner. Shivering in the cold, she curled up into a ball on the ground knowing that the trembling would use up energy she couldn't spare.

To distract herself she began a prayer to the *Lady* for strength to resist the blood-fever and when she finished that she recited all *Her* scriptures, those she'd learned from other human-slaves and the ones Hesia had enjoyed quoting. Listing every known plant and herb, their uses and benefits followed. Then her lessons with Rissa.

Glancing at the candle, a puddle of wax lay at its base and half of it was gone. Annika had no idea how long that had taken but it was the only marker of the passage of time.

Beneath her the cold of the stone floor seeped slowly through the layers of her clothing. Across the room she could hear Rissa's soft breathing and her human scent was strong in the cool air. Tempting, alluring. Annika licked her lips, almost able to imagine the warm, sweet flavor of human blood on her tongue. Her stomach cramped and she stifled a groan.

Look at her! Who'd have thought she'd growl with hunger like a juvenile Vorc. Annika flinched as a voice from her past echoed in her mind. *Hold the human near the door, see if she tries to grab him.* Mocking laughter followed a child's terrified scream.

Put him in. The image of her father staring at her from behind the steel barred door was vivid. *I want to see her feed.*

Even with her five-year-old enhanced senses, Annika saw his violet eyes glowing with satisfaction as his warriors unlocked the door to the room and shoved the boy inside. She couldn't stop the memory. Hot tears burned beneath her eyelids as she remembered wrestling the older boy to the ground, the sound of her ravenous hunger coming out as a savage snarl. Shuddering, shame burned through her as she denied the final death scene to replay in her mind.

A groan rumbled up from deep inside her. Her stomach clenched then spasmed. Mid-formation, the groan became a growl; frustration and hunger escalated. Over by the door she heard Rissa's breath catch. Annika curled even tighter in an attempt to control the animal growing stronger inside her. Her soul shriveled at the thought of history repeating itself.

The boy had been a stranger, one of the many slaves in the fortress. Too young, too innocent. Tears slipped from her eyes.

Rissa was a friend. One of too few, precious and cherished. More tears tracked over Annika's cold cheeks at the thought of attacking her. She'd welcome death at the blade of any sword if she killed her friend.

With all her heart, Annika prayed that Kalan would find her in time.

"I'VE had a dozen Patrols scouring the countryside since the first report was made this morning." Kalan waved at the map spread before him as his gaze swept the table.

All the Councilors were present as were many of the more senior warriors of the Light Blades. With the final search report in less than two hours ago he wanted to squash any rumors before they became evening gossip over the dinner table. The delegation of Guild-officials had been an indication of the panic that could swell if half-truths were allowed to spread. He didn't need a city full of frightened people, not now.

"You can see where they've been searching. The valley, the hills and farmlands beyond. None have seen or found any evidence of *Na'Reish* attack force."

"They may be farther away . . ." Davyn's calmly delivered comment drew his gaze to the man. "Who knows how far those scouts traveled?"

The older warrior wore a self-satisfied smirk as he sat back in his chair, relaxed, the only Councilor not leaning over the map. The map he'd been so intent on seeing when he'd stormed in at the earlier meeting.

"Councilor, none of the Outposts have sent a report of a *Na'Reish* army making its way toward us." This came from one of the Light Blade warriors to Kalan's left. He nodded his thanks.

"They wouldn't if they'd been caught by surprise." Yance sucked in his cheeks, making his gaunt face seem emaciated. "They could've been slaughtered by several raiding parties. That would leave the way open for Savyr to move an army across the border in the dead of night. Have you sent riders to check?"

"Yes. Our fastest ones have been dispatched." While Kalan's reassurances did little to ease the worry on Yance's face, his thin lips flattened out from their tightly pursed position. "I expect the first to report to me early tomorrow morning."

The doors to the Inner Council Chamber opened. Kalan glanced up as one of the guards entered, the expression on her young face a combination of apology and surprise.

"Pardon the intrusion *Lady's Chosen*. The *Temple Elect* wishes to address the Council."

"Send her in." He'd received word that Kymora had still been occupied in the temple when he'd called the meeting. Unwilling to disturb her at her duties he'd started without her.

The young guard cleared her throat and looked back over her shoulder. "She's not alone, *Chosen*."

He nodded. "It's all right, Shanna."

Yance drummed his fingers on the table, impatience obvious. "If there's no evidence of an invasion force then how do you explain what the original Patrol saw?" He tugged at his tunic, the only indication he was uneasy. "They gave detailed descriptions of four *Na'Reish* warriors. Did they imagine them?"

"Not at all, Councilor Yance." Kymora's voice spoke clearly over the mutterings his comments drew. "They did see four scouts, only they weren't *Na'Hord*."

People shifted in their seats to face the Handmaiden. Kymora entered the chamber, her hand resting on the arm of a tall, broad shouldered companion. The hooded cloak was pulled low over the face of her escort so that it concealed their identity. He saw her hand tighten on her escort's arm. A large, masculine hand lifted to push back the hood.

A gentle smile lit Kymora's face. "Our warriors saw four *Na'Chi* scouts."

Chapter 24

KALAN heard the blades of nearly a dozen warriors being drawn and chairs scraping back as almost everyone shot out of them. Shouts of surprise and anger filled the Inner Chamber.

"Varian has the *Lady*'s protection!" Kymora's cry could be heard over them all.

"Stand down!" Kalan hurried around the table. Alarm flooded him when he saw the dark-haired *Na'Chi* pull his sister in front of him as a human shield. A dagger was clutched in his other hand, and his lips were drawn back in a silent snarl. Kalan stopped short at the implied warning.

"That animal threatens our *Temple Elect*!" The growled comment came from Davyn. "Kill him!"

Kalan flung out his arm, staying the warriors who moved. "There will be no blood shed in this chamber!"

"Varian only threatens me because you're all blinded by emotion!" Kymora made no move to struggle or free herself from the *Na'Chi*. "He seeks sanctuary for his people, just as Annika did."

"There are more of them?" Candra's astonishment was reflected in the expressions of those around her.

"She lied to us!" Corvas hissed, his dark eyes flashing with anger.

"Annika never knew about the other *Na'Chi*." Kymora frowned. "There is so much I have to tell you . . ."

Kalan's gaze connected with the *Na'Chi*'s. His violet eyes were cold, intelligent, assessing and confident, the flecks of color barely distinguishable, like he had tight control over his emotions. Thin temple woven braids held his jet-black hair back from his hard, angular features. A jagged scar ran from the corner of his eye to the bottom of his dark stubbled jaw.

The man stood eye to eye with Kalan, his lean, hard body exuding the lethal strength of a warrior. The relaxed grip of his arm around Kymora's waist was deceptive. Had he wanted to, he could've slain her the moment the first blade had been drawn.

Kalan was the first to break the stare. He looked around at his warriors. "Why are you all still armed?" Startled gazes met his; a few had the grace to look shamefaced. "The *Temple Elect* has granted Varian *Her* protection. Sheath your weapons and resume your seats."

He waited until everyone had followed his direction.

"Yevni, two more chairs. We'll continue this meeting and listen to what the *Temple Elect* has to say."

Ignoring the fact that Varian still held his sister hostage, with a gesture he invited the young *Na'Chi* to join them and went back around the table to his own seat. The tension was palpable as they all waited for Varian to make a decision.

"Today I've observed your people in the streets, at the market, and now here." Scorn laced the *Na'Chi*'s quiet statement. It thickened as he continued speaking. "You all fear what you don't understand and it dictates your actions. A warrior must be in control of his emotions at all times if he's to make sound judgments." His lips curling in disgust, he released Kymora and sheathed his dagger. "Are you sure these are the leaders of your people, Handmaiden?"

Kalan almost grinned as Varian's deserved insult reminded him of the day Annika had squared off with the Council. Candra was not so restrained. Her hearty laughter filled the chamber and she slapped her hand against the table.

"*Lady's Breath*, are all *Na'Chi* so forthright in their opinions?" the woman asked, her eyes sparkling as she met his gaze. "Kymora, you said there were more where this young man came from? Then I, for one, look forward to meeting them."

Her lighthearted comment eased some of the tension. His stance and gaze still wary, Varian helped Kymora to the seats set aside for them.

"Does anybody care that this . . . *Na'Chi* has admitted to being in the city all day and only now has he chosen to reveal himself?" Davyn raked his gaze around the gathered warriors. "Or that sympathy toward these demons seems to run in the Tayn family?"

Davyn's antipathy and deliberate provocation stroked Kalan's temper, especially as it ratcheted up the tension Candra had worked so hard to dispel.

Kymora turned her head toward him, her glare heated. "I suppose you'd walk into the *Na'Reish* fortress bare-handed asking to see their *Na'Rei*, Councilor? Who would blame Varian for being wary of a people who ignore the promise of sanctuary to draw their weapons against him?"

"Davyn." Kalan's voice carried clearly across the table.

"*Chosen?*" The man stiffened in his seat, his gaze locking with Kalan's.

"Show the *Temple Elect* the respect due her. I won't warn you again."

Silence fell, broken only by the sound of someone's chair creaking. Davyn's pupils dilated, a darkness flickered in his eyes, and, for a moment, Kalan believed he was about to be challenged but then the man's face blanked of all emotion.

"My apologies, *Temple Elect*." The smirk returned as Davyn deliberately leaned back into his chair. His behavior caused the hairs on Kalan's neck to rise. What did he find so amusing? "Address the Council. Take as much time as you want . . ."

His sister straightened, her lips pursed, and Kalan wondered if she would rebuke Davyn, but then she inhaled a deep, calming breath. "I believe I'll begin with reminding you all of the words the *Lady* spoke to me . . . *Another Journeys with him. Her presence is necessary. She threatens all we know but must be welcomed. As do those who come after her. My children must survive.*"

"So, the *Lady* was referring to Varian and the other *Na'Chi*?" Candra asked.

"Varian's arrival and the story he's told me makes *Her* meaning very clear, Councilor," Kymora said. "The *Na'Chi* were saved from death by a human slave called Hesia. You'll remember that name from the time Annika told us about how she learned to heal.

"Hesia assisted with many of the *Na'Chi* births. The mothers, overcome with the shame of delivering crossbreed children, would plead with her to kill the child. Instead of giving in to their demands, Hesia secreted the children away and helped them survive. Varian and Annika were two of the first she saved."

"But why?" Yance demanded, his cheeks flushed. "They're an abomination, an affront to the *Lady*."

"*My children must survive.*" Candra's strong voice rang out. "Listen to the *Lady*'s words. She claims the *Na'Chi* as her own, just as she did us."

A smile curved Kymora's lips as she inclined her head. "*Her* words are clear, Council."

"Hesia helped us survive." Varian's deep voice broke through the stir caused by the revelation. "For a while she had the eldest of us pose as *Na'Reish* to blend in but when one of us was discovered he was killed. It was too risky to remain among them, so Hesia hid us away from the fortress. She took many chances to bring us supplies. We grew up as ghosts, learning to hide from those who would kill us, *Na'Reish* and human alike."

"Annika was led to believe all *Na'Chi* babies were killed at birth." Kymora picked up the tale. "Hesia couldn't tell her about them. Not when her father was the *Na'Rei*. The risk was too great.

"But she was determined to show Annika there was hope for her in her situation. She taught her about the *Lady* and remained strong, praying for an answer to the *Na'Chi* problem."

Kymora's head turned in Kalan's direction. Her gentle smile warmed him. "Had you not been captured, *Chosen*, the *Na'Chi* would still be hiding from persecution."

Varian folded his arms and his expression grew tense. "Hesia knew our one hope lay with Annika seeking sanctuary with you so she encouraged her to bargain with you. Your freedom for hers." He cast a dark look toward some of those seated around the table. "While Annika had faith in Hesia's belief of your compassion, I don't know whether what she bargained for was worth the trade."

Candra chuckled and this time a few of the warriors joined her. Kalan couldn't stop the grin that shaped his lips.

"There is no doubt these are uncertain times, Varian," he said. "Until I met Annika none of us ever knew the *Na'Chi* existed. We believed you to be a myth."

"How many more of you are there?" Benth asked curiously.

"Including me, forty-seven." Varian's tally drew a murmur. "Thirty one of us are aged fifteen and older. We have another nine young ones, and seven under the age of four."

"Where are they now?" The silver-haired Councilor looked slightly bewildered. "Are they all hiding in the city somewhere? How could our Patrols have missed them?"

"I'm the only one within your city and the location of my people remains a secret until I decide whether I can trust you or not with their lives." Varian then issued a dry chuckle. "When you've spent all of your life hiding from the *Na'Reish* it's very easy to avoid being seen, even by those trained to spot the *Na'Hord*."

Candra's laughter came from deep inside her belly this time. She shared a look with Kalan but didn't say anything. He knew what she was thinking and was surprised Varian had so diplomatically told them their Patrols weren't worth the leather their boots were made from.

"I would like to learn how you evaded our Patrols so easily." Kalan's request drew agreement from several of his Commanders.

Varian's sharp gaze pinned him where he sat, then the corner of his mouth twitched. "There are many skills among the *Na'Chi* we'd be willing to share with you. Our scouts might be younger than many here but I'd pit them against yours any day."

The not-so-subtle challenge was reflected in his gaze. Kalan decided he liked the brash young *Na'Chi*. "Well, we'll have to see what can be arranged."

"Are you serious, *Chosen*?" Yance enquired. "You can't be offering them all sanctuary."

"The *Na'Chi* are hunted by the *Na'Reish*. They've placed their faith in a human woman who helped them survive, they hold no allegiance to their demon parentage, and the *Lady* claims them as her children." Kalan held the man's gaze for several heartbeats before speaking. "Why wouldn't I extend an offer of sanctuary to them?"

The old warrior's mouth opened and closed, as if he struggled to find the words to express his outrage.

"And what blood source will they slake their hunger from when the need arises?" Davyn's soft demand cut off whatever Yance had been about to say. "Do all of you claim to drink the blood of animals like Annika? What will you do if none is available?" The warrior raised a mocking eyebrow. "You can't guarantee their nature won't put all our lives in danger. How many of us are willing to run that risk? You might ask that before making any decision, *Chosen*."

Kalan didn't like the grumble of support his comments received.

"Every *Na'Chi* monitors their hunger," Varian broke in. "Just as you know when it's time to eat—your stomach growls and grows hollow—we know when to hunt."

"Our hunger never runs the risk of taking a life if we can't eat."

Varian leaned slowly forward, his gaze narrowed and Kalan saw the flicker of black in his eyes. "We are not animals."

Kymora reached out to lay her hand on his arm. Kalan was ready to interrupt the brewing argument when the doors to the room were flung open.

"Commander!" Arek stood in the open doorway, his tanned face noticeably paler, a large tome clutched in his hands. "You have to see this!"

Davyn shot from his chair, his face red with outrage. "You have not been granted permission to address the Council, Second!"

Kalan rose, inwardly grimacing. Arek's grand entrance gave the Council the perfect excuse to deny him. What had him so apprehensive to forget his warning not to antagonize the Council?

"Your pardon, Councilors." Arek's penitent tone and low bow startled quite a few. He immediately turned on his boot heel and stepped back outside to speak quietly to the two Light Blade guards.

The young woman, Shanna, returned, her expression bemused. "Councilors, *Temple Elect*, *Lady's Chosen*, Second Barial requests permission to enter."

"Could the day get any more interesting?" Candra's dry question amused quite a few.

"Councilors?" Kalan asked. Candra inclined her head. Davyn shook his, as did Yance and Corvas. Benth hesitated a moment, made eye contact with Davyn then his features hardened. He shook his head. Kalan ground his teeth. "*Temple Elect?*"

"I'd like to hear what Arek has to say."

"Four votes to two." Davyn's tone oozed satisfaction. "Close the door, Shanna."

"Hold." Heads turned as Kalan rose from his seat. "As *Chosen*, it's my right to overrule the Council's decision. I do so now."

Kymora gasped. "Kalan, do you realize what you're doing?"

The consequence of abusing this power was dire enough that any leader needed to consider carefully his decision to use it. The system ensured that no one *Lady's Chosen* could gain ultimate control and turn the leadership position into a dictatorship.

"I'm prepared to step down as the *Lady's Chosen* if Arek's address is deemed a waste of time." His sister nodded and said nothing more. Kalan met Arek's solemn gaze over the heads of those at the table. "Come in, Second."

The warrior strode into absolute silence. He advanced around the table and placed the tome before him. Kalan retook his seat as the book was opened at a marked page.

"If you'll read this page and the next two, *Chosen*." His friend's expression remained neutral but an intense light burned in his eyes.

Kalan read the pages indicated. His whole body went rigid with shock and it took another reading to take in everything contained in the writing. His mind clouded, his focus narrowed until everything but the words on the page claimed his attention. The flames of anger ignited deep inside and it took every shred of willpower not to react immediately. He sucked in a harsh breath and the hand resting on the table curled into a fist. Precious minutes passed as he strove to contain it. Not until then did he look up from the book.

Kalan's gaze took in the Council members, his lethal stare pinned each one where they sat. "On your oaths as Light Blade warriors, which of you have concealed the truth about the history of humans and demons?"

Chapter 25

THE sound of Rissa's breathing seemed loud to Annika's sharp hearing. Even without opening her eyes, she knew exactly how far away the child was and the precise position of where she leant against the door. She could also hear the beating of her heart. The rapid pace increased every time she groaned and the sound of it intensified her predatory need to claim what she needed to survive.

Her whole body now shook with the need for blood, every cell throbbed, her limbs ached with the pain of withdrawal and her moods were becoming harder to control the longer she went without. The cutting pain of curling her fingers into the palms of her hands drove back the terrifying sensations for a while. But the time between her lucid moments and the agony were growing shorter.

Annika lifted her head aware that the cheek she had pressed to the floor had gone numb with cold. She peered toward the door, able to see Rissa huddled there, her pale face turned blindly in her direction. She was trying not to show fear but total darkness wasn't helping. The candle had sputtered and burnt out some time ago.

"Listen to me, Rissa." Her voice was hoarse, strained with concentration it took to form each thought. "In a little while you're going to hear some . . . strange sounds . . ." Her throat tightened with shame. "You might even hear me moving over here. Just stay there. Don't make a sound. Nod if you understand."

She did. Annika released a soft sigh and slowly sat up. Her limbs were stiff with cold but the movement awoke the pain in her shoulder. It cleared her mind a little. She leant back against the wall and fumbled one-handed with the belt around her waist.

"I'm going to throw my belt toward you," she said. The sound of it hitting the stone floor made the child flinch. It slid to a stop near her boot. "It's near your right foot."

Rissa groped around for it, then her hand closed around the leather strip. She hugged it to her chest.

"It has a good, metal buckle on it. If I . . ." Annika's voice faltered. She swallowed dryly. "I want you to use it as a weapon. If I come near you, swing it as hard as you can and aim high for my face." The soft whimper nearly broke Annika's heart. "I'm sorry, Rissa. I know you're frightened of me."

The girl shook her head hard. "I'm not scared of you . . ." Her reply cut off as if she remembered the instruction not to speak. She bit her lip and her chin lifted. "I just don't want to hurt a friend."

Annika drew in a shuddering breath. Her words meant so much to her. The small human girl was braver than any child should ever have to be. Anger at what Davyn was forcing her to live through burned in her veins. Healer or not, she wanted to kill him for putting Rissa through this.

"Nor do I want to hurt you." She forced a reply past the tightness in her throat. "I'll do everything I can to stop myself. Pray for us both—"

A wave of intense hunger assailed her. Her innards twisted hard. Every muscle locked tight as she arched back against the wall. It drove every logical and rational thought from her mind. She gasped and tasted the scent of Rissa's fear.

Flinging out her arms, Annika dug her fingers into the cracks between the stones in the wall. Panting only flooded her senses with more of Rissa's scent, accelerating her desire for blood but there was nothing she could do except ride out the pain and fight the urge to leap across the space dividing them.

Annika squeezed her eyes shut, hoping the lack of sight would ease the need. It didn't. She heard a feral growl and could barely believe she'd made it. She threw her head back hard.

Pain exploded inside it as her skull cracked against unforgiving stone. The next wave of hunger seized the breath in her lungs and ripped another animalistic sound from her throat. It took all her strength to drive her head backward again. Light shattered behind her eyelids. She did it again. More pain. And again. A groan tore from her lips.

The hunger receded to a tolerable level.

She slumped against the wall, the ache in her head now as strong as the one in her shoulder. Her stomach heaved and she vomited on the ground beside her. The sudden weakness made her whole body shake.

Annika forced herself back into a sitting position. Tears slid down her cheeks as she prayed to the *Lady* for the strength to save a friend.

KALAN slowly rose from his seat, the legs of his chair scraping loudly on the stone floor of the chamber. The sickening feeling in his stomach grew as the silence in the room drew out. Candra and Benth wore confused frowns. Corvas was looking to Davyn while Yance's tanned face was devoid of color. Davyn still wore that self-satisfied smirk and of all the Councilors, he looked the least perturbed by his demand.

"*Chosen*, what's Arek found?"

Kymora's soft voice calmed the fury racing through his veins. Drawing in a deep breath, Kalan glanced back down at the book.

"Arek has brought me a record of our past history written by the then, *Lady's Chosen*, Irat Zataan. He led the Blade Council four hundred years ago during the time we know as the Great War.

"He says . . . *'Will future generations understand the series of events that have transpired here today? I think not, but as my final Journey draws to an end I feel compelled to reveal the truth . . .'* He goes on to say he regrets his part in what happened and seeks forgiveness from the *Lady* for his actions . . . *'I don't know the origins of our racial pride but the decision made by the Blade Council to enslave our demon allies was passed today in chambers.*

'Perhaps we became too obsessed with our own self-importance or believed our greater numbers gave us the right to exploit them. Maybe we grew to fear them. Certainly our resentment of our dependency on them and our jealousy of their physical superiority played a part in this—'"

Several curses interrupted his reading; one of the most vehement came from Candra. She wasn't the only one with a look of horror on her face.

"The entry goes on to tell how they raided the homes of the *Na'Reish* in their attempt to enslave them. Many fled and those captured preferred death to servitude."

His voice shook as he paraphrased Zataan's entry.

"He revealed that the *Na'Reish* once coexisted with us for centuries. We were two races who shared a dependency—they needed our blood to survive, we needed their bloodlines to nourish the *Lady's* Gifts. The Gifts belonged to the offspring of those who joined and partnered with the *Na'Reish*."

"Only those who joined?" Candra asked. "That means all Light Blades have *Na'Reish* blood!" She wasn't the only one with a look of shock on her face.

Kalan nodded as a sense of irony curled in his gut. "We've bastardized their original use. The Gifts were never meant to be used against the *Na'Reish*. We began the war. Our history has been distorted and hidden from us for centuries."

"*Mother of Mercy.*" Kymora smothered her soft cry with her hand. The devastated expression on her face was certainly shared.

"We've caused our own problems?" Benth's voice came out as a weak croak. "Our dwindling numbers of Gifted people are our own doing?"

"*You shall reap what you sow.*"

Candra quoted the *Lady*'s words. The hard truth was a bitter one but Kalan nodded. "The arrogance and corruption of our own leaders led us down the path we find ourselves on today."

"Where was this book found?" Kymora asked.

"Among the personal journals in a storage room of our library," Arek said. "When you asked us to look for evidence of the *Na'Chi* among the histories I found nothing but dry facts. I thought to cross-check the personal journals of each Councilor and *Chosen* from the time of the Great War."

"What I'd like to know is just how far that corruption has spread." Kalan stabbed a finger at the book and glared at each Councilor. "Who among us knew about this?"

Yance was the most shaken. As the weight of the stares of everyone turned on him, he crumbled. "The information was kept from everyone for the good of all . . ."

Kalan's anger thickened. "Benth?"

"No, *Chosen*, on my honor as a Light Blade I knew nothing about this history."

Kalan gave a curt nod and looked to Candra. The older woman met his gaze levelly. "I've never read this account, *Chosen*."

He gazed at Corvas. The silver-haired warrior looked to Davyn, found no support there. His jaw clenched then lifted. "I've read it. The decision was made not to reveal its contents for fear of widespread panic."

"I don't see what you're all so upset about," came Davyn's calm reply. "The Council responsible died four hundred years ago. Too much time and blood has been spilled for us to ever rectify what was done. What good would revealing the truth do?"

Kymora's staff clattered to the floor in her haste to stand. "What good comes of telling the truth? You sit here at the highest level of leadership and profess that truth-saying means nothing?" Her voice shook. "Today I'm ashamed to be human and I weep for the lives of our loved ones, past and present, who've died senselessly in this war. How can you call yourselves Councilors when you deliberately chose to continue the corruption that is destroying us?"

Davyn slammed his fist onto the table. "Our paths have split with the *Na'Reish*. They hate us as much as we hate them. Telling them about this won't stop them from raiding. Savyr would rather see us all dead than talk peace."

"The distortion of history is an unforgivable abuse of your leadership." Kalan gritted his teeth against his disgust for the ex-warrior. "What chance have you given us to rectify the mistakes our forbearers made? You decided our futures for us by perpetuating generations of their fears and prejudices. We made the *Na'Reish* what they are today through our ancestors' choices."

Davyn leapt to his feet, his face distorted by anger. "They're animals! All of them!" His eyes flashed with a wild light. "Whether we like it or not to survive we must continue killing every demon, full-blooded or half-blooded."

Varian surged to his feet, his face tight with cold anger. "You deny your heritage and the facts." His lip curled. "Now you live the lies you've told."

Kymora reached out to grasp his arm as others rose around the table. "Do you all realize that the *Na'Chi* may be the answer to our problem with the *Na'Reish?*"

"I won't tolerate an alliance with half-breeds!" The light in Davyn's eyes grew wilder. "I'll see them all dead first."

Kalan sucked in a sharp breath as his words triggered a memory. *Will it take the death of an innocent to convince you, Chosen?* He stared at Davyn as the hairs on his neck lifted. The warrior had come to the meeting unnaturally calm, composed, and until now, hadn't lost that self-satisfied smirk.

"Where's Annika?" Kalan watched the anger fade from Davyn's face until only the wild look in his eyes remained. Coldness raced through Kalan.

"Rissa escorted her home to your apartment this evening," Candra commented. "We parted ways at the garden."

He glanced at Arek. "Check my apartment."

Confusion clouded his Second's gaze but he nodded. "Yes, Commander." The warrior left the chamber at a jog.

"Kalan, what's wrong?" Kymora asked.

Something dark and unpleasant flickered in Davyn's eyes as the smirk reappeared. He began chuckling, softly at first, and gradually it became louder.

"What's got into you, Davyn?" Benth demanded, his brows pulled down low. Others eyed the man with disbelief. "This situation is no laughing matter."

"Oh, but it is, my friend." His chuckling stopped and he stabbed a finger in Kalan's direction. "Can't you see what he's doing? He's already offered sanctuary to the half-bloods. He'll demand an alliance between the *Na'Chi* and us next." He shook his head. "Such a decision would be suicide."

Running footsteps sounded out in the corridor. Arek appeared in the doorway, out of breath. "Commander, the guards at the door said Parnolli was escorting them to this meeting at your request."

"I gave no such instruction."

But Kalan wouldn't put it past Davyn to do it. A sickening sense of dread scraped along his scalp.

"If Annika and Rissa were supposed to be brought here, then where are they?" Kymora asked, a frown on her forehead.

"He knows." Varian's quiet comment drew their attention away from Arek. The young *Na'Chi* had his violet gaze locked on Davyn. "Annika's scent is all over you."

As Davyn's chuckling began again Kalan's temper exploded. He leapt across the distance between them and wrapped his fists in the man's tunic. With a strength born of anger he slammed the older warrior back first onto the table then leaned in against him.

"Where is she?" he hissed.

A malicious smile curved Davyn's mouth. "By the time you find her, it'll be too late. You'll realize just what sort of animal you've given sanctuary to, *Chosen*." Fanaticism crazed his gaze. "You'll see she's just like the *Na'Reish*."

Fear ripped through Kalan as his imagination went into overdrive. Was Davyn insane enough to kill Annika? Bitterness had twisted the older man's mouth into a sneer; every breath he exhaled reeked with hatred. There was little doubt he'd defy the promise of sanctuary.

Kalan's chest tightened until he thought it might explode from the pressure of the hollow feeling building inside him. *Mother of Light*, he'd promised to protect Annika, to keep her safe. Had he failed her? Again?

She couldn't be dead. He needed her. He couldn't imagine the future without her beside him.

Face the truth in your heart and embrace it. His sister's soft words echoed in his mind. Annika had tangled herself in his thoughts, wrapped herself around his soul, and slid right in next to his heart.

Merciful Mother, Kymora had been right. Against every convention, against everything he believed possible, he'd fallen in love with Annika.

His gaze slashed to Arek. Voice hoarse, he forced out an order. "Find Parnolli!"

Chapter 26

TIME narrowed to the smallest of measures. Annika counted every breath in and out of her lungs in an effort to combat the incessant heat burning inside her. Sweat gathered in the hollows of her body and soaked into her clothes. She barely felt the cold against the cheek she had pressed to the stone wall.

Her tongue rasped over dry lips as the feverish sensation in her body increased. She moaned. It felt like her skin was peeling off her body. Hunger drove its claws into her stomach in response to the faintest sound of a boot scraping on stone.

"Don't move, Rissa."

Her plea came out as a distorted growl. The air in the room thickened with the bitter odor of fear. The scent tormented the beast inside her. Annika shuddered, her long drawn-out moan smothered as she pressed her forearm to her mouth and sank her teeth into her own flesh again. The pain was nothing compared to the hunger. The saltiness of her own blood filled her mouth but it tasted so weak compared to her memories of the sweet, heavy flavor of human blood.

"Annika? Rissa?"

She heard Rissa's breath catch at the faint sound of a voice calling their names on the other side of the door.

"In here!" The girl's small fist pounded against the door.

Her cry shattered Annika's tenuous control. Limbs that once shook now felt the incredible rush of inhuman strength and she turned her head to fix her gaze on her prey.

"You're mine!" Her wild, rasping cry jerked the child around until she pressed her back to the wall next to the door. Hunger overrode every rational thought and, with a snarl, Annika lurched to her feet and staggered toward her.

The door burst open. Light spilled into the room, blinded her. The impact of a heavy body drove hers to the floor. A masculine scent, not quite human, filled her lungs. Rage at being denied her prey surged and Annika twisted and bucked in his hold.

"She's mine!" Her scream echoed in the enclosed space.

"She's strong," grunted the unfamiliar voice.

"What's wrong with her?"

"It's blood-rage." Annika raked her fingers along bare flesh, heard her assailant's breath hiss through his teeth. She heaved in his hold as she became aware of another masculine scent, one more familiar. "Help me hold her!"

Another pair of hands grasped her shoulders. She barely felt the searing pain of her wound. A redhaze obscured her vision as she peered up at the people restraining her. The strong, steady beat of the human's heart so close it was a torment. Every muscle in her body strained in the attempt to break free.

"She needs to feed now!" The urgency in the male's voice penetrated her crazed mind.

"Arek! The kitchens. Get a fresh carcass!"

"Her eyes are pure red," said the second male. "The blood-fever has peaked. She needs blood now!"

"Annika?" The familiar scent grew stronger. "Annika, look at me!"

Snarling, she turned her head toward the sound of the voice. His scent finally registered.

"Kalan?" Her voice was a hoarse croak. She shuddered. Her vision blurred, blackened at the edges. The struggle sapped the last of her energy and she was left trembling beneath her assailant. Her limbs became heavy, her eyelids closed, and she began to drift.

"We're losing her, *Chosen*." The voice sounded like it was coming from far away.

"*Mother of Mercy*, please don't take her away from me." There was the soft hiss of a blade being drawn from a sheath then the rich, metallic scent of human blood filled Annika's nostrils. It drew her back to consciousness. She issued a weak groan. "Annika, drink my blood."

She forced her eyes open. Every instinct urged her to take what she needed but fear swelled within her. She turned her head away from him. "No . . ." Wracking spasms stole her breath and vision again. She gasped as they stopped. "Can't . . . Kalan . . . don't make me . . ."

Kalan gathered her limp body into his arms, fearful at the sudden change in her behavior. He glanced at Varian who knelt the other side of her. The warrior's mouth flattened and he shook his head. His heart clenched hard. His hand trembled as he touched her face.

"She's ice cold." A deep groan welled from his chest. She'd gone from wild to unresisting in a matter of heartbeats, as if her strength had been drained from her body. She couldn't die, not now. They'd just found one another.

His arms tightened around her. He wanted her to live, for them. And, *Lady* forgive him, so she could hear the words he'd been too afraid to acknowledge. He hadn't told her he loved her.

"Annika, hang on and fight it, please." His voice dropped to a whisper. "My heart is yours."

She remained silent in his arms. In the light thrown from the braziers Arek had lit in the chamber he could see the ominous dark stain of blood on the bodice of her dress. Unadulterated rage ripped through him at Davyn's betrayal but he pushed it back to focus on Annika.

Cradling her head on his shoulder he placed his slashed wrist against her mouth. "Drink!"

"You're offering her your blood?" Varian sounded surprised.

His nod was sharp. "If becoming her blood-slave means it'll save her life, I'll do it."

Annika's soft groan pierced his heart. It beat harder at her refusal to drink.

"She's never told you, has she?" Varian asked, his normally stoic face slackening in astonishment.

"Told me what?"

"If she drinks your blood the addiction becomes hers."

Shock washed through Kalan. Annika's insistent need to hunt after the *Vorc* attack suddenly made sense. "She told me she once fed on human blood then managed to wean herself."

"*Na'Chi* children have the capacity to recover. We don't know why. But no adult has ever survived withdrawal."

Drinking human blood would condemn Annika to a life dependent on others. But not feeding now meant she'd die. His vision blurred as his soul filled with black, bitter fury for Davyn. Consumed by blind hatred, the warrior cared nothing for the suffering he'd caused. He'd been willing to sacrifice the life of two innocents and the trust of their people to keep a truth from being revealed.

"Please, Annika, you've got to drink." With a shaking hand Kalan smoothed disheveled hair away from Annika's face and leant in close to her ear. "I love you."

Her eyelids fluttered closed and her head rolled against his shoulder.

"Annika?" His voice broke. Kalan touched her face but she didn't respond. Anguish sliced through his body, tearing him until he truly believed his heart bled. *"Lady's Breath*, no!" She couldn't die. He wouldn't let her. His gaze linked with Varian's. "Help me! Open her mouth!"

The young *Na'Chi* raised an eyebrow at his harsh order but complied. Kalan pressed his wounded wrist to her lips. He wasn't strong enough to allow her the choice of living or dying. She'd claimed his heart. He needed her. "Drink!"

Long moments passed, the silence in the room only broken by the sound of his ragged breathing. Annika stirred, the faintest movement of her lips against his wrist, then he felt a faint sucking sensation against his skin. A small shock tingled through his body at the feel of her feeding, drinking his blood. He saw her swallow. Once, twice, then a third time.

Her body convulsed and she tried to pull away from him. He didn't let her. She moaned softly. "Keep going, Annika."

While her sucking was weak at first, it slowly grew stronger until he swore he could feel the blood rushing through his veins as she fed on him. Behind him he heard one of his other warriors hiss in distaste.

He glared at the man. "Leave if this offends you, Light Blade, but remember I owe this woman my life."

The warrior grimaced. "My apologies, *Chosen*, there've been too many shocks in one day . . . the *Na'Chi*, Zataan's journal, the dismissal and imprisoning of Councilors, and now this . . ." He shook his head. "I'm having trouble keeping up."

"I know, Warnas, I know." Considering the implications of all that had transpired could wait until he knew Annika was safe. "Place your faith in the *Lady. She* guides us. And rely on the wisdom of the remaining Blade Council members until we can sort this all out."

Varian grunted. "Your people are divided," he said, so softly only he could hear. "Dissention will follow."

"Perhaps," Kalan agreed, wearily. "I'll worry about it later."

The young warrior nodded then motioned to Annika. "She'll regain her strength shortly." His tone became terse. "Her instinct will be to drain you. You have to stop feeding her the moment you begin to feel light-headed."

They both heard running footsteps out in the other room. They glanced up as Arek entered the room, the feathered carcass of a *geefan* in his hand. He drew up short as he took in the scene.

"What have you done?" Alarm lit his face.

"Saved Annika's life." Kalan met his eyes, his gaze level. "She might hate me for it once she recovers, but I'll deal with that then. Give Varian the beast."

He let Varian take over Annika's feeding once he'd prepared the substitute blood source then dealt with the wound on his wrist.

"Commander, Annika needs my help." Candra's comment came from the other side of the room. She gestured with one hand, dark gaze shining with concern. "That wound has to be sealed."

With a potential disaster averted, Kalan could feel the fury he'd kept contained begin to rise. "You and Rissa are the only healers I'll allow near Annika until she's well."

Nodding, the older woman approached. Varian discarded the drained carcass and Kalan carefully laid Annika down on the floor, his mouth tightening when he saw that her eyes were closed again.

"She'll sleep now," the *Na'Chi* warrior murmured. "It'll help her heal faster."

They made more room for Candra as she began treating Annika but Kalan made sure he kept hold of her hand, unable to stand being separated from her just yet. His gaze shifted to Arek. He couldn't keep the growl from his voice.

"No one will enter my apartments unless you sanction their visit. I'll not see Annika harmed again." His gaze swept the room, hard and uncompromising. "The other *Na'Chi*, all forty-seven of them are being granted sanctuary within human territory. I expect you to consult with the *Temple Elect*. She'll compose the announcement that I expect to be delivered to every crofter, village, and Outpost."

A few shared, startled gazes at his sweeping order but no one said anything.

He turned to look at Varian. "Will you trust Kymora to accompany you to bring the *Na'Chi* to Sacred Lake?"

The young scout regarded him gravely for several, long heartbeats as he considered his question. "If I assent, we reserve the right to defend ourselves against anyone who threatens us."

"Agreed." Arek stirred but Kalan quelled him with a glare. "Take a good look at Annika, Second. Put aside your dislike and ask yourself if she deserved this. Davyn's actions have proven that he, and others who share his views, threaten the *Na'Chi*."

His friend reluctantly inclined his head. "I'll arrange for one of the storage buildings within the compound to be cleared and made into a dormitory for them."

"And I'll protect Kymora with my life as we bring back the others." Varian's solemn promise was reflected in his gaze.

"You all have your tasks." Kalan received murmurs of assent and the room emptied quickly until only a few Light Blades, Arek, Candra, Annika, and himself remained. The Master Healer's expression was grim. A frisson of fear licked the length of his spine. "Candra? Is something wrong?"

"I've used my Gift to seal the wound but Davyn's blade went deep." The woman finished tying off a new bandage around her shoulder. "Annika's lost a lot of blood."

She gently turned Annika's head to reveal the scalp wounds and swollen knots on her skull then lifted the sleeve of her dress to show him one of her forearms. Kalan winced at the teeth marks, torn flesh, and bruises marring her skin.

"I believe she did all this to herself to fight the hunger," Candra said, quietly. "If she hadn't, Rissa would probably be dead."

He released a shaky breath. Annika's courage and strength continued to astound him. "How is the child?"

"I'm fine, *Chosen*." The young girl's voice came from behind him. He turned to see Rissa standing next to Arek, her small face pinched with worry. "Is she going to be all right, Master Healer?"

"With rest, she'll recover."

The frown on Rissa's face cleared. "Good." She glanced to him, her gaze direct. "There's just one thing I don't understand."

"What's that?" he asked gently.

Her lips pursed and she lifted her arm to point at one of the walls in the room. "Why does Councilor Davyn have a picture-weaving of Annika in his apartment?"

Chapter 27

ANNIKA didn't want to wake. Instinct warned her that rousing would be unpleasant. A memory hovered in the darkness between the drowsiness of sleep and alertness. Her body urged her to remain warm and at peace but she could hear voices talking, one in an elevated tone, both some distance away.

She was aware of the softness of a bed beneath her and a thick blanket tucked under her chin. Her body felt heavy and, for a while, she drifted in and out of sleep but the nagging memory and sound of voices kept rousing her.

Inhaling deeply, she grunted as the muscles along her neck and shoulder protested. She cracked her eyes open. The only light came from a brazier on the wall but its soft glow made her eyeballs ache and throb. She grimaced. Blinking, she discovered that she lay in Kalan's bed.

"Good, you're awake." The whisper came from her left. "Kalan's been worried."

Turning her head slowly, Annika saw a fatigued looking woman sitting in a chair beside the bed. Her name slowly emerged from the fuzziness in her head. "Candra?"

"Easy, don't move yet. Let me help you." The bed dipped as the older woman climbed onto it to help her rise.

Annika's breath caught as the action of being propped on pillows sent pain ricocheting from her shoulder throughout her body. As Candra untangled the soft-worn nightshirt from around her, her memory came flooding back. A wave of ice slid through her. "*Lady's Breath*, did I hurt Rissa?"

"It's all right, Annika, she's fine."

She sighed. "How long have I been asleep?"

"Nearly four days."

She stared at Candra, trying to make sense of the jumble of vague images and hazy recollections in her mind.

"You lost a lot of blood. Don't be surprised if your recovery takes a little time." With a smile, Candra tucked the blanket over her lap then raised her voice. "Kalan!"

The sound of the voices stopped. Rapid footsteps sounded outside the room then a tall figure appeared in the doorway. Annika's breath hitched again and warmth spread throughout her at the sight of him standing there.

Gone were the fine, velvety clothes of the *Chosen*. Instead he wore black leather breeches and the body armor of a warrior, his lean, muscular arms bare. Around his throat he wore the *Lady's* amulet. The ambient light caught on the sun symbol as he entered the room.

He looked so weary, so exhausted, but with his long, dark hair drawn back into a ponytail it lent a severe look to his unshaven face. His aura seemed dangerous, lethal, something she hadn't seen since their escape from the fortress.

Kalan stared at her in the flickering light, then joy and relief filled his face, and in three strides he was kneeling at her bedside. His arms went around her and he buried his head against her chest. She ran a hand over his bowed head, her throat tightening as she felt him tremble.

"Thank the *Lady* you're all right." His voice cracked then he lifted his head to stare at her, his tired, green eyes glittering. "How do you feel?"

"Sore, a little weak, but all right." Her smile shook as she tried to reassure him. Inhaling a ragged breath, she fought the urge to look away and kept her gaze on him.

The knowledge that Kalan had seen her dark side made her more than a little uncomfortable but the emotion wasn't as intense as she expected. His touch, the expression on his face, the look in his eyes eased her fears.

She stroked a hand across his rough cheek. "Thank you for finding us in time."

Something shadowed flickered through his gaze and he swallowed hard. He took her hands in his and pressed a kiss to her fingertips. "Forgive me. I was weak."

"I don't understand."

"I forced you to feed from me." He showed her his wrist and the newly healed-over wound.

A tingle of shock shot through her. The blood addiction scared her, there was no denying it but the thought of relying on him for her survival wasn't as frightening as she thought it would be.

She searched her memory. "I don't remember anything after you and someone else stopped me attacking Rissa—"

"You didn't want to feed from me, but I made you do it anyway," he admitted, his mouth pulling down at the corners then he closed his eyes. "You hold my heart. I love you, Annika. I couldn't bear losing you."

He loved her?

The words stuck in her mind, repeating themselves over and over. She raised an unsteady hand to his face, her fingertips brushed his cheek. Emerald green eyes opened and blazed with a fierce heat and an intensity that burrowed deep, lighting all the dark places, warming her soul.

Her heart contracted. For the first time in her life, she was something special to someone. She pressed her forehead against his, her breath hitching. Tears burned in her throat and she began to shake.

"Kalan . . ." Heat raced through her quickly followed by a chill. *Merciful Mother,* did he expect her to tell him how she felt when she didn't know? "I . . . don't . . ."

One side of Kalan's mouth curved upward. He knew. "Only when you're ready, Annika."

Her cheeks flamed. Annika bit her lip and glanced at Candra. A wide grin split the healer's face. Over by the door Arek stood stiffly with his arms folded, the flesh over his cheekbones pulled tight. His blue eyes pierced hers as his lips thinned in disapproval.

"This is between us, Annika." Kalan's arms tightened around her, drawing her attention back to him. "This is our Journey. Not theirs."

"The *Lady* doesn't always provide clear paths for us to tread but with *Her* guidance we'll make it. You told me that once." Her whispered words drew another smile from him. "I'm not alone." She sent a swift prayer heavenward, grateful for his patience. "As for forgiveness for making me feed from you, there's no need to ask for any. I don't blame you for saving my life."

Kalan's embrace grew tighter as profound relief eased the crinkles of stress around his eyes. She lay her fingertips over his curved lips.

"Candra tells me I've been asleep for four days," she said and tugged him to his feet. "Why are you dressed in warrior leathers? What's happened in that time?"

His leather breeches creaked quietly as he climbed into the bed behind her and tucked her in against him, using the solid warmth of his body as support. His arms went around her, as if he couldn't bear not to be touching her in some way. While his demonstration of affection felt odd, especially in front of the others, she liked the security of sitting between his legs, her back pressed against his broad chest.

"There's so much to tell you," he said, entwining his fingers with hers. "Candra, I don't want to wear her out. Is it all right to talk?"

"As long as she tells us when she gets tired." The woman took her own seat and Arek moved to the foot of the bed and sat on one corner.

Annika listened as each told of the events that had transpired from the time when she and Kalan had parted in the marketplace. The disclosure of what Arek had found in the journal and the corruption of the Blade Council astounded her. To think humans and demons had once lived together was shocking.

In part, Davyn had been right to predict Savyr's reaction to such information. The *Na'Reish* bordered on fanatical when it came to matters of bloodline purity. As did some humans, she thought wryly.

Kalan stroked her wrists with his thumbs as he told her about Hesia, Varian, and the other *Na'Chi*. His touch grounded her as a wave of intense emotion overwhelmed her. She didn't know whether to cry or laugh.

"Hesia didn't kill the *Na'Chi* babies?" He shook his head. "Thank the Mother of Mercy . . ." Her voice caught. She dragged in several deep breaths. "Where are they now?"

"In the compound." Kalan's voice was a gentle rumble inside his chest. His hand cupped the back of her head and pressed a kiss to her forehead. "Light Blades and *Na'Chi* alike are watching each other warily. It's going to take time for everyone to get used to one another. Kymora and some of the other Servants have moved into their makeshift barrack to help ease the tension."

"The children are leading the way in making new friendships," Candra said dryly. "Rissa's been visiting them since they arrived and she's dragged several of her friends with her. The children from both races are playing in the garden as we speak."

Annika issued a shaky laugh. "When can I meet them?"

Candra lifted an eyebrow and gave her her best Master Healer's stare. "Not today. Maybe tomorrow, *if* you rest and eat well."

"There's one more thing you should know . . ." Kalan's strange, neutral tone alerted her to a subtle tension that had been growing in the room since the revelation that the *Na'Chi* weren't the bloodborn disgrace either race believed them to be. "Arek, would you go and get the wall hanging?"

She frowned. "Wall hanging?"

The blond warrior left the room without saying a word, returning a few moments later. In his hands was a rolled-up piece of woven cloth. His face was a stony mask; only his eyes showed any sort of emotion and she found it hard to interpret. She glanced to Kalan then Candra, uneasy with the strain she could feel radiating from Kalan's Second.

"What's wrong?" she asked.

Kalan nodded to Arek and gripped her hand more securely. "Show her."

The skin around the Light Blade's eyes tightened then he unfurled the hanging like a blanket across the bed. Annika gasped as the picture was revealed. Blue eyes as bright as glacial ice stared at her from the visage of a woman who bore the same facial features she'd seen reflected in the mirror during the last twenty-five years.

"That's me! But her eyes, they're blue . . . and there's no marking on her face—" Confused, she reached out to touch the pale cheek of the portrait then left her hand hovering over the fabric as doubt gnawed at her stomach. "Who is she?"

"My mother, Jarella . . ." Arek's voice was hoarse. Annika's head snapped up at the brittle sound of it. She sucked in a sudden breath at the tormented expression on his face. A muscle ticked in his jaw. "Our . . . mother . . ."

Her jaw loosened.

"Jarella was Davyn's daughter," Kalan said softly. "Arek was three when she was taken by Savyr. Too young to remember, he never knew what she looked like and Davyn never let him see this hanging. We found it in the room where you and Rissa were imprisoned."

"I'm her daughter?" Annika's hand shook as she touched her mother's face, and wished the rough texture felt more like skin. A tear slid down her cheek. She swallowed hard. "Davyn knew this? And he still tried to kill me?"

Candra issued a low-pitched sound of disgust. "It was Yance who revealed the truth. Davyn refused to speak. Being two of the eldest surviving Light Blades, they knew who you were the moment they saw you. Yance remembered Jarella from the days when he trained her as a warrior.

"Setting you up to kill Rissa was Davyn's insane attempt to cover the truth and erase the family shame before others recognized Jarella in you. If there was no reminder of his perceived shame he could go on living the lies he'd told so many others."

Kalan watched a myriad of emotions flicker across Annika's face as she struggled to comprehend the facts in a situation none of them had a hope of ever fully understanding. It hurt to see her cry but he was glad he could offer her the comfort of his presence because no words would reassure her.

He glanced over at Arek, and winced inwardly at the tortured expression on his friend's face. The last four days hadn't been easy for him. For almost thirty years he'd grown up resenting the loss of his mother, adopted many of his grandfather's beliefs and much of his hatred for the *Na'Reish*, and now he was faced with the tangled puzzle of figuring out how to cope with having a younger, half-blood sister. One he'd hated from the moment he'd first seen her.

Annika stiffened in his arms and he heard the soft catch of her breath. He watched her steal a glance at Arek and knew she'd made the same realization. But before she could say anything, Arek turned on his boot heel and disappeared from the room.

"Arek!" Candra called and she started after him, her brow creased in concern. They all heard the outer apartment door slam shut.

"Let him go." Annika's soft plea stopped the other woman's pursuit. "This has to come as quite a shock. I know I hardly believe it."

"How I'd love to have just five minutes alone with Davyn," Candra hissed, her dark eyes flashing. "His hatred has infected too many lives."

Kalan met her gaze, his own anger tightly restrained. "He'll be judged for his actions, be assured of that."

The woman let out a short sigh and shook her head. "I don't envy you your position, Kalan. The days ahead will be tough. A new Blade Council should be appointed as soon as possible. Reports are already coming in of unrest and turmoil among our people. They need strong guidance and leadership to erase the instability brought about by Davyn's and the others' actions."

"I know. Over the last few days, I've been busy reassuring and explaining the situation among our own warriors." Annika stroked his arm, the simple action easing his frustration. "Some have left the Barracks and returned home." He pressed an apologetic kiss to Annika's cheek before he spoke his next words. "They refuse to live or serve alongside the *Na'Chi*."

Candra's troubled gaze locked with his. "Whatever decisions you make, *Chosen*, present them sooner rather than later. The more time our people have to worry, the more likely unpleasantness will occur."

She excused herself then to return to her duties at the hospice and left them with instructions to call her if they needed her. Kalan was content to hold Annika in his arms, aware that she was beginning to flag. The emotional toll had wearied her.

"I should leave you to rest," he murmured.

"Would you stay with me?"

Her plea warmed his heart. "Let me take off this armor and I'll join you." After setting it aside, he stripped, aware that she watched him through sleepy eyes. The soft smile on her face was for him as he settled alongside her under the covers and she snuggled in against his side.

He listened to her breathing slowly even out and, while he was just as exhausted as her, having not slept more than a few hours each. night since the attack, his mind wouldn't settle. Candra's valid comments kept replaying in his head.

"I can hear you thinking, Kalan," Annika murmured, her words slurring. "You need to sleep. Dedicate your worries to the *Lady* and close your eyes. You can deal with them tomorrow."

He chuckled and did as she asked, also thanking the *Lady* for Annika's indomitable strength. Tomorrow was indeed soon enough to plan and consider the options available. He'd need a clear head and sharp wits if he wanted to avert civil unrest. War between his people would be catastrophic if the *Na'Reish* chose to attack.

Annika's hand lay over his heart and he placed his on top of hers, finally able to relax, and in between one breath and the next he fell asleep.

Chapter 28

V ARIAN listened to the squeals of laughter from the children, human and *Na'Chi* alike, coming from the garden and the infectious sound curved his lips into a small, rare smile. In the few days they'd been there the youngsters had learned it was all right to make that amount of noise and he'd never seen them laugh out loud so much. He leant against the tall rock at his back and cast his gaze around the compound as he heard the familiar *tap-tap-tapping* of a staff on pavement coming from his left.

"Are you coming to join the others for noon-meal?" Kymora's melodic voice grazed his hearing and brushed like a caress across his nerves. "Some of the Councilors' families are joining us today."

"In a little while," he replied, wondering how she'd known where to find him amidst all the noise. Behind him he could hear the Light Blades training, as they did this time every day. Conversations came from several directions and, over by the hospice, a supply cart from the city delivered barrels and crates. The people unloading them were not particularly gentle.

Kymora's staff drew level with him and he deliberately stretched out a leg so that it hit his boot. Her delicate eyebrows rose. "You do know it's rude to trip a blind person. Once you spoke I knew exactly where you were."

He snorted. "You wouldn't have fallen. For someone without sight you're remarkably coordinated and agile. I've also seen you train with that staff."

"Have you been spying on me?" She wagged a finger at him and a teasing smile lifted the corners of her mouth. "Where were you this time?"

"On the wall running around the back of the *Chosen*'s apartment closest to the temple. It makes a good lookout." He liked how the sun lit her long, dark hair. Today she'd left it free and it fell around her face in gentle waves. "You're quite skilled with that staff. I'm glad you didn't use it on me the day we met."

This time both her eyebrows rose. "Two compliments in one day." She stepped closer and her light, florally scent teased his nose as her expression grew more somber. "You seem constantly surprised by my skills . . ."

The enjoyment he received from their conversations continued to startle him. They were as direct and straightforward as the ones he had with Lisella. He quite liked talking with Kymora, probably more than was prudent.

Her not so subtle query had him considering how to answer without offending her. "Physical deformities are frowned upon," he said, gently.

"By whom? The *Na'Reish*? The *Na'Chi*?"

"Both."

Her head tilted as she considered his answer. "Your tone was clipped, short. Did my question bother you?"

Varian grimaced. She was also superb at reading people's voices, much the same as he picked up on facial expressions and scents. "I know what it's like to have people judge you."

"You're not just referring to your *Na'Chi* markings are you?"

"You don't remember, do you?" Stepping toward her Varian took her hand and placed it on his jaw. Her soft touch tingled as she traced the scar on his skin. "I received this in a fight against a *Na'Reish* guard. It never healed cleanly."

Kymora's sightless green eyes blinked and a frown pulled her brow down low. "The *Na'Chi* judge you because of this?"

"We've inherited a few of the more unsavory personality traits of our parents."

"Is that why you choose to stand in our memorial garden alone?"

"Memorial garden?"

She nodded and waved a hand at the rock behind him. "There are names carved into the rocks behind you. They're the Light Blade warriors who've died in the war against the *Na'Reish*."

Varian wondered if that explained the unhappy looks he'd received from several humans as they'd passed him on the way to the temple or *Chosen*'s apartments. He'd interpreted them as looks of disgust for what he was, not because he'd been using the stones as a convenient place to lean, and ignored them. Warmth flushed his cheeks.

"I didn't mean any disrespect." His words were stiff. "I didn't know—"

"It's all right. Annika didn't know either." Kymora's hand slid to his shoulder then along his arm until her hand grasped his. He wanted to draw away from her but found he couldn't. She seemed to enjoy invading his personal space and wondered if she did it deliberately. "You don't like mixing with others, do you?"

The *Na'Chi* had learned not to bother him but she poked and prodded and pushed his limits every time they met.

"You prefer it," he retorted. "Much like Lisella."

"You still haven't answered my question."

"What's wrong with a little solitude?"

"Nothing. I spend a portion of my day in quiet reflection. It helps calm the mind, gives me time to gather my thoughts, but I don't deliberately spend hours alone."

"Are you saying that I do?" He found it hard to inject any anger into his voice.

She issued a soft chuckle. "You know you do."

"So? Perhaps I'm more discriminatory about whom I mix with."

Her chuckle turned into a laugh as if she truly took pleasure in their debate. "You seek out Lisella, one of the younger scouts, and you enjoy the company of the children but very few others."

"Now who's been spying on someone?"

"I like to listen." Kymora flashed him an impish grin that he felt right to his toes. He blinked at the image of him kissing her smile from her face. It came from out of nowhere and left him at a loss for words. "Are you ready to come to noon-meal yet?"

Varian shook his head, unsure if he was protesting his attraction to the human woman or at the desire for him to accompany her to the meal. "You're not going to give up and leave me be, are you?" His tone was a little gruffer than he'd intended.

Her smile faltered. "I will if that's what you want, Varian." She let his hand go and gripped her staff, her face resuming its usual polite look; the expression she reserved for her meetings with the Blade Council. "I'm sorry. I didn't mean to make you feel uncomfortable."

Varian cursed himself for his abruptness, not liking the absence of her warmth but he'd brought this on himself. He raked a hand through his braids, uncomfortable now in the silence between them. He had no idea what to say to reestablish the rapport he'd come to expect and like with her. But when her staff moved so did he, before he even realized he was going to stop her leaving. He gently pried the wooden staff from her fingers then tucked one of her hands into the crook of his arm. His heart beat faster at the startled look on her face.

"I'd rather sit at the end of a table." Varian didn't know whether his voice shook with the anticipated nervousness of being among so many people or because he was afraid of how she'd respond to his rudeness.

"You truly don't have to go to this if you don't want to, Varian." Her fingers tightened on his arm. "I don't want you to come because you feel guilty for snapping at me. I shouldn't have pushed you like I did. We could have noon-meal at the temple kitchen if you like."

Her words eased the rapid beat of his pulse. He heard Lisella calling the children to noon-meal. "I don't know why you put up with me," he muttered.

"It's part of my job," she replied with a gentle smile. Her other hand patted his forearm when he tensed. Her voice softened. "It's also because you're my friend."

He searched Kymora's face for any sign of untruth then inhaled to test her scent. Her floral scent was deeper, stronger. Her sincerity was genuine. The tension inside him lessened and the warm sensation that replaced it left him feeling uncertain.

"It's not easy letting others in, Kymora," he said quietly. Lisella turned in his direction and he waved to indicate they were coming. "I'm not a people person. Circumstances have never fostered the level of trust needed to form that sort of bond. I let very few people close to me but, with you, I'm willing to try."

Her smile returned. "*Lady* willing you'll succeed." He grunted. "And we'll work on your faith while we're at it."

His lips twitched. "You've definitely been speaking to Lisella," he said dryly.

She laughed softly but didn't reply. Varian kept their pace steady and they headed to the Barracks for noon-meal.

KALAN felt Annika move closer to him as she entered the building that had been converted into a dormitory for the *Na'Chi*. He heard her sudden intake of breath and knew her excitement at meeting them had changed to nervousness. Scattered around the room, some in groups, others seated on their pallet beds occupied with tasks, the *Na'Chi* went about their nightly routines with quiet efficiency.

It was one of the first traits he'd picked up during his many visits here. Very few loud noises were made. No raised voices, conversations were kept low-pitched, children played. Smiles were present but laughter was rare. Even moving around the room was done on silent feet, children included. When he'd questioned Varian about it, he'd learned that the habits were ingrained from a very young age. After living under the noses of the *Na'Reish*, the behavior was second nature.

Barely a step inside the doorway, Kalan watched as three young men moved to block their path and several others took up flanking positions. While none were overtly hostile, all were alert, their stances indicating they were ready to react if the need arose. It was a move he'd seen them use outside in the compound many times.

"*Chosen*, welcome."

Varian's deep-voiced greeting seemed to be an indication to the others to stand down. They stepped back and resumed whatever they'd been doing when they'd arrived but their watchful gazes never eased. Their discipline impressed him and was part of the reason he'd brought Annika for a visit. She'd been keen to meet her people and he wanted to speak to Varian about a matter he hoped would benefit both races.

"Annika, it's so good to finally meet you." A woman with long, dark hair accompanied him. Her smile was warm and he felt Annika's tight grip on his hand ease. "I'm Lisella. Please, come in and join us. I've just put on a kettle for an herbal tea."

Annika's gaze flickered to him, an eyebrow raised in question.

"Go on, I'll join you in a moment," he said, with a smile. "I need to speak to Varian. Shouldn't take long."

Kalan watched as Lisella took charge and hustled her farther into the building, her light chatter putting Annika at ease. Introductions were made and a small group gathered around the open fire pit to share tea and talk.

"You wanted to discuss something with me?" Varian asked, his quiet tone drawing Kalan's attention back to him.

Kalan nodded. "I'd like the *Na'Chi* to join us for our training sessions."

"Is it a wise move? Our presence here is tolerated. I doubt many of your warriors have had the time to accept us yet."

"It's a calculated risk," he conceded. "It'll probably mean a few tense encounters but if it works then it'll help ease fears out in the city and farther afield." He'd thought hard about how to best integrate the two races. Defending themselves against a common enemy was a good start. "I'm not saying hundreds of years of hatred can be wiped away overnight but mistakes can be reconciled if there are willing people."

The young *Na'Chi* grunted. "Kymora tells me you've been in meetings all day with village leaders. Hearing that your history was altered has to be unsettling."

"There has been significant unrest." He'd spent many hours defusing volatile situations but he hadn't let those meeting with him hide from the truth.

"And the new Blade Council?"

"I've approached three possible replacements for Davyn, Corvas, and Yance and also two of the Guild-leaders. The new Blade Council should be inducted in the next couple of days if the *Lady* approves."

"Will your people accept the changes?"

"In time. The *Lady* will guide us."

He issued a disbelieving grunt. "How can you place hope in something you cannot control?"

Kymora had mentioned the *Na'Chi* scout's reservations concerning the *Lady*. "What other alternative do I have? There are limits to what I can do. The rest I leave to *Her*."

Varian said nothing more for a while and Kalan took the time to glance around the room for Annika. The group of *Na'Chi* seated at the fire had grown to include children. Whatever she was telling them had them all captivated. Her gaze lifted as if she'd sensed him watching her. While her smile warmed him, he realized that this was the first time he'd seen her so relaxed and content. It caught him off guard.

"*Chosen*." Varian's use of his title distracted him. The hint of tension refocused his interest on the scout. "I don't wish to offend but I need to speak plainly."

"Call me Kalan," he said. "Titles outside the chamber are unnecessary."

The man inclined his head then hesitated and the obvious sign of unease was surprising considering he'd grown used to the scout's stoic personality. "I find it . . . unusual that you would so freely speak of your plans to us—"

"As opposed to the *Na'Reish* style of doing things?" Varian nodded. "Open communication is important to me. How else can I show my trust in others if I hide something from them?"

For a long moment violet eyes regarded him with solemn contemplation then Varian nodded as if he'd reached a decision about something. "How long will we live within the compound?"

"You don't like it here?"

"It's not a matter of liking it." A slight frown marred his brow. "I understand the need for our two races to adjust to one another. The protection you offer us is essential but the surroundings and scrutiny is daunting for some."

"Coming from almost total isolation to coping with so many has to be hard."

"Yes." Relief flashed briefly across the young *Na'Chi*'s face. "I'm worried the stress of adjusting might prove too much for some and misunderstandings may occur. That would only harm our cause. Is there a place we can go outside the city?"

The issue was something he hadn't anticipated. "I'll see what can be done," he promised. "I'll discuss it at the next Council meeting and have a solution for you in less than a week."

"Thank you."

Annika's soft laughter drew his attention away from Varian. Again he was struck by the peaceful expression on her face. She'd truly relaxed among the *Na'Chi*. Even while living with him there'd been an air of cautiousness about her, as if she was unsure of her place in his world. Here she held no doubt and he discovered that disturbed him.

The longer he watched her interacting with the others, the more he recognized the emotion growing inside him. Jealousy. She hadn't found complete happiness with him, among her mother's people, yet in less than an hour she was as comfortable here as if she'd lived with them all her life.

For a heartbeat he regretted bringing her here tonight and then flushed at the thought. His negative emotions were unjust but, if he was honest with himself, he couldn't suppress them as easily as he wanted to.

A shiver skittered along his spine as another thought arose from the darker side of his mind.

If the *Na'Chi* left the city, would she want to go with them?

Chapter 29

ANNIKA finally gave up her practice of writing words and glanced at the balcony door of the apartment for the fifth time in less than an hour. Since returning from their visit to the *Na'Chi* Kalan had been quiet and withdrawn. She'd put it down to weariness but then he'd disappeared outside. Without his cloak.

Shifting in her chair, she chewed on the end of her pencil and stared at the wooden door. The quiet crackling of the flames in the fireplace and the cozy warmth in the room highlighted the fact he was standing out there with little protection from the elements.

Was he worrying about the reports of unrest coming in daily from his Commanders? Since riders had delivered the message about the Blade Council's corruption and deceit he'd been inundated with meetings with village leaders who'd traveled to Sacred Lake to confirm what they'd heard. That coupled with Light Blades leaving the compound had to be playing on his mind.

While he hadn't told her about what was going on, claiming she needed to focus on regaining her strength, others had. With a sigh,

Annika placed the pencil down and closed her journal. It didn't help knowing that her arrival had been its genesis. Kymora's reminders that the *Lady* had foretold her arrival, along with the other *Na'Chi*, helped but it still didn't sit well that Kalan now dealt with the ramifications.

She rose and stretched out the kinks in her spine. The muscles in her newly healed shoulder pulled. A reminder of another problem only Kalan could help her sort out.

Throwing on her cloak, and after grabbing his, she joined him on the balcony. The clear, moonlit night and bracing cold made her wonder how he'd lasted outside for so long without it. His hands spread wide, his tall form stood leaning against the wall overlooking the compound.

"I know Light Blades are supposed to be tough but isn't this a bit extreme?" she asked stepping up alongside him.

His somber expression didn't change at her attempt at humor but he accepted his cloak with a nod. "Thank you."

His cold-stiffened fingers fumbled with the tie so she took over. "You should come inside." Moving closer, she took his ice-cold hands in hers and tucked them in against her body under her cloak. Their frosted breaths mingled. "Why are you standing out here freezing?"

"I needed to think."

"About what?" She relaxed a little as he cradled her against him. His scent surrounded her, all earthy male and winter's breath, and with their shared body warmth it didn't seem as cold.

"The *Na'Chi* want to leave the city." His quiet statement seemed hesitant. "Varian's worried some of your people are having trouble coping with living here."

Annika nodded, her cheek brushing against his chest. "I know. Lisella mentioned the same thing tonight. The children seem to be adapting easier."

"There are caverns in the foothills of the mountains on the other side of the lake." He turned in that direction so that she could see the darkened mountain range beyond the city wall. "It's isolated enough to suit the *Na'Chi*. They wouldn't have to worry about crofters intruding because of the geography. With enough supplies they could live there."

"Didn't you want them to begin training with your warriors?"

"Yes. It's only a few hours' walk from the city so they could return here on foot or we could visit them." He took a deeper breath. "If the *Na'Chi* leave the city, I was thinking of sending some of my warriors to live with them. Varian and his scouts have skills we could benefit from learning. I'd also like to establish an alliance between the *Na'Chi* and us. This would be a good way to start."

Annika liked that he was willing to discuss his thoughts with her. "Perhaps you could begin with an exchange of warriors and ideas. If you send some of your Light Blades with them, why not a few of your healers and crafters?"

He grunted. "Kymora and some of her Servants already live with the *Na'Chi*. It wouldn't be much of a stretch to take that idea further."

She warmed to his plan. "Tell the Light Blades and the others what you hope to achieve then ask for volunteers to go with the *Na'Chi*. Someone keen to learn will accept the idea more readily than someone forced to go."

"Maybe they can go for a few months to start with," he murmured. "Then they can return to train others. If it's successful we'll send more . . . yes, it could work."

Through their shared touch Annika could feel the tension leaving Kalan's body. She smothered a yawn and wondered what it would take to convince him indoors.

His arms tightened around her. "You should rest."

"I will." She glanced up at him. "If you do, too."

His brows drew down low and his fingers cupped her chin. "When were you going to tell me about your hunger?"

She pulled back from him slightly, her cheeks heating. "It was why I came out here."

"I wish I could give you back your independence." Kalan's statement made her stomach clench, more out of uncertainty than hunger. He sounded like he regretted his action of making her feed from him back in Davyn's apartment.

"I only need a little . . ." Annika glanced away, across the compound, wishing she could recall the time she'd first fed from him but her memory still hadn't returned. "I'm sorry. I won't trouble you for long."

The heat in her cheeks intensified and goose bumps broke out all over her. Kalan caught her face between his hands. His dark gaze locked with her and his lips thinned as if he'd confirmed something by looking at her.

"Annika, I made the choice to feed you freely. I don't regret it. I was merely implying that I wish I'd been the one addicted, not you. You're never to be ashamed of needing to feed from me, do you understand?" Low-pitched, hard-voiced exasperation filled his words. The sincerity and conviction in them shook her. "I won't go through the experience of losing you again."

No human will ever let you drink from his or her vein willingly. If you want to survive you have to take what you want. Savyr's fierce demeanor as he'd held her by the neck and forced her to look at the body of the human boy she'd killed still had the power to make Annika shiver. Her tears had earned his disgust but that had been nothing compared to the shame she'd felt for being *Na'Chi.*

For so many years she'd been reviled, and now, here was a man who understood. Kalan's gift of love and acceptance was worth a lifetime of addiction to him. The unconditional acceptance she saw in his gaze left her with a strange, freeing joy and it gave her the courage to face the memories of her past and shove them down where they belonged—the back of her mind.

Letting Savyr's hatred and anger make her feel less than worthy would always haunt her but Kalan's love would help combat it. It didn't make the nerves in her stomach any easier to squash but she could say the words in her mind out loud without cringing. "I need you, Kalan."

A slow smile lit his face. "I'll always be here for you." He tugged a lock of her hair. "Let's go inside where it's warm. I've had enough of the cold."

Once inside he helped her out of her cloak, shed his then pulled her in close to him. The hard feel of his body against hers, and the faint throb of his pulse at the base of his neck stroked both hungers. She swallowed hard then shivered as a spiral of need curled deep in her, tightening so fast it bordered on painful.

"So, how do you want to go about this?" he asked. "In here, or in the bedroom?"

She detected a sudden increase of heated spice in the air surrounding them and stared up at him in surprise. He steered her toward the bedroom, making the decision for her. "This . . . excites you?"

His smile turned into a wicked grin. "Your mouth on me anywhere excites me, *Na'Chi*."

Her pulse leapt at the way he drawled her name. She let herself be drawn into his room. He lit the single brazier. "Wouldn't you prefer I do this in the dark?"

"I can handle watching you feed, Annika."

She blinked as he stripped out of his shirt. "But—" He stepped toward her and cut off her protest with a kiss. The unexpected dominance of his action thrilled her. He was neither gentle nor rough, just demanding. The pressure of his lips and the way his tongue teased then thrust into her mouth ignited her desire like a striker placed to dry tinder.

Annika's soft groan and the way she melted against him gave Kalan immense satisfaction. That she'd been hesitant to approach him to discuss her need and now her obvious anxiety over feeding from him tore him up inside. Kissing her had been his only solution. But if he worked this right, the experience would be pleasurable for both of them.

He backed toward the bed, drawing her with him, never breaking the kiss. He felt the edge of it behind his legs and slowly eased them both down onto it. The delicious weight of her lying on top of him had him hard in a heartbeat. The softness of her breasts pushed against his chest with her every breath. The curve of her hips fit in perfect alignment with his and the way she writhed against him brought him close to the edge.

"Slow down." He caught her bottom lip between his teeth, gently nipped it then threaded his hands through her hair, loving how the soft strands slid through his fingers. "We've all night."

Her eyelids lifted slowly and the blue within her hungry gaze only became darker as she scowled at him. "You started this, Light Blade."

He chuckled and slid one hand along her body until he reached her thigh then, keeping his gaze locked with hers, he pulled the hem of her dress slowly upward. His fingertips grazed the softness of bare skin as he drew the material up over the curved swell of her buttocks. Annika's pupils dilated then her eyelids fluttered shut. Using both hands he gripped then kneaded her flesh, pushing her hard against his erection. She gasped and her fingers dug into the muscles of his shoulders.

"Kalan, I need more . . ." Her hissed admission then the unconscious undulation of her hips against his wrenched a groan from the back of his throat. The scent of her filled his head as he inhaled. Hot musk.

In less than a minute he threw their boots and clothes onto the floor and they were skin to skin. Annika still straddled him, a shy smile on her face as she settled herself over him. She clasped his hand in hers and took it to where her softness was pressed against him.

Bare flesh parted and his heart thumped erratically as her wetness coated his fingers.

"I like the feel of you here." Her husky whisper deepened as her fingers trailed over his length, her touch feather light, a torment and a pleasure. "There's an ache, a burning tightness that gets hotter when I think of you filling me here."

Her eyes widened as he delicately parted her folds and pushed himself inside her. She shuddered, her eyes closing. Kalan ground his teeth together as her inner muscles clasped him hard. Nothing could ever compare to how her body responded to him. He loved her uninhibited response.

His hand shook as he reached for the dagger he'd set aside as he'd undressed. With a flick of his wrist he sliced the fleshy part of his thumb and returned the blade to its sheath.

He felt Annika stiffen and glanced up to discover her just sitting there, her eyes closed tight. Her nostrils flared and he knew she could smell the blood trickling from his thumb.

"It's all right."

"No, it's not." He saw her swallow hard and ached as she shook her head. "I can't do that now, Kalan."

"Why not?" he asked, quietly, wishing she'd open her eyes. They both needed to experience this together. He wanted to erase the last of her doubt and fear. Was he pushing too hard? He hoped not.

She let out a sharp, ragged breath and finally opened her eyes. The violet color was gone, obscured by the red of hunger, flecked with blue. "I don't want it to spoil what we share . . . there's no intimacy."

"Is that a challenge?"

The thought of proving her wrong heightened Kalan's desire. He lifted his hips and drove himself deeper inside her. She cried out and he took great satisfaction in the way her muscles grasped him then released. He did it again, liking the way she trembled. A slow smile spread across his face.

"That's pleasure, *Na'Chi*, and until you feed from me you'll never know whether there's any intimacy." He stilled, wanting her to make the choice to continue. "You mightn't have any memory of before, but I remember the rush of heat inside me when you fed and I know it'll be the most intimate, most erotic thing we can share."

The sight of Kalan's defined muscles straining as he held himself in check, his cheeks flushed with desire, the hard thickness of him inside her body, proved almost irresistible. Annika swallowed hard, too aware of his scent; a combination of molten spice and the metallic odor of his blood flooded her senses.

He wouldn't force her to feed from him. The choice was hers. He'd always given her that power.

She reached for and linked her fingers with his then lifted his hand toward her mouth. The scarlet trail of blood ran down his inner forearm and if she let it, it would reach his elbow in a matter of heartbeats. Locking her gaze with his, needing to see his reaction, she caught the trickle with the tip of her tongue and followed it to its source.

Her tongue exploded with flavor. *Lady's Breath*, he tasted so sweet. Hot and sweet. His scent and taste ran through her, and her hunger grew. She swallowed and licked her lips. The heat in Kalan's green eyes burned brighter, his long fingers tightened around hers.

"I need more." Her voice was hoarse with need. She felt him jerk inside her, and her muscles contracted around him. They both groaned softly.

"I'm all yours, Annika." Kalan's deep voice stroked her almost like a physical caress. "All you have to do is claim me."

She let herself go, giving herself permission to do as her body demanded, just this once. She fed both hungers, rocking her hips so she could feel him moving inside her and her mouth latched onto the shallow wound he'd made at the base of his thumb.

"That's it," Kalan hissed and began to push in a rhythm counterpoint to her, his desire reflected in his eyes. A shudder shook her at the feel of him buried inside her.

Annika bit into the fleshy part of his thumb, instinct driving her and she suckled hard. Hot sweetness filled her mouth and as she swallowed she swore the taste of him added fuel to the fierce burning consuming her from the inside out.

Kalan curled his fingers around the curve of her cheek, his own teeth bared as if he too felt the flames. He moved faster against her, heightening their pleasure until all she could feel was the inferno overwhelming them both.

With a swirl of her tongue over the wound, she swallowed one last time then pressed his hand to the bed next to his head. One hunger satiated, and with a need to satisfy the other, she leaned over him. It changed the angle of his thrusting and the deeper penetration made her cry out.

Kalan eased back on the force, but not the speed, of his strokes. She shivered, so close to her release, touched heart and soul by the incredible awareness this man had for her needs. The rapid thump-thump of her heart made the flames twist higher, burn brighter. Biting her lip, she smoothed a hand over his chest, and felt the pounding of his heart beneath hard, damp flesh.

She brushed her lips over his, heard the softest of groans then he kissed her. Too late she realized her mistake. Tears filled her eyes as his tongue traced her lips and darted between them to play with hers. He would taste himself and she waited for him to pull away. Annika thought her heart would stop as he groaned then deepened the kiss.

"There's nothing I don't love about you, *Na'Chi*." His guttural, whispered words sent her over the edge. White-hot pleasure tore her apart. Her head swam as she heard him cry out and felt him shudder beneath her as he spilled his seed inside her then she collapsed on top of him. Tiny shock waves drew out her release. She was so sensitive, just their ragged panting ignited them. All she could taste and feel and smell and sense was him, inside and out, touching her skin, her heart, her soul.

Kalan didn't believe she was worthless. He wasn't repulsed by her. He didn't push her away when she needed solace. He made her feel wanted and special and loved.

She would always be *Na'Chi*, neither human nor demon, yet the best of both resided within her. He'd taught her that. She still couldn't believe the way he felt about her but it was becoming easier and she was sure that if she took the time she'd discover many more heart-gifts given to her by this man. She knew without a doubt there was nothing she wouldn't do for him.

He had claimed her. Tenderness and warmth encircled her heart. It left her feeling weak yet strong at the same time. She wasn't aware of her tears, not until Kalan began kissing them from her face and brushing them away with the pads of his fingers. He made soft, soothing sounds and just held her, comforting her.

His compassion and endless love tightened her throat even further and it was a long time before the tears stopped. Then, as she calmed and her mind drifted through the myriad of new memories, she understood the strange emotion inside her.

She loved him.

Her heart beat so hard she wondered if Kalan could hear it. For long minutes she lay there in his arms, content to hold onto the incredible sense of peace and satisfaction the knowledge gave her. When Annika raised her head she found him watching her. A gentle smile curved his lips as she ran her fingers across his cheeks and stubble-roughened jaw.

"Are you all right?" He caressed the side of her face with the back of his hand.

"I love you, Kalan." Her whispered declaration shocked her as much as him. She swallowed hard and spoke in a more confident voice. "I love you."

His eyes closed and she wondered at the pained expression that flickered across his face. The intensity of his green gaze seared her when his eyes opened again. "Your love humbles me, Annika. I'm truly blessed."

Chapter 30

THE inner chamber was as full as Kalan ever remembered seeing it. Nearly sixty people had walked through the doors this morning, all invited to see the induction of the new Councilors. The Blade Council's reputation and honor had been badly damaged by Davyn and the others. The open invitation was his attempt to rebuild everyone's trust.

Light Blade Commanders and their Seconds gathered as a cohort at the back of the room. Varian, Lisella, and several other *Na'Chi* sat with Annika while small groups of crafters who worked within the compound filled the remaining seats.

Kalan seated himself at the table and it was the signal for those on either side of him to convene. Kymora took her position to his right, Candra and Benth to his left. Five empty chairs remained at the table, two more than usual and another deliberate effort to restore confidence in the Council. He hoped the gamble would pay off.

"I welcome you all to the first meeting of the new Blade Council." Kalan made sure his voice carried clearly to every corner of the room.

Conversations ceased and silence followed. *"Temple Elect*, would you please open the session with a prayer."

As Kymora began the traditional benediction, Kalan added his own petition to the *Lady* for strength and guidance. A lot rode on the issues being discussed. He wondered just how many present would realize the decisions they made today would determine their people's future.

When Kymora had finished he nodded to Benth and the silver-haired Councilor stood, a sealed parchment in hand.

"Today the Blade Council calls on the following provincial leaders to take up the responsibility of leading all our people," he said. With a flick of a thumbnail, the seal was broken and he unfolded the piece of parchment. "Rellyn Nyon."

The warrior who rose from his seat near the front of the crowd stood a head taller than those around him. He was known for his deliberate decision-making skills.

Beside him Candra made a soft sound in the back of her throat. Kalan's glance flickered to her. Her dark eyes sparkled but her expression remained serious. He wondered if it would change when she saw who else had been selected. She'd wanted younger, more energetic leaders and he'd considered that during the selection process.

"Jho Elamm." A small waiflike woman in her middle years from their southernmost province stood. Her strength lay in her connections with the outlying crofters. Benth greeted her with a nod. "Ophesius Witham."

Rising from among the Light Blade ranks, the older Commander was highly respected by warriors and city workers alike. Kalan hoped his knowledge of both communities would serve the Council well.

"The *Lady's Chosen* has also included two new tenures and these positions will be filled by members from the Guilds," Benth announced. "Master Weaver Shellana Lin and Master Trader Ilon Evel."

Both were well into their seventies but Kalan knew neither would have risen to their present positions within their own Guilds without developing the skills needed to serve as Councilors.

Benth turned to face Kymora. "Has the *Temple Elect* presented these candidates to the *Lady of Light*?"

She inclined her head. "I have and *She's* given *Her* blessing."

Kalan wasn't surprised when clapping and several cheers erupted from those gathered. All were well liked within their own communities. Each new Councilor pledged their oath to serve the *Lady* and their people with faith, integrity, and honor then took their seats at the table.

Annika was aware of Varian shifting impatiently and had to agree that most of the business discussed in the first hour was less than riveting even though Candra kept the pace of the meeting flowing.

Leaning closer to the scout she whispered, "Kalan said he wanted the new Councilors to feel comfortable in their new roles."

"If Evel was any more comfortable he'd be snoring," Varian replied dryly.

Annika glanced at the Master Trader's heavy-lidded gaze and relaxed posture then bit her lip to smother her smile.

"Councilors, I'd like to discuss an issue affecting our current situation." Kalan's opening had Annika straightening in her chair. Varian leaned forward, his gaze intense as the problems of the *Na'Chi*'s living arrangements were presented and a possible solution suggested. It drew several favorable murmurs from the new Councilors.

"You say the caverns are a distance from the nearest crofters?" Master Trader Evel inquired. "If the *Na'Chi* would feel more comfortable then I have no objection to them moving there."

"If you'll pardon me for saying so, *Chosen*," said Witham, the ex-Light Blade Commander. "Their request to move is advantageous all round. It could encourage those warriors who left to return if they knew the *Na'Chi* were settled elsewhere."

"So, it's out of mind, out of sight?" Varian murmured.

His sarcasm wasn't lost on Annika. "Kalan's not finished speaking yet."

"Regular supplies would need to be delivered to the *Na'Chi*," Kalan stated. "It would require the cooperation of some of your members, Guild-leaders."

"I'm sure some sort of arrangement could be made." Lin inclined her head but a frown creased her brow. "But I'm curious, *Chosen*, who would monitor them?"

Varian snorted, none too softly, and several heads turned in his direction. Kalan narrowed a warning glare in the young scout's direction. "The *Na'Chi* don't need monitoring, Councilor. They've been granted sanctuary."

"But . . ."

"Your question raises another point of discussion," Candra said, with the barest of smiles as she cut the new Councilor off. "We should consider an alliance with the *Na'Chi*."

There was a murmur of reaction to that statement and Annika sensed sudden tension. Scanning the faces closest to her, she discovered several wore scowls. Varian must have seen them too as his posture changed to one of coiled readiness as if he expected an attack.

"Why?" Nyon's simple question was accompanied with a folding of his brawny arms.

"They have fighting and scouting techniques that would benefit our warriors." Kalan leaned forward to meet the older man's light-eyed gaze. "Any advantage in the war with the *Na'Reish* should be welcomed."

"Agreed." The word was spoken in a deliberate manner. "But is that reason enough to suggest an alliance?"

"Not at all. Varian, you might like to address the Council on this matter." Kalan's invitation had the warrior rising from his seat in less than a heartbeat.

"The *Na'Chi* would freely teach your warriors our skills, *Chosen*." He glanced around the room. "We've spent the better part of twenty years learning how to avoid the *Na'Reish*, and to some extent, the human-slaves they kept at the fortress. Our skills are highly specialized, designed for a smaller group so that they can deal with or avoid a larger one, their age notwithstanding."

"Quite applicable considering our diminished numbers, don't you think?" Candra asked of the table in general.

"I'm proposing we send volunteers with the *Na'Chi* when they go." Kalan leant forward onto the table. "A trial exchange of sorts."

Varian spoke up. "We'd request no more than a dozen people during the initial exchange."

"Why not send as many who wanted to go?" Nyon asked. His chair creaked as he shifted his heavy weight around to speak directly to him.

"For the original reason the *Lady*'s *Chosen* has outlined. Both our peoples need time to adapt."

"You raise a valid point, *Na'Chi*," Elamm spoke up for the first time. The diminutive woman tapped a finger on the table. "Your plans are certainly ambitious, *Chosen*, but surely you can see we all need more time to get used to the idea of having the *Na'Chi* among us. Letting them all settle outside the city is a good idea but rather than rush into a hastily devised plan we should wait. Maybe in several months we could revisit this issue—"

"Nothing was said of relocating them all, Councilor Elamm," Kymora said, gently interrupting her. "Annika is staying with Kalan."

The woman shook her head, seemingly taken back by her words. "Why? Wouldn't she feel more comfortable among her own people?"

Varian's soft chuckle wasn't pleasant. His violet eyes flashed black as he met Annika's gaze. "And now we see their true colors."

A shiver worked its way along Annika's spine as Lisella admonished him in a whisper.

"Annika's choice and reason to remain is her own. You should all know though that I intend accompanying the *Na'Chi* when they leave," Kymora stated. "In her wisdom, the *Lady* has asked that I undertake my fourth Journey with them—"

Protests rose up from around the table, the Councilors' voices drowning hers out. Beside her, Annika noticed Varian reseating himself, a startled expression on his normally serious face.

"Who would replace you as *Temple Elect*?" Kalan seemed surprised by the news.

"Too many changes." Again Elamm shook her head.

"It's too soon, too fast, *Chosen*, *Temple Elect*," Witham agreed.

"You see?" Varian's cynicism carried only as far as Annika's ears. The coldness within Annika spread.

With a frown on her face, Kymora rose from her seat and banged her staff on the stone floor to regain order. "Have you no faith in the *Lady*?" she asked, her tone scathing. "Am I to refuse to follow the path *She*'s set me? What sort of leader would I be to ignore *Her* wisdom just because I was afraid or felt it too hard a decision to make? If we're to survive then it's what I'll do for the good of us all."

"Survive?" Witham's heavy eyebrows shot high on his forehead. "We don't need help from the *Na'Chi* to survive in this war against the *Na'Reish*. Our warriors—"

"Our ranks are shrinking in numbers!" Candra's biting comment matched her angry gaze. "Or haven't you been listening to everything this Council has been told?"

"The *Na'Reish* outnumber us, Councilor Witham." Kalan's calm voice restored a modicum of civility to an escalating situation. "What we must address is our survival." His gaze swept the room, taking in everyone. "This Council once hid from the facts and now we're all paying for it. Have the respect to face the events that led us here rather than deny them, and let's consider the options before us." He paused a moment to let his words sink in. "Candra and the *Temple Elect* are right, we can survive with help from the *Na'Chi*."

There were protests from Elamm and Nyon, and the brawny warrior even leapt to his feet to argue Kalan's point. A few of the Light Blades in the room joined in. The cold feeling that had crept along Annika's spine settled at the base of her stomach. It saddened her to see that the Council were still unwilling to accept the truth. She wondered if Kalan had anticipated this level of opposition to his plans.

"They're not interested in surviving," Varian muttered. "They still think they can take on the *Na'Reish* alone."

"Change is never easy," she replied, meeting his gaze.

"And do you think if these leaders reject change that Kalan will ignore their wishes? Look around you. He has few supporters, Annika. Not enough to effect and secure the future he sees for his people. If he ignores them now how long do you think he'll remain as their leader? Once he's gone will the safety he promised us exist anymore?"

Annika rubbed her arms, trying to dispel the grim picture he painted for her as the arguing continued. She could see Kalan trying to restore order to the room, his hands raised, a frown on his drawn face as the Councilors ignored his efforts.

She closed her eyes. His people needed him, now more than ever. It didn't matter that they were still afraid of the *Na'Chi*, of her. The greater threat came from the *Na'Reish* and any attack her father might initiate if he ever got wind of this unrest. Kalan needed to focus on that.

Perhaps she could go with the *Na'Chi*, give everyone the time they needed to cope with their new situation, maybe Kalan could convince the new Council of his plans later. But even as she considered the idea, she knew he'd be unlikely to agree, not when she relied on his blood for her survival. He'd have to choose between her and his people. She knew what his heart would decide and that was something she refused to let him do, not when it would cost him everything he held dear. She couldn't do that to him.

Annika clenched her jaw tight as tears burned in her eyes. For the first time in her life she'd found true acceptance and love and now circumstance was forcing her to choose between happiness and the survival of a people.

Annika stared at Kalan across the room, her heart aching so hard she thought it would break. He'd given her his friendship, acceptance, and a thousand memories she'd always cherish. Letting him go would mean watching her own dream die but she was willing to sacrifice that for him. She loved him too much not to. But *Lady's Breath*, why did it have to hurt so much?

The consequences . . . well, she'd survived withdrawal once. Perhaps, with the *Lady*'s blessing, she'd succeed again.

Swallowing hard, she linked gazes with Varian. "It's time the *Na'Chi* left." Her voice sounded as hollow as her chest felt. "Let's go."

His eyes narrowed at whatever he saw in hers but made no comment. He spoke quietly to Lisella and the other *Na'Chi* then as one they headed for the door.

Tears made their way down Annika's face as she followed them. She looked neither left nor right, nor back toward the man she loved more than life itself.

Had she, she doubted if she'd have had the strength to leave her heart behind.

Chapter 31

ANNIKA was gone. So were the other *Na'Chi*. The voices around Kalan faded as he stared at the empty seats where they'd sat. How long had they been gone? Heart pounding in his chest, he glanced toward the doorway and saw only the two warriors standing guard. Where were they? What were they doing?

One possibility occurred and it sent a wave of fear shooting through Kalan. The blood drained from his face and he shot from his chair so fast it kicked out from under him to scrape across the stone floor.

"*Mother of Mercy, no!*"

Kymora turned in her seat to face him. "*Chosen*, what's wrong?"

There was no time to waste.

Kalan slammed his fist against the table. The sharp sound drew the attention of every Councilor, new and old, seated there. His action also silenced the arguments from the Light Blades to his left.

Without a word he unbuckled the belt around his waist then gently set the leather-sheathed dagger in the middle of the table.

"Kalan, no!" Candra gasped, her gaze widening.

Benth paled to the color of his hair. "What are you doing, *Chosen*?"

"Find another to lead you." His voice was hard, impatient, but he didn't care.

Gut instinct told him Annika and the *Na'Chi* were leaving. If they left the city . . . he shuddered. They'd use all their skills to evade detection, and he had no assurances that their final destination would be the caverns. Not after what they'd witnessed today.

His gaze lifted and surveyed everyone in the room. "I'm tired of your dissention, your fears, and your attempts to exile the *Na'Chi* and Annika. I've done everything I can to follow the *Lady*'s will and give you a choice of how we move on from our mistakes.

"A new Blade Council, a plan to survive against the *Na'Reish*, a way to build our numbers. But even now you refuse to acknowledge the need to change.

"How can you expect me to lead you when you've asked me to choose between the two things I love most in this world? You people are my soul and I've done as my faith and honor demanded and led you into our next Journey, but without my heart . . ." and here his throat tightened, ". . . without Annika, I find I can't continue." His voice dropped, deepened with anger. "And while you argue the *Na'Chi* are leaving the city. Annika included." Heads turned to discover the empty seats he'd seen several heartbeats ago. He inhaled a slow breath. "I choose to go with them."

The Inner Chamber erupted into a second round of chaos; this time it included his warriors, not just the Councilors. Ignoring all pleas and cries Kalan left the chamber, his long stride changing to a dead run as soon as he made it to the corridor.

The building that had been turned into a dormitory for the *Na'Chi* was eerily empty. All that remained were the bed pallets and scattered crates of supplies given to them on their arrival. Packs and blankets and people were gone.

Ignoring the cries of Arek and others as they pursued him through the compound, Kalan headed into the city. With every pounding step, his mind filled with the emotions and memories of his time with Annika.

Her laughter. The many colors of her eyes. Her touch. The uninhibited way she loved him. Every incredible kiss.

Merciful Mother, he couldn't live without her.

He needed her. He loved her. More than he ever imagined possible. He couldn't picture life without her.

And that's what she risked by leaving him now. Her life.

"Fool *Na'Chi!*" The curse ripped from his lips as desperate anger drove him faster through the city streets, his boots thudding on the cobblestones.

His hurried passing drew startled and puzzled looks from the city folk but he ignored them, his thoughts and mind focused on reaching Northgate as quickly as possible. It was a gamble to assume the *Na'Chi* would head there but it was the closest exit to the trail into the mountains where the caverns were located. The fastest way out of the city.

Finally the huge wall came into sight. Breath sawing in and out of his lungs, Kalan spotted a large group of cloaked people almost through the double gates.

"Annika!" His shout turned heads. A familiar blond one caught his attention. Relief almost brought him to his knees. "Annika, wait."

Three young *Na'Chi* scouts blocked his way. Kalan's temper sparked and his fists clenched. Just for satisfaction's sake he was tempted to engage them but held back. His anger wasn't aimed at them but those coming up behind him. "Varian, tell them to stand down. I just want to speak to Annika."

The dark-headed scout made his way through the group of *Na'Chi* to stand beside his warriors.

"Perhaps," he said in his usual, stoic voice, "she doesn't want to speak to you."

Chest heaving, air hissed in through Kalan's teeth as he fought not to plant his fist in the young man's face. "Why not?"

The *Na'Chi*'s eyes flickered, the dark flecks changed to green. "Don't make this any harder for Annika than it already is. She's made her decision. Let her go."

"And let her die?" Kalan took an aggressive step forward. "I think not." The rear guard of four tensed. He let out an aggravated breath. "I'm not here to stop her. I'm coming with you."

"Oh, Kalan, no!" Annika's cry came from a huddle of *Na'Chi*. He whispered a prayer of thanks as she pushed through them, her face pale, her eyes red from crying. "What have you done?"

Another tear tracked down her cheek as he tried to angle his way past the scouts. Varian gave the order to let him through.

"*Mother of Mercy*, what possessed you?" Kalan snatched Annika in against him and buried his head against her shoulder. "I nearly lost you!"

"Your people need you, Kalan." Her violet eyes shone with tears as she pressed a hand to the side of his face. "You can't abandon them."

"I can and I will." His anger flared. "I've done what I can for them. If they can't see past their fear or place their trust in the *Lady* then that is their choice. If they want me as their leader they accept the Journey we share. There'll be no side trails or detours."

"Don't you tell me what I can and can't do!" Candra's outraged voice echoed through the street.

They turned to discover a large crowd of people hurrying along the thoroughfare, the Master Healer in the lead, shaking off a very upset Councilor Elamm from her arm. Relief filled Candra's face as she caught sight of him. She pivoted on her boot heel and stabbed a finger at each of the new Councilors and the Guild-representatives following in her wake.

"Less than one day in your seat and you think that we can remove those who remind us of our mistakes and all will be well." She snorted loudly and shook her head. "As I said in the chamber, you can do without me as well."

She dusted her hands as she joined the small group gathered in front of the gateway.

Benth, looking every year his age, his face red from exertion, led Kymora along the street. As they reached the back of the crowd, he shoved his way through then took a moment to catch his breath.

"Kalan, you were right to remind us that the *Lady* has always guided your hand. There may have been times I found your decisions difficult to understand but you've never given me reason to doubt your leadership. Now is no different." He guided Kymora over to join them then pinned the crowd with a glare. "If you can find another leader more suited than Kalan, then may the *Lady* favor your choice."

The remaining Councilors glanced between themselves, and the expressions on their faces were priceless.

"While I don't speak for all my warriors, unless Kalan remains as the *Lady's Chosen*, my service to this Blade Council is also finished." Arek's declaration caught everyone by surprise.

Kalan's heart lifted as Arek met his gaze. He nodded to acknowledge his decision.

"Your hatred for demons is legendary!" Nyon's confusion was laced with astonishment. "You'd side with the *Na'Chi*?"

"Since reading Zataan's journal I've discovered I was wrong about many things, least of all my beliefs. Annika and the *Na'Chi* don't deserve my hatred. They've done nothing to earn it. Nor are the marks on their bodies and the color of their eyes reason enough to hate them. Until they give me one, I'll follow Kalan." He turned to face Varian. "If you'll accept me I'd like to train with the *Na'Chi* as a scout."

"You'd follow my orders?"

Arek's jaw tightened. "Yes."

"Then there's hope for you yet, Light Blade." Varian's eyes gleamed even though his expression remained stoic. "I look forward to training you."

Somehow Kalan doubted the first few weeks for either man would be easy.

As if Arek's declaration was merely the stopper in a flask, more and more of the Light Blade Commanders and their Seconds came forward to join them, clearly stating their intentions. Kalan sent a swift prayer for forgiveness for dividing *Her* people heavenward; yet he couldn't help but feel fierce satisfaction as he watched his people choose.

"I think you'd better consider your options carefully now, Council," Candra said, her voice clear and hard. "I'm sure once it becomes known Kalan has stepped down as *Chosen* many more will follow. I can't speak for everyone in the hospice but there will be quite a few healers who'll also withdraw their service from the city and throw their lot in with the *Na'Chi*."

"You'd leave our people without services?" Elamm sputtered, the first to find her voice. "There'll be riots in the streets. We'll be inundated with complaints—"

"What about the *Na'Reish*?" The wide-eyed and pale-faced expression of Lin, the Master Weaver was almost comical. "Once they hear of this, they'll flood across the border and attack."

Annika's hand squeezed his. "Kalan, you can't let this happen."

"It's their choice." His tone brooked no argument.

"Perhaps we've made too hasty a decision." Evel glanced swiftly at his peers to gauge their reactions. All nodded and the grey-haired

Councilor gestured to him. "Please, *Chosen*, Councilors, we need your experience and leadership."

His contrite plea did little to mollify Kalan. He was aware that Candra, Benth, and Varian all watched him closely, ready to follow his lead. Kymora stood beside Varian, her head tilted to one side, a serene smile on her face.

For a moment his sister's expression reminded him of the times she'd received a visitation from the *Lady* but then she moved and her head turned toward him. She was listening carefully to all that went on around her.

"We could discuss the issue of Annika remaining, couldn't we?" Elamm's weak smile to the other Councilors faltered. "Surely one *Na'Chi* within the city . . ."

"No." Kalan made sure his voice carried. "If you want me back, there'll be no negotiation. You agree to the plans discussed in the chamber or I won't return."

Annika's indrawn breath was sharp but she said nothing.

"That's blackmail! An abuse of your power as *Chosen*!" Elamm protested.

"I tried to give you a choice before. You refused to consider it, so now I'm making the decision for you, Councilors. You either agree to my terms or I leave." He speared them all with his gaze. "I've decided the *Na'Chi* need a representative on this Council. I find that after the way you've dismissed them, they're going to need an equal voice, someone to speak to their interests. Annika, would you take on this position?"

Goose bumps prickled Annika's body and for the longest moment she said nothing, shocked by his proposal. Kalan's power and determination to save his people and hers made her love him even more. Standing up to the Council, abandoning them if they refused to follow him was an enormous sacrifice but she had little doubt he'd do it.

She swallowed hard as she considered the role he offered her. Her first instinct was to refuse. She could barely read and write their language, how would she fulfill the role without those skills?

Her gaze flitted to the men and women standing in the street, the ones who had followed from the chamber and those from the city drawn by the commotion. She considered the anxiety and concern etched into the faces of the new Councilors. They all waited for her answer. Instead of feeling intimidated, she realized their hypocritical intolerance, their lack of faith in the *Lady* and *Her* chosen leader left her feeling angry.

But, *Lady's Breath*, the responsibility of the position was enormous. Should anyone have been chosen, Lisella would've been the better alternative. She'd already established a rapport with the Councilors' families in the time she'd lived here.

"The *Na'Chi* would wholeheartedly support you." Varian spoke softly, so only they could hear him.

Annika took in a ragged breath and glanced at the circle of friends surrounding her. Varian's gaze blazed violet and green, his look fierce and encouraging. Lisella's small smile was full of hope.

"There's no one I'd rather have championing our people, Annika," she murmured. "Hesia would be proud to see what you've already accomplished for us. You've helped us find a home and, *Lady* willing, many friends to share it with."

Annika's throat tightened with her timely reminder of her mentor and friend's dream for them. Her heart ached that she wasn't there to see it, too.

"The Journey hardest traveled is always the most rewarding, Annika," Kymora reminded her.

Candra grunted and nodded. She even waggled her eyebrows as if in challenge, daring her to take on the position.

Kalan's gentle smile warmed her heart. "Many travel this Journey with us. More will join us. We're not alone."

His words vanquished her doubts. Annika took a deep breath. "I'd be honored to be a part of the Blade Council."

Kalan's hand tightened around hers as he faced the Council. "With the *Lady* as my witness, if you agree to follow my plans, and if after a year there has been no significant change in the people's attitude or acceptance of the *Na'Chi*, I'll step down again and you can appoint another *Lady's Chosen*."

"If we agree to this, will you all remain in the service of the *Lady*?" Nyon asked, his frown deepening as he addressed the Light Blade warriors and crafters who'd supported them.

"We stand with Kalan." All who stood by them echoed Candra's affirmation.

The new Councilors all nodded and just like that the new Blade Council was reformed. Annika's stomach danced with nerves but her heart soared as she contemplated her future.

It didn't matter what it held as long as she was by Kalan's side. She was proud to accompany him on this Journey. Both their races would survive this transition period. She was under no illusion that the road would be filled with many holes and steep rises but, with the *Lady*'s blessing, their love would shape not only their destiny but also the destinies of all.

Tightening her grip on his hand, Annika smiled at Kalan. There was such renewed strength and purpose burning in his gaze.

"You would have truly sacrificed your future for me, wouldn't you?" she said.

"Yes. My life, my heart, my soul." A slow, tender smile curved Kalan's lips. "I would've given it all, because without you there's nothing of worth left living for." His fingers traced the side of her face, lingering to caress her *Na'Chi* markings. "Besides, you put the needs of everyone ahead of your own life. How couldn't I do the same for you?"

Annika lifted herself on tiptoe to press a gentle kiss to his lips.
"I love you, Kalan."

His green eyes burned brighter and his spicy scent filled her lungs.
"I'll never get tired of hearing that." His lips brushed hers. "Say it
again, *Na'Chi.*"

"I love you." His next kiss curled her fingers into fists in his shirt.
"Again."

"I love you."

He drew her hair off to the side and kissed her neck. Annika hissed
at the touch as lightning sizzled through her body, and wished they
were alone together instead of standing in the middle of the street
in front of two dozen pairs of eyes.

Kalan's voice dropped, deepened and she felt his lips curve against
her skin. "Again . . ."

She made him wait until he caught her up and swung her around.

Annika swallowed her laughter and threaded her fingers through
his hair. "I love you, Light Blade," she murmured as her mouth met
his and, without words, she showed him just how much.